# TRAITOR

## IN THE SCOTTISH ISLES

INSPIRATIONAL ROMANTIC SUSPENSE

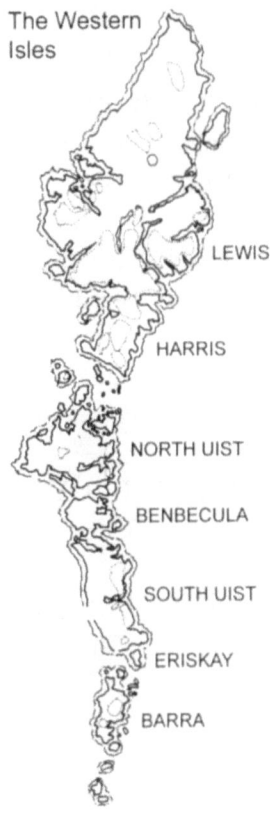

The Western
Isles

LEWIS

HARRIS

NORTH UIST

BENBECULA

SOUTH UIST

ERISKAY

BARRA

# Books & Audiobooks

## by Paige Edwards

**PRESSLEY-COOMBES SERIES**
Catherine's Intrigue #1
Deadly by Design #2
Danger on the Loch #3
Skye Fall #4

**ROXBURY HEIRS SERIES**
Facing the Enemy #1
Flat Deception #2

**ROXBURGH SCIONS SERIES**
Traitor in the Scottish Isles

**STAND-ALONES**
Heirs of Falcon Point (creator)

**ANTHOLOGY**
Sinister Secrets

**SOLDIERS LEAP SERIES**
A Royal Request (Coming 2025)

ROXBURGH
SCIONS

# TRAITOR

## IN THE SCOTTISH ISLES

INSPIRATIONAL ROMANTIC SUSPENSE

# PAIGE EDWARDS

BALQUHIDDER

Cover Design: Cynthia Edwards

Published by Balquhidder Books, LLC

ISBN: 978-1-966494-01-0

Library of Congress Control Number: 2024927511

# PRAISE FOR PAIGE

"A modern-day spy thriller set amongst the windswept and remote Scottish Isles of Uist. *Traitor in the Scottish Isles* is a fast-paced, riveting story that takes readers into worlds they can only imagine. Paige Edwards has created two wonderfully unique and completely different characters in Cairstie and Sheridon. The contrast between the pampered girl and the hard-bitten, slightly cynical, dangerous MI6 operative couldn't be more apparent. A fun, exciting story. I highly recommend this read." – Reader's Favorite 5-star Review.

"The action is non-stop in Paige Edwards' romantic adventure novel. Her plot is uniquely complex, informing an astute audience that there is more than one moral at the end of this story. *Skye Fall* is an exciting novel in a class of its own." – Readers' Favorite Five-Star Review.

"Paige Edwards has woven a gripping and riveting multilayered story that grabs one's attention in the first few pages of the book and just doesn't let go!" – InD'Tale Magazine Crowned Heart Review

"*Danger on the Loch* grips your attention with its mix of romance and mystery to which any reader regardless of age can relate in terms of identity, family, and relationships. Castle Rannock is a brilliant setting that breathes with a life of its own. With its stone walls, secret passages, and staircases, it exudes an air of mystery and foreboding that you want to unravel. Paige Edwards has created a mystery case worthy of someone like Sherlock Holmes to crack." Readers' Favorite Five-Star Review

"Paige Edwards' romantic suspense novels never disappoint. I know when I pick up one of her books, I'll be drawn into high adventure with characters who come to life off the page."– Kathi Oram Peterson, author of Danger Unknown and Treacherous Legacy

"The estate is a character in itself made only more haunting by the diverse characters within it. As part of the Pressley-Coombes Series, this meets reader expectations and terms of offering high-tension suspense and feel-good romance." — Readers' Favorite Five-Star Review

"Filled with vivid description, unique characters, and page-turning tension, Paige Edwards is the perfect blend of suspense and romance."— Sian Ann Bessey, USA Today best-selling author

"Edwards knows precisely how to blend suspense, romance, and depth of feeling in such a thrilling manner it will leave readers anxious for more." – Esther Hatch, award-winning & best-selling author.

"I can't wait to read more from Paige Edwards." — Sarah M. Eden, USA Today Best-selling author

"Paige Edwards has created an exciting world of high society, complete with dark secrets, budding romance, and heart-breaking decisions that will keep every reader turning the pages." – Traci Hunter Abramson, award-winning & best-selling author.

"Fabulous characters, great heart, and a determined villain all combine to make *Skye Fall* a novel fans of romantic suspense won't want to miss!" – A. L. Sowards, author of Codes of Courage *for David*

# Acknowledgments

Special gratitude and deep appreciation go to the men and women who dedicate their lives to provide freedom against those who seek to destroy it.

To LeAnn Gutierrez, a professional reading instructor and expert on all things dyslexic.

Beta readers are gold in this industry. A special shout-out goes to Dani Pettrey, Ellie Whitney, Cassie M. Shiels, Mandy Biesinger, Tasha Bradford, Kaila Douglass, Christina Biasca, and Sally Johnson for their input. Thank you to my critique group, Ellie Whitney, Kyla Beecroft, J. C. Wade, and Cindy Ray Hale, for early eyes on the story.

My editors, Bev Kaz Rosenbaum and Ellie Whitney, have such a way with words and know how to make my stories shine. To Cynthia Edwards for the amazing cover. And to my husband, Ladd, who keeps me on track in myriad ways. I'm so lucky to have him in my life.

To my street team, thank you for your amazing friendship and talents in promoting clean fiction. You have no idea how much I appreciate what you do. Readers—it's you who make this solitary journey a joyful one. Thank you. Lastly, to my Heavenly Father, who loves His children and desires our greatest happiness. Thank you for the inspiration to write.

# Scottish Vocabulary Words

|  |  |
| --- | --- |
| A mhuiranín | Irish Gaelic for darling |
| Addle-pated bairn | Stupid or confused child |
| Bairn | Small child |
| Balivanich | Largest town & former Royal Air Force Base on the Isle of Benbecula |
| Bampot | Idiot |
| Banshees | Shrieking ghosts |
| Barking Mad | Thoroughly insane or crazy |
| Bass Rock | A huge rock island in the Firth of Forth Estuary |
| Benbecula | An island in the Outer Hebrides also known as the Uists, or Uist. |
| Bin Man | Trash man |
| Bits and Bobs | This and that, things |
| Bonnet | Car hood |
| Bonnie | Beautiful, pretty |
| Caravan Park | Campground |
| Carriageway | Highway – two lanes |
| Ceilidh | A Scottish gathering of live music, singing, and dancing |
| Cracker | Cookie |
| Crisps | Chips |
| Cullen Skink | Fish chowder |
| Dinnae Ken | Don't know |
| Easy-peasy | Easy |
| Eriskay | Island in the Uist chain of the Outer Hebrides |
| Flymo | A type of lawnmower |
| Galashiels | A city in the Scottish Borders |
| Ghillie | Attendant on a hunting/fishing expedition. Also, laces on Scottish dancing shoes |
| Gombeen | Irish word for corrupt underhanded businessman or politician |
| Gorse | Prickly bush with yellow, gold blooms |
| Hebridean | Native inhabitant of the Hebrides, islands off the northwestern coast of Scotland |
| Hen | Term of endearment, honey, girl, women |
| Hen dos | Bridal showers, girls' night out |
| Honesty Box | An unattended receptacle that relies on customers leaving money for goods taken |
| Incomer | A person not born in the Western Isles |
| Irish Gaelic | Pronounced Gay-lick |
| Irn Bru | Scottish soft drink |
| Jackeen (Irish) | Self-assertive but worthless man. |
| Jings | Wow |
| Kelpies | Shape shifters, often in the shape of a horse that pull you underwater when you touch it |
| Ken | Know |
| Lad | Boy, man |
| Lark | A joke |
| Lass | Girl, woman |
| Layby | A place to pull over on the side of the road so cars can pass |
| Loch | Lake |
| Loch Morar | A freshwater loch in the Highlands |
| Loo | Toilet |
| Machair | Vast planes of long grass & wildflowers that grow in sandy & seashell soil |
| Mallaig | A town in the Highlands |
| Mod Cons | Modern conveniences, usually appliances |
| Oban | A coastal town in Western Scotland |
| Outer Hebrides | Farthest Western Islands in Scotland |
| Peely-wally | Looking pale and sickly |
| Primogeniture Laws | Las that passes the entirety of an estate to the closest living male relative |
| Pure Dead Brilliant | Something is excellent or the best |
| Pure Gallus | Bold or cocky or impertinent |
| Raasay | Inner Hebridean island |
| Ring a peal over yer head: | Scolding someone |
| Row | Fight, argument |
| Scottish Gaelic | Scots pronounce Gaelic as "Gal lick" |
| Skerry, Skerries | Small, uninhabited island(s) generally comprised of rock |
| Snug | Small tv room with comfortable furniture |
| Sticking plaster | Bandage |
| Tatty Jumper | Ratty-looking wool sweater |
| Telly | Television |
| Tenner | Ten pounds |
| The Minch | The sea between the Inner and Outer Hebrides |
| Uists | Southern islands in the Outer Hebrides |
| Verra | Very |
| Wee | Small or little |

# CHAPTER 1

## DEEP SEA RANGE, OUTER HEBRIDES, SCOTLAND

MI6 AGENT VICKY WANG inserted a hard drive into the Royal Air Force's base computer and hit the download button. She and Agent Mansfield, her partner, had worked most of the night inside the small SCIF, a secure office on a top-secret military base, to locate the files and schematics for the developmental weapons tested there.

"It's not on this one." Mansfield returned to the safe and exchanged his portable hard drive for another.

She clenched her fist. Mansfield had more than adequate skills, but if Agent Sharidon, the twenty-five-year-old whiz kid, had accompanied her, they could have cut through these hard drives in half the time. Too bad he was convalescing from an injury.

Mansfield checked his watch. "Time's running out. The guards return in seven minutes."

She didn't need a reminder. They were cutting it close.

Yesterday, she intercepted a transmission that sent her and Mansfield to the control room on Benbecula, an island in the Outer Hebrides that served as headquarters for the missile range testing in the Western Isles of Scotland.

China intended to steal their dark op weaponry files. If they succeeded, the UK and other Western societies would be open to a planned takeover. Thus far, European intelligence had not informed the general population of the rising threat. If she and Mansfield failed, it was only a matter of time before hostilities broke out, and China, with its massive stockpile of subpar missiles, high speed jets, and naval war ships, would crush them by sheer numbers alone.

Wang checked her watch, urgency rising within her. No one had labeled the blasted hard drive, one of dozens inside the safe. What she and Mansfield anticipated as a snatch and go had taken most of the night, delaying their departure. They couldn't take the lot because the base needed the specs in case a glitch occurred during testing.

She glanced at the clock as a metallic clang in the outer corridor alerted her to someone's presence. Since the guards weren't due for seven minutes, who had accessed this quadrant?

Wang withdrew her MI6 issue and motioned for Agent Mansfield to take the wall position beside the SCIF door. Mansfield nodded and tossed her his hard drive. He withdrew his gun and inched toward the door, his shooting arm extended.

She pressed the console key and disconnected her hard drive, then, pivoting, she sprinted to the safe, secured both drives, and spun the dial. The tumblers clicked in place.

An explosion rocked the room and blew the SCIF door off its hinges. Wang took cover behind a desk, her ears ringing. Mansfield needed backup. She used the plaster-coated air to her advantage and crouch-ran, then dropped beside the central console and hit the silent alarm.

Two hazy forms stood near the door, Mansfield, and their intruder. Mansfield's weapon boomed. The intruder staggered backward but somehow remained upright. Wang shifted to get a bead on the infiltrator, but her position was off.

Two pops followed in quick succession—a silencer. Agent Mansfield grunted and fell.

Wang aimed across the desk then squeezed the trigger. The target crashed into the wall, and his rasps filled the room, but he didn't fall. She'd hit him square in the chest. He had protective gear. Blast.

Keeping low, Wang debated taking another shot when he pushed away from the cinderblock wall and swung in her direction. Wang hit the tiles, and combat crawled to a new location, determined to shoot it out—only the intruder arrived first and planted his boots three feet from her hand. She rolled onto her back and raised her weapon.

Pop.

Fire burst through her chest. She gasped and glanced at her shirt. Two agents down. Two agents . . . Wang's head flopped back and images of her daughter, Lily spilled through her mind.

Lily. Poor Lily.

Helpless, Wang lay on the cold tiles as the intruder stepped close, and his face came into focus.

A face she knew.

# CHAPTER 2

## TORWOODLEE CASTLE, SCOTTISH BORDERS

WEDDINGS WERE USUALLY JOYOUS OCCASIONS. But Lady Cairstie Henderson had nothing to celebrate as she scanned the castle's ballroom from her position in the bridal party's receiving line. Oh, she delighted in her sister and new brother-in-law's happiness, but Cairstie strongly objected to the tall, dark-haired groomsman with the Irish accent.

A string quartet played from a raised dais at the far end of the room, and scents of jasmine and lilies wafted from the centerpieces on the damask-covered tables. Mother, the Marchioness of Roxbury, had assured that everything looked perfect.

Cairstie glared at the Irish groomsman during a lull in the receiving line. He caught her stink eye and winked. Pure gallus, that one! The tall Irish groomsman had caused her public breakup with her boyfriend, Lord Ahern. Even now, weeks after Ahern's arrest, Cairstie burned with resentment at the Irishman's part in making her a pariah among her social set.

Who did he think he was, anyway? The Irishman had arrived at the castle minutes before the ceremony began. Frowning, she tossed her hair over her shoulder and caught her sister, Elise, eyeing her with a pucker between her brows. Not much rattled Elise, but she appeared too interested in Cairstie's response to the Irishman.

Until that night at the restaurant, Cairstie had never laid eyes on the fellow, yet her brother-in-law had included him as a groomsman. When had they become such good friends? And the fellow also seemed well-acquainted with Elise.

Angling her body toward her flame-haired sister draped in white Brussels lace, Cairstie raised a questioning brow. Elise glanced at the Irishman, then back at her, rolled her eyes, and nodded.

"You sent him to the restaurant?" Cairstie mouthed to her.

"Sorry." Elise mouthed back.

Cairstie's heart stuttered as shock gave way to indignation. Elise sent the Irishman to sabotage her evening with Ahern? Cairstie clenched her bouquet, and the plastic handle scored her palms.

Throughout the next hour between greeting guests, she fumed. Doubtless, Elise had asked the Irishman to split her from Ahern to circumvent a scandal, but sissy dearest had miscalculated her timing. The Irishman's behavior had humiliated Cairstie—a precursor to her ultimate disgrace.

If her family hadn't approved of Ahern, they should have told her. Why use that cloak-and-dagger method to remove him?

As the youngest Henderson sibling, Cairstie's brother and sisters often treated her like an addle-pated bairn. Cairstie tapped the toe of her shoe, heartily sick of the lot of them. Just then, her gaze collided with the Irishman's, and she narrowed her eyes to slits. He personified everything wrong with her life.

"I'm going to give that Irishman a piece of my mind," Cairstie whispered to Sophie, her next oldest sister, who stood beside her in the reception line.

"Shhh," Sophie hissed. Tonight, with her wild curls tamed and her blue eyes sparkling, Sophie outshone every female in the room, including the bride—and Cairstie had a good idea why. She glanced at the canary diamond Sophie sported on a significant finger. Dad's hedge fund manager had obviously put it there.

"What's bothering you?" Sophie asked when the queue bottlenecked in front of Elise and Harry.

"Who's the Irish groomsman? The one on the end. I never caught his name." She wouldn't need to ask if the fellow had attended the wedding rehearsals.

"That's Sharidon."

"Sharidon?" A much too dignified handle for such a despot. "Is that his given name or surname?"

"No idea. He and Harry met through work."

"Hmmm." Harry held a hush-hush government job. "Sharidon showed up at the restaurant where Ahern and I were dining and pretended to be my boyfriend. He was so convincing that Ahern caused a scene and broke up with me right there in the restaurant, then left me to find my way home."

"I'm so sorry about that." Sophie edged close and squeezed Cairstie's arm, her blue eyes filled with dismay.

"You knew?" Sophie, the kindest of all her siblings, had plotted against her, too?

Color flooded Sophie's face. "We suspected Ahern was involved in a horse racing syndicate and were desperate to separate you from him."

"Why didn't you just tell me?" Hurt and anger warred within Cairstie. How dare her sisters arrange that incident. She'd been the laughingstock of the Scottish Border towns for months—and that Irishman, Sharidon, had colluded with them.

"We weren't sure you would listen." Sophie bit her lip.

"Yes, I would—" Och . . . Perhaps not. Cairstie pinched the bridge of her nose and acknowledged that her family had the right of it. She hated being bossed about and often did the opposite to prove her independence. She opened her mouth to say more, but Lord and Lady Cavanaugh, an older gentleman with a comb-over and his "oh-so-proper" wife, paused in front of them.

"Lady Sophie, what a delight to see you." Lady Cavanaugh took Sophie's hand in hers.

"Aye. It is." Sophie nodded, all sweetness. It wasn't even an act. She had the kindest heart imaginable.

Cairstie bared her teeth in the best imitation of a smile she could muster when Lord Cavanaugh dipped his head to her, his manner cool. "Lady Cairstie."

His wife kissed Sophie's cheek, then faced Cairstie, the feather in her hat bobbing. "Lady Cairstie, how becoming you look in that blue silk. Is that by Stella Walker? We missed you in her Spring Fashion Show last week."

Cairstie's insides twisted, but she kept a straight face. "I was involved with Elise's wedding preparations."

In truth, Stella Walker canceled her contract for the Spring Fashion Show when Ahern's arrest made national news, but that was none of Lady Cavanaugh's business. Even weeks later, Stella's words had scorched her like a branding iron. "I've pulled you from the Spring Show, Lady Cairstie. I won't have anything sordid attached to my brand."

Sordid. With one word, Stella had sacked her. Cairstie's innocence did not matter, only that she had appeared once too often on Ahern's arm in the tabloids. Guilty by association, they called it. The upper echelon of British society did not soil their reputations despite their poor behavior in private. It was the image that counted. As a result, all Cairstie's contracts as a high street influencer and fashion model had dried up overnight— along with her so-called friends.

Such shabby treatment of the daughter of a Scottish marquess still astonished her. And seeing that Irishman, Sharidon, today drove home her issues like an iron stake to the heart. Fury snarled within her at the unfairness of it all. Sharidon was here for the evening, and she had no intention of letting him slip away without giving him a piece of her mind. When she finished with him, her sisters were going to get an earful, too.

Needing an outlet, she fantasized about giving Sharidon a dose of his own medicine by knocking his cane out from under him and leaving him sprawled on the ballroom floor.

"You're planning something," Sophie said. "Please don't cause a scene."

Her? Cause a scene? How hypocritical after the scene Elise and Sophie had orchestrated, Cairstie would love nothing more than to do just that. "Elise only consented to this event to make Mother happy."

Sophie couldn't combat that; it was true. Elise didn't care about wealth or social standing and had proven it by dropping her title and changing her name to avoid preferential treatment in the workplace.

While Sophie retained her title, she was so humble and down-to-earth that people were often surprised when they discovered she lived at the castle. What Roddy, their brother, felt remained a mystery. He lived somewhere in the Aegean—or was it the Caribbean—and had only flown home for the wedding.

While her handsome renegade brother strolled the ballroom, chatting up the prettiest women, Mother had insisted that Cairstie keep a stiff upper lip against the sharp comments shooting her way.

As a model and influencer, Cairstie adored parties and the socialite lifestyle, jetting from one runway or photo shoot to the next. But that life had ended, and she was imprisoned every bit as much as those who had once graced the castle's dungeons—only her cell had gilded walls.

⚜

Sharidon leaned on his cane as the reception wore on and kept a careful watch on the gorgeous blonde bridesmaid. Her blue eyes shot daggers at him every time he glanced her way. Should she attempt a confrontation, he needed an exit plan. As much as he'd enjoy a sparring match, keeping a low profile in case he ran into members of the upper echelon while on assignment seemed prudent.

The groom, his friend, Harry, had transferred from MI6 to MI5 a few months ago, and the bride, a former top MI6 operative and the most brilliant hacker he knew, positively glowed with happiness. Sharidon wished them joy, but marriage wasn't something that mixed well with his life as an MI6 operative. He had to admit, Harry had the right of it by transferring out. No woman deserved marriage to a spy, and Sharidon did not intend to tie himself to someone who made him vulnerable.

McFarlane, Lord Roxbury's rather stuffy butler, stepped forward. "My lord. My ladies. Guests. Thank you for coming. Please advance into the ballroom, and supper will commence."

The mobile inside Sharidon's trouser pocket vibrated as the throng surged forward. He stepped to the side and retrieved it. Restricted. His heart thumped double-time. Nigel?

Nodding to Harry, Sharidon slipped behind an enormous tapestry as the blonde bombshell bore down on him. He grasped the brass knob embedded in the wall paneling and entered a darkened stairwell, one that had seen little use of late, judging by the musty scent. He locked the door behind him and leaned against it to get his bearings.

The doorknob rattled almost immediately. *Take that, my lovely.* He grinned and stepped onto the small landing to answer his call. "Sharidon."

"Sharidon. How strong is your leg?"

"Nice to hear from you, Nigel." His interest spiked. Something big was up. Nigel Thatcher, the legendary spymaster, never contacted him without a purpose.

"The leg?" Nigel, in typical form, bypassed the pleasantries.

"It's healing, sir. I'm off the crutches and only need the cane when standing for long periods." Things must be serious at the home office.

"Good. Good. I'm recalling you."

Shock rippled through Sharidon, arctic as ice water. "That requires a field physical."

What was going on? Agents never reentered the field without undergoing rigorous examinations to prove they'd reclaimed peak physical and mental performance.

"No tests. We have a situation that requires your abilities."

"Nigel speak" for linguistics or weaponry. Nigel would never retract him unless things were dire, which meant, national security was on the line and MI6 needed his specific skill sets. Tingles of anticipation hummed through him.

The doorknob rattled behind him again, accompanied by small scraping noises inside the old-fashioned lock. Lady Cairstie didn't give up.

Sharidon grasped the handrail and leaned on it for support as he started down the stairs, using his mobile to light the way.

"We've been testing developmental weapons in the Uists, weapons the Chinese want so they can stay ahead of the world with their hypersonic missile program."

"Didn't they shut that RAF base down?"

"The Ministry of Defense uses it on a need-to-know basis and keeps only a skeletal crew of military and civilians there."

Translation: civilian locals without connections to the mainland. With jobs at a premium in the Outer Hebrides, signing a disclaimer to work on base doubtless kept the site under wraps.

"And?" he prodded. What was Nigel asking of him?

"Someone breached the base last night."

"Casualties?" Sharidon asked.

"Two missing agents. One sounded the alarm before they disappeared. Base guards showed up within five minutes, but the infiltrator had cleared out, along with our agents. We need to find who did this."

Sharidon creased his brow. "Were the guards in on it? That seems quite fast for an intruder to caper off with two agents."

"Possibly. With such a small staff and population base, everyone is a suspect, even our military personnel. The base will not be notified of your presence."

Sharidon exhaled. He was right. This was big.

"The UK, Americans, and Australians are testing low and slow missiles along with High Energy Liquid Laser Area Defense Systems aimed at neutralizing surface-to-air missile threats with the capacity to destroy enemy ground targets," Nigel continued.

"Lasers and low and slows in addition to hypersonics?" Sharidon's eyes bugged.

"Yes. Radar can't track low and slows, which allows them to approach any city without warning. We've kept this under wraps by testing hypersonic rockets into the Atlantic along with the HELLADS. The heat plumes showed up on satellites. Unfortunately, they made someone curious."

"Who's after those plans?" Sharidon asked.

"Our intercepted transmission revealed that China plans to destroy our hypersonic CAD files and schematics to prevent our creating defensive measures against future attacks."

Sharidon groaned. The Chinese. Most civilians believed North Korea, Russia, or the Middle East were their most significant worries, but China intended to take over Western cultures. By destroying the West's laser missiles and rockets, China could annihilate their defenses. For the last few decades, the Chinese had stockpiled weapons, experimental planes that flew faster than the speed of sound, and more warships than anything the West had in numbers.

"China's Ministry has denied the home office's accusations, but one of our agents on Benbecula unscrambled a recent transmission that stated otherwise."

"Does China know about those radar-proof missiles?" Sharidon rubbed his chin, the rough stubble already poking through his skin after this morning's shave. The hypersonic and HELLAD programs were common knowledge, but discovering those low and slows would finish the West if those plans fell into the wrong hands.

"Hard to say. The low and slows are the best offense we have and are almost ready for production. If China gets their hands on those hard drive files, we have no way to counter against their sheer number of stockpiled weapons."

And China had no compunction about harming civilians to achieve their objectives. Their global cyber-hacking campaign, a forerunner to their spy balloons and power play with their Russian ally off U.S. coastlines, lent credence to Nigel's words.

Sharidon reached the bottom of the stairwell and pressed against the wall to rest his leg while the situation sank in.

"How good are your Gaelic and Mandarin?" Nigel asked.

"Gaelic's brilliant. Mandarin, less so, but I know enough to get by." Sharidon's heart rate picked up.

"Excellent. Pack your bags."

"When do I leave?"

"Tonight. I'll have someone meet you at Waverly Station with your packet. Give Agent Benson my regards."

"Yes, sir." Sharidon's mobile went dark.

He pushed away from the wall and placed weight on the leg he'd injured on a prior mission. His knee held. He exhaled. For a time, he'd worried about permanent disability, but physical therapy had dramatically improved his mobility.

The home office was desperate if Nigel deemed him, bum leg, and all, valuable enough for recall.

He started for the basement exit, but a stray thought stopped him cold. He wasn't the only operative who spoke Mandarin. Mansfield and Wang did as well.

Disquiet stirred, dark and wary. Wang adored her five-year-old daughter, and Mansfield was still a newlywed to a woman he'd pursued for years until she said yes. Were they the missing agents?

# CHAPTER 3

CAIRSTIE LEFT Torwoodlee's river trail and cut through the pasture when she spotted a pair of anglers fishing the Upper Beat of the River Tweed under the guidance of Dad's ghillie. A few steps further, a ring-necked pheasant darted out of the long grass ahead of her, flushed from its lair. Winkle, her Goldendoodle puppy, darted after it.

She cupped her hands around her mouth. "Winkle. Heel. Winkle," she called. But Winkle was long gone and would doubtless return covered in burrs when he gave up the hunt.

The sun's haphazard appearance cut through the morning mist and raised the humidity as the temperature climbed. Her family had slept in after the wedding festivities ended in the early hours. Try as she might, she had lost Sharidon and ended up dancing with one of Roddy's old friends whose advances precipitated her premature departure from the ballroom.

Cairstie shaded her eyes and glanced about for Winkle one last time. The year-old pup burst through the tree line and loped in her direction. Her shoulders relaxed. A few minutes later, she reached the single track that led to the castle, with Winkle trotting at her heels. They passed Mother's formal gardens, fenced by tall brick walls.

A loss of products to promote or catwalks to strut, the day stretched before her without even a wedding rehearsal to break up the monotony.

She jutted her chin and narrowed her eyes. Not that she'd attend one after discovering her sisters were behind that humiliating incident with Sharidon. Their betrayal had cut deep.

She passed the formal gardens and reached the castle, tugging open the scullery door. Mrs. McNab, the cook, poked her head around the doorframe, her triple chins wiggling.

"Lady Cairstie, your mother's been tearing the castle apart looking for you."

"Is something the matter?"

"You've company in the morning room."

"Company?" Cairstie sat on the wooden bench and tugged off a mud-caked boot.

"Aye. A solicitor. He's been here an age." Mrs. McNab nodded.

Cairstie glanced at her filthy clothes and her even dirtier dog. "Could you have someone bathe Winkle? Please tell Mother I'll join them directly."

"That I will," Mrs. McNab said.

Cairstie shot across the limestone tiles and up one of the servants' staircases. Mother had a hard and fast rule about appearing in public properly dressed. Cairstie didn't have time to shower, but a midi with a wide-brimmed hat and espadrilles, all products she had received as an influencer, should do.

When she reached her room, she dumped her walking clothes into a heap, slipped the dress over her head, jammed the hat over her messy hair, and put on her wedged heels.

She rushed down the first-floor corridor to the main staircase and descended, gripping the polished oak handrail. What did a solicitor want with her? She glanced at the clock on the landing as it chimed half-ten. How odd that he had arrived unannounced.

Speeding along the tartan-carpeted corridor, she slowed when the muted rumblings of Mr. Anderson, her family's solicitor, reached her.

McFarlane, the butler, stood waiting in the hall before entering the morning room. "Lady Cairstie," he announced.

Cairstie crossed the threshold into the yellow and blue room her mother favored.

"Here she is." Mother beamed as she approached Cairstie with her arms wide.

Dad set his teacup on a side table. "For a while there, I thought we needed to call a military unit from Glenkinnon to find ye."

"Very funny. I took Winkle for a walk." Cairstie's stomach growled, and she eyed the tea trolley's pastries and yogurts. Turning away, she acknowledged the solicitor. "It's good to see you again, Mr. Anderson. I understand you're here to see me?"

"Aye. And I'm out of time to do this correctly," Mr. Anderson grumbled, nodding toward his briefcase.

"I was unaware that we had an appointment." Cairstie wrinkled her brow.

"When I rang last week, I left a message with Roderick."

"Well, that explains a lot, doesn't it, dear?" Dad winked at Mother. "Our son left after the wedding and didn't pass on the message," he explained.

"I'm terribly sorry about the mix-up." Mother collected Dad's teacup and saucer off the side table and placed them on the trolley.

"Why don't we convene in the dining room?" Dad rose from his chair and led the way.

The ochre-colored walls and elaborate plasterwork in the family dining room proved less formal than the one they used for large functions. Mr. Anderson pulled out a chair at the end of the table for himself, and Cairstie sat across the table from her parents.

Mr. Anderson pressed two brass snaps on his old-fashioned briefcase and retrieved a folder, then passed her several clipped papers and kept a copy for himself.

"I am the bearer of sad news, I'm afraid. Your godmother, Mrs. Caroline McDougal, has passed," Mr. Anderson said.

Cairstie frowned. Her godmother had died? Cairstie scarcely knew the woman, but on the few occasions they met, Mrs. McDougal struck her as a person of robust health.

"I'm sorry to hear this," Dad said.

Mrs. McDougal was a distant cousin of her father's. Cairstie glanced down and squinted at the top sheet Mr. Anderson had given her. "Last

Will and . . ." The words writhed before her eyes, and she couldn't make out the rest.

"As you may have guessed, I am here to see to your inheritance," Mr. Anderson said.

"Mrs. McDougal left Cairstie a bequest?" Mother asked, her voice expressing the surprise. "Caroline never once mentioned that she intended to leave Cairstie anything."

"Mrs. McDougal's husband passed away two years ago. She had no direct heirs, so she left Lady Cairstie her entire estate."

Cairstie leaned forward. "I beg your pardon?" The solicitor must have it wrong. Mrs. McDougal, Dad's second cousin, served as one of Cairstie's six godmothers. Save for the occasional holiday, Cairstie rarely saw her, but every now and then, gifts arrived in the post—the address from the Uists, a string of islands in the Outer Hebrides off the west coast of Scotland.

Cairstie always sent Mrs. McDougal a thank you note, but that was the extent of their relationship. Sadly, in the early days, those notes were more from Mother's insistence than from her own contrivance.

"Your godmother has left her house, bank accounts, and personal and real property on the isle of Benbecula to you. Do you know where that is?" Mr. Anderson steepled his fingers.

"Somewhat." She fought back an eye roll at his condescending attitude. Though she struggled with dyslexia and had not pursued a university degree, she was well-versed in geography and could read a map.

"Caroline McDougal left one stipulation. To inherit, you must live on the island for six months—"

"Six months?" Cairstie's jaw dropped. Less than thirty thousand people lived in the entire Outer Hebrides. Her family had visited once. Due to storms and limited ferry service, the co-op grocery stores struggled to keep basics on their shelves during the winter months. Not one high-end dress shop, other than Harris Tweed, existed. As for restaurants and entertainment—she might as well join a convent. The only thing the Hebrides abounded in was cold, wind, and rain. What was she to do with herself?

"Six months," Mr. Anderson stated, his manner firm. "Should you not accept, the property goes to your brother, Roderick Henderson, Earl of Clovenfords."

"Roderick receives my inheritance if I refuse to live in the back of beyond?" Cairstie surged to her feet, unable to remain seated.

"Mrs. McDougal insisted her estate stay in the family. Should you forego the inheritance, I shall notify your brother."

"How much is the estate worth?" Cairstie asked. It couldn't be much. Mrs. McDougal wore nothing but tatty jumpers and outdated trousers. And her house, though charming, was sadly old-fashioned.

"In pounds sterling, it's valued somewhere close to six million, two hundred thousand pounds. Of course, the property has likely increased in value since its last appraisal."

"So much?" Dad rubbed his chin.

Cairstie dropped into her chair, her knees like rubber. Leaning back, she stuck her legs out in front of her and stared at the ceiling. Six months in the Outer Hebrides to earn her inheritance. And what an inheritance. That, coupled with her trust fund, placed her comfortably off indeed. And it allowed her to get away from her traitorous sisters.

"Are you quite all right, Cairstie?" Mother rose from the table; her heels clicked, then silenced, as she crossed the thick rug to her side and pressed a hand on Cairstie's shoulder.

"Did you know that Mrs. McDougal had that kind of cash?" Cairstie rolled her head to the side without lifting it from the back of the chair to see both parents.

"Not in the least. Caroline always wore those moth-eaten jumpers. I think she even used rope to hold up her trousers when she got on in years," Mother said.

Aye, her godmother had never dressed to impress.

"When do you need my decision?" Cairstie lifted her head to meet the solicitor's gaze.

"The first of the month."

Five days? No use dithering. "I don't need five days." Cairstie tucked a strand of hair behind her ear.

"Well?" Mr. Anderson tapped the side of his briefcase.

"I accept."

"Very good." The solicitor pushed out of his chair and snapped his case shut.

"That's it? When do I take possession of the house?" In other words, how long before she began her self-imposed exile?

"The first of the month."

Her heart stuttered. That barely gave her time to pack. "How will you know if I stay on Benbecula for the full duration?" Maybe she could fly home on weekends.

"Mr. and Mrs. MacRae, along with their son, work at the Benbecula Airport and the ferry terminals on North and South Uist. If you leave the area, they'll alert me."

Dad surged to his feet and pressed the wall button for McFarlane. "Good to see you again, Mr. Anderson."

"My pleasure." Mr. Anderson bowed to Dad.

McFarlane appeared in the doorway.

"I look forward to hearing from you." Mr. Anderson nodded to her, then to Mother, and followed McFarlane out of the room.

Silence followed his departure for the space of three beats.

"How certain are you about this, Cairstie?" Mother's soft blue eyes clouded with concern. "There isn't much shopping in the Outer Hebrides, and their winter gales cut off supplies and communication."

"I'll be all right." Then Cairstie voiced the real reason she had accepted. "It might be best if I leave the area for a while and let the gossip about me and Ahern die down." Not to mention getting away from her sisters.

"I think it's a sound decision and shows your maturity." Dad hugged her tight. "I'm proud of you, lass. When you return, I'm sure the scandal will have blown over."

"I hope so," Cairstie muttered under her breath. The ostracism hurt more than she cared to admit. Six months on the edge of civilization did not appeal to her, but she had only two options: stay caged at home to ride out the gossip or go to Benbecula. The latter had a six-million-pound incentive.

She might be frivolous, but she'd never been a fool. For better or worse, Cairstie was going to the Western Isles.

# CHAPTER 4

A WALL of heavy mist hugged the steep, windy road. The clouds lay so low that Sharidon couldn't see more than ten meters ahead. Fog lamps did not help. He took the tight curve on the switchback, his tires close to the edge of the tarmac. The Sprinter van squealed.

"Easy there, Betsy." Sharidon patted the dashboard. "Don't burn up yer brakes."

His contact had met him at Waverley Station and handed over the keys to this unique house-on-wheels, along with new identity papers and his brief, then hopped on the high-speed train for London.

Shelter in the Uists during the summer proved nonexistent, so the converted "van" was his home for the unforeseeable future. Kudos to the home office for creativity. He was grateful they hadn't handed him a tent; wild camping, though fun for a few days, did not appeal overmuch with Scotland's unstable weather conditions.

After a long stretch that skirted the coast, he entered Mallaig, a seaport with ferry access to the Outer Hebrides. An enormous sea-worthy ship lay anchored at the terminal. Upon further inspection, he found that it was his and queued up behind a lorry.

The ferry didn't load for another thirty minutes. So, he locked the van, crossed the road to a small grocery store, stocked up on tinned food, fresh veg, and several liters of lemonade, a sweet fizzy drink, and then returned to the van.

A few minutes later, the lorry ahead of him lurched forward, so he fired up Betsy, then rolled down his window and gulped in the salt-laden air before he entered the ship's belly. The ferry closed around Sharidon and swallowed him whole. His shirt stuck to his back. His mouth watered and his stomach cramped. Sharidon groaned as he set the parking brake, then darted up the metal stairs to the nearest loo, praying for relief.

For the entire three-and-a-half-hour crossing, he knelt over a white porcelain bowl—and longed to die. He would have cursed Nigel for this assignment if he had the energy. Flying to Benbecula hadn't been an option, not if this mission took time to solve. Hence, the cumbersome home-on-wheels that needed transport via the ferry.

Blast his queasy stomach. Without fail, whenever he set foot on a boat, his stomach revolted. Thank heavens causeways joined the Uists, the southern islands in the Outer Hebrides. Those connecting roads prevented him from entering another boat until he completed the mission.

Earlier in the week, a storm ripped through the islands and shut down the ferry service. Fortunately, the squall had moved north. Otherwise, this crossing would have been worse.

When the ferry docked on the island of South Uist, he dragged himself to the van and exited the ship, armed with a plastic seal bag and a one-liter bottle of fizzy lemonade. Rain splattered the windscreen, and gray clouds hovered sixteen meters above the ground; spotting a petrol station, he pulled in and sipped the drink until his body equalized.

While training as an operative, he'd jumped from planes, mastered defensive driving skills, and learned the art of disguise. He had even beaten his instructors in hand-to-hand combat and weapons training, but water defeated him—always had—even as a lad growing up on a coastal farm in Ireland. Place him in a vessel, large or small, and he emptied his stomach.

The wobbly feeling slowly eased, and he fired up the engine, programmed his satnav, and headed up the single-track road for Benbecula's campground, his home for the unforeseeable future.

The causeway between South Uist and Benbecula appeared in good order, and he drove across without an issue, the clear sea lapping at the rocks. Benbecula, a flat island covered in long grass and wildflowers the locals called *machair*, boasted one hill of considerable size. Other than the *machair*, Benbecula appeared devoid of vegetation.

Wind whipped in from the sea and buffeted the van, and he tightened his grip on the wheel to keep from veering off the tarmac. Ten minutes into his half-hour journey, his sat phone rang with a restricted number. He pulled to the side of the carriageway, careful not to sink into the sandy, sea-shelly soil.

"Sharidon," he answered.

"I see you've made it to the Uists," Nigel greeted him.

His spymaster monitored his travels via his sat phone.

"Any news on our two missing agents?" Sharidon leaned back, still a mite weak from the crossing.

"No contact. We've checked all the CCTV footage for Wang and Mansfield. It's possible they left the island by private boat."

"Anything else I should know?" Sharidon tapped the steering wheel. Wang and Mansfield were valuable agents. They would not have gone silent. Something was wrong.

"Put that Irish charm to good use with the locals."

Mingle with the locals? "I'll do my best." According to his brief, islanders did not socialize with incomers, those not born and raised on the Hebrides. Gaining the natives' acceptance might prove difficult.

"Satellite masts are often down out there. Report when you can. You're my eyes on this, Sharidon. Don't let me down." Nigel rang off.

Since his officer did not waste time with small talk, if Nigel said to mingle, he meant ASAP. Sharidon swung back onto the road and headed for Balivanich, the one town in the Uists of any size. Its thriving population boasted just over four hundred souls.

He had intended to set up camp first off, but time was of the essence if he hoped to find Wang and Mansfield alive. And he'd bet his cane that one or more of the islanders knew what had happened to them.

The second prong of this mission appeared more problematic if the Chinese obtained those top-secret files. The home office needed leads, and his boots on the ground were the sole supplier on this assignment. In such a tight-lipped community that closed ranks to incomers, the culprit could be anyone.

From memory, Sharidon called up what they had on the populous.

Most natives and incomers were Caucasian, save for one Asian family. He'd start his investigation there, though he didn't believe for one second the Chinese would be that obvious.

No. This situation smelled of a deep plant, someone who never had raised an eyebrow. Sharidon rubbed his jaw, his fingers snagging on the stubble. He could be wrong. Because of that, he'd handle a systematic investigation—everyone guilty until proven innocent.

As he moved up the carriageway, small white cottages dotted the gently rolling landscape before the road curved, and he got his first view of Balivanich. No other word but ugly did it justice. The utilitarian buildings were once part of a military base until civilians took over most of the property. Today, the repurposed structures boasted homes and shops. What remained of the original Royal Air Force Base, or RAF, lay behind fenced-off buildings with barbed wire across the top and an airfield that the military and locals shared.

Beneath a wooden water tower, a homemade sign stated: Meeting at the community center. Below it, today's date was written in bold. Sharidon checked his watch. The gathering started in thirty minutes. That gave him enough time to tour the thriving metropolis.

He read a sign for a military rec center, but when he passed the building, it now housed one of the island's two small co-op markets. Turning down a side street toward East Camp, those former structures now accommodated a radio station, horse-riding stables, and miscellaneous small businesses.

He circled back to the gray and white community center at the end of a paved street and parked beside a dumpster. Lonely. The entire windswept island made him lonely. If this was the biggest town in the Uists, finding excuses to meet the outlying residents might be troublesome.

After sitting for so long, Sharidon didn't need his cane. He hopped out and entered the large, open room. A podium and microphone stood at one end, two refreshment tables at the other, and portable seating occupied the middle of the floor. Men clad in flannel shirts and jeans and ladies in joggers stopped chatting and turned in his direction.

A lovely, warm welcome indeed. Sharidon pasted on his friendliest smile and nodded to the men closest to him. "Hello." He used the local dialect.

A gentleman, a thin fellow with stooped shoulders and faded gray eyes, disengaged from the crowd, and approached him. "Are you lost?"

"I'm not lost," Sharidon replied in Scottish Gaelic, ready to share the cover story Nigel had prepared for him.

"Are you an incomer?" The man switched to English.

"In a manner of speaking. The government has sent me to check the boundary lines between the military base and the co-op's land." Again, Sharidon responded in Scottish Gaelic.

According to his brief, the islanders had formed a community-owned organization that managed Benbecula, save for the RAF base, along with the islands south in the Uist chain.

"Do you intend to appropriate more land from us?" The man's mouth flatlined.

"Just the opposite. The government believes they've acquired too much property. I'm here to verify that they've exceeded their boundaries. Yer organization stands to gain more acreage when I submit my results." Sharidon projected his voice to reach the others in the room.

His inquisitor's mouth curved, and the suspicious glances inside the center softened.

"Is that why you're here, then?" A man of middle years joined the stoop-shouldered man.

Sharidon nodded. "Aye. I want to ensure that no one takes alarm if they see me out with my surveying equipment."

"You speak the Gaelic well," Middle-aged Man said.

"Some of it escapes me." No one liked a braggart, Sharidon least of all, even if he was a linguist.

"We'll have you sounding like a native in no time. What's your name?" Stoop-shouldered Man asked.

"Will Sherwood." Sharidon thrust out his hand.

"Angus Gillies." Angus's stooped shoulders did not affect his grip.

"Good to meet ye, Angus." Sharidon longed to flex his hand after the older gentleman let go.

"Meet Malcolm Kennedy." Angus jerked his chin toward Middle-aged Man.

"We've a bit of time before the meeting starts," Angus continued. "Come meet the lads. They'll be happy to know the Ministry of Defense has admitted to keeping our property."

Sharidon accompanied them around the room. The islanders' unspoken words were hard to miss. Life would be grand if they could get incomers to leave the Uists.

# CHAPTER 5

## PRE-DAWN, OUTER HEBRIDES, SCOTLAND

DARKNESS ENVELOPED him in its chill embrace as he maneuvered the small watercraft through the Atlantic off the coast of North Uist. Cutting the engine, he clicked on his torch and ran the beam over the rocky cliffs, searching for a sea cave only visible during low tide. He refused to think about the cargo he carried, a person he once served with.

The boat rose and dipped as it rode the swells. A dark crevice, no more than a shadow, appeared in his beam. He dropped anchor, the water too treacherous with rocks to bring the boat closer. With a rope secured around his waist, he heaved his burden over the side and jumped in, inflating his buoyancy control device so he didn't sink.

Setting off, he cut through the waves with strong, measured strokes, towing his load. By the time he reached the entrance, he had gone through half a tank of air. His regulator echoed inside the rocky chamber reminiscent of Star Wars' most famous villain.

The thing he towed snagged, forcing him to backtrack and free it. Water lapped, rising with the tide, the temperature much too cold without a dry suit. He shortened the rope and towed the body the last few meters to the far reaches of the cave, then wedged it behind an outcropping of rock.

He couldn't look at the tarp. Couldn't think about what he had done. Yet, despite his best efforts—he did.

A while back, he and Wang worked together. Today, she was an assignment. Too bad she had been in the wrong place at the wrong time. He compartmentalized away his actions, along with behavior that made him a traitor—the only way he could function these days.

Once, he considered himself a patriot. That was before the atrocity. He had returned to the Uists a changed man after witnessing an overseas cover-up by the admiralty when their ship poisoned local waters by dumping toxic chemicals near a small fishing village. Over two hundred Chinese died within days after ingesting poisoned seafood. And what had the admiralty done? Swept the entire thing under the rug.

After some investigative digging, he discovered that was not an isolated occurrence. The incident ate at him and corroded his allegiance to God and country. Not long after the incident, he'd returned to the Uists and married Nicola. Then, the Chinese approached him and made his wishes a reality.

He checked his psi levels and blinked. His tank had run low. Without a backward glance at Wang, he took off for the boat, swimming on the surface to conserve air.

When he reached the borrowed watercraft, he tossed his scuba fins over the side and climbed aboard. Water poured off his dry suit and puddled on the deck as he removed his tanks and flopped into the captain's chair. That forty-five-minute dive in the North Sea had pushed his physical limits.

Leaving on his insulated undergarment, he scanned the gray horizon, where the ocean divided from the sky. Time to leave before the local fishermen marked his presence in the lightening sky.

Once he hoisted anchor, he started the engine and headed south, sea spraying out from both sides of the bow, and the headwind stinging his eyes. As he drew closer to shore, he dropped anchor where someone would notice the skiff and report it to the owners. Doubtless, the police would chalk the missing boat to a drunken vacationer's joyride.

Tossing his bag overboard, he dove over the side and dragged it to shore where he changed into the clothes he'd left behind. As he tugged on his sandy socks, the sky pearled, and two fishing boats headed out to sea. That was close. Too close.

He drew the hoodie over his head, swung the dive bag over his shoulder, and started for home across the *machair.*

The Chinese had set him up for life. All they asked for in repayment was to ring a restricted number when the RAF base ran tests. Then, two years ago, China upped its demands. When he attempted to back out, they threatened Nicola's safety and left him no recourse but to do their bidding.

Nicola was his world. He'd do anything to keep her safe.

A stiff breeze blew in off the sea and plastered Cairstie's clothes to her body. She zipped up her coat and disconnected from the charging station outside her red convertible when the preprogrammed EV clicked off. In the distance, the ferry pulled away from the terminal and started for the next port.

She checked her watch. Fifteen hundred. She had left home at first light, just shy of four o'clock, and her bones ached from the long drive.

"Stay here, Winkle. I'll be right back." Cairstie leaned over the passenger door and patted his soft, furry head.

The Goldendoodle whined when she left him to enter the petrol station and purchase a drink. When she reached the counter, she smiled at the lad beside the register.

"How long a drive is it to Benbecula Island?" she asked, referring to the island north of South Uist, where the ferry had docked.

"Depends on where you're going."

She ran her card. "Balivanich."

Mrs. McDougal's home abutted the military base on the island north of the ferry terminal.

"No more than three-quarters of an hour, perhaps less."

"Thanks." Cairstie tucked up her collar and leaned into the wind as she walked to her car.

With one eye on the darkening clouds, Cairstie hopped inside and pressed the button to close the soft top on her convertible. Dad offered her the use of one of his 4x4s, but she paid for this beauty and intended to drive it during her exile. Her car symbolized the life she intended to regain when she returned to the mainland.

"Ready, Winkle?" she asked her dog.

The Goldendoodle raised his tired eyes, not even bothering to lift his head. Her pup had worn himself out on the ferry, dragging her from one external deck to another as he barked at the gulls circling the ship.

She took the A865 and headed north on the single-track carriageway toward Benbecula Island. A-roads on the mainland were double carriage-ways—not in the Uists. That would take some getting used to, especially if a farm tractor pulled out in front of her.

On the west side of the tarmac lay nothing but *machair*, the long grassy plain dotted with wildflowers that grew from the fertile soil of seashells and sand. White beaches stretched beyond to greet the mighty Atlantic's turquoise water. Hills rose to the east, the wee glens she made out, peppered with lochs.

Cairstie clutched the wheel as the wind buffeted the car and swept across the vast countryside devoid of humans. Fifteen minutes into her drive, a single lorry passed her, its engine roaring as she pulled into the layby. Never in her life had she felt so alone. How did people cope with the quiet out here?

She turned on the radio, but the station spoke only Gaelic, a language she did not comprehend, so she switched on her playlist as she maneuvered her way over the causeway, sea lapping both sides of the road.

A campground with sea views forked off the main road. When she overtook a second vehicle, the driver raised an index finger off his steering wheel in greeting. She returned the favor and smiled to herself. After the empty road, the human interaction almost felt like a conversation.

The green flag of the Outer Hebrides, with its blue and white cross, snapped in the breeze as she entered Balivanich, an ugly town with boxy terrace homes that once served as enlisted residences. No trees. No flowers. Just endless *machair* broken here and there by a white cottage and an occasional stone ruin.

The satnav's directions led her past one charging station, two small markets, a radio station, and a small hospital no larger than the village surgery at home. Cairstie's spirits plummeted. The town, if you could call it that, did not have one dress shop in sight. Thank goodness Dad warned her to stock up on groceries before she left Clovenfords.

The airport road led to Muir Tigh, her godmother's two-and-a-half-storied stone house that abutted the military base on one side and sat on several acres that overlooked the Atlantic. Its tall hedges separated it from the other homes further down the road.

Cairstie eased the car onto the dirt drive and parked by the side door. Mr. Anderson had assured her a detached garage existed, but so many weeds clogged the driveway that she stopped for fear of getting stuck.

After she snapped on Winkle's lead, she grabbed her Louis Vuitton suitcase and purse and stumbled to the door. Panting, she heaved the heavy case onto the stoop and inserted the house key in the lock.

She let herself in and flipped on the lights, having prearranged to turn on the power after some coaching from Dad. The Outer Hebrides depended almost entirely on electricity, which often went on the blink due to storms.

The house's musty odor made her wrinkle her nose. This would never do. She unfastened Winkle's lead and smiled as he darted from room to room, tail wagging and sniffing everything in sight.

"You silly bairn," she said with affection.

Her heels clicked as she crossed the tile floor and cranked open the kitchen windows. Cold air billowed the curtains as she plugged in the old-fashioned fridge. After lugging inside another suitcase and groceries, she opened the first kitchen cupboard.

"Ew. Ew. Ew." She stepped back and shuddered.

Mouse droppings lay at the bottom. She slammed the door, retrieved her checklist, and sketched a catch-and-release trap at the top. No beady-eyed rodents were getting into her food. To ensure they didn't, she stored her groceries inside the fridge before she exited the house to walk the property's exterior.

Muir Tigh proved smaller than a manor but more extensive than a parsonage. Picture windows lined the overgrown back garden, which faced the North Atlantic. The house's pointed gables and stone exterior held authentic charm compared to other structures in the area. Mrs. McDougal must have hired someone from the mainland to build it.

Cairstie rubbed her arms and went inside to tour her new lodgings.

The eat-in kitchen with its round, wooden, drop-leaf table and chairs seemed good-sized and modern with its cooker oven combo and microwave. But then, she was no judge, having never spent time in a kitchen, save when Mother and Sophie went on a baking spree and needed someone to sample their creations.

The adjoining lounge, with its floral chintz sofas draped in dust covers, appeared rather grand for island life, as did the dining room that seated twelve. She entered the corridor to access the snug, a small, cozy room with a sofa, telly, overstuffed chair, and a wood burner, just the place to spend an evening. A family bathroom with pink porcelain fixtures received no more than a cursory glance. At the far end of the corridor, she located a study with built-in bookshelves, an overlarge desk, and her godmother's set of golf clubs.

One last door remained on the ground floor. Cairstie pushed it wide to find a small solarium that faced the beach. Frigid air whooshed in from several broken glass panes, and she closed the door with a bang.

Upstairs, she discovered three dormered bedrooms, each with sea views, and a second family bathroom—another flight of stairs led to the attic.

Cairstie twirled in delight, laughter bubbling out. Winkle joined in the fun. He barked and zoomed about the dusty attic until he sneezed. Mrs. McDougal's home held real charm, and even though it was old-fashioned, Cairstie found the atmosphere delightful, minus the mouse droppings.

With a lightened heart, she returned to the ground floor and closed the windows, then cranked up the heat. A fine coat of dust covered the worktops, floor, and exposed furniture. Thankfully, someone had covered the sofas.

Even with Winkle for company, the quiet weighed upon her, much like a library with a vigilant librarian on duty. Before her exile on Benbecula ended, she'd probably become one of those women who talked to themselves and kept a dozen cats.

She retrieved her mobile and found that she had reception. After snapping a selfie of herself in her new home, she sent it to her parents.

Cairstie: Arrived safe and sound. Will call soon. XO.

Mother: Glad you made it in one piece.
Love you.

Winkle, worn out after his adventures, curled up inside his kennel and was out in minutes. Might as well unpack. She had nothing better to do. She tottered upstairs with her suitcases. Feeling much like Goldilocks, she tested all three beds, chose the most comfortable mattress, plugged in her electric blanket, and settled for a late afternoon nap.

Hours later, she sat up groggily and rubbed her eyes. Her throat was parched, so she trotted downstairs to retrieve a glass from the kitchen cupboard. She reached inside and closed her hand around a film-covered cup. Ew. She made a face and let go. Moving to the tap, she leaned over the basin to drink from the faucet. Nothing came out. She twisted the opposite handle and had the same result. Why didn't she have water?

Stumped, she faced the kitchen, her backside against the counter, and shivered. The place was an icebox. Why hadn't the house warmed? She pressed her hand on the radiator. Cold.

She frowned. The solicitor assured her that the house was in perfect working order. She glanced at Winkle, who lay watching her from the kennel.

"Thirsty?" she asked.

Winkle sat up and barked.

He needed water, and so did she. No hope for it. She latched Winkle's kennel shut and blew him a kiss. "I'll be back soon, laddie."

He thumped his tail.

She grabbed her purse and walked up the street toward the restaurant she had noted earlier. Perhaps someone inside could recommend a furnace repairer or handyperson to check her plumbing. But the sign said closed. Who closed their restaurant at nine o'clock, especially in summer, with the twilight lasting well after eleven?

Pivoting, she scanned the street for other options and came up empty. Both grocers had shut down for the night. She retraced her steps and happened upon a pub with a cluster of vehicles parked outside. Live music sounded from within.

She smiled at the tune as she pushed the handle and entered. Two fiddlers and an accordionist stood in a corner playing a rousing melody.

Seated at tables scattered around the room, people clapped to the beat. Several men at the counter glanced her way. A tall, dark-haired man leaned against the bar, a glass of brew raised halfway to his lips, a cane beside him.

Cairstie stopped dead in her tracks. Her heart roared, and a great rushing filled her ears. The cad who had turned her into a laughingstock was *here*. The very same bampot who disappeared from her sister's reception—the Irishman called Sharidon–the bane of her existence.

"Sherwood, care for a game?" A fellow with a solid upper body at a nearby table called.

Sharidon set his drink on the bar, his green eyes fastened on her face. "I'm a wee bit busy just now, Hank." He grasped his cane and crossed the room toward her.

Cairstie balled her fist, and her breath rasped.

"Come now, Sherwood. I need to win back my money after last night's game," a short, stocky man with a red beard said.

"Another time, Gordon," Sharidon tossed over his shoulder.

Cairstie narrowed her eyes. "Sherwood?" she bit out. "What kind of name is—"

Sharidon dropped his cane and snatched her into his arms. Before she could protest, he covered her mouth with his.

# CHAPTER 6

ONE THOUGHT and one thought alone, pierced the panic cresting inside Sharidon. He had to get Lady Cairstie out of the pub before she blew his cover. He clutched her elbows and backed her to the door.

But Lady Cairstie jerked free, her eyes like blue flames, and knuckled him in the mouth.

"Ouch." Sharidon tasted blood and dabbed his bottom lip.

Laughter erupted in the room behind him.

For such a feminine woman, Lady Cairstie did not hit like a girl. "Nice punch."

"Do that again and see what I do, Sh—" She drew back her fist.

He clamped her arm to keep it from plowing into his face a second time.

"Shh." If anyone overheard her spout his real name . . . "Go with it." He silently begged her to cooperate as he leaned down and kissed her a second time.

Her eyes remained open and bored into his. For the briefest second, her mouth responded, then she drew up her knee. He shifted a split second before it connected with its target, and his bad leg took the brunt of it. He staggered, then tripped on the raised threshold, knocking the pair of them to the ground inside the pub's vestibule and slamming the internal set of doors between them and the pub proper.

"Get a room, Sherwood," a drunken male guffawed, his voice muffled by the divider.

"I'm most sorry," Sharidon grunted, pitching his voice low.

"Haven't you damaged my reputation enough?" Lady Cairstie spat, then rolled off him and regained her feet, her face the color of a ripe tomato. "What are you doing here, anyway? And why did you kiss me?" Her eyes narrowed to slits as her gaze traveled over his body.

He sat up and rubbed his elbow.

"Did you hurt your leg?" Worry lit her blue eyes. Worry he didn't deserve after how he'd used her.

"Could ye fetch me my cane?" He'd never admit to the hot pokers shooting inside his femur.

She slipped back inside and returned with his walking stick a moment later. When she handed it over, he made rather a show of rising to his feet. The musicians switched to a new song, their music somewhat subdued through the closed doors.

"I suppose you have a reason for using an alias?" Lady Cairstie asked sweetly—too sweetly.

His heart rate ticked up a notch. "What makes ye think my name isn't Sharidon Sherwood?" he asked.

"Because it isn't. I asked Elise when you disappeared from her reception. Sharidon's your surname."

Her smug retort rubbed him the wrong way.

"What are you up to, Mr. Sherwood?" Her voice dripped with sarcasm.

"Nothing that concerns ye, me darlin.'" He tapped his cane on the ground. She was going to be a problem; he could feel it in his bones.

"If you think you can brush me off, you don't know me very well."

He exhaled. "If I call yer sister and have her speak with ye, would ye let this alone?"

"Not in the least. My sister's MI6, and so is that husband of hers—which makes them both liars." Cairstie tilted her head coyly. "Much like you."

Shock sizzled his brain cells like a 220 volt. How had she figured that out? Elise and Harry would never share that information.

With difficulty, he kept his reaction from showing. "Yer sister is no more a spy than yer mother."

Cairstie snorted. "You'll need to do better than that, Irish. My family is a veritable nest of spies." A crafty look slid over her features. "If you expect me to keep quiet about who you are, you'll need to fix some things where I'm staying."

"Yer staying on the island?" This was bad—more than bad. This was a problem.

"Aye."

He needed her off the island ASAP. "What kind of things? Why are ye here anyway?" Sharidon pushed open the external doors and moved outside to the lot. He leaned against the building and rubbed his thigh. She followed. Roxbury's youngest wasn't as naïve as her family believed.

"I inherit my godmother's estate if I live here for the next six months."

His body tensed like a coiled spring, and he squeezed his cane's handle until his bones all but cracked. If she stayed on Benbecula, she'd destroy his mission.

"What if I'm not handy?" he asked, suppressing the turmoil swirling inside him.

"I find that hard to believe. Your kind are excellent improvisers."

"My kind?" Her tone made it sound like he had an incurable disease.

"I'm no fool, Sharidon. Harry and Elise are adept mechanics. If you don't help me, I'll put it about who you work for."

There it was. The threat he expected. He glowered at her for a full minute. She had him over a barrel, and she knew it.

"What sort of things do ye need help with?" He'd roll with it for now, but Lady Cairstie's days on the island were numbered.

"For starters, the tap doesn't run, and my heater's on the blink." She folded her arms.

"Are the waterworks on?" he asked.

"We're on wells here, aren't we?" Her brow puckered.

"This is an island, not a castle. The local water works handle all potable water."

She blushed but recovered quickly enough. "What about the other?"

"Yer heating?" Tenacious. He liked that. The lass was like a dog at a bone, rather like her sister, Elise.

"Aye." A gust blew her long, fair hair into her eyes.

Attraction stirred, startling in its intensity. Sharidon glanced away before he did or said something stupid. "I'll give it a look. Where are ye staying?"

"Muir Tigh. Do you know it?"

"I do. I'll walk ye home and see to it now."

"Just like that?" Suspicion colored her voice. "You want me to leave the pub, so I don't rat you out, is that it?"

The lass was clever, he'd grant her that.

"I'm a dab hand at most things." He sidestepped her question. Despite the precarious situation, he was enjoying their head-butting a mite too well.

"So, I was right?" Lady Cairstie all but crowed with victory.

"I'm a farm lad from Ireland. If ye can't mend broken tools and machinery, ye don't eat."

She rolled her eyes, a look he rather enjoyed.

"Why'd ye come to the pub?" he asked.

"I'm parched, and so is my dog."

"Ye came for a whiskey?" Roxbury's family were not heavy drinkers.

"No." A feminine gurgle of amusement escaped her lips. "I don't drink alcohol, but I'd adore a glass of water just now. Everything else in town is closed."

"They've water inside. I'll fetch it for ye." He left before she could argue and went to beg a liter off Randy, the bartender, a well-made man of indiscriminate years.

"I'll be needing some water. Can ye sell me a liter?" Sharidon leaned on his cane. He had spent the day scouting the area and chatting with the locals, and his leg was complaining.

"Ye've blood on yer face." Randy handed him the bottle from across the bar.

Sharidon tossed a tenner at him and dabbed at his swollen mouth. "That lassie has a wicked left. Watch yerselves, lads." He warned the room at large. "Don't be getting too friendly with the likes of her. She's liable to pop ye one too."

Raucous laughter erupted around him.

Tucking the water under his arm, Sharidon started for the door. So, the lass intended to blackmail him, eh? A reluctant smile tugged at his mouth. Well, two could play at that game.

# CHAPTER 7

RAIN PATTERED against the windows and woke Cairstie the following day. She rolled over, flung her arm wide on the queen-sized mattress, then arched her back and stretched. Winkle whined and scratched at her bedroom door.

"All right. All right." How did he get out of his kennel? She must not have latched it properly.

She slipped a hoodie over her sleepwear and padded barefoot downstairs to let him out. When she opened the kitchen door, frigid air rushed inside her toasty home. It had taken half the night for the furnace to warm the house after Sharidon showed her how to bleed the radiators.

Winkle hesitated.

"Go on."

Needing no further encouragement, her Goldendoodle dashed out. Cairstie folded her arms across her chest and shivered on the stoop until he darted back after the swiftest potty run in history. He circled her feet and whimpered.

She brought him inside and dug through a kitchen drawer for a tea towel.

"Poor Winkle. You don't like the cold? I agree with you. It's midsummer and feels like November out there." She dried him off, then brought him upstairs, where he jumped onto her bed. He shouldn't be on the duvet, but what did it matter? Muir Tigh House was her place, not the castle.

Cairstie removed her damp hoodie, tossed it on the floor, snuggled under the covers, and stared at the ceiling—her first day in exile.

She retrieved her mobile from the bedside table and marked a big fat x through yesterday's date, much like she had as a child when she cut off paper chain rings to count off the days before an anticipated event.

Homesickness swirled within her, and its weight expanded inside her chest.

Out of habit, she checked her friend's socials. Last night, they had visited her favorite dance club. Cairstie scrolled through previous posts of them riding vespas in Rome, eating chocolate croissants at a Paris bistro, and whale watching in Iceland. Not one of her "close friends" had texted her since Ahern's arrest.

For years, Mother had insisted Cairstie's friends had no depth and encouraged her to associate with people who cared about things that mattered. But Cairstie adored magazine shoots, runway shows, parties, and trotting the globe, so she ignored her mother's counsel.

When she introduced Ahern to her girlfriends, they had enjoyed hanging with the handsome aristocrat, but the instant a whiff of scandal attached to her, those so-called girlfriends tossed her aside like last season's couture. Now thoroughly sorry for herself, Cairstie switched to clips of Stella Walker's latest runway show and the model who replaced her. Stella had designed those clothes for her.

Cairstie dropped her mobile on the duvet as the ache inside burst. Tears poured down her cheeks, and she buried her face in her pillow. No one needed her.

When Ahern had humiliated her, she didn't cry. When her friends ghosted her, she pretended it didn't hurt. When Stella made her redundant, Cairstie kept it together. Until now. Now she had proof that her world had moved on without her. She padded to the bathroom and retrieved the tissue box, then jumped back in bed and cried even harder. Winkle crept forward on the duvet and licked her face. Was it so wrong to enjoy parties and pretty clothes? Or foreign travel? Or admit that she basked in the social media likes and interactions on her platforms?

She was stuck on this flat, forsaken island with nothing but grass, sea, and rain for company—along with that horrid Sharidon–the harbinger of all her troubles. Cairstie scrunched the soggy tissue and tossed it onto her bedside table, then snatched another and blew her nose.

Her head ached from weeping, and she doubtless looked a fright. It didn't matter. No one cared how she looked out here. No one cared at all.

Cairstie flopped back onto the mattress as fresh tears poured down her cheeks. She wanted Sophie, her next oldest sibling by almost five years. Sophie always made her feel better, except when she had collaborated with Elise and made her the laughingstock of the Borders. Despite all that, she needed to hear Sophie's voice.

She patted the blankets until she located her mobile and pressed her sister's number.

"I was about to call you." Sophie sounded nothing short of joyous. "Zander and I are setting our wedding date."

"Oh." That large canary diamond on her sister's finger had obviously sped things along. "When are you thinking?"

"This autumn. I know that isn't much time." Sophie rushed on, "Only a few months, but Elise encouraged us to make it soon, so Mother doesn't turn it into an extravaganza, but I'd like to wait until you return. Do you know when that will be?"

With her feelings still raw from both of her sisters' betrayals, Cairstie left for Benbecula without wishing either goodbye. After what Sophie had done, it would serve her right if she didn't attend her wedding. But despite their deception, Cairstie missed them.

She bit back a fresh sob. She couldn't pour out her heartbreak and mess with Sophie's happiness, even if she longed to retaliate.

"Are you there, Cairstie?" Sophie asked.

"Aye." Cairstie wiped her eyes.

"For a moment, I thought we'd lost connectivity."

"No, I'm here. That's awfully kind of you to hold off until I return, but . . ." Cairstie swallowed, fighting the hard lump in her throat. "If you want to get married this autumn, I think you should. Elise is right. Mother will turn your wedding into something edging on a royal event."

"But I want you here for it."

That was all it took. Her chin trembled, and silent tears oozed from under Cairstie's lids. Sophie wanted her.

"I'm stuck here for the next six months, and I refuse to be the reason you place your wedding on hold. I won't return until January, and you know how difficult winter weddings are to plan. We have too many storms, and travel is unreliable."

"I'll think about it." Sophie, for all her sweetness, had the disposition of a mule when she dug in her heels.

Cairstie muted her mobile and blew her nose. Missing the festivities that led up to a family wedding made Benbecula even more unbearable.

"Are you okay, Cairstie bug?" Sophie used her childhood pet name.

"Just a wee bit homesick, is all."

"It must be dreadfully dull for you. I know how much you love the city."

"The wide-open spaces are an adjustment." Cairstie picked at a piece of lint on the duvet. "Do you think you can outmaneuver Mother taking over your wedding?"

"I hope so. Zander and I like simple."

"Mother is anything but." Cairstie cleared her throat, then voiced the unthinkable, "I think you should pick a date and go with it. Why did you take so long anyway?"

"Everything happened so fast. I wanted to be sure our feelings would last after the newness wore off."

"You picked a splendid fellow. He's handsome and verra, verra rich," Cairstie whispered sotto voce as the knot inside her eased.

"That's not why I'm marrying him," Sophie responded like a prim schoolmarm.

"No, but it certainly doesn't hurt," Cairstie teased.

They both laughed.

"I'll let you know what we decide," Sophie said. "Cheers, love."

Cairstie reclined against the pillows. Despite the betrayal and hurt, Cairstie longed to attend Sophie's wedding. Perhaps Mr. Anderson would allow it. After she'd witnessed Elise's struggles during her engagement, Cairstie didn't want that for Sophie. The less time Mother had to plan, the better.

Someone pounded on Cairstie's kitchen door and drew her upright.

Who on earth could that be? Winkle lifted his head and woofed, then ran to her bedroom door and looked at her expectantly. She couldn't meet the neighbors with her hair, a rat's nest, and mascara under her eyes.

The pounding continued. Whoever it was knew she was inside. Flinging back the covers, she tossed her hair into a messy bun, then charged downstairs in her tank top and sleeping shorts, ready to give the door pounder an earful.

She snatched up her godmother's nine iron from the study, then swung the door wide, Winkle barking at her heels. Sharidon stood on the stoop, his hand raised for another round of door beating, grocery bags and a tool kit at his feet.

A slow smile tugged up his lips. "Ye look like ye've been working out really hard."

"Whoever taught you how to give compliments, Mr. Sharidon? The bin man?" Cairstie gave him her politest smile.

"If it's compliments ye want. Okay." He scratched his head and assessed her again. "It looks like yer leg exercises are paying huge dividends."

Ugh. Cairstie spun on her bare heels and marched into the kitchen. Sharidon followed, carrying several bags and a tool kit. Winkle sniffed his ankle, looked up at him, and wagged his tail. Cairstie rolled her eyes. Great watchdog.

"I assume ye'd like me to shut the door?" he asked.

Only if he was on the opposite side of it. Cairstie set down the golf club.

Not appearing the least abashed by her silence, Sharidon nudged the door closed with his boot. "I brought the cord for yer cooker and a heating element for the oven."

"Was that bad too?"

"Haven't ye used either of them?" He placed the shopping bags on the worktop, pushing yesterday's toast crumbs aside and depositing her dirty crockery and knife in the basin.

"I don't cook."

"What are ye subsisting on? Toast and carrots?" He glanced at the plate, unwashed due to her lack of water and an even more considerable dearth of skill sets.

She folded her arms and gave him the stink eye.

"Are women born with an innate sense of how to do that?" Sharidon indicated her expression.

She chose not to respond.

"Have ye checked the tap to see if yer water is on?" he asked.

"I haven't called them yet." She'd meant to, but her morning hadn't gone as planned.

"That's quite all right. I handled it." The fellow puffed out his chest like he'd done something heroic.

"How? Don't I need to appear in person?" she asked.

"I impersonated ye on my mobile and filled out the online form. This is a small community; they don't stand overmuch on ceremony here." He winked, then moved to the cooker and hauled it away from the wall, the corded muscles in his arms rippling.

She caught herself just before she performed another eye roll. She'd never understand how this fellow worked for the same employer as her brother-in-law. Spies were stealthy creatures, strong and athletic. Sharidon used a cane, the complete antithesis of everything spyish. Perhaps he applied that overabundance of charm in an office setting, away from the action.

"And how did that go?" She couldn't imagine his deep voice passing muster for a woman's.

"See for yerself." He jerked his chin toward her kitchen basin.

"I will." She moved to the sink and turned the lever. Air bubbles hissed, then a blast of cold water shot from the tap. It sprayed the counter and soaked her tank top. She inhaled sharply through her nose and shut off the water.

Sharidon's green eyes sparkled with suppressed humor, and he brazenly gave her the once-over.

She gasped. No one ever treated her with such an utter lack of manners. With her arms crossed over her chest, she sped from the room, serenaded by Sharidon's laughter.

# CHAPTER 8

STILL CHUCKLING from Lady Cairstie's dousing and subsequent flight from the kitchen, Sharidon stepped onto the weed-filled driveway and battled his way through the overgrowth to the white, sandy beach at the end of her back garden.

Waves rolled, spread across the sand, then receded in its lulling melody. He glanced over his shoulder toward the house as he withdrew his sat phone and rang Nigel. A shadow moved in one of the upper windows.

"Thatcher," Nigel answered, his tone clipped.

"We have a slight hiccup."

"Let's hear it." Papers shuffled through the speaker.

"Roxbury's youngest is here and knows who I am." He'd held off updating Nigel last night, thinking he could convince Lady Cairstie to return home.

Movement. Sharidon shifted and eyed the upstairs windows. Sure enough, a curtain twitched. Lady Cairstie was watching him. He waved. Not much got past the lass; he'd give her that.

"The youngest, you say? The one caught up in that horse syndicate?"

"She had no part in that, just the misfortune to date the chap who did." Why did he feel the need to defend her? Since her arrival, Lady Cairstie had been nothing but a thorn in his side—albeit a lovely one.

Those legs. He blocked any further images of Lady Cairstie's gorgeous gams and waited for Nigel's verdict.

"If she's a problem, I'll have Harry Benson speak with her." Nigel didn't sound concerned.

"That's another issue."

"How so?"

"Lady Cairstie is aware that her sister, Harry, and I are, or were, affiliated with MI6." It didn't matter that Elise had left SIS for the private sector and Harry had transferred to MI5.

"How did she work that out?" Nigel asked.

"Very little gets past her."

"Hmmm. Should I contact C?" Nigel referred to the head of British Intelligence, who also happened to be Lady Cairstie's uncle.

"I don't think it's dire, but I felt ye should be aware of the situation."

Cairstie moved into plain view, and he blew her a kiss.

"Are you keeping close?" Nigel asked.

"Aye. Lady Cairstie threatened to expose my identity if I didn't repair her place."

Silence.

"Nigel?"

"She blackmailed you?" Humor laced Nigel's words. "I might recruit her myself. Henderson's make fabulous agents."

"Don't encourage her. She's a spoilt baggage with a will of iron."

"Hmmm. Any leads?" Nigel switched to the more immediate issue.

"I've been meeting with the locals."

"How's that going?"

"Rather well. They shun most incomers, but my case is different. Since the inhabitants stand to gain more property due to my cover job, they've been quite friendly."

"Don't beat too many of them at cards, or that friendliness will evaporate."

"Roger that." Growing up in a large family on the north coast of Ireland, money was scarce. Sharidon had learned to count cards and a few other unsavory skills to keep food on their table during lean times.

"I only joined last night's game to meet more islanders."

"Any whiff on Wang and Mansfield? The forensics team located blood on the control room floor, but thus far, no bodies."

"Not so much as a sniff. The natives were edgy when I asked about recent crimes. They insist that their issues come from mainlanders."

"That's likely true when it deals with petty theft," Nigel said, his voice once more accompanied by the swish of papers.

"I'll let you know what I find. Right now, I've got a date with a cooker. Ta." Sharidon repocketed his sat phone and turned back toward the house.

Lady Cairstie stood on the stoop near the side door. She had changed into trousers and a bright blue jumper that emphasized the color of her eyes. He missed the shorts and messy bun. This woman appeared too grand.

"Is everything all right?" she asked when he reached her.

"Aye. What other items do ye have for me to fix?"

"Why do you believe I have more projects?" She raised an arched brow and tapped the toe of her shoe.

"I can't think of another reason ye'd follow me out here unless it was my handsome self ye were missin'." He laid on his Irish brogue.

She flushed a becoming shade of pink. "If you must know, I'm off to hire a housekeeper and gardener. Do you need me to bring back anything?"

Touched at her consideration, he left off teasing. "That's most thoughtful of ye, lass, but folks here work three jobs or more to make ends meet. They don't have time to take care of ye. Ye'll need to do that yerself or hire someone from the mainland."

Her expressive eyes filled with dismay at his words. "Take care of this myself?" She motioned to her tangled garden.

"Aye." Was this woman entirely helpless? "After I fix the cooker and oven, I'll show ye how to start the Flymo. Ye have one, don't ye?"

"If I do, it's in the garage." She picked her way through the long grass to the detached garage and withdrew a key from her pocket.

Sharidon gained the stoop and placed his hand on the knob. What had brought this pampered lass to Benbecula? Lady Cairstie could no sooner care for herself than a wee bairn.

He fumed at the way she coerced him to play nursemaid. He didn't have time for this. He had a traitor and two missing agents to locate.

A scream shattered the silence. Sighing, Sharidon turned back. "What's the matter?" he asked when he reached the open garage doors.

"A mouse." She pointed to a dark corner.

"Ye probably scared the life out of him with those shrieks of yers." Was she for real?

"I hate mice." She shuddered.

"Yer in the country; they're everywhere." He forced back his mounting exasperation.

"I almost stepped on it."

"Then wear boots." He shook his head.

She searched his face. "You don't like me much, do you?"

"I'm here to do a job, Lady Cairstie. Liking ye has nothing to do with it." He pivoted and marched to the house. This time, no shrieks followed him.

# CHAPTER 9

CAIRSTIE OPENED her eyes in the darkened room, her heart hammering. What was that? She checked her mobile for the time. Three o'clock. Hours ago, the ebb and flow of waves hitting the shore had lulled her to sleep.

The ocean wouldn't have woken her. So, what had? With only three flights a day to Benbecula's bustling airport, the town rolled up its proverbial pavement at nine o'clock. She flipped onto her side while her eyes adjusted to the gloom. Sound carried for miles across the flat grassland, even those unrelated to wind and waves.

She glanced at Winkle, who snored at the foot of her bed.

Beneath her room, the study door creaked. She locked the house last night and covered the windows with the triple-lined draperies to keep out drafts. Someone had let themselves in.

Were kids downstairs having a lark at her expense? Or was it something more sinister, like the thing that had brought Sharidon to the island? Whoever he rang in her back garden yesterday, their exchange had wiped the charm from his features. No, Sharidon's reason for being here had nothing to do with her house. This was a dare. One she intended to stop.

Grabbing a torch from her bedside table drawer, she tiptoed down the stairs, not bothering with the light as she intended to scare the wee beggars

from entering her house again. Blood pounded like kettle drums inside her
ears, and she could scarcely hear her thoughts. When she reached the
bottom step, she peeked around the wall. The study door at the end of the
corridor stood wide, a door she had closed before she went to bed.

A grunt came from within. Wood splintered—a soft curse.

Her heartbeat pinged, then ricocheted off her ribcage. She narrowed
her eyes. How dare someone tear up her house.

Like a ninny, she had left her phone upstairs so she couldn't dial 999.
Did this backwater town even have emergency services? She crept down
the hall and leaned around the opening to retrieve one of her godmother's
golf clubs, the study black as pitch. A soft padding behind her on the
stairs. Then Winkle brushed against her leg and plunked himself at her
feet.

Sharidon didn't think she could take care of herself? Well, she'd handle
this teen vandal on her own. Snapping on the torch's high beam, she
shone it on the shadowed figure.

A male whirled, clad all in black with a lumpy thing around his head.
She shrieked, dropped her torch, and swung Mrs. McDougal's metal club
like a cricket bat. It connected with the fellow's shoulder and upper back.
He swore and fumbled with something on his person.

She raised the nine-iron to strike again, twisting as she did so.

Pop. Pop. Pop.

Plaster cut her face from the wall beside her. She gasped. A gun? The
fellow had a gun. This was no teen out for a lark. She opened her mouth
to scream, but nothing came out.

Winkle burst into the room, growling.

The fellow swore and shoved her into the desk, knocking her with
such force that she dropped the club.

The intruder put the desk between him and Winkle's teeth, then
leaped through the doorway, Winkle on his heels. A second later, the outer
door banged, and cold air swept down the corridor into the study.
Rubbing her backside, Cairstie straightened and hit the light switch.

No power.

The fellow must have cut the electricity or taken advantage of one of
the numerous outages on the islands. Her knees buckled, and she leaned
against the desk to hold herself up.

"Winkle." Her voice was nothing more than a breath of air.

Her dog returned, still growling under his breath. She sank to the floor beside him and wrapped her arms around his neck.

"Good, lad." That's when the trembling started.

Raised with firearms on her father's estate, she knew a thing or two about guns. She and her family helped keep the pheasant, grouse, and deer populations under control.

Those pops were much too quiet. The intruder must have used a silencer on his handgun. Both items were illegal in the UK. If she called 999, it would take ages for the police to arrive. They'd doubtless send someone from the mainland in a few days. Elise or Harry were much better options, but again, it would take half a day before either arrived.

Unfortunately, Sharidon was her best option.

Cairstie exhaled a shaky breath. She had determined never to speak to him after his discourteous behavior. This was different. He worked with her sister and brother-in-law, which meant he carried a weapon and knew how to use one—definitely her safest option, more so than the baton-toting constables.

She fetched her mobile and returned to Mrs. McDougal's study. What had that fellow been about? Searching the floor, she located her torch and shone it on the wall in question. Splintered wood inside the cupboard disclosed a cavity beyond. She inched forward and peered inside. What on earth?

A tunnel—an old one, by the look of it.

Her knees wobbled, and she leaned against the wall as reaction set in with a vengeance. She didn't have Sharidon's number, but she had a good idea where he lived after he mentioned living in a Sprinter van near the causeway.

Gathering her purse and coat, along with her bottle of mace and several golf clubs, she bundled Winkle into the car and took the B-892 toward the caravan park, praying Sharidon's van was the only one at the site.

Atlantic breakers rolled, lace-edged, onto the sand a few meters from the road. On the horizon, clouds scudded above the sea as dawn pearled the sky. Sea birds skimmed the waves, and their discordant cries filled the air.

She had surprised the intruder tonight; that alone had given her the upper hand. Few carried guns in the UK—save for the military or special police, or Sharidon's people—not unless they were up to no good.

Cairstie hadn't gone looking for trouble—it had come calling. Now that it had, Sharidon had best fill her in on what was happening here because nothing could convince her that the intruder was an affiliate of Sharidon's. Undercover agents did not shoot at civilians.

A caravan park loomed ahead. She slowed and entered the facility, scanning the vehicles and tents facing the Atlantic. Only one van occupied the campground, so she pulled in behind it and turned off her engine.

The first rays of sunlight limned the clouds and silhouetted them in gold. Cairstie opened her car door and climbed out, keeping a tight grip on Winkle's lead. He leaned into his leash in an effort to chase the birds.

"Come, Winkle."

He looked at her, then at the gulls, and barked.

"Shhh. No birds." She stepped to the van on steadier legs and rapped on the door.

The white Sprinter van rocked, and the side door cracked open.

"What do ye want?" Sharidon snapped.

She gave him a perky smile and congratulated herself. The fellow had gotten up on the wrong side of the bed, a fact which filled her with delight after her night of terror.

"I'm returning the favor for the other morning."

"It's half four." He protested.

"Thank you for the update." She took in his dark, tousled hair and sleepy green eyes. "May I come in?"

He grunted and moved out of her way. "Hurry it up. Yer letting in the cold."

She lifted Winkle, then climbed aboard. Sharidon shut the door and placed his gun inside a drawer. Her eyes bulged. It was one thing to assume your companion was a spy, but it was quite another to see his firearm and prove it.

Tension drained from her body, and she felt safe for the first time in the better part of an hour. Cairstie didn't like Sharidon, but he'd protect her. Of that, she did not doubt.

Cairstie took in the white shiplap that covered the van's walls and ceiling. Every window appeared draped in blackout material. Upper and lower cabinets stretched down one side with a built-in two-burner cooker, miniature oven, basin, and mini fridge. A shower stood on the opposite wall, along with a small table with two built-in chairs. Across the rear section, a raised bed stretched from wall to wall, the blankets mussed.

Sharidon clicked on the lights and indicated that she utilize one of the chairs. She plopped onto the padded cushion and gloried in the heat.

He edged past her, removed a jumper from a cupboard above the bed, and tugged it over his head, covering a T-shirt that said, "North Rim, Grand Canyon."

Grabbing two mugs from another cupboard, he filled the kettle and clicked it on high. "Tea? Coffee? Hot chocolate?" His matter-of-fact tone put her at ease and allowed her to gather her thoughts after her flight from Muir Tigh House.

"Hot chocolate, please."

After the water heated, he turned, exposing a livid scar on his leg–a scar the dark hair couldn't conceal.

"What happened?" she asked to postpone the inevitable questions. Of reliving the fear. The surprise. And the anger for the fellow who shot at her.

"Surgery to repair some damage." Sharidon's tone flatlined her curiosity.

"On-the-job injury?"

His eyes met hers as he set both mugs on the table, then slid into the seat across from her, bumping her knee with his own. "Now, what's brought ye out here at this ridiculous hour?"

He sipped his tea while she shared her tale, his green eyes intent. "Do ye think the fellow could identify ye?" he asked.

"Possibly. He wore an apparatus around his head, similar to what Dad uses on the estate." She squeezed the mug between her fingers, its warmth not communicating to her brain.

"Night vision goggles, most like." Two furrows scored Sharidon's brows.

"Was I right to come to you? Or should I notify the police?" she asked.

"I'd like a look before the local constabulary gets involved." Sharidon didn't elaborate, but suppressed excitement emanated from him in waves.

She sipped her hot chocolate as she considered his response. Could what happened tonight in the study be linked to Sharidon's presence on Benbecula? If so, had her experience at Mrs. McDougal's landed her in the thick of it?

# CHAPTER 10

SHARIDON TOOK THE COASTAL ROAD, following Lady Cairstie's red convertible to Muir Tigh House, and parked behind her on the weed-infested drive. The lass ought to switch out that Mercedes for something practical, but far be it for him to mention the fact. That woman had definitive ideas about things.

He secured his weapon, then added two ammo magazines to his pockets before he hopped out and locked the van.

Lady Cairstie stood outside her kitchen door, her hand on her dog's lead. Though she appeared composed, he sensed the fear that sent her to his campsite at first light—a fear that kept her from entering her home.

When he reached her, she unlocked the door and followed him inside.

"Where's yer power main?" he asked after pressing the unresponsive switch.

"Just here, beside the refrigerator."

Using his mobile torch to light the way, he flipped the breakers, and the kitchen lights clicked to life. He scanned the room, his hand on his waist holster. Observing the neatly stacked dishes in the basin, he couldn't resist needling her to break the tension. "No luck finding a housekeeper?"

"Not yet." She pushed her reluctant dog inside his kennel.

Winkle barked in protest.

"Until ye do, might I suggest ye invest in paper products?" Either that or learn how to clean up after herself. If she didn't, mice would come calling. The idea made him grin despite the circumstances.

Lady Cairstie led him past a bathroom on her way to the study. She shut the door, but not before he caught sight of trousers and blouses hanging from every conceivable surface.

"What happened in there?" He jerked his chin toward the closed door.

"Nothing."

She did not elaborate, so he dropped the subject. "Where's the tunnel?"

"Just through here." Cairstie opened a door at the end of the hall. He stepped inside and scanned the study, where a large desk sat before a picture window facing the Atlantic.

The space contained floor-to-ceiling bookcases stacked with random books and binders on one wall. On the near wall, three gouges in the plaster drew his attention. Solid metal filled the center of each one. A chill raced through him.

"Are these new?" He touched the bullet holes and glanced at her.

"Aye."

"Why didn't ye mention the fellow shot at ye?" Was the lass daft?

"Because you'd call my sister, and then my family would force me to leave the island."

"Do ye have a death wish or something?" Was she for real? "Whoever shot at ye is still at large. Until they're apprehended, ye aren't safe."

A mulish expression flitted across her features.

"Lady Cairstie, I mean no disrespect, but—"

"I can't go home, even though I'd like nothing better." She pressed her hands together.

"Why not?"

"Have you watched the news lately? That nonsensical act you pulled at the restaurant for my sisters didn't work, because the scandal around Ahern's arrest has spilled over on me anyway. I'm here to escape it. Returning home is the last thing I need. Besides, I'll lose my inheritance if I go."

"Ye could lose yer life if ye don't."

"There's nothing for me at home. At least here I can ride out the scandal, no thanks to you," she huffed, her eyes blue fire.

*Ach.* He'd done her a favor getting rid of Ahern, scandal or no, and she held it against him? He folded his arms across his chest. The lass was the stubbornest Scot he had ever encountered, and that was saying something, considering he knew her older sister. "What's this about an inheritance?"

"My godmother left me her entire estate if I stay for six months."

"Hmmm." Despite being shot at, he sensed that her fear of public opinion, more than physical danger, kept her rooted on the island. Since her career dealt primarily with public scrutiny, her arrival on Benbecula had likely more to do with starting fresh than anything else.

Pivoting, he approached the study's cupboard. Though old-fashioned, the house had spectacular sea views from almost every window.

"Do ye have a torch?" He'd left his inside the van.

"Aye." She scrounged about the floor and retrieved an impressive military model.

"Thanks." He clicked it on and shone the beam into the dark recess beyond. "Looks like the tunnel heads onto the base."

He placed the torch on the floor, gripped the edge of the hole, and ripped the paneling back to access the tunnel. Damp, pungent air rushed into the room.

"You're tearing up the house," Cairstie squawked. "Someone could enter through the hole you just made."

"I'll repair your cupboard, but I must see where this goes." He stepped into the rock-hewn shaft, not much taller than his six-foot frame, and started forward. Doubtless, at high tide, the passageway flooded with seawater. A noise made him spin toward the cupboard, his hand on his waist holster. Lady Cairstie stood in the opening, blocking the study's natural light.

"I suppose asking ye to stay behind is wasted breath?"

"Aren't I safer with you than in the study? That's where I encountered my attacker."

She had a point. Sharidon grunted his assent and moved on, careful of every step. The place looked old, like WWII tunnels he'd encountered in Jersey and in northern Norway.

After one hundred meters, the tunnel twisted, and the rock floor gave way to sand and puddles. Water dripped and seeped down the walls, shimmering in the torchlight. His beam caught an object lying on the ground ahead—the pungent odor emanating from it, most foul.

"Lady Cairstie. Please wait while I investigate." His voice echoed in the narrow space.

For once, she cooperated.

His stomach tightened, and he covered his nose as the scent of a decomposing body overwhelmed the narrow space.

Fifteen steps later, he reached the tarp-covered object and lifted a corner. His torch picked out what was left of Agent Mansfield. Sharidon forced down the rising bile in his throat. Mansfield had taken two bullets to the chest at close proximity—a pro.

His heart plunged. He had hoped for a different outcome. He placed the tarp back over Mansfield and retraced his steps. "I need to ring someone."

"It's bad, isn't it?" Cairstie covered her nose. "Someone's dead."

"Yeah. Let's go." He squeezed past her and headed to the study. "I'm going to install deadbolts on your doors and seal up that tunnel. Yer not to go anywhere on the island without me. Do ye understand? My guess is that whoever shot at ye killed that man."

Her eyes rounded. "Okay."

"Come along now and have a seat." He led her to the snug and sat her on the sofa. "Ye've had a bit of a shock."

No use pretending around her. She knew his line of work. "I'll be close by." He retrieved his sat phone and hit speed dial the second he left the snug.

"Thatcher."

"I found Mansfield. Two bullets to the chest."

Nigel didn't comment for three beats. "I'm sorry to hear that. I was hoping..."

"Yeah. We all were sir."

"Any sign of Agent Wang?"

"No, sir." He updated Nigel about the tunnel and Lady Cairstie's narrow escape.

"Have you explored the rest of that passageway?"

"Negative."

"I'll send a team out. Sharidon, I need to know where that tunnel leads."

"Ye don't want anyone on the base involved I take it?"

"The killer could be military personnel. I'd prefer to leave them in the dark. Our initial questioning revealed that no unofficial personnel visited the base at the time Wang and Mansfield disappeared. Whoever did this knows their way around weapons. And that base."

"We have a problem." Sharidon kneeled on his good leg and poked a finger through the kennel grate to pet Winkle.

"What is it?"

"Lady Cairstie." Winkle licked his hand.

"Return her to the mainland," Nigel snapped.

"That's where things get tricky. Whoever attacked Lady Cairstie last night wore night vision goggles. It won't take much investigative work to find out her identity in this community. She's no safer at home than she is on Benbecula."

Nigel swore. "This has set our mission sideways." Computer keys clicked.

"Are ye pulling up Lady Cairstie's file?" Sharidon asked. MI6 profiled all agents and officers' families.

"Yes. This is interesting. Do you know anything about Lady Cairstie's background?"

"Other than she can scarcely feed herself? No." He had never encountered a more helpless female.

"I'd say she did just fine with that golf club," Nigel said in his mild way.

Lady Cairstie had taken the traitor by surprise. Sharidon granted her that. "A primary school lad knows more about how to care for himself than that lass."

"Lady Cairstie has a black belt in martial arts. Jujitsu."

Sharidon blinked. "What?"

"And she helps her father thin his pheasant and deer population on the estate."

"She can shoot?"

"That's what it says. Not such an albatross, after all?" Nigel asked.

"No, sir." Sharidon rubbed his face. "I'll take her shooting and see what she can do."

"Very good." Nigel paused. "Watch your back, Sharidon. Mansfield was a crack shot, much like you."

# CHAPTER 11

A FIRE BURNED inside the snug's wood burner, but Cairstie felt none of its heat. She huddled on the sofa, her arms wrapped around her legs. A dead body was inside her house—okay, not directly in her house—in the tunnel attached to her house. And that was almost the same thing. She'd never seen a dead body before. Thanks to Sharidon, she hadn't viewed this one, either, but the odor would stay with her forever.

Unable to withstand the clinging stench on her clothes, she fled upstairs to change. She reeked of corpse. Afterward, she went in search of Sharidon. They had been up for hours. He must be hungry.

When she searched the ground floor, she found herself alone. Sharidon must still be on that call. The skin around his eyes had tightened when he pulled back that tarp. Afterward, he said little, but his soberness inferred that he had known the person.

She found a tutorial on her mobile on how to scramble eggs. That didn't appear too complicated, so she turned the cooker on high, placed a dab of butter in the pan while she cracked six eggs, then swished them about the bowl with a fork.

The butter sizzled, and dark smoke rose. The next step was to cook the eggs, so Cairstie poured them into the skillet, where they hissed and bubbled. She stared at the writhing mass, attempting to recall the next step. Och, aye. She snapped her fingers and retrieved a short-handled, flat, metal thingy to push the eggs around the pan.

In seconds, the blob turned a muddy color. Done. Cairstie dumped them onto a platter. Weren't they supposed to be yellow? She poked the eggs with a fork, and some parts oozed. They must be okay. She had followed the instructions.

Since Dad enjoyed cheese with his eggs, she placed several slices on top of her creation, then covered them with a lid while she set the table. McFarlane had taught her how when she was a child and wanted to be a butler when she grew up.

With breakfast ready, all she needed was Sharidon. She peeked inside the solarium. Nope. Surely, he wouldn't leave after finding bullets in the wall and a dead body in the tunnel. She opened the front door and looked outside. The van stood on the drive, so he hadn't gone far. Maybe he was in the garden. She trudged through the lounge and opened the kitchen door.

The spy stood on her stoop, wearing the same tight expression around the eyes. Once again, she received the impression that Sharidon knew the person who had died.

"You must be hungry. I made eggs," Cairstie said.

"Thanks. I am." Sharidon followed her inside.

She motioned toward the table, and he took a seat.

"This looks rather fancy." He motioned to the tablecloth and floral dishes.

"It's nothing much, just eggs and cheese." She sat across from him and lifted the lid off the eggs. They were not the bright yellow she had grown up with. Maybe it had something to do with using brown eggs.

Sharidon held out his plate, and she used the flat metal thing to divvy out the food. After a quick blessing on the meal, she picked up her fork and took a bite. She gagged and dashed for the sink, spitting the contents into the basin.

"Don't eat it," she shrieked.

Instead of joining her, Sharidon threw his head back and laughed. "Have ye ever made eggs before?"

"It didn't look hard on the tutorial." She wiped her mouth with the back of her hand and leaned her backside against the cabinet.

A funny expression flitted across Sharidon's rather expressive face and was gone. "I'm touched ye took the trouble."

"You looked like you'd had a tough morning. I wanted to do something nice."

"That was kind of ye." Again, that peculiar expression returned. "Would ye like me to teach ye how to scramble an egg?"

"Aye. I'm verra tired of toast and carrots."

"Well then, let's start by using a spatula."

She picked up the flat metal-ended apparatus. "This?"

"That is an ice cream spade, a rather unique one."

Sharidon didn't so much as crack a smile. If he had, she would have fled the room. As it was, she flushed to her very toes. Would she ever do anything right in front of this man? She set the ice cream spade on the counter.

He did not mock her, which seemed out of character. Instead, he hopped up, retrieved the last of the eggs from the refrigerator, and set them on the worktop. Then he scrubbed the pan and mixing bowl before he helped himself to a few seasonings in the cupboard, along with cheese and milk.

"Why don't ye crack those eggs for me?" Sharidon asked.

At least she could manage that. She cracked the remaining eggs, making sure the shells didn't enter the bowl, while Sharidon scrounged through the fridge and cupboards. He used the last of her bell pepper and chopped it into tiny pieces, his movements deft.

"You put veg in your eggs?" She came up beside him.

"I picked that up in America. They put all sorts of things in their eggs, much like their sandwiches." He made a face, letting her know what he thought of American sandwiches. "But they're spot on with their eggs."

She eyed his concoction. "You're sure?"

"Trust me. Ye'll like it."

"If you say so."

He added seasoning and a dash of milk, then nudged the bowl toward her. "Give it a good stir with that fork until the yolks are blended."

She followed his instructions while he added a dab of butter to the pan and turned the heat on medium-low, not high like she had done. Was that where she'd gone wrong?

"Now, pick up that spatula." He indicated a long-handled utensil he'd plopped on the countertop. "Now scoot the eggs around the pan, and don't let them stick to the bottom," he said over his shoulder as he popped two slices of bread into the toaster.

She followed his directions. "They're yellow. I thought they'd be brown like the shells."

Sharidon's face contorted, and he coughed as though something was stuck inside his throat. "All scrambled eggs are yellow," he said in a strained voice. "Now turn off the heat and remove the pan from the cooker." Sharidon added thin slices of cheese and set the lid on top. "This will help it melt."

She stared at the pan of eggs, and something akin to wonder swelled inside her.

"Yer a right dab hand at it, Lady Cairstie. All ye needed were a few more instructions." The toast popped, and Sharidon buttered, then plated the bread.

They seated themselves at the kitchen table, and she blessed the food —again. "You're an excellent teacher. Where did you learn to cook?" she asked.

"I've seven siblings. We all took turns helping Mum in the kitchen."

"Eight children?" She stabbed a forkful and paused with it halfway to her mouth. "I thought my family was large with four."

"It was a tight squeeze in the farmhouse. I left at sixteen to make my way."

She digested that silently while she finished her eggs and toast in record time. The food was delicious.

"Have you traveled much since you left home?" She placed her utensils in the four o'clock position on her plate.

"Here and there." He shrugged.

"University?" If he continued to evade her questions, she'd pin him down.

"Two years at Trinity."

"You dropped out?" At sixteen, she had given up on higher education after not finding a key to her dyslexia. Her modeling career took off at that time, and she never looked back.

"I finished in two years." Sharidon ducked his head and shoveled more eggs in his mouth.

"No gap year?"

"No." He swallowed, then bit into his toast.

That would make him eighteen, or thereabouts when he graduated from university. His jovial act hid a keen intellect. Though Cairstie had a high-paying career until recently, her lack of education bothered her. She longed to learn, but her reading issues had proved a major stumbling block in her thirst for knowledge.

"What did you study?" His long, dark-lashed, green eyes were gorgeous.

"Linguistics and Chemistry."

"You doubled?" No wonder the home office had recruited him. His IQ must be off the charts.

"I remember what I read." He shrugged, then fiddled with his cutlery.

A photographic memory. Figured. Life wasn't fair. But then, her so-called girlfriends complained about her lucky break when she signed with Stella Walker at sixteen. In her heart, a university degree topped a modeling career any day.

Mother's words rang in her ears whenever she bemoaned her lack of education. "You cannot alter the cards life deals you, but you can influence how you play them. Make them count."

Sharidon hopped up from the table. "I can do these."

It didn't take much to read the tea leaves. Sharidon needed privacy, probably to make another one of those calls on that sat phone of his.

"Thank you." Taking the stairs, she entered her room and gathered her shower things.

People wore masks. Cairstie sensed a sadness in Sharidon after discovering that body in the tunnel. Had they been friends?

Sharidon might appear the happy-go-lucky drifter, but that was a front. Thoroughly intrigued by her handsome guest, she conceded that Sharidon might be much more than he seemed.

⚜

Pipes groaned inside the kitchen wall. Sharidon glanced at the ceiling and cocked his head. Lady Cairstie must be in the shower. With sisters of his own who had a penchant for the bathroom, he took advantage of the time.

Snatching the torch off the worktop, he hurried to Mrs. McDougal's study and entered the tunnel. Covering his nose, he approached Mansfield's body and paused to tuck the tarp more carefully around him.

"I'll find whoever did this to you. They won't get away with it." He stepped past Mansfield and continued with caution. How had Mansfield ended up in this tunnel? The distress ping indicated it had originated from the SCIF on base.

Twenty meters later, the passageway curved, then dipped, seawater rising to his knees. With the rock-hewn wall supporting him, he trudged through fifty feet of slimy water before the shaft rose, and a glimmer of light shone up ahead.

He approached with his MI6 issue drawn. Nine meters later, the tunnel ended, and iron rungs, bored into the rock wall, formed a built-in ladder. Above, outlined by the merest fragment of light, lay a wooden trap door.

This tunnel must have been a relic from WWII. No one would construct such an elaborate escape route these days, assuming that was this tunnel's purpose.

He gripped the first rung and ascended the metal ladder to the hinged door. Pausing, he strained for sounds of activity. All seemed quiet. He pushed the wood panel a few centimeters and peered out. The tunnel led to an old bunker that housed a conglomeration of tires, steel drums, and old airplane parts.

On finding himself the sole occupant of the space, he climbed out. The Ministry of Defense, or MoD, had sold many of its RAF buildings to the community-owned group when the MoD "shut down" the base.

Very few were aware of this top-secret test site. How had the Chinese caught wind of it? He crossed to a grimy window to get his bearings. A dozen yards to the right stood the control center where Mansfield or Wang had triggered the silent alarm. No wonder the traitor had disappeared with the bodies so quickly. He had an escape hatch within easy distance.

That meant the traitor had killed Mansfield and dumped his body in the passageway. Drag marks near a side door with a broken pane of glass backed up his theory. The intruder let himself inside the derelict building and hauled Mansfield with him.

But where was Wang? Sharidon examined every inch of the bunker but found no sign of her. Could she still be alive?

His sat phone dinged.

Nigel: On approach.

That was quick—less than eight hours after he made the initial call about Mansfield. Sharidon let himself out and scoured the sky. A dark speck appeared on the horizon, flying beneath the clouds.

He had never delivered a body before, and proper protocol escaped him. Did he return to Lady Cairstie's and wait for a knock? Or did he meet the crew at the airfield? He glanced at Muir Tigh House across the *machair* and chose the second option.

Limping, he set off for the helipad, his leg aching from overuse. As the chopper closed in, its propellers flattened the grass. The engine throbbed, and his clothes flapped.

With a high mechanical whine, the helicopter touched down, and two men jumped out with a stretcher between them. Nigel followed. Sharidon clamped his jaw to keep his mouth from falling open. His spymaster rarely made field appearances. The severity of the mission's success drove home even further.

The chopper's propellers slowed to a stop.

"Sharidon. I figured you'd be nearby poking around." Nigel crossed the last few steps to his side.

One thing about Nigel, he had his agents pegged. The man was legendary, yet his unremarkable gray hair, eyes, and average height concealed this fact. But Nigel Thatcher had caught more spies and double agents during his time in the field than anyone in the last half-century. Because C, the head of British Intelligence, considered him too valuable an asset, he removed Nigel from the field, and promoted him to run his own teams.

"Any news on Wang?" Nigel asked.

"No, sir."

"Did you contact the local police constabulary?"

"The incident occurred on the base, and Mansfield's body, as far as I can determine, is within MoD boundaries."

"Dillardson and Burke are our clean-up and investigation crew." Nigel nodded toward the two men holding the stretcher.

Sharidon acknowledged the pair. Burke's eagle-eyed reputation at a crime scene preceded him. The young, ginger-haired Dillardson must be his trainee.

"Is base command aware of your arrival?" Sharidon turned back to Nigel.

"Yes. I'll speak to them after we retrieve Mansfield. Do we need to commandeer a lorry?"

"Negative. But I've got to warn ye; that stretcher will be a tight squeeze where we're going."

# CHAPTER 12

WHERE HAD SHARIDON GONE? Cairstie marched outside to his Sprinter van and banged on the door, then folded her arms and tapped her foot while she waited for him to answer. If she was in danger, why had he left her to deal with a killer by herself?

Sharidon did not answer to her pounding, so she went back inside and barred the door. She couldn't wait all day for that flighty Irishman. She had things to do, like clean her dirty underthings.

Grabbing her godmother's nine iron and the container of liquid soap, she approached the contraption in the kitchen. Sharidon deemed it a clothes washer. A dozen buttons lined the unit's face. Which ones did she push?

She opened the washer and focused on the instructions, but the words wiggled so badly that Cairstie gave up trying to read them. Resting the nine iron on her shoulder, she hefted her laundry basket and carried it upstairs. After she plugged the claw-footed tub, she added a squirt of washing-up soap, then turned the tap on hot. Upending her basket, she tossed everything into the suds—unmentionables and woolens alike.

"I can do this the old-fashioned way," she muttered.

With her nine iron, she swished her clothes in the soapy water, humming to avoid jumping at every creak and groan in the house. When

she finished rinsing the bubbles from the material, she draped her underthings on the shower rod to dry. She raised her favorite wool blazer next,
the water pouring off it. Why did it look so small?

Movement from her peripheral vision. She spun, raising the nine iron
to strike.

"Woah, lass. It's just me." Sharidon threw up both hands.

With a hammering heart, she lowered the golf club, blushing at her
items strewn about the small room.

He rested against the basin, and she got her first real look at him. His
trousers were filthy to the knees, his hair tousled, and the dark stubble on
his ordinarily clean-shaven face made his eyes stand out like emeralds
against black velvet.

An unwarranted zing of attraction stirred within her. She beat it down
and took the offensive. "Some protector you turned out to be. Where have
you been?"

"The crew came for the body." Sorrow flashed in Sharidon's eyes and
was gone.

"Oh." She deflated like a leaky balloon. "I'm dreadfully sorry. He was a
friend of yours, wasn't he?"

"A mentor. And thank ye." He took in her dripping clothes and the
tub full of water. "What are ye doing?"

"Washing my clothes."

"Why? Ye've a perfectly decent clothes washer in the kitchen."

Heat rose up her neck. Lifting her chin, Cairstie declined to share her
humiliating secret. Let him think the worst of her. At least he needn't find
out about her struggle to read.

"Has no one taught ye how to clean clothes?" His gaze sparkled with
humor. "Why did yer parents turn ye loose when ye don't know how to
care for yerself?"

Heat suffused her entire body, and she glared at him.

"I've put my foot in it, haven't I?" The teasing left him entirely, and an
expression she could only term hangdog slid over his features. "I'm sorry. I
am. My tongue got away with me. It does that sometimes. If ye'll forgive
me, I'd be most happy to show ye how to work the clothes washer."

Right now, she'd love nothing more than to dump a bucket of dirty
tub water on his head, but she swallowed her pride and nodded. She

didn't have the luxury to refuse. No one had answered her housekeeper advertisement on the Uists' job website.

"Care to accompany me after I shower? The islanders should see me performing my 'day job.'" He made air quotes.

"And what job would that be?" Sharidon must feel badly about inviting her along.

"I'm to survey the base's boundary to confirm the government absconded with some of the people's land."

"They've spoken to you? Dad told me the inhabitants don't socialize with incomers."

"I've been lucky."

"Why did they welcome you? You're an incomer."

"Because I stand to offer this community-owned island free land. Keeping me on their good side is in their best interests."

Depend on Sharidon to figure out how to get in with the locals.

"I'd like to go." If Sharidon intended to leave the premises, she refused to stay behind with a murderer at large.

It only took him a few days to find the material for an explosive device, not a difficult task for someone who knew where to look.

He settled into bed and opened his eBook as the wall clock ticked away the minutes.

Inside the bathroom, Nicola, his wife, gargled and spat into the basin, then turned on the tap, crooning to herself. He smiled at the familiar bedtime ritual. His sweet Nicola. Everything he did, he did for her to provide her with the life she deserved.

He had just returned from a trip throughout the Hebrides to collect materials to relieve himself of a problem. Nicola accompanied him on the first leg of the journey, ferrying from North Uist up to Harris and Lewis to visit her sister until he returned for her.

By purchasing the ingredients on three different islands, the authorities would never suspect him. And Nicola, bless her, thought he had signed with other suppliers while she was at her sister's.

Nicola peered around the loo door, a white cream mask plastered on her face, reminiscent of that Phantom of the Opera character she went on about in that London show.

"You're already in bed? That trip must have knackered you out."

"Hmmm?" He glanced up at her from the thriller novel on his electronic device. If he didn't engage in conversation, she'd grow bored and come to bed. And the sooner she fell asleep, the sooner he could build that bomb.

She washed her face and patted it dry, watching him in the mirror.

Crossing the room, she climbed into bed beside him, turned out the light, and leaned across his chest. "I didn't get a kiss last night."

He lowered his eReader and pecked her lips, wishing he could give her a better one.

She emitted a deep sigh. "I intend to accompany you next time you search for new products. We need a getaway to spice things up. We're getting much too settled in our ways."

"Mm-hmm." He chuckled. She was right, of course. He intended to rectify things with her when he took care of a wee bit of trouble.

Nicola turned her back on him, and in a few more minutes, she was snoring like a top. He grinned at the endearing sound she made. One thing about Nicola: she slept like the dead once she passed out.

He ran a hand down her arm. "Nicola?"

"Wha—?" she cut off mid-word, soft snores filling the room.

"Sleep well, hen." He kissed her cheek and tucked the blanket around her shoulders to ward off the chill. Clicking off his eReader, he lay another ten minutes before he slipped out of bed and donned his tracksuit and jacket. He had obligations to attend to.

A few minutes later, he drove to work and parked around back in case someone drove by and noticed his car. With his bags in hand, he hauled his stockpile upstairs and sat at the small folding table beside the adder and frog aquariums. Nicola chose not to come up here because of his pets. "Disgusting things," she called them.

Many people had issues with reptiles. Personally, they fascinated him.

Setting out the copper cathode and other supplies, he got to work. His years in the military proved a blessing when it came to projects like this. Meticulously, he mixed the ingredients, humming that song Nicola had earlier. Then, he attached the wires much like an artist, adding a final touch to their masterpiece.

He leaned back, his chair creaking, and admired his work. It paid to have the skills. He hadn't lost his touch and remembered it all—like it was yesterday.

❖

The wind whipped over the *machair*. Leaving Cairstie in the van, Sharidon set up his equipment within view of the B892, a secondary road outside Balivanich. To provide legitimacy to his "job," the locals needed to observe him about his duties.

Sharidon checked the dimensions, then peered through the theodolite, rotating the telescope on the surveying tool to measure the horizontal angle. The numbers he collected would triangulate the military base's boundary. A smirk lifted the corners of his mouth. So far, it appeared the numbers were in favor of the islanders. This pleased him to no end. Too often, Downing Street pulled rank. Not this time. When he submitted his calculations to the authorities, he was confident the islanders would receive an additional chunk of acreage.

Mentally cycling back to the creeper who broke into Lady Cairstie's place as he performed his "fake job," Sharidon had long since deduced the chap did it for a reason. But why break into Muir Tigh House to access the passage instead of entering it from the base unless the intruder had been unaware that someone had moved in. Or he couldn't access to the base after they heightened security?

Sharidon eyed his nearby vehicle. Lady Cairstie sat in the passenger seat, her face tilted toward her mobile. He invited her to accompany him rather than leave her behind for a possible second attack. The lads in the pub, the majority of which were hammered when Lady Cairstie arrived on the island, were the only people aware of her existence, and they had no idea where she lived.

Only locals and a handful of military personnel knew of that subterranean route. Even fewer claimed knowledge about the unoccupied homes in Balivanich. So, whoever killed Mansfield and abducted Agent Wang must have strong ties to the island.

A niggle ate at his stomach lining like Thai sauce. That old tunnel had doubtless provided an escape route for islanders if Germans invaded the base.

How many locals—or military personnel, for that matter—knew about that tunnel? And the traitor had used a silencer, pointing to weapons experience, a definitive clue he needed to pursue.

The vehicle door slammed, and he swung toward the road as Lady Cairstie picked her way through the *machair*. He dragged his gaze from those long legs of hers to keep from salivating. The lass's attractiveness proved a distraction. She needed to leave for her own safety and his mental health. He couldn't mind her day in and out, not with a traitor on the loose.

He tweaked the theodolite and jotted down another number. Just before he fell asleep each night, he entered his latest readings into the government form. He might be working undercover, but after being raised on a farm, he understood that a few extra acres often eased a meager subsistence on a lean budget.

"How are things?" Cairstie came abreast of him. "Have enough cars passed to satisfy the locals that you're a surveyor?"

He grunted, his eye once more pressed to the lens. "May I ask ye a personal question?"

"You can ask me anything, but I'm not obligated to respond." The hint of a laugh tinged Cairstie's words. "I've one of my own as well."

He lifted his head and shifted to stare her in the face. "A man broke into yer house and took a few shots at ye. Why are ye still here? Do ye have a death wish or something? Or are ye just stubborn?"

"Are you deaf? I told you before that I must remain at Muir Tigh for six months. If I don't, my inheritance goes to my brother."

Ah. Her inheritance, again, a foreign commodity in his world. "Why six months?" That seemed an extraordinary amount of time, but the posh never made much sense to him.

"I haven't the faintest notion why Mrs. McDougal insisted on it, but I'll lose my inheritance if I don't stay on Benbecula."

"I'm not sure ye understand how dangerous this man is. Is the estate worth more than yer life?"

"There's nothing to return to." She shrugged, but tears clouded her eyes.

"What about yer job? Don't influencers promote products?" Did the lass not understand the danger?

Her blue eyes sparked. "We've already covered this. Thanks to Ahern's arrest, I am no longer employed."

Even he, a complete novice in stylish dressing, had seen her decked out on social media.

"They canceled my modeling contracts and endorsements because they were unwilling to link their brands to someone who might damage their reputation. Since Lord Ahern and I dated . . ."

"They deemed ye culpable." And he'd played a role in her public humiliation. Guilt coursed through him at what she had suffered, even if his "assignment" aimed to prevent that very thing from happening.

"No one cared if I was guilty or not, only that their association with me might stain their fashion line." Her mouth dipped for a brief second, but she covered her hurt rather well.

"I assume the inheritance is vast enough to tempt ye to risk yer life?"

She shrugged.

"Lass, isn't yer life worth more to ye than things?" Why was she really here? Her family was loaded.

"You don't understand. This isn't only about my inheritance. Not really. I've been shunned. My friends dropped me, and my parents' peers barely tolerate my existence. I can't leave home without someone snubbing me in the village. So, yes, I came to earn my inheritance, but I need a place to wait out the scandal."

Now, they were getting somewhere. He hadn't expected such candor or the sudden rise of sympathy that swamped him as she lifted her chin. Benbecula proved her sole opportunity for a fresh start. Not even a traitor or her lack of homemaking skills deterred her from her goal. He needed to turn her into an ally if she refused to leave.

"I understand ye've taken self-defense classes."

"Aye." She moved toward his equipment and peeked through his telescope.

"It might be an excellent idea if ye brush up on them later today. Ye never know when they'll come in handy."

She stepped back from the theodolite, her expression puzzled. "How did you hear about my self-defense training?"

"A little bird might have mentioned it." He placed his hand on the theodolite to keep it from tipping, then squinted through the lens. "A wee set-to might prove useful."

"Where do you suggest we do this? In the back garden or on the beach?"

"Somewhere less conspicuous. Yer garage."

Her gaze widened. "There are mice in there."

"I doubt they'll be running about while we face off."

"You're challenging me?" Her mouth dented the corner of her lips, and a sly expression flitted across her features.

"I want to see what ye can do." He met her gaze with an unflinching stare.

"So be it. But I warn you. I was taught by the best."

"So was I."

# CHAPTER 13

CLAD in joggers and ankle boots, Cairstie opened Mrs. McDougal's rickety garage door and assessed the interior. Gardening tools leaned haphazardly against one wall, and an old 1990s Vauxhall Nova took up the other half of the space, its key in the ignition.

Cairstie rolled her eyes. People never locked anything in the Uists. They didn't see the point. Everyone knew who owned what. How long had Mrs. McDougal's vehicle been sitting there? Probably for quite a while. Did the thing even run? Cairstie had only driven her Mercedes once since her arrival. With the shops so close, walking seemed a better option.

She hopped in the Nova and turned the key. Despite sitting idle for two months, the engine sputtered to life on the second try. Shifting into reverse, she ground the gears before she backed out of the building.

Sharidon, tasked with loading tools in the barrow, trotted to the driver's door.

"Easy on that, lass. Ye might hurt the gearbox."

She really couldn't care less.

"What do ye plan to do with the car?" Sharidon stepped back and scanned the Nova's exterior.

"I hadn't considered."

"If yer selling, I'll pay ye three thousand to take it off yer hands."

"For this old thing?" Her brows shot up. Was he mad?

"That's a classic, and it's in mint condition." Sharidon accessed Edmunds' Kelly Blue Book on his mobile and showed her the value.

"Sold." She had no intention of driving Mrs. McDougal's car. With it gone, she had a place to protect her convertible from the elements.

They cleared out the remaining debris, then laid out the moth-eaten rugs she found rolled in a corner to soften their landings.

"I want to see what ye can do. All I ask is that ye go easy on my bad leg." Without waiting a beat, Sharidon grabbed her forearm above her wrist.

Cairstie blinked. Reading his intent to flip her, she placed her opposite hand on his fingers, then pulled him toward her. With both hands gripped on his arm, she swung it counterclockwise, then pushed him down by his captive arm onto his knees and twisted it behind his back.

"Nice beginning." Sharidon dipped his chin with approval. "What about this?"

His speed stole her breath as he snatched her from behind and placed her in a headlock, his opposite forearm across her shoulder and clavicle.

She grabbed Sharidon's wrists and slumped, making herself heavy. It threw him off-kilter and gave her the advantage.

To prevent Sharidon from crushing her windpipe, she turned her head aside and dropped into a squat. She twisted, then encircled his thighs with her arms, lifted him off the ground, and dumped him onto his back. The entire sequence, done in quick succession, took him off guard.

"That's for the restaurant," she crowed. "Trust me, I haven't forgotten."

Sharidon gaped up at her.

"Didn't see that one coming?" She lifted a brow.

"I expected something different." Sharidon laughed good-naturedly, making it hard to dislike the man. "For what it's worth, I am sorry I embarrassed ye that day. Elise was only trying to save ye from being linked to Ahern in the news."

"It didn't work," Cairstie gritted out.

"Word hadn't gotten around yet about yer split when Ahern was arrested. Ye know how toffs are when one of their own is linked to anyone associated with a public scandal."

Ostracism. The upper echelon ran from anyone with unsavory associations. Even the royals were not immune.

Sharidon cleared his throat. "Ye ready to make this interesting?"

He did not get distracted from his goals. Sharidon ceased going easy after that, and they went at it like two prize fighters looking for any weakness in their opponent. When they finished, they both lay sweating on the foul-smelling rugs, panting to catch their breath.

As a favor to her sister, Sharidon had gone to that restaurant to save her from scandal. The real culprit was Ahern. What an eejit she'd been to date him. In retrospect, the red flags were there all along, but she had ignored them.

The last of her anger drained away. Elise had good motives, but she should have told her, even knowing how much Cairstie hated being bossed. The loss of her agency still rubbed like sand against raw skin. Aye, she'd have likely continued dating Ahern just to be ornery. Och. She had a lot of growing up to do.

"Ye've set my mind at rest, Lady Cairstie."

"It's Cairstie to you, Irish. After being up close and personal, don't you think we should skip the formalities?" she asked, throwing out an olive branch.

"I've no issue with calling ye Cairstie."

"And what's your first name?" She raised up on her elbow. Perhaps, this time, he'd share it with her.

"Sharidon will do." He winked, reading through her attempt to discover his handle. "Heaven help the chap who takes ye for an easy target. I'm a mite curious. Why self-defense? I figured ye'd be more into dance or music lessons."

"Mother enrolled us in both." Cairstie flopped back down and stared at the cobwebs in the eaves above her. "When I was younger, I watched Elise practice her moves on my brother. She got the better of him every time. Then, when Roderick decapitated my dolls later that summer, I needed revenge, so I took up jujitsu."

"Did ye ever take yer brother down?"

"By the time I learned enough to attempt it, Roderick had a few moves of his own, so I poked a hole in his car tires instead." She sat up and tipped her head to the side. "So, what's your name? Is it something horrid? Is that why you won't tell me?"

He rolled onto his stomach, his eyes twinkling. "Ye don't give up easy, do ye, lass?"

"Never."

"I'm afraid yer in for a disappointment, then." The smile he gave her could charm the venom from a snake. Her stomach fluttered despite her best effort to squash it.

"I'm a Scot. We're notoriously stubborn." Cairstie showed her teeth.

"Nobody knows my first name."

"No one?" He couldn't be serious.

"Only my family and boss call me anything but Sharidon."

"That's ludicrous."

"I suppose one day, the woman I love will have leave of it."

Sharidon held out his hand. When Cairstie touched his fingers, an electric volt zapped her. What was that? Her eyes widened, and the perpetual twinkle in Sharidon's wiped clean.

"I'll be needing my cane after that workout." He turned away.

"How's your leg?" Still discombobulated from that jolt, she grabbed the cane he propped against the wall and passed it to him.

"Stronger every day."

His flat tone discouraged further questioning. Evidently, Sharidon's injury was off-limits. He remained an enigma, and she was no closer to understanding him than the day they met. For some reason, that irritated her.

Not that he interested her. He wasn't her type.

Jutting her chin, she gripped the Flymo that cut the grass and returned it to the garage, then gathered the other gardening tools, hanging them on rusty nails along one wall. Curious why Sharidon had not assisted her, she glanced around and saw him limping up the beach with that confounded sat phone pressed to his ear.

Hadn't he experienced the same jolt when their hands touched? If so, he'd recovered quickly, but that charge surely hadn't only affected her.

Sharidon had stopped, and his eyes locked with hers. The air crackled, even from that distance. She spun away.

He did not interest her—not in the least.

What spyish person did Sharidon make all those mysterious calls to? And why did he refuse to talk about his leg? Or give her the use of his first name?

She set the last shovel against the garage wall, her gaze darting about the corners for small rodents. Not one furry creature stirred. Perhaps she and Sharidon scared them off.

Retracing her steps to the house, she snatched her Mercedes's EV fob off the worktop so she could park her car inside the newly organized garage. At least the shelter would save her paint job and soft roof.

She went back outside and climbed behind the wheel.

"Stop, Cairstie. Stop." Sharidon raced toward her, limping badly, and waving his cane.

She paused with her hand over the starter. Something appeared dreadfully wrong. She opened the driver's door to find out what the yelling was about.

"Don't turn on the engine," Sharidon bellowed as he rounded her car's bonnet.

"Why?"

"Because I didn't check to see if it was booby-trapped." He reached her door and hauled her out with such force that he lost his balance. They fell to earth, a place they always seemed to end up. This time, they landed on wet, overgrown weeds.

Cairstie spit out a mouthful of prickly grass. "Why, you . . ." she sputtered. He had no right to handle her so brusquely. She'd have bruises tomorrow.

Sharidon didn't apologize but popped up like a Jack-in-the-box toy. He reached inside her Mercedes and released the bonnet catch.

"I need to check something before we drive it." He lowered himself to the ground and emitted a stream of Irish Gaelic. Doubtless, the foreign words had terrible connotations.

"Can ye bring me diagonal cutting pliers?" He asked after a time.

"That's it?" No apology for knocking her down?

"Hurry, lass." This time, his urgency connected.

She rose, wiping off the wet grass, then went to do his bidding. When she returned, he hadn't moved, but his sat phone was once more glued to his ear.

Shocker.

"Which colored wire? I haven't done one of these since Fort Monckton." Sharidon gave Cairstie a corner eye. "Bother. Yer sister's returned."

Cairstie glared at him, but her efforts were wasted. The fellow had returned to whatever he was doing.

"You might as well level with her. I think you can trust her." Elise didn't have a quiet voice, and it blared through Sharidon's sat phone speaker as Cairstie handed him the tool.

"Thanks," he grunted. "You better be sure about this, Elise."

"Just do it, Sharidon. We don't have time to fly there before it goes off."

Goes off? Cairstie's stomach quivered. What exactly was Sharidon tinkering with under her car? And why was Elise coaching him?

"Got it." Deep satisfaction sounded in his voice. "Sophisticated workmanship, that. Whoever perpetrated this wired two detonators. The last bit was confusing. Thanks. Yer the best." Sharidon hung up.

Cairstie waited for him with folded arms when he edged out from under the Mercedes. "What exactly did you do a moment ago?"

His green eyes did not sparkle. Nor did they dance. Sharidon's entire expression remained solemn. "I disconnected a bomb."

"A bomb?" She stared at him as her blood froze and clogged her veins.

He nodded.

"Why didn't you make me take cover if it was so dangerous?" The question tumbled from her.

"Because whoever did this wired enough explosives on yer Mercedes to turn yer driveway into a swimming pool."

Her legs threatened to crumble beneath her. "Don't you think it's time you filled me in on what you are doing here? Why did someone place a car bomb on my Mercedes? And why did Elise help you dismantle it?"

"Let's go inside." Sharidon took her elbow gently and escorted her to the kitchen door. He opened it for her, then led her to the table. She pulled out a chair and sat, fisting her hands in her lap to hide their trembling.

"Tea?" Sharidon asked.

"Aye." She drew her feet onto the chair and clasped her arms around her knees.

He clicked on the electric kettle, opened a cupboard, and removed tea packets. Busying himself while the water heated, he accessed her godmother's porcelain tea service, filled the floral pot with the heated water, then placed it on the table. Deftly, he poured out and dropped a bag of herbal lemony zip into both cups.

Cairstie set her feet on the floor and wrapped her hands around the painted teacup while the herbs steeped. Delicious warmth invaded her body.

A dark lock fell onto Sharidon's forehead as he added sugar to his tea and stirred.

Butterflies erupted in her stomach, and she glanced away. Of all people, why did he have this effect on her? Sharidon was the absolute antithesis of anyone she had previously dated.

"Ah." He sipped from his cup and closed his eyes. "Nothing like a warm drink to celebrate not being blown to smithereens." Sharidon set the teacup on its saucer. "Where would ye like me to start?"

"The beginning."

"I can't share national secrets, lass, but I can tell ye that two of my colleagues went missing. I was sent to find them and complete their mission. One of them was in the tunnel."

Cairstie straightened in her chair.

"And Elise? How does she figure into all of this?"

He lightly touched the side of the teacup. "Until her last injury, we were colleagues. She works in the private sector at present but has security clearances should the need arise."

Cairstie digested that in silence. It was one thing to suspect your sister was a spy but quite another to have it boldly stated as such.

"When ye surprised yer intruder the other night, ye must have seen something for him to take such drastic measures to get rid of ye."

"It all happened so fast. I didn't notice much." Cairstie lifted the creamer and added a dollop to her tea.

Steam rose from Sharidon's cup. Though he sat across from her, his mind appeared far away. She'd witnessed a similar phenomenon in members of her own family from time to time.

Sharidon leaned back in his chair, stretched his long legs before him, and bumped her foot. "Sorry." He tapped the handle on his teacup. "It's pointless for a pro to revisit the site of a dumped body. He has unfinished business; otherwise, he'd keep well enough away. He must be after something inside yer home. Heaven knows there's nothing in the tunnel. May I give yer study a once over and see if anything's there to lure him back?"

"By all means." She swept her arm toward the doorway.

They both rose and tramped down the hall.

"Why set an explosive in my car if he wants something in my house? That's counterproductive."

"He might have found what he was looking for and tried to off ye afterward." Sharidon shrugged, a Gaelic movement she now associated with him. "We won't know until he's interrogated."

Sharidon appeared confident that he'd capture her intruder, but the man had already murdered one MI6 agent and almost blown up another in her driveway. What made Sharidon think he could outsmart him?

He followed Nicola out of the church pew, moving at a snail's pace up the aisle among neighbors and friends as they spilled out of St. Mary's. He buttoned up his coat inside the vestibule before he stepped out into the rain and put on his hat. Umbrellas were useless in this wind.

With Nicola close beside him, he led her to their car on the single-track road.

"I'm so happy you accompanied me today. It's been months since you last came."

He only attended services on occasion to make Nicola happy.

"I don't like you driving in this weather." If Nicola discovered his role with the Chinese, it would destroy her. He spoiled her to make up for not being the man she thought she married.

He opened the passenger door and rounded the boot to the driver's seat. His burner vibrated, so he leaned against the fender and read the text.

> Where are the CAD files you promised? Do I
> need someone else to retrieve them?

Someone else meant a replacement—as in a permanent one—making Nicola a widow. He glanced at his wife through the windscreen. She was the light of his life.

> He texted back: It's under control. I'll have
> them tonight.

Even if he had to kill again.

# CHAPTER 14

THE SEA TUMBLED onto the fog-shrouded beach, its steady rhythm soothing in the deepest hours of the night. Sharidon lay prone in the *machair*, gloved, and armed to the teeth, as he monitored the sentries making their base rounds. He timed each circuit outside the main building where Mansfield and Wang had sent their distress signal.

Until he narrowed the suspects, he couldn't risk the traitor being one of the guards. Anyone with access to the base or had prior access to the base could be selling plans to the Chinese.

Though no moonlight shone, his night vision goggles provided adequate visibility. He had locked Cairstie inside the van and set his observation cameras and alarms. A flea couldn't twitch without his knowledge.

The guards moved off to handle their sweep. Sharidon jumped to his feet and sprinted to the building, pushing his leg to the limits, timing his run to avoid the security cameras. Panting, he attained the cinderblock structure and punched in the code Nigel had provided—one the base changed daily.

Snick. The catch unlocked, and he was in.

He slipped inside and scanned the corridor. Empty. Having memorized the floor plan from the packet he'd received at Waverley Station,

Sharidon advanced toward the control room, his footsteps silent. A camera rotated in his direction. He dodged around a corner, his heart slamming against his ribs. His nerves stretched as he counted the seconds until the lens shifted.

Too close. He stopped twice more to take cover. When he reached the SCIF's new door, another camera rotated, its slight hum his only warning. Sharidon punched in the combination and dove inside as the camera moved in his direction. He had less than an hour before the guards made their circuit.

After a quick assessment of the room, he set his timer and plugged in an ear device before approaching the safe. His heart plummeted like a chopper with disabled blades when he noted the brand.

This safe model—a Greek Trojan Horse—was the Rolls Royce of all safes. He needed to drill through the unit's Achilles heel, a wee spot in the door tumblers to crack it. If he didn't get it right, titanium rods dropped into place, making the safe impossible to breach. And if he tripped the relocker or broke the sheet of glass, not even the proper combination would open the lock.

The intruder, or intruders, who blew off the SCIF door had left safe-cracking tools behind in order to escape. MI6 had retrieved those tools from the military, but they were wiped clean—no prints. That, along with the intercepted transmission, betrayed China's aim. They wanted the schematics and files so they could replicate the West's defensive weapons and render their enemies helpless.

Sharidon removed a small battery-operated drill from his large camo pocket and kneeled before the lock. Despite Nigel's contacts, he hadn't obtained the code to this high-tech model, which left Sharidon cracking this the old-fashioned way.

Sweat beaded Sharidon's forehead underneath the safety glasses he wore. If he slipped up, he couldn't access the hard drives inside. He angled the drill and pressed the switch, going through three battery packs before he reached the tumblers.

His alarm vibrated, and he stuffed his equipment into his pockets as footsteps came down the hall. He rose to his feet, his breath suspended. The guards were early.

Ducking, Sharidon rolled under a workstation with its back facing the safe as the SCIF door beeped and a swath of light stretched across the floor. A click, and the overhead lights flickered to life.

"All clear," a man with a gruff voice barked.

"What do you suppose they were after in here the other night?" a younger man with a nasal tone asked.

"Not my job to question," Gruff Voice snapped, subduing the younger man.

Muffled footsteps on the tiles covered the room's perimeter. Sharidon held his breath and withdrew his weapon. If the guard saw him, he might need to use his sidearm.

Blood surged, and his pulse raced.

If the man reached the safe, he would notice the metal shavings. Rising to his knees, Sharidon peeked around the workstation as the young soldier rounded the last corner of the room. Having never killed anyone in friendly fire, Sharidon prayed that held true in this situation. This mission required utter secrecy. The traitor could be anyone—even one of the guards.

One step. Two steps. Three. Please, God. No. Sharidon cocked the MI6 issue he carried just as Gruff Man's shoulder device erupted into life.

"Movement on the outer perimeter. Repeat. Movement on the outer perimeter."

"Let's go," Gruff Voice called.

The lights blinked off, and both men dashed out, the door slamming behind them.

Sharidon exhaled. Thank you, God. He re-holstered his sidearm, sprang to his feet, and returned to the safe. Had the traitor returned? Was that the reason for the alarm?

Retrieving a thin wire, Sharidon threaded the fiber optic viewer into the hole so he could watch the tumblers as he lined up the notches.

The minutes ticked like eternity. If he made one misstep . . . Sharidon held his breath, his shirt sticking to his torso.

The first tumbler fell into place. Two more to go.

A faint noise in the hall.

Sharidon raised his head, ears straining, the precious minutes fleeing. Nothing. Perhaps that was the heating system?

The second tumbler clicked.

With his attention divided, he almost missed the third tumbler and barely stopped in time. He hadn't expected this one situated so near the second.

He wiped his face on his arm and filled his lungs. Spinning the dial, he opened the door and faced a stack of unmarked hard drives. His heart skipped a beat. Which one held the CAD files and schematics? He didn't have time to sort through that pile.

All but two were positioned on the right. Had Mansfield and Wang already sorted through those? Going with his gut, he booted up his computer and inserted the hard drive. After a quick scan, he switched it out for the remaining drive.

The screen lit up with a CAD drawing of a missile. Bingo. He checked his watch. This was cutting it way too close. He still needed to sabotage the file, so he rang the best hacker in the business, Lady Elise—Cairstie's older sister.

"This better be good, Sharidon," Elise answered. "I'm on my honeymoon."

"I need yer help. I have about ten minutes before our company returns."

"Where are you?"

"I'm on The Deep Sea Missile Base. I need ye to hack into the base's mainframe so I can alter CAD files on the missiles and rockets being tested on Benbecula."

"The Chinese are after them, aren't they?" she asked. "That's why Nigel recalled you."

"Elise, I'd love to chat, but I'm a little pressed for time."

"You're asking me to hack into a government facility, so you had better answer my question."

"Ye know I can't give ye that information."

"If you're worried about sharing too much, I have the necessary clearances. Nigel's requested my aid as Cyber is tied up with a conundrum."

He exhaled loudly. "Brilliant. Yer talents are missed at MI6."

"Why are you interrupting my honeymoon?"

"We intercepted a Chinese transmission and sent two agents over to protect the weapon files we're testing with the Americans and Australians.

A break-in occurred at headquarters on Benbecula, and now our agents are missing."

"Did the Chinese get what they came for?" Elise asked.

"Negative. The agents sounded the alarm in time, but I need to copy these CAD files ASAP and leave a fake one in case they make another attempt."

"You think they'll try?"

"I do." Cairstie's intruder and the ensuing car bomb on her Mercedes left him with zero doubts.

Computer keys clacked in the background. "Who went missing?" Elise asked.

"You know I can't share that information until their families have been notified."

"Never mind. I'll find out myself."

And she could, too.

Harry's deep voice murmured in the background, coming through the line.

"You need to leave," Elise murmured to her disgruntled husband. "I don't want you in trouble if Nigel questions you. That way, you can honestly say you don't know what I did. This shouldn't take long. Promise."

"Good to know," Sharidon said. He needed to move this along.

"I wasn't talking to you," Elise said. More key clicks . . .

"I'm in a hurry here." Didn't Elise understand his time constraints?

"Give me a second. I need to access the MoD through their back door, then tunnel through to the RAF on Benbecula."

More typing.

Sharidon rose from the desk and paced in front of the workstation. In reality, it had only been a few minutes, but if the traitor had infiltrated the base or the guards reappeared, he had no way out of the SCIF.

"And you're in," Elise said.

"Brilliant. With a brain like that, I'm grateful yer on our side." Sharidon inserted his pen drive and copied the original files before he retrieved his technical alterations for the magnesium and alloy of aluminum for the slow and low missile file.

"Better make it snappy. I still need to cover your entry when you finish," Elise said.

"Yes, ma'am." Typing fast, he reconfigured the malleable elements of the missile's outer hull, then added the adapted detonators and homing devices. If the Chinese wanted these, they were welcome to them.

"I owe you one," he said.

"Aye, that you do," Elise said.

"Name your price." Sharidon switched out the low and slow missile files for the hypersonic rocket. With his alterations, if the Chinese assembled the rocket, it would disintegrate within minutes after take-off.

"Won't someone notice the modified files?" Elise asked.

"Test & Evaluation won't check them unless something goes wrong on the physical tests."

"Mmmm," she responded, a sure sign he had lost her attention.

"This is interesting," Elise said after a time.

Suspicions rose inside him. "Are you poking around the mainframe?"

"Of course."

"Don't let them catch you." He altered the last tweak to the rocket's propulsion system.

"That's for amateurs. Give me more credit than that."

"I'm done." He pushed back from the workstation and scored the hard drive with a drill bit to differentiate it from the others in the safe. Rising, he crossed the room and placed back inside its lock up, then cleaned up the metal shavings. Hopefully, no one noticed until its replacement safe arrived in the morning.

"Did you find anything?" he asked.

"The infiltrator attempted to hack into the mainframe but didn't have time to access it. Whoever did this is rather good." Her tone held respect.

"I need to slope off." Sharidon dropped the shavings into an empty pocket and regained the console. "There's movement on the outer perimeter. It could be a cat or an unwanted visitor."

"Give me a second. I'm triggering the system. If they hack it, I'll know."

"Ye've got half a minute. Make it good." Sharidon kept his eye on the wall clock's second hand. "Ten. Nine. Eight," he counted.

"And I'm done."

"Whew." Sharidon sighed. "Thanks. Gotta run." He disconnected.

With tools in hand, he slipped into the corridor, his mouth tight. Even if the traitor returned, the Chinese couldn't get their grubby paws on the files. Now, all he needed to do was keep Lady Cairstie alive while he located the person behind the disappearances of two seasoned operatives.

# CHAPTER 15

CAIRSTIE PULLED BACK the blackout curtain beside her and peeked outside Sharidon's van window. The single shower house light shone in the campground. Sick of solitaire on her mobile, Cairstie tapped her nails on the minuscule table. Sharidon had left hours ago in Mrs. McDougal's Nova, right after he "jailed" her and Winkle inside the van.

She needed to use the toilet but had no intention of accessing the composting one inside the shower. The very idea made her shudder.

When Sharidon dismantled that bomb, it hadn't looked especially hard. How difficult could it be to deactivate Sharidon's security system? She accessed several tutorials on how to install alarm systems. Easy-peasy. All she needed to do was work backward.

Rising from the table, she scrounged through the cupboards to locate a tool kit. She massaged her temples. Sharidon must have hidden it somewhere. How else did a spy manage all their spyishy things?

She took apart the cab's headliner. Nothing. Placing both hands on her hips, she scanned the van's interior. Her eyes narrowed on the space above the shower. She might not be good at reading, but mathematics was her strong suit. That space appeared dimensionally off. She climbed inside the shower and pressed up on the ceiling. It gave way quickly.

"Take that, Sharidon!" Chortling, she stretched her arm into the space and removed Sharidon's bag of goodies, along with his motorbike key.

Using some rather unique tools, she disassembled the interior cameras and those on the exterior door. It took a while, but it gave her something to do. When she shut down the last camera attached to a tripwire, euphoria, unlike any prior achievement, washed over her. She had freed herself without assistance or using her looks to skate by.

A fluke? Perhaps. But the elation was absolute.

After a lifetime of low grades due to her reading struggles, she accepted the labels her boarding school professors and peers placed on her.

Below average.

Stupid.

Lovely, but dim.

Her self-esteem had plummeted until several high street labels approached her to represent her brands after viewing her social media posts. One thing led to another, and her influencing turned her into an overnight sensation with more runway contracts than she could accept. She had never looked back.

Until now.

This one small victory felt like she had scaled Everest. It also made her pause. What if she wasn't wholly unintelligent?

If she needed the toilet, Winkle might, too. So, she let him out to do his business and stretch his legs before she returned him to the kennel.

"I'll be back soon, Winkle."

She locked the van and approached Sharidon's motorbike. Growing up on the Torwoodlee Estate, she was accustomed to quad bikes. This two-wheeled contraption couldn't be all that difficult.

To make sure, she accessed an online motorcycle tutorial. She climbed aboard, turned the key, and kicked the engine to life. Pure dead brilliant. Placing it in first gear, she let out the clutch and stalled almost immediately. After a few more tries, she got the hang of it and started up the coast road for Mrs. McDougal's.

Navigating by the lightening sky, she drove without headlamps to Muir Tigh and let herself inside via the kitchen door. Careful not to turn on lights to give away her presence, she stumbled into the sofa and stubbed her toe.

"Ouch." She sucked in through her nose, holding her breath until the pain receded. Afterward, she used the main floor facilities, then closed the thermal-lined draperies.

If the intruder had returned twice, he must be after something specific. Sharidon believed the fellow had already located what he came for, hence the car bomb. But what if he hadn't? She trembled as the thought took hold. What secrets lay hidden inside Muir Tigh House that were worth killing for?

She clenched her fists. After losing her career, friends, and reputation, she drew the line at Muir Tigh House. No one was driving her from her home until she claimed her inheritance—including that gun-toting burglar.

Time to dig through her godmother's belongings. Marching down the corridor, she reached the study. Since she had surprised the prowler there, it seemed a good place to start.

The mantle clock chimed four in the morning.

One glance at the bookcases, and she groaned. Those would take forever to sort. Tired from staying up all night, she didn't have the patience to tackle them. The desk didn't hold much, only papers and odd bits of stationery supplies.

Turning, she left the room and entered the snug. She had previously sorted the lounge and dining room, tossing out ancient stacks of yellowed newspapers. If anything important existed there, the sanitation worker had hauled them away long ago. She jogged upstairs and scoured the bedrooms, family bathroom, and attic. Nothing of interest came to light.

Running her hand through her hair, she returned to the kitchen. The room remained much as it had when she'd arrived. She hadn't yet ordered replacement appliances for the ancient fridge, cooker, and oven. And the clothes washer duo Sharidon taught her to use wasn't much of an improvement over her own methods, as the dryer left everything damp and required her to peg them on the line, anyway.

She faced the sea of painted cabinets and rolled up her sleeves—no time like the present to sort through them. Opening the cupboard nearest her, she removed an odd assortment of jumbled pots and cooking para-phernalia. Another contained crockery. And the drawer beside it held measuring devices and mouse droppings. Ew.

Continuing down the stack, she reached the last one. Behind a pile of tea towels, her fingers brushed against a loose backing. Was it broken? She dumped the lot beside her on the floor for a better view. The back appeared deliberately made that way.

She slid the panel sideways, which revealed a small cavity beyond. Holding her breath, she shone her mobile torch into the dark space. A metal tin sat in the back, much like the ones Mother filled with sweet bread at Christmas. Carefully, she reached into the recess, her flesh quivering at the thought of mice, and retrieved it.

Sitting on her heels, she pried off the lid. Inside lay a small stack of passports and an aged missive. She opened the first passport. Her godmother's picture jumped out at her with a different name and nationality. Two more passports did as well.

What? Her mouth dropped open. She snapped it shut. Had Mrs. McDougal been involved in something illegal?

The note inside the tin was addressed to Mrs. McDougal but contained no return address or signature—save for a green initial C at the bottom.

C?

Surely, C was a nickname. One that rang a bell. Where had she heard that before? Because she had. She was sure of it. But where? She ran her fingers over the yellowed paper as a memory flirted just out of reach.

C. C. C. Of course. Everything clicked into place.

Mother had been chatting with Uncle Roger in the blue salon, just the two of them. He teased her about something, and she had laughingly called him C.

"Never call me that, Janet. It's not safe."

"Not even here at Torwoodlee?" Disbelief laced Mother's tone.

"The very walls have ears," Uncle Roger said.

Cairstie had been young at the time, playing in the corridor with her dolls. She had stolen away from the nursery to find her mother, but she was occupied, so Cairstie had waited until Uncle Roger left, so she could claim her cuddle. Only Nanny found her and marched her back upstairs before her uncle left.

Was Uncle Roger C? If so, why did he sign that correspondence with green ink? Strange.

Cairstie unfolded the fragile paper and struggled until the words wiggled and ran together.

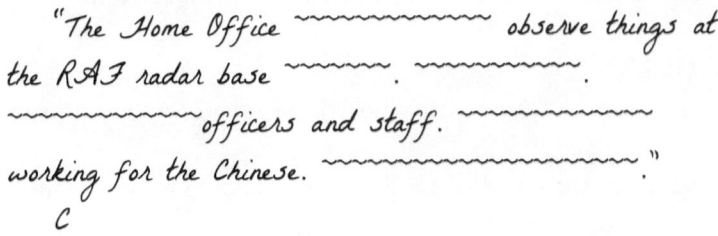

"*The Home Office* ～～～～～～ *observe things at the RAF radar base* ～～～～. ～～～～～. ～～～～～～～*officers and staff.* ～～～～～～ *working for the Chinese.* ～～～～～～～～～."

C

The date at the top was thirteen years old.

Had Mrs. McDougal worked for SIS, the Secret Intelligence Service? Why else would the mysterious C request her observance of military personnel and staff?

Cairstie was still kneeling on the floor mulling over the letter when Sharidon let himself inside the kitchen door, his face like a thundercloud, all dark mushed eyebrows, and spark-shooting eyes. "How the devil did ye get out of the van?"

She blinked up at him, mentally shifting gears from her discovery to the angry man above her. Winkle rushed into the room with a happy yip and butted her, his tail swishing. She draped her arm around his furry neck as relief and equal parts attraction stirred at Sharidon's return. "I turned off the cameras so they wouldn't notify you. You were gone almost six hours."

"I left ye there to keep ye safe. When I returned and found ye and my motorbike missing, every monstrous scenario went through my mind, especially since ye left Winkle."

"Missed me, did you?" She batted her eyelashes at him, trying to lighten his mood. When his expression didn't soften, she sighed. "I'm sorry I gave you a fright."

"So ye called yer sister, and she walked ye through the steps, did she?"

"Wrong. I figured it out for myself." Cairstie lifted her chin haughtily. Why did everyone think she was incapable of handling things on her own?

Sharidon opened his mouth for a rebuttal, then paused. "You tripped several wires."

"I thought I got them all." She grimaced.

"Ye shouldn't have figured out how to leave." His green eyes snapped, but something else came and went in them, too. Admiration? Dare, she hope?

"But I did."

"I wasn't sure if it was you who tripped them or our murderous intruder."

She swallowed that in silence as guilt pinned her to the floor. Sharidon had raced here, not knowing what he would find.

"I'm sorry." She picked up Mrs. McDougal's secret stash as a peace offering. "I discovered some interesting papers behind a drawer with a false back. An initial C is signed in green ink at the bottom. Do you know anything about that?"

Sharidon plopped down beside her. "May I?" He extended his hand.

"Be my guest." She presented the stack to him with a flourish.

He fanned through the passports without a word, then opened the letter. "How did your godmother die?" He folded the letter after he finished reading. "A lingering illness?"

"No. It was quite sudden. Surprising, really. Mrs. McDougal enjoyed robust health. Her death came as quite a shock."

"I'm sorry to hear that." He tapped the letter, his face decidedly blank of any expression.

"I'm going to the mainland tomorrow. Would ye care to accompany me?"

She blinked at the sudden change of topic, but the enticement of mainland shops distracted her. To leave the islands, even for a few hours, would be absolute heaven. "Of course. We would return tomorrow night?"

"That's the plan." He pushed back from the table. "I'm going to assemble an online grocery order and pick it up in Mallaig."

"Good idea." Mainland prices were much more reasonable.

He left the room. Instead of entering the snug to pack his things, he went outside.

That's when it hit her. Sharidon had cleared out shortly after his question about Mrs. McDougal's death.

Did he suspect foul play?

# CHAPTER 16

THE GRAY HEBRIDEAN Sea lay calm as glass around the ferry, but one look at the greenish hue of Sharidon's face filled Cairstie with alarm.

"Are you all right?" Cairstie approached him, unsure of what to do.

"I need fresh air, is all." He faced the sea and closed his eyes.

"Okay . . ." She left Sharidon on the rear deck and purchased him a chocolate croissant and hot cocoa.

She returned to the outer deck a few minutes later. The wind snatched the metal door and banged it against the ship's exterior. She kicked it shut without spilling the piping hot drink.

Raindrops spattered and stung her cheeks as she rejoined Sharidon at the rail. She placed her purchases on the bench behind him and touched his back. "Seasick?"

He grunted.

"I'll get you a patch in the ship's store." She dropped her arm and slung her purse over her shoulder.

"I'm already wearing one."

"Oh." That pulled her up short.

"Could you . . ." He leaned away from her. "Could you ditch that hot chocolate? The smell." He put his back to her.

"Sorry."

She chucked the drink into a bin just as he leaned over the rail and retched. Cringing, she left him there and reentered the ferry's interior. Poor Sharidon. He had another two and a half hours before they docked. If he suffered from seasickness, why hadn't he booked a flight from Benbecula to the mainland instead of insisting they take his van? Didn't the home office cover the price of a plane ticket?

Cairstie took the stairs to the next deck and gazed out the ferry's lounge windows, a massive seagoing vessel that connected the Western Isles to the mainland.

An occasional cloudburst appeared over the distant peaks.

She frowned. Did Sharidon insist on the ferry because he needed something inside the van? Come to think of it, Sharidon carried a gun, but when she'd searched for his tools, she found no evidence of ammunition. Elise and Harry kept a regular arsenal. Sharidon must have one, too. But where? She mulled that over for a bit. The overabundance of security cameras on that van gave her an idea.

"Mummy, look. Dolphins!" a wee lad shouted.

Several children clustered at the lounge windows and jabbered excitedly, bouncing on the balls of their feet. Having never spotted a dolphin in the wild, Cairstie approached the glass-plated windows and bent toward the wee lad.

"Where are they?" Cairstie asked.

"Just there." The lad pointed not ten meters from the starboard bow of the ship.

Sure enough, soft, gray-colored dolphins skimmed the water under the surface. Cairstie counted. One. Two. Three. Four. Five. Six. Seven. An entire pod. One leaped from the water. His body made a perfect arc before he disappeared under the waves.

A thrill rocked her. "It's like they're playing a game."

"Aye," the lad agreed, looked up at her, then scuttled to his mother's side and tugged her hand. "Mummy. I showed the pretty lady the dolphins."

The lad's mother winked at Cairstie. "Aye. That kind of you, Jemmy."

"Thank you for your help, Jemmy."

Jemmy's dark eyes rounded, but speech apparently overwhelmed him, and he hid his face in his mother's trousers.

Chuckling to herself, Cairstie continued on her way. Having never lived by the sea, she found the ferry a delightful mode of travel. No one rushed about. Many of the islanders chatted to one another, much like the villagers did at home—except there, they excluded her.

Stopping at the ship's store, she purchased a clear fizzy drink and hard ginger candy for Sharidon's queasy stomach. Afterward, she checked on him and found the poor fellow had not budged from the rail.

By the time the ferry docked at Mallaig, Sharidon was in no condition to drive, so she took the wheel and adjusted the mirrors while they waited their turn to disembark.

"Why did the government assign a seasick agent to the Western Isles?" she asked. That question had burned within her throughout their crossing.

"Because two other Mandarin speakers are dead and missing." Sharidon punched an address into the satnav, then semi-reclined in the passenger seat.

"You were their backup?"

"Something like that. I'm a linguist with a specialty in weapons."

She chewed on that for a bit, monitoring him in case he needed to hurl. "I've a fizzy drink and ginger drops in my purse for you."

"Thanks." He picked up her orange leather handbag that matched her wedged shoes, then retrieved her purchases.

He popped the fizzy bottle's lid and sipped in silence.

The lorry in front of her pulled forward, and she followed the stream of vehicles exiting the ferry. "Where are we going?" she asked.

"Loch Morar. I've made a reservation at their campsite."

Cairstie white-knuckled the wheel. "I need to return tonight." She did not intend to spend the evening off the island or share this minuscule van with him. She could lose her inheritance if she didn't return.

He glanced at her hands and smirked. "Relax. We're catching the ferry back this afternoon."

"Will there be time to pick up our food orders in Mallaig before we board?"

He nodded. "And catch a bite to eat. If yer very lucky, ye might spy Morag on Loch Morar while I handle my business."

"Morag?" She glanced at him, then back at the road. "Who's Morag?"

"Do ye not know yer own country's legends?"

"I've never spent time in this part of Scotland. Legends exist in every corner of the country. How am I to keep track of them all?" She side-eyed him, then quickly looked away. "Besides, I'm not superstitious."

"Brilliant. Then ye won't be worried about spending time by the loch?"

She stiffened at his hint about something sinister. "What's down by the loch?"

While a wee lass, Nanny's bedtime stories of kelpies, fairies, and banshees scared Cairstie so badly that she had burrowed under the covers. Elise scoffed at the tales and insisted Nanny used them to keep them in bed. So Cairstie had scoffed too, but secretly, she admitted to believing in those legends, especially on nights when the castle windows rattled, and the wind moaned down the chimneys.

The glint in Sharidon's eye told her he was feeling better.

"What's down by the loch?" she asked again.

"Ye'll see."

"Sharidon." A threat warmed her voice.

"Morag's a close cousin to Nessie."

"A sea monster?" Cairstie rolled her eyes.

"The locals believe in her. They've more pictures of Morag appearing on Loch Morar than Nessie's world-famous ones."

Was that true? She slid her gaze in his direction, but his expression gave nothing away. "I'll take my chances."

"A brave lass indeed."

"So, I'm to wander about alone while you play spy games?"

"I never said I was a spy."

"Yawn." She fanned her mouth. "What if I get lost? Or whoever left that friend of yours in the tunnel follows us?"

"No one's following us."

"How do you know? You had your head over the rail throughout the entire crossing."

He looked at her, his green eyes glinting. "Touché."

She shrugged.

"I'd best stay on my toes around ye." He laughed outright. "Yer much more than a pretty face, aren't ye, lass?"

Warmed by the compliment, she continued another five hundred yards until the satnav guided them down a narrow dirt track, the steep hills rising around them. Brown heather and gold-blossoming gorse grew in ravines alongside evergreens twisted by westerly winds. By and large, though, the landscape lay barren, covered only by short, stubby grass.

"You have reached your destination," the satnav announced through the car speakers.

Cairstie set the parking brake when a roofline appeared through the trees. That must be Sharidon's meeting place.

They exited the van and crossed a junction where several trails branched in different directions: one to the beach, another zig-zagged up to the ridge, and the third led toward the small glamping pod overlooking the loch below. Unsure what to do, she followed him to the cedar-clad pod.

Sharidon rapped smartly on the door. No response came from within. He grasped the handle, and it turned beneath his hand. Lifting his finger to his lips, he withdrew his gun from his waist holster.

Her eyes fastened on the weapon, and her heart ricocheted off her ribs as Sharidon entered the pod. What if someone shot him? What if someone lay dead inside, just like the man in the tunnel?

"All clear," Sharidon called.

Cairstie sagged with relief. Her imagination had gotten the best of her. She entered the one-room structure to find a double bed in the back corner, separated from a shower room by a thin partition, and to her right stood a wee kitchen that contained a tap and basin, a two-burner cooker, a microwave, and a refrigerator. A table and two chairs took up the floor space.

No dead bodies lurked in the corners. "Is this the right place?" Cairstie asked.

"Positive. The area's safe. I'll need some privacy for a while. I'll meet you down on the beach after my meeting concludes." Sharidon gave her a pointed look.

Heat filled her cheeks. No one ever told her to make herself scarce. No, but they'd ghosted her and removed her from modeling contracts.

"I'll see where one of those trails leads." Lifting her head, she marched outside and took the track farthest from the loch, the one leading up the hillside.

Below, the white sandy beach with its clear sparkling water drew her eyes, but she had no intention of luring Morag from the loch. She did, however, have every intention of sighting Sharidon's missing party.

She picked her way up the rocky trail. Her wedged soles snagged on a root, and she stumbled to her knees, grasping at a prickly gorse bush to save herself from tumbling down the steep incline. She clenched her teeth to keep from crying out.

Her knees stung, and she rubbed the raw flesh before locating a clump of heather two hundred meters above the glamping pod. She ducked and took out her mobile camera, curiosity burning through her. Who was Sharidon meeting? Was it another agent or a potential threat who could harm them?

Shifting to a more comfortable position, she waited. Bees hummed as they flitted from one bloom to the next. The loch below glinted when sunlight broke intermittently through the clouds.

A shadow crept along the pod's outer wall. Cairstie zoomed her camera and snapped a grainy picture just as the fellow slipped inside. She picked up a large rock and removed her shoes. Scrambling to her feet, she crept down the trail toward the pod. A sharp stone cut her foot. She covered her mouth to keep from whimpering. Blood dripped onto the soil, and tears stung her eyes.

Gritting her teeth, she hobbled down the trail to the pod, then sidled along the cedar exterior to the door. All seemed quiet within. She stepped a wee bit closer, and the door suddenly jerked inward. Sharidon stood on the threshold; his dark brows snapped together, and his eyes blazed green fire.

She shivered at his expression—so dissimilar to the man she knew. Or was that happy-go-lucky attitude just an act? She caught movement behind his shoulder. The opening of the deck slider. A gust of air.

They were alone.

Sharidon's lips had lost all their color. "Never surprise me again. I could have—" Still blocking her entrance, he slipped the firearm into his waist holster.

"You can let me in. They're gone." She dropped the rock and placed a hand against the rough exterior to keep her knees from knocking together.

His eyes darted to the thicket, then he gripped her arm and tugged her inside.

Still shaken by his response and hobbling from her injury, she tripped on the threshold and sprawled on the floor. "Oomph." Could this get any worse?

"Ye've cut yerself." Sharidon kneeled and inspected her bare foot.

Her face flamed as she rolled over and took in the blood smears.

"Where are yer shoes, lass?" Concern softened Sharidon's expression.

"I took them off to sneak up on you. I wanted to make sure you were all right."

Sharidon cocked a brow, and his mouth dented at her lie. He didn't believe her. Brilliant. "Since you refuse to tell me what's going on, I thought I'd find out on my own," she confessed.

"Ye almost got yer head blown off." His dark brows lowered. "And how would I explain that to yer family? Eh?"

Since he didn't appear to expect an answer, she didn't give him one.

He assisted her to the table, then fetched a bowl of warm water. "Let's clean that foot of yers, then have a look, shall we?"

Obediently, she dipped her foot in the warm water. It stung, but she refused to let it show, choosing instead to watch the fellow whose mercurial behavior changed as quickly as the Scottish weather—one minute, a charming, devil-may-care Irishman; the next, a hard-eyed operative. Who was the real man?

Sharidon returned with a handful of napkins. "It's just a scratch. Without a sticking plaster, this will have to do.

"Thank you." She made a pad of paper and pressed it to her foot until the bleeding stopped. "Did you get what you came for?"

Humor curved his mobile mouth. "Yer a persistent thing, aren't ye?"

"I'm told it's a virtue," she said primly.

Sharidon threw his head back and laughed. "In yer case, I'd argue that point." He sobered almost immediately. "Yer brave. I give ye marks for that, but I've never met such a stubborn lass. Do ye never do as yer told?"

Though his words weren't complimentary, his eyes lingered on her face, then dropped to her lips. Sharidon might say one thing, but his eyes told a different story. She glanced away. Did he ever intend to act on the attraction between them?

She took herself to task. What was she thinking? This Irishman had humiliated her in front of a restaurant full of patrons. Loneliness had scrambled her brain. She would never have glanced in Sharidon's direction at home.

Not true, her heart protested as the air thickened between them. She pressed her hand to her chest, which rose and fell with alarming speed the longer he stared at her lips.

Even Sharidon's limp did not detract from his impressive physique. If looks were the only thing going for him, she could fight her attraction, but the fellow had fixed her cooker and refrigerator, taught her to make eggs, and played bodyguard since the intruder's first invasion.

Initially, she blamed him for her troubles, her stubborn pride blinding her to the real issue between herself and her family. Sharidon wasn't her problem. He had responded to her sister's request. Her dilemma lay in the lack of trust her family bore her and the shattered trust she now bore for them—not the thing stirring between her and this Irishman. She wet her lips, and her eyes fastened on Sharidon's.

He touched her face, the softest of grazes, muttered something in Gaelic, and rose to his feet, breaking the crackle of electricity arcing between them. He cleared his throat. "Where did ye leave yer shoes?"

She pulled herself together. "Just up the trail toward the ridge," she answered with calm composure, even though her senses hummed like she had touched a live wire.

"I'll fetch them, and we'll be on our way." He left the glamping pod without a backward glance, a guarded expression slamming over his features.

Cairstie fanned her face. Blast. She stood a strong chance of falling for the Irishman if she wasn't careful. And that was something she refused to do.

He would not be her rebound.

# CHAPTER 17

Two hours later, Sharidon still chided himself at how close he had come to shooting Lady Cairstie, then almost kissing her afterward. What kind of agent did that? A lunatic. That's who.

He strolled Mallaig's narrow streets back to the Sprinter van after dropping Cairstie off at a dress shop. When he recalled the rock she'd dropped on the ground, his heart softened a bit. She had intended to protect him with that? Luckily, her blonde hair had betrayed her presence through the partially open door. Why had Cairstie snuck up on the glamping pod? Didn't she understand that what he did wasn't a game?

Despite it all, a glimmer of admiration endured. Cairstie had crept all the way to the door before he caught her. Impressive.

He needed to catch the traitor who had killed Agent Mansfield and possibly harmed Wang. Twice now, the traitor had attempted to dispatch Cairstie. And it worried him. A lot.

Compartmentalizing his emotions, he got to work. Sitting at the table inside his van, he booted up his computer and inserted the pen drive Agent Snodgrass passed to him at Loch Morar.

A list of residents, from North Uist to the Isle of Eriskay, filled his computer screen with addresses, occupations, and backgrounds from age eighteen to the present.

He groaned at the massive amount of information. Sorting and checking into this would take days, much more than the allotted hour before he met Cairstie at Mallaig's Cornerstone restaurant on Station Road.

Best get on with it.

He created a spreadsheet, then sorted the jumbled information, first by island and then by occupation, color-coding anything that raised suspicion. Bo and Grace Chen, the couple who owned one of the two grocery stores and the Chinese takeaway on Benbecula, spoke Mandarin and were originally from Beijing. Sharidon doubted China would plant such an obvious saboteur. Whoever it was, they had gone many years without detection.

National safety relied on the success of this mission. If he didn't stay on top of his game and steel himself from the distracting Lady Cairstie, he might wind up like Agent Mansfield.

⚜

Groceries and shopping bags jostled in the van as the sun gilded the island gold in the evening light. Cairstie glanced at Sharidon from the passenger seat. His pallor looked better now after surviving another ferry crossing. She clenched the van's door handle and forced herself not to fidget as Sharidon slowed for the last turn into Balivanich.

"Squeezing that won't get us there any quicker, lass." Sharidon glanced at her white-knuckled fingers.

"Sorry. It's just that Winkle's been in his kennel far longer than usual."

"Another minute won't hurt him."

How could the nomadic Sharidon understand how much her twelve-month-old puppy meant to her? Sophie had brought him home, and Cairstie immediately fell in love with the Goldendoodle and begged him off her sister. It never occurred to her that Sophie meant to keep Winkle for herself—not until months later when she overheard Elise's remark about her taking Sophie's dog.

In her defense, Sophie never once mentioned her desire to keep Winkle. Remorse consumed Cairstie for weeks. By then, Winkle had bonded with her, and returning him to Sophie proved impossible. She had learned her lesson, though. Now, she asked before she begged her sister for anything.

Sharidon turned onto her street and pulled into the driveway. "It should be safe. I haven't received any alerts from my surveillance cameras. Let me bring in the groceries while ye let the dog out."

"Lovely." Skirting the bonnet, she unlocked the kitchen door, leaving it wide for Sharidon. "Winkle. Hiya."

Winkle whined. She crossed the room and kneeled beside his kennel, which had moved several feet from where she kept it. Tufts of golden fur stuck to the wires. "What's wrong, my lad?"

She unlatched the door, and the pup cautiously stepped out, then promptly piddled on the floor. Winkle whined, then climbed onto her lap, trembling. "Poor bairn. Did you think I wasn't coming back?"

Sharidon bustled into the kitchen and plopped the first load of groceries on the worktop. The hackles rose off Winkle's spine.

"Ye were right. Poor pup." Sharidon looked pointedly at the fresh puddle of urine.

"Something's wrong with him." Cairstie placed the pup on the floor and gathered cleaning supplies. "His crate was partway across the room, and his fur . . ." Winkle growled at Sharidon and bared his teeth. "No, Winkle. You know Sharidon." She cuddled him close, but it did no good.

"Easy. Yer dog acts as though someone upset him. Stay here while I have a walk-about." Sharidon whipped out his gun and left her huddled on the kitchen floor with Winkle in her arms.

His footsteps entered the lounge, snug, dining room, solarium, and study; then he went upstairs, the floorboards creaking overhead. After a few minutes, he descended but didn't immediately return. Just when her fears had reached breaking point, Sharidon reentered the kitchen.

He holstered his gun but appeared to be looking for something. She opened her mouth to remark, but he put a finger to his lips, shook his head, and motioned for her to go outside.

Hoisting Winkle into her arms, she entered the garden where the dog marked his territory on every living plant before his ruffled fur lay flat once more, and he flopped at her feet with his face on his paws. The rhythmic ebb and flow of the waves gradually soothed her as she stared out at sea.

The minutes ticked, long and slow, until Sharidon returned. "Ye were right, lass. Someone paid ye a visit while we were gone. I found a bug upstairs in yer bedroom and one in the lounge. There's also one in the snug and another in the study. I can't destroy all of them, or whoever planted those listening devices will know we're on to them. We need to be mindful of what we say."

"Can you destroy any of them?" She fought the sudden trembling in her limbs. Who wanted to spy on her?

Sharidon squeezed her shoulder. "I'll destroy two. May I suggest that we leave the one in yer bedroom?"

"Why my bedroom? I'm in there the least amount of time."

"That's why I suggested it. Also, I should warn ye, the lads at the pub think we've patched up our quarrel." Sharidon cleared his throat and didn't meet her eyes. "They've noticed my van in yer driveway, and the locals believe I've moved in with ye. That kiss at the pub sealed yer fate. They assumed we'd had a row, so I let it about that ye followed me here."

"That makes me sound rather desperate."

"Or emotionally involved with yer boyfriend." He gave an expressive shrug.

Och. Her face burned with embarrassment. Did no one believe in abstinence before marriage these days? Or were she and her siblings the rare few who had taken to heart what their minister preached? "I see."

"Sorry, lass, but I think for yer own safety, it's best to keep up the pretense."

"I'll make up one of the spare bedrooms," she offered, trying to be practical when she longed to cover her face. Mother would have a coronary if she ever caught wind of this.

"I'll sleep in the snug or lounge."

"You're a might too tall for the sofas," she pointed out.

"Trust me, I've slept on worse. People will notice lights upstairs in the other bedrooms and think we've rowed—again."

"Have it your way, then." Her face flamed, and she longed to change the subject.

"Where should we keep the second bug?" he asked, reading her perfectly.

"Definitely not where you're sleeping; you ring too many people on that sat phone of yours."

"I vote we leave it in the lounge. We can turn on the telly and keep it running to help cover our conversations. They'll either think we don't use the other rooms much or that one isn't working."

"Won't they return to change them out?" The very thought of another break-in made her quiver.

"It's possible but unlikely if we play our cards right. If we talk about our being here because of yer godmother's will and my job, perhaps whoever's involved will choose to let well enough alone."

"But I clobbered the fellow who broke into the house."

"Let it about that someone broke in the first night and scared ye so badly that ye clubbed them."

"That will take care of the issue? What about my Mercedes?"

"Mention that yer battery died when ye arrived, and ye haven't driven it since. Tell them yer having it towed to the mainland for servicing."

"Will they remove the explosives if I let that about?"

"I haven't the faintest idea, but it'll be fun to find out." His green eyes danced and sparkled.

Fun? Her and Sharidon's ideas of fun varied widely. "What about your van?"

"Ye think they'll break into it?" The corner of his mouth ticked up.

"Why not? They've tampered with everything else on the property." Did he not take this situation seriously?

"Monitors and alarms are all over the van. I doubt they'll touch it."

"He bypassed your surveillance cameras in the garden," she reminded him.

"I only placed a handful on the grounds. The van's another thing altogether."

"And my godmother's car?" She raised both brows at him.

"I'll look it over before I drive it."

"What will happen when they find out who I am?"

"That yer an aristo?" His mouth curved.

"An influencer. What if someone on Benbecula follows me on social media?"

"For fashion trends?" Sharidon's eyebrows disappeared under his dark locks.

She laughed. "Put that way, probably not." The islanders were a thrifty, hard-working lot who thought little of incomers and their fancy ways. "What about Winkle?"

"I'd keep him with ye when yer out and about. Purchase more dog food. If the grocer inquires about yer increased consumption, explain that the last batch didn't agree with him."

Sharidon let very little rattle him.

"You're a clever one. You make everything sound easy," Cairstie said.

"I don't believe in overcomplicating things. Simple is always best."

A strand of hair blew into her face. He pushed it out of her eyes, sending tingles down her neck and arms. Flustered by her response, she stepped away.

"What is this house to our intruder?" That had weighed on her for some time. "Why did he return and try to blow me up?"

"I don't have the least clue, but I believe someone connected your godmother to the business on the base, and that's why she died."

"And I think the answer lies inside yer house."

❖

He shut the blinds, then switched the electric sign to closed. At last, his clients cleared out. They had lingered after hours until he fidgeted with impatience. Turning out the main lights, he slipped into the back room, pulled down the attic ladder, and ascended. The steps creaked beneath him as he climbed the rungs.

Pressing play on the sleek electronic device, he listened to the conversations inside Muir Tigh House as he busied himself with the reptiles. Sherwood and Miss Henderson enjoyed loud music, making conversations challenging to hear.

Using both hands, he caught two frogs and fed them to his snakes. Nicola would have his head if he didn't turn up soon. He had delayed supper the last few days to check the recordings for anything of value. Nicola possessed the mildest of tempers and rarely put her foot down, but she expected him home for the evening meal. And he had no intention of disappointing her again.

Upping the recording to double speed, he zipped through the

remaining conversations at Muir Tigh House. All those two spoke about was that mutt, Winkle, or cooking.

Everyone who saw the lass's arrival at the pub knew she and Sherwood were a couple. How could they not? Sherwood had pounced on her and planted enough kisses to raise more than a few eyebrows in their profoundly religious community. After listening in, he was prone to agree. Those two sparked off each other like flint to gunpowder, but thus far, nothing worth overhearing had occurred.

Nor did they mention any files. As far as he could detect, neither appeared professionally connected to that old snoop, Mrs. McDougal. Perhaps the lass was who she claimed.

But he had to know. To be sure.

Months ago, Gordon let it slip while in his cups that Mrs. McDougal had a work computer file about a deep plant passing on weapons information being tested here.

That very night, after he checked Mrs. McDougal's workstation computer on base, he slipped into Muir Tigh and helped her pass from this world. Mrs. MacLeod discovered her friend's body the following day. Chaos, in the form of solicitors and appraisers, had descended on Muir Tigh House. When the place finally emptied of people, he'd let himself in to search for the file, but the Henderson lass popped up out of nowhere, swinging a golf club like an ancient broadsword. He rubbed his arm where a considerable knot lingered from the encounter.

Perhaps he'd been a bit mad when he wired that bomb to her car. But he needed that file. With two of them now living inside Muir Tigh House, he could not access the place via the tunnel or solarium.

His stomach churned, and he popped an antacid. What if Sherwood and Miss Henderson stumbled across that information? If he were arrested, his sweet Nicola would never recover from the humiliations—nor would he from their separation.

He needed to search that house, and for that, he needed time. Sherwood and Miss Henderson must go, but two more deaths at Muir Tigh House would never do. Getting rid of them called for something different, something that took planning.

# CHAPTER 18

SHARIDON RAN HIS GPR, a ground penetrating radar, over the snug's external wall, scanning the surface to find if anything lurked behind it. The electromagnetic pulses of radiation imaged sub-surfaces, a handy gadget he had used on multiple missions. If Mrs. McDougal had hidden something inside her floors or walls, this thingamajig would find it.

A soft footstep sounded behind him. He spun on the balls of his feet.

"What are you doing?" Cairstie asked.

Sharidon placed a finger to his lips, walked to the desk, and switched on an old transistor radio to high. Gaelic music filled the room. He smiled at the tousle-haired beauty, who took up too much of his thoughts of late.

"What are ye doing up at this hour?"

"I asked you first." Cairstie tipped her head to the side, a smile pasted to her lips.

"I heard something." By now, he had learned a thing or two about Cairstie. That smile spelled trouble with a capital T.

"Do you plan to zap it?" She indicated his GPR unit as she edged into the room, clad in tracksuit bottoms and an electric blue jumper. The ensemble shouldn't have looked fashionable, but she pulled it off with ease.

"Lady Cairstie, it's not the right time for ye to be here."

"The name's Cairstie. Remember? Besides, this is my home. I have every right to be here."

Involving a civilian on a mission was strictly taboo. It endangered the operation. But the lass had iron in her spine, ears like a lynx, and too much spirit for her own good. Short of tying her to a radiator or shipping her home in a body bag, he was stuck with her.

"I can't involve ye in the case, lass."

"Then give me a nonclassified task." She mouthed the words, even though no bug under heaven could pick them out with the radio on high.

He rubbed his jaw, the stubble snagging his fingers. Grabbing his rucksack, he withdrew the list he jotted from the pen drive Agent Snodgrass transferred to him at Loch Morar.

"Can ye hop on social media and see who these people associate with?"

She took the handwritten sheet from him with a frown in her eyes.

"Is there a problem?" he asked.

"No."

She left the room with that same clouded expression. He continued to run the GPR over the wood burner wall, but his mind lingered on Cairstie. What had caused that troubled look? Until he handed her the list, Cairstie had seemed her old self. Surely, she didn't expect him to loan her his equipment? Not when social media was her forte. An influencer of her magnitude could whip through that list in no time.

He reached the corner. Nothing there. Kneeling, he plugged in the battery pack to boost the charge before he moved to the next room. Cairstie's voice, a soft murmur of unintelligible words, traveled down the corridor from the dining room. Who would she be calling at this hour? It was going on half one.

Curious, he crept toward the dining room and stood outside the door.

"So that's an S? What about the fifth line? I can't make heads or tails of that first word."

Scratching, like a pencil on paper, drew him closer still. She couldn't read his writing? One thing he prided himself on was penmanship. His mum insisted that he and his siblings turn in tidy schoolwork.

Sharidon peered through the crack between the door and the wall. Cairstie sat at the table, her back to him, holding a pencil. She had drawn pictures beside the list of names on the paper.

Retreating to the snug, he checked his battery and found a green light. After he inserted the pack inside his device, he went into the solarium and started on the wall attached to the house. Why would Cairstie draw pictures beside the names on his list? Was she illiterate?

He found that hard to believe. Elise had several degrees. So did Sophie. The Henderson family was well-educated and up-to-date on the latest political issues. Cairstie, however, had not attended university. Her career took off in her mid-teens, providing an enviable income for someone twice her age.

When they were alone, rather than talking about her famous self, Cairstie quizzed him about his education until he shared his ability to recall what he read or saw. Maybe she struggled with reading like his sister had. Should he ask her about it? Or let it come up naturally?

Squatting, he ran the GPR across the floorboards, but nothing unusual appeared. What did the intruder want? Something in the study?

Could something else be concealed in there? He left the solarium and crossed the lounge to enter the study via the adjoining corridor. Stopping in the middle of the room, he scanned the large desk, bookshelves, picture window, and the cupboard he used to access the tunnel.

Mrs. McDougal wouldn't hide anything in those bookcases. Too obvious.

He barely gave them more than a cursory glance, then ran his GPR beneath the window, and now shifted to the wall which contained the bullet holes. Nothing dinged.

That left the floor and cupboard wall. No one of intellect would place something of value underneath Muir Tigh House. The water table on Benbecula was too high, and storms occasionally flooded the island. That left the cupboard wall and ceiling. He doubted she'd leave anything there. Not with a tunnel . . .

A tunnel.

He marched to the far end of the paneled wall, checking seams in the woodwork. Every panel had a seam worked into the design. The clever construction had kept the intruder guessing, choosing to tear into the cupboard wall first. Interesting.

Good thing Cairstie chased the intruder off before he found what he was after. Excitement coursed through him as he swept the GPR over the panels.

Beep. Beep. Beep. His GPR lit up and imaged a niche less than two meters from the cupboard. His mouth dried out like a desert. Whoever dug the tunnel must have started another one, then given up.

Rather than pry off the paneling and further destroy the room, he set down the device and leaned against the desk, his eyes roving the wall. Mrs. McDougal doubtless accessed that niche, so it stood to reason that a hidden mechanism opened it.

At a soft footfall in the corridor, he rose before Cairstie entered, her blue eyes alight with success.

"I found the information you asked for." She waved the paper before her.

"Brilliant. Think ye can help me locate a way to access your godmother's hidey-hole?"

"You found something?" Her voice rose with an excitement that matched his own.

"I did. See how cleverly the paneling hides the cracks? They've integrated the woodwork to conceal it, rather like an artist's shading."

She went to the panel and examined both edges of the woodwork.

"What are ye doing?" he asked.

"Checking if anything appears to have seen more use than the rest."

He came alongside her. "Anything?"

"No. But Torwoodlee Castle has several passages. I'm just looking to see if–"

Stepping toward the wall, she gazed up at the ceiling, rounded the desk, and opened and closed drawers, muttering to herself. She removed a piece of plastic the size of a credit card inside the pencil drawer. "Hmmm. I wonder . . ."

She trotted to the panel and ran the card up and down each crack, pushing on the woodwork repeatedly. He had seen a few Murphy doors in his day and understood her theory of a magnetic lock. Unfortunately, that did not appear to be the case. Dismay shrouded her features when she stepped back. He bit back a smile at her expression.

"Let me have a go at it." He held out his hand.

"Good luck." She placed the card in his palm, her fingers barely brushing his, but the charge of her touch buzzed through him like a power surge. He locked his jaw, disgusted with himself. What a fine time for attraction to spark. He had more important things to handle than giving way to a pretty face.

He rubbed his finger down the rough edges of the plastic, then slipped the card partway into the crevice and lowered it toward the floor. Nothing impeded his progress. He switched to the opposite side of the panel and inserted the plastic into the crack. About chest high, the card stopped, and a snick of metal sounded within the wall. Gently, he pushed on the panel.

It moved four inches inward, then slid to the left, barely leaving enough room for one person to enter the niche behind.

Victory surged through him. "Have ye a torch?"

She ran to the desk and retrieved a light, then handed it over.

"Thanks." He pressed the switch and clicked on the torch, illuminating a plastered cubby hole two meters high by one meter wide. On the three shelves inside were a file folder, an ancient typewriter, a Bible, and two pen drives. The hair rose on his arms. Could it be? "When did ye say your godmother passed?"

"Last month. It was all verra sudden. No one knew she was ailing."

He blocked the opening and secreted the pen drives into his cargo trouser pocket. "Do ye recognize any of these items?" He stepped back from the niche so she could peek inside.

She glanced at the contents inside the cubby hole. "No."

"Would ye mind if I take this folder and have it analyzed?" he asked.

"Not at all." She hesitated, then said, "This tunnel and cubby hole are a rather strange addition to a home. Do you think Mrs. McDougal was a spy?"

"No one's mentioned her. She might have been a deep plant." He shoved his hand inside his pocket and enclosed his fingers around the pen drives. "How long did she live on Benbecula?"

"For as long as I've known her, perhaps longer. I'll ask Mother."

He nodded. "We've been a mite busy the last few days to handle this, but when the store opens, I plan to block that tunnel. I'm not happy leaving ye here. Would ye care to join me?"

"Aye. I'm not all that comfortable staying." She rubbed her arms, her pupils dark.

"Ye've had a bad time of it. Can ye sleep with what's left of the night?" he asked.

"I'll take Winkle upstairs with me."

"He's not much of a watchdog."

"No. But you are." She tossed him a smile and departed, looking more than a mite pleased.

"You are a rotten watchdog." Cairstie toed off her shoes, hoisted Winkle in her arms, then padded upstairs to her bedroom. "But I love you, anyway."

Peeling off her jumper and track bottoms, she changed into a tank top and shorts, then climbed into bed and snuggled beside her pup. Winkle swiped her face with his tongue. Cairstie grimaced and pushed him away. "You need a bath."

The puppy placed his head on her chest and closed his eyes, his breathing evening out almost immediately. Unfortunately, sleep eluded her after the recent find downstairs.

Had Mrs. McDougal been a spy? And what was in that file Sharidon requested? And the two pen drives he had pocketed? Should she demand them back? For now, she'd let it pass until she had more time to think about it.

After a long ten minutes, she grabbed the mobile off her nightstand and voice to texted Mother.

> Cairstie: How long did Mrs. McDougal live on Benbecula?

A few seconds later, her mobile pinged.

> Mother: Why do you ask?

> Cairstie: Just curious. Didn't she move here after my christening?

> Mother: She was well established on the island before your father, and I married.

> Cairstie: Did she work on the base?

> Mother: I believe so. She and her husband never had children, so she took a civilian job. Are you terribly bored, darling?

Bored? Cairstie snickered. Winkle raised his head and gave her a mournful glare. "Sorry, Winks." She stroked his fur, and he moaned in puppy ecstasy.

> Cairstie: I'm not bored.

Not with intruders and a fit MI6 agent to keep her company.

> Mother: I'm so happy to hear that.

> Cairstie: What are you doing up so late?

> Mother: Baking.

Ahh. Mrs. McNabb, their cook, frowned on anyone in "her" kitchen. So, when the baking bug bit, Mother and Sophie invaded Mrs. McNabb's domain after she left for the day.

> Cairstie: What are you making?

> Mother: Meringues. Sophie and I are trying out different desserts for her hen dos.

Cairstie's chin wobbled. Sophie was getting married, and she wasn't there to attend the pre-wedding festivities.

> Cairstie: I'm sure they will be delicious. I need to go. Night.

> Mother: Night, dear. xx

An ache squeezed Cairstie's chest, and her throat constricted. She missed her family. Mother and Sophie most of all, but she daren't share what had occurred since her arrival. Her family would rush to her aid and postpone Sophie's nuptials. No bride deserved such treatment.

Cairstie rolled onto her side and closed her eyes, but it was a long time before she fell asleep.

# CHAPTER 19

"THIS IS THE LAST OF THEM." Sharidon slid an eight-foot piece of wood from the van and balanced it against a side panel until Cairstie slammed the back doors and relieved him of one end. Together, they started for Mrs. McDougal's front porch.

"When I finish blocking the tunnel, would ye care for some target practice?" With a murderous traitor on the loose, he'd rest easier if Cairstie confirmed that she knew her way around a weapon.

"Halò," a young man called from the road and started down Mrs. McDougal's drive toward the front steps.

Sharidon halted, adjusting the wood to glance over his shoulder at the newcomer. A fair-headed lad stood eyeing Cairstie like a dog drooling over a bone.

"And who might ye be?" Sharidon responded in Scottish Gaelic.

"I'm Colin MacKenzie." The lad tore his eyes away from Cairstie just long enough to answer. "Are you new to Balivanich?" Colin asked in English.

Cairstie set her end of the board on the porch, forcing Sharidon to do the same.

"I'm Cairstie Henderson, and this is—"

"Will Sherwood," Sharidon cut in, using his alias.

Cairstie pressed her lips together, clearly irritated. Too bad. They couldn't undo the damage if she blundered his name, not on such a sparsely populated island.

"Nice to meet you. You must be the chartered surveyor we've heard so much about." Colin eyed him with open curiosity.

"Could be." Sharidon remained non-committal.

"Are you summer visitors or new residents?" Colin was clearly fishing to see how long Cairstie intended to stay.

"I'll be here a while. I don't know what Will's plans are after he completes the survey."

Colin brightened. "That's grand. It'll be nice to have young people at Mrs. McDougal's place. Did you know her?"

"She was my godmother."

"I'm sorry for your loss." Colin's words were polite, but he spoiled the effect by ogling her some more.

"Thank you." Cairstie's darkened lashes swept onto her cheeks.

Sharidon growled as a flash of resentment raised its ugly head. "I don't wish to be impolite, but we're busy at present. Doubtless, we'll see ye around." Sharidon hefted the board, giving Cairstie no choice but to grab her end or gouge the plaster as he dragged it inside the front hall.

"Cheers," Colin called after them, then sauntered back up the drive whence he came.

"Must you be so impolite?" Cairstie hissed as she nudged the door closed with her heel.

"The lad eyes ye like a Sunday dinner after a week of fasting," Sharidon growled. Couldn't the lass see that?

"He was being neighborly."

"Too neighborly if ye ask me." He resented anyone who ogled her like that.

"He said nothing impolite." Cairstie huffed.

"If ye want that pretty lad mooning about, keep encouraging him with yer smiles and fluttery eyelashes." Truthfully, Cairstie had done nothing save to look the way she did. He was behaving like a Jackeen. The situation vexed him, and he had a fair idea why—which put him even further out of sorts.

He backed down the corridor and laid the board on the stack. The clerk at the local hardware store, which sold random building supplies, had pre-cut the wood to Sharidon's specifications.

Cairstie left him to it without another word. The side door opened and closed a few seconds later, and Winkle dashed past the windows, barking madly, and heading for the beach. Gulls took flight as the Goldendoodle obtained the sand. Cairstie followed at a sedate pace, bracing against the wind.

"Ach." Sharidon tugged on his hair. He owed her a very large apology. Stress and jealousy didn't excuse his behavior. One could hardly blame the lad for appreciating her beauty.

If looks were the only thing going for the lass, temptation might not have come knocking on his heart. But Cairstie had proven herself more than a pampered princess. She didn't complain when she had every reason to, and her resourcefulness flat-out shocked him. His mouth quirked at the memory of how she blackmailed him into fixing Muir Tigh House. Plus, the lass kept her wits about her when it mattered. Whacking the intruder with Mrs. McDougal's golf club proved her courage when under fire.

The lass had a steely spine underneath the fluff, and the combo pierced him with the accuracy of Cupid's arrows.

All right. So, he more than liked her. He couldn't do anything about it or shouldn't anyway—not with Harry for her brother-in-law. To act on his attraction might prove a death sentence, and to act on it while on assignment was mad.

Compartmentalizing his emotions, he screwed each piece of wood into the cupboard's back wall while he practiced his apology. No matter what he came up with, it sounded stilted and false. *Ach.* For good measure, he added a horizontal row of lumber, from floor to ceiling. No one could access the house via the tunnel now, not unless they used an electrical saw or explosives.

Unable to endure another minute of discord, he went in search of Cairstie. He found her at the end of the garden, speaking to a middle-aged woman dressed all in black and carrying a battered basket.

"I assure you, Mrs. McDougal let me wander her property to collect pottery and sea glass," the woman said, shifting her basket to her opposite arm.

"That may be true, but I own the house now, and it upsets my dog to have you mucking about. The beach is open to everyone, but you need to keep clear of the garden."

"I don't see why. It's not like I'd be tearing up the grass. The place is a disgrace," the woman argued.

Sharidon halted alongside Cairstie to lend his support. "Is there a problem?"

"Mrs. MacLeod, Will Sherwood." Cairstie clipped out his alias while making the introductions. When her eyes met him, they were hard. "Mrs. MacLeod used to dig about Mrs. McDougal's garden and intends to continue, even though the property now belongs to me."

"I'm sorry, Mrs. MacLeod, but Cairstie has plans for this space. She can't have ye digging holes in her garden whenever ye please. Her dog will likely go after ye."

Mrs. MacLeod stared him down but acquiesced when he refused to cower. "You're that man here to help us reclaim our land from the government, aren't you?"

"Aye."

"I suppose I can leave the garden be. It'll be nice to see this place put back to rights. Drop by for tea any time. I'd love to chat." The woman nodded and moved down the beach.

"Thank you, Mrs. MacLeod. We will," Cairstie called after her.

"Why did ye deny her access to the garden?" Sharidon lowered his voice in case the woman was still within range.

"I caught her peeking through the kitchen window." Cairstie's entire manner remained stiff. "Thank you for backing me up."

"We can't have people snooping about the place."

"Definitely not."

He took her arm. "I'm very sorry for what I said to ye earlier. It was uncalled for."

She looked up at him. "It's forgotten, especially since you are going to help me put this garden to rights."

"What?"

"You heard me, Mr. Sherwood. I trust I don't need to repeat myself." Cairstie started for the house. "Come, Winkle; Mummy has a treat." Winkle's ears perked, and he circled her with a wagging tail.

Sharidon stood stock still, mesmerized by how she had just played him.

Reaching the kitchen door, she glanced at him with a pert smile on that pretty mouth, then disappeared inside, the door slamming behind her.

He tugged at his hair and exhaled loudly. He was in very great trouble —very great trouble indeed.

The gray morning had given way to a break in the clouds that afternoon. Taking advantage of the weather, Cairstie clipped Winkle's lead to his collar.

"I'm going for a walk," she called, not that Sharidon paid her any attention. Today, after their shooting match, he ran a Flymo over her lawn to cut the grass and create some semblance of order. Afterward, he'd holed up in the dining room with his computer.

Winkle barked excitedly and ran in circles, tangling his leash around her legs. She tripped and supported herself against the kitchen worktop while she laughingly disengaged herself from the leash. "All right, laddie. Let's go."

She grabbed the nine iron for added protection, then stepped outside. The sun might be shining, but the weather remained cool. Filled with restless energy, she set off with Winkle, towing her along the road like a champion sled dog.

White cottages dotted the green swales, not stacked against each other like in the city but here and there with property all around. The vast sea, sky, and grass-covered plains had filled her with uneasiness when she first arrived on Benbecula, but now, she welcomed the almost spiritual aspect of the island's quiet and unique beauty. The road stretched before her, empty. Silent. She could well believe herself the only inhabitant on a day like this. She now relished the slower pace and lack of demands.

Caught up in the busyness of her former modeling career, she had rushed from one event to the next with little to no downtime, never allowing herself the occasion to ponder.

If the looming threat of the murderer's return didn't hang over her, she might enjoy the island. Her nine iron should keep her safe enough during daylight hours.

After meeting Mrs. MacLeod that morning, Cairstie had busied herself removing dust covers off the furniture and wiping down the wood-work—something she had observed the staff do at Torwoodlee Castle. When she finished, the house smelled of beeswax and lemons. She gazed at the gleaming surfaces, and a spark of accomplishment filled her. She had done something on her own and done it well. Later, she had squirted the basin with washing-up soap and cleaned the dishes.

Winkle slowed from his mad dash to a happy trot, allowing her to catch her breath. The lull of breakers hitting the beach made her sigh, but a loud bang spun her around as a large bin truck lumbered down the road in her direction. She tightened Winkle's lead and stepped onto the *machair* to let them pass.

Instead, the truck halted beside her, and Colin MacKenzie leaned out the window and gave her a boyish grin. "We meet again."

"So, I see. Is this your job?" Winkle edged up beside her and emitted a low growl.

"One of them. I work at the airport, too. We've three flights a day," he huffed out.

"That must keep you busy."

"Aye." Admiration filled his gaze and made her shift. No one else was about. They might have been the only two people on earth.

"I'll not be keeping you then." She nodded to him.

Colin seemed poised to continue, but Winkle growled and stopped him. Colin set the lorry in gear and moved off toward the next house almost a quarter mile away. A flock of gulls flew overhead, and Winkle strained on his lead when one alighted in the *machair*, forcing her to jog to keep him from choking himself.

Collin behaved as though he had never seen a female before. Though few women his age lived in Balivanich, she could not be the only lass in the small community.

Not caring to catch up with Colin, she followed a trail that cut through the *machair* to the beach, where she let Winkle off his lead. The puppy raced up and down the white sand, barking at birds. She slipped off her trainers, then dipped her toes in the frigid Atlantic. Goosebumps prickled her skin until it numbed from the cold. The ebb and flow of the sea, the bright sunlight, and the soft sand worked their magic on her soul. She wandered the beach, stopping now and again to admire colorful rocks and shells beneath the water's surface.

Her thoughts drifted to Sharidon. After their unfortunate meeting, he'd grown on her, and she suspected that he had become necessary for her happiness. Underneath his easygoing exterior lurked a determined patriot. The glitz and glamor of her former career did not impress him, nor did her aristocratic title, as he treated her without deference.

Of late, an awareness buzzed between them like an improperly grounded electrical appliance, and though he never acted on it, she knew he felt it, too.

Making her way up the beach, she selected a pebble, the water running down her forearm and dripping off her elbow. How many years had it taken to smooth these rocks so perfectly? Before she knew it, she had a small pile, but once removed from the water, their vibrancy dulled. She tossed them back one by one, plopping them into the waves.

She whistled for Winkle. He gamboled back, his tongue lolling. "Did you have a fun time scaring the birds?" His fur had matted from dashing in and out of the sea, and he desperately needed a bath.

He sat beside her while she put on her shoes and clipped his lead onto his collar. Rising, she dusted off the sand. A lone figure holding a basket stood half-bent further down the beach—Mrs. MacLeod. Cairstie caught her breath. Did she ignore the woman and take the trail back to the road, or should she do the neighborly thing and greet her?

Determining the latter, she started in the woman's direction. Mrs. MacLeod straightened and watched her come with no sign of welcome in her expression. Cairstie inwardly tensed. Until the last few months, people had fawned over her wherever she went. Mrs. MacLeod's disapproval filled her with an all too familiar dismay.

"Hiya, Mrs. MacLeod," she said more cheerily than she intended. The woman worried her with her peeping and digging.

Winkle dropped at Mrs. MacLeod's feet and gave her a puppy smile. The woman visibly melted and patted his head. "There's a good lad. Out walking your dog, I see?"

"Aye. The weather was too fine to stay inside."

"That it is."

"Have you found anything interesting today?" Cairstie indicated the woman's basket.

"A few bits and bobs." Mrs. MacLeod allowed her a peek at the smoothed pieces of pottery and blue and green glass inside her basket.

"What do you do with them?" Mrs. MacLeod must have an ulterior motive if she spent so much time combing the beach.

"I make table tops and picture frames and sell them on consignment at The Sea Hut. Have ye heard of it?"

"I don't believe so."

"Tourists love the place. It's one of the few shops on the island that sells local art and is a nice way to earn some extra cash during the summer months."

"I'll be sure to stop by. Thank you for telling me about it."

Mrs. MacLeod nodded. "We islanders don't associate much with incomers like yourself and that Irishman of yours, but Mrs. McDougal was a friend of mine. If you're her goddaughter, I can make an allowance this once. Why don't you come to tea on Thursday and bring that Irishman along."

Warmth filled Cairstie at Mrs. MacLeod's offer of friendship. Cairstie had disliked standing up to Mrs. MacLeod earlier, but they couldn't have someone spying on them for both her and Sharidon's sake.

"Thank you, Mrs. MacLeod. I can't answer for Mr. Sherwood, but I would be delighted to come."

"Three o'clock. Don't be late."

"I won't. Ta."

Smiling to herself, Cairstie followed the trail back to the road. There beside the tarmac stood Sharidon. Two indentations scored the flesh between his dark brows and marred his usual cheery disposition. Her heart sank as she closed the distance between them.

"Where have ye been?" Sharidon crossed his arms.

"I told you I was going for a walk."

"That was ages ago."

"I was safe." The intruder had only attacked inside her house.

"Out on the beach by yerself? With no one the wiser as to yer whereabouts? Anyone could have come along." He tugged at his hair, making it stand on end.

"Nothing happened." She folded her arms, golf club dangling from one hand and stuck out her chin.

Sharidon leaned forward, his green eyes shooting sparks. "Have ye forgotten we have a murderer on the loose?"

"That has nothing to do with me." This situation dealt more with MI6 or the military.

"I beg to differ. Ye've been shot at, and the intruder's seen yer mug. And while we're at it, let's not forget that little ticker he placed under yer Mercedes. I'd say that has a good deal to do with ye."

They stood toe to toe now, glaring at each other. Cairstie's chest tightened as his words sank in. He had searched for her, which proved his concern. Unfortunately, her stubborn pride balked, and it took everything in her to shove it back down. Cairstie refused to meet his eyes. "I'm sorry. I was restless and didn't think about the ramifications. It won't happen again."

He placed a finger under her chin and lifted her face. "Ach. Lassie, I didn't mean to ring a peal over yer head. Ye gave me a scare when I couldn't find ye, and I'm afraid I reacted badly. It's I who am sorry."

His sincere apology softened her even further, and she blinked several times to erase the sting in her eyes. Glancing away, she searched for his van, finding only a half-hidden motorbike on its side in the *machair*.

"Did you ride that?" she asked.

"I wasn't sure which way ye went and thought ye might have taken one of the trails. It seemed the quickest way to find ye."

He walked over and righted the motorbike, pushing it alongside her as they turned as one toward Muir Tigh House. She noted his limp had all but gone.

"Did you have time to look at my list?" She referred to the names she had checked on social media.

"I glanced at it. Several of them have backgrounds that require further investigation. I'd like to put a visual to their names. Why don't we visit the local pub and grab a bite to eat?"

"Are you deputizing me as a spy?" She warmed at the prospect.

"I wouldn't go that far, but two of us can interact with more locals than just one."

"Admit it. You need my help." Her smile widened.

"I do—within limits."

Taken aback by his lukewarm response, she walked in silence for several hundred yards. A bird shot out of the *machair*, and Winkle barked, straining on the lead. "Stop that, Winkle."

"Limits?" Cairstie asked after settling her dog. What exactly did that mean?

"Yer observant. I'll give ye that. But yer every bit as much a worry as ye are a help."

"You know, Sharidon, for a smart fellow, I think you could have worded that a wee bit differently. Women don't appreciate hearing that they're a bother."

She marched down the drive to the side door and stopped on the kitchen stoop.

"Did ye expect me to lie?" He came alongside her after setting the kickstand on the motorbike.

"Aye. Isn't that what spies do? I would think you were verra good at it by now." Grasping the brass knob, she turned it and yanked the door open. Winkle dashed inside.

Cairstie followed, then slammed the door behind her.

# CHAPTER 20

WEAK SUNLIGHT FILTERED through Mrs. MacLeod's kitchen windows and highlighted the cat hair on every conceivable surface. Cairstie fought back a sneeze as she set her teacup on its saucer.

"That was lovely, Mrs. MacLeod. Thank you for inviting me." Cairstie picked up her napkin and dabbed her lips.

"It's a shame that man of yours could not attend." Mrs. MacLeod wore bright yellow today and had coordinated her clothing with her table-cloth and tea set. Even the plastic flowers she used for a centerpiece were the color of butter.

"He had to work."

One of Mrs. MacLeod's five cats jumped onto the table and drank the last dregs from Mrs. MacLeod's cup.

"Sissy, say hello to my company." The cat, a black and white tabby, blinked at Cairstie, then proceeded to clean herself.

A tickle burned inside Cairstie's nose, and she sneezed.

"Are you coming down with a cold?" Mrs. MacLeod's eyes rounded.

"It's nothing." Or would be when she left Mrs. MacLeod's dander-infested house.

"Best have a word with Dr. Campbell. He's the best diagnostician in the Uists."

"I'll keep that in mind." Another sneeze burned Cairstie's nose, but this time she squelched it.

"We're having a Sunday School hike up Reuval tomorrow." Mrs. MacLeod referred to Benbecula's only sizeable hill. "You should come and bring that Irishman."

She must have looked skeptical, for Mrs. MacLeod continued, "Reuval doesn't look like much, I'll admit, but the views from the top are remarkable. On a clear day, you can see all the way to St. Kilda in one direction and across the Little Minch in the other to Skye."

"The Little Minch?" Cairstie had never heard that term.

"The sea separating the Uists from the Inner Hebrides."

"What time are you leaving?"

"Nine. We're meeting at the landfill depot. It's the only place near the trailhead with parking. Will you come?"

"I will if I'm free. Thank you for the invitation." Cairstie rose from the table. "Do you need help clearing things?"

"Leave it. The cats will enjoy what's left."

Inwardly cringing at the response, Cairstie collected her coat and said her goodbyes. Sharidon could cross Mrs. MacLeod off his list of suspects. The woman was pure dafty. Or was her behavior just a ploy by a consummate actress?

After all, she had caught Mrs. MacLeod peeking through Mrs. McDougal's windows instead of digging about the garden for sea glass.

Kneeling in the *machair* behind a boulder, he raised the rifle and focused his scope. His wife's figure magnified behind the lens. He moved to the right and captured the Irishman, Sherwood. Not his target. Lastly, Cairstie Henderson trudged up the trail with the other members of St. Mary's strung about in clusters, chatting.

The hike up Reuval took several hours, enough time to accomplish his errand. He stroked the rifle's barrel. Hopefully, this would give him the bonus he needed.

Though he preferred the cover of darkness, he refused to pass up this opportunity. Setting the Henderson lass in his crosshairs, his pulse raced. He exhaled and forced himself to focus.

Allowing for the breeze and distance . . . He held his breath and—

The Irishman looked his way just as he squeezed the trigger. Sherwood grasped the lass and fell. Cries and shrieks rose in the distance.

His breath rasped from the adrenalin rush. He congratulated himself. That had worked well.

Rising from the *machair*, he climbed into his EV and eased onto the A865 toward Balivanich. He left his car in the village car park, where if anyone noticed, they might assume he was visiting the shops.

Drawing on his hoodie, he cut across the windswept grass, shaving off a mile to Muir Tigh House. At the top of the drive, he spotted the first camera embedded in the hedge, the second mounted on the porch. He swore under his breath.

The lass must have installed them after their encounter.

Mulling it over, he avoided the main road, choosing a path leading to the beach. A lone figure bent over the sand some distance away. Not Mrs. MacLeod, she and Nicola were scaling Reuval. Her niece must be scavenging for bits and bobs to help her auntie.

No one at the pub or community center mentioned Muir Tigh House's break-in. Odd that. Why hadn't the lass said anything? Break-ins were big news in these parts.

He spotted another camera under the garage eaves when he approached Mrs. McDougal's back garden. His pulse drummed, and he drew up short. Bother the cameras. Just how many had the lass rigged up?

Retreating to the fence line, he scanned the garden as he drew on his gloves. The grass appeared freshly mowed, but the Mercedes EV had not moved since his last visit. He averted his face from being photographed and approached the solarium.

Three shimmies and the old lock gave way. It looked sturdy enough but wasn't, or doubtless, Miss Henderson would have changed it out. Even if she did, though, it wouldn't have stopped him.

Thankfully, she took that poor excuse of a dog with her today, or his barking would alert the neighbors. That mongrel went off his nut the last time he entered Muir Tigh House.

After Mrs. McDougal's demise, he had scoured every room for that file, but his search proved fruitless. She must have hidden it somewhere. Perhaps in a book on a handwritten note? Or a pen drive?

Though hammered at the time, Gordon insisted it existed. Whatever "it" was.

He'd searched the tunnel from one end to the other, even after the body he'd dumped in there began to smell. Did other tunnels connect to Muir Tigh? During the last world war, tunnels riddled the countryside. If one reached the house, perhaps another did as well.

Using the desk chair for a step stool, he started on the bookcase, hunting behind and inside each volume. Nothing. Fury bloomed, and he jumped off the chair and kicked the desk.

Where was that file?

He scanned the room again, his eyes returning to the carved panels. Crossing the floor, he opened the cupboard to access the tunnel. New lumber enclosed the hole he had created.

Well, he hardly blamed the lass for sealing off the area. Heating costs would prompt similar behavior from any Scot. He stiffened as a stray thought struck. If Miss Henderson enclosed the tunnel, had she found the body? He had hidden it some distance from the house.

No. Of course not. Police Scotland would descend in droves if she had.

He returned to his search. Mrs. McDougal had not secreted a file in that tunnel. He eyed the rather elaborate paneling on the remaining section of the wall. Too elaborate.

On a whim, he thumped the wood beside the cupboard, then continued along the wall. Tap. Tap. Tap. Partway across, the sound changed, and he clicked on his mobile torch app and shone it into the crack. Nothing but darkness. He duplicated the process on the opposite side, moving his light vertically over every section.

Metal glinted inside the gap. His breathing intensified.

If a metal hinge moved the panel, Mrs. McDougal wouldn't keep the key to its access very far. Rounding the desk, he tugged open a drawer and shifted a few papers aside for a lever. Not seeing anything close, he sorted through the bits and bobs for something thin and long enough to reach the mechanism.

An old razor blade? Too rusty. What if he nicked himself? He hadn't had a tetanus shot in years. He tossed it aside. A letter opener?

He returned to the panel and attempted to insert it into the crack. Too thick. Perhaps a paperclip? He unbent half of a paper clip, inserted it into the gap, then wiggled it around. Click. The panel jolted.

*Aye. That's the ticket.* He pushed on the wood, and it slid to the side on some sort of track. Behind it lay a niche. His heart banged like a drum corps. Inside, an old typewriter, the kind his great gran used until her death, complete with black ribbons and separate metal keys. Beside the typewriter lay a Bible.

That was it? Two ancient relics from the past? The Bible was massive, its pages yellowed and unpleasant smelling. Had Mrs. McDougal placed her files inside its pages?

Voices coming up the walk alerted him. "Bring her into the lounge."

"Shouldn't we take her upstairs? She needs to rest," Mrs. MacLeod's voice crackled.

"Please stop fussing," a younger woman responded.

Miss Henderson? She lived? He snatched the Bible and eased the panel shut. Tiptoeing across the corridor, he entered the solarium, exited into the garden, and dodged around the garage, pressing his body against the base's fence. The camera rotated in his direction. He swore and ducked out of the way.

Mrs. MacLeod's niece stood at the bottom of the garden. "What are you doing?"

The confounded woman must have seen him cut through the garden. She couldn't identify him from one hundred meters away, but her noise would draw attention from those inside.

He clasped his firearm by the handle, then hesitated. After today's shooting at Reuval, killing Mrs. MacLeod's niece was not the answer. Authorities would swarm the island and likely discover the other body. And if they did too much digging, he'd be compromised.

"You there. By the garage. I see you." Mrs. MacLeod's niece started in his direction. If she reached the flower beds . . .

He hunched his shoulders and tied the hoodie to cover most of his face while removing his mobile from his pocket. He had wired the Mercedes' bomb to the starter, but his mobile contained a secondary AP to trigger it.

Opening the app, he pressed the ten-second countdown as Mrs.

MacLeod's niece gained the flowerbed. He sprinted past the Mercedes and van to obtain the road. Instead of keeping to the tarmac, he raced through the *machair* to the back of Robertson's bakery. Gasping, he rounded the building and bent with his hands on his knees, gasping for air.

He waited for the blast, then checked the timer. The bomb should have detonated. Something was wrong.

Ripping off his coat and hoodie, he chucked them into the dumpster bin and edged around the bakery to reach the car park. His app worked. Someone had disarmed his bomb.

He glanced across the fields toward Muir Tigh House. Something didn't add up about that pair. He'd best discover who they were and what they were doing on Benbecula.

# CHAPTER 21

FEMININE LAUGHTER CARRIED across the pub to where Sharidon stood at the bar, nursing a fizzy drink as the dueling fiddlers concluded their song. Enthusiastic applause broke out across the room.

"Looks like Colin MacKenzie's making inroads on your lass," Randy, the bartender, commented as he filled two shots of whiskey.

Sharidon glanced at the table where Cairstie played cards with Colin, Gordon, and Harry. She'd been quiet all afternoon since their aborted hill walk.

He hadn't meant to hurt her. But while scanning the area, a flash, like sunlight on a rifle scope, drew his attention, and his instincts had taken over. He had tackled Cairstie to the earth and skinned her arm in the process. She didn't need stitches, so he had cleaned the wound and bandaged her up. The easy explanation was that no shot had been fired. But silencers on the black market came in all shapes and sizes.

Since his flying tackle made him look the fool, she had kept her distance. He had been hard-pressed to set things right between them afterward, so he hiked back up the hill to find the bullet to vindicate himself by way of explanation.

An accordionist started a sweet melody, and one villager lifted his voice in a beautiful, clear tenor. The Gaelic lyrics quieted the room. Malcolm

Kennedy added his own, harmonizing with his gravelly baritone. His voice shouldn't have blended with the other singer, but somehow, it did. Then, a lad, no more than thirteen, tuned his violin and joined in.

"The lad's good," Sharidon commented to Randy, who was drying a batch of empties.

"He's not so bad—about average in these parts." Randy nodded.

Sharidon raised a brow. "Is he yers? Is that why yer being modest?"

"He's not mine. We start our bairns early on instruments. Most of them play."

"Ah." That explained the Ceilidh signs posted everywhere. The locals enjoyed a musical gathering, and their talent, whether professional or amateur, provided a real draw.

A rousing folk tune followed, and Sharidon clapped to the beat. Cairstie stepped forward and spoke to the young fiddler who sat the song out. He handed her his instrument, and Cairstie plucked a few strings, then applied her bow to the strings.

Sharidon goggled. Well, wasn't she a lass for surprises? Cairstie's arm did not appear to trouble her much, but he kept an eye on her in case she started to bleed.

When the song concluded to uproarious applause, Cairstie's smile bloomed, and she glanced in his direction. He raised his glass to her in a silent toast. Never once had she mentioned her musical skills, but then, his brother Paddy, who sang like a dream while he worked about the farm, rarely sang in public. Perhaps Cairstie was much the same.

The fiddlers spoke to her, then started into another tune, with Cairstie joining in. *The Braes of Balquhither's* ballad swelled, and something inside Sharidon went right along with it, stirring his heart with nostalgia for the green hills of home. A wave of emotion, fierce and powerful, tumbled his heart like a sea roller approaching the shore. He gripped the bar, his fingers pressing tight.

How had that stubborn lass burrowed her way inside his soul? The shock rendered him speechless—a man accused of having a double-hinged tongue.

Cairstie swayed to the music, her eyes sparkling as her gaze swept the room and met his over the heads of those seated at the tables. She sobered immediately but kept her gaze on him as she played.

His pulse raced, and blood pounded in his ears. Time ceased to exist in the bubble between them.

A woman lifted her voice in song, penetrating the room's corners.

*I will twine thee a bower*
*By the clear, silver fountain*
*And I'll cover it o'er*
*Wi' the flowers o' the mountain,*

Shifting ever so slightly, Cairstie played the chorus of *The Braes of Balquhither*, with the other fiddlers and never glanced his way again. The enchantment lingered long after she handed the lad back his violin and retook her seat beside young Colin.

"You going to do something about that, lad?" Randy indicated Cairstie.

Gordon came up and slapped Sharidon on the shoulder. "If I had a lass like that, I sure wouldn't be leaving her to young Colin's attentions. Although young, the lad has some insights about women. The first is attentiveness. Lasses have a liking for that, for some reason."

Sharidon glowered at the pair from under his brows, then tossed back the last of his spritzer water and smacked it onto the polished surface. Half-growling at the dare, he waded through the throng to reach Cairstie's table.

He arrived in time to hear Colin say, "The movies are in town. Would you like to come with me and see what's playing?"

"You make it sound like a traveling circus." Cairstie didn't look up from her cards.

"That's basically what it is. A clever Scot turned an eighteen-wheeler into a movie theater that seats eighty with a full-sized projection screen. We bring our own crisps, but it's loads of fun."

Sharidon cleared his throat and was almost certain Cairstie saw him, though she kept her eyes on her cards before she lifted her chin ever so slightly. "I'd love to, Colin."

"Brilliant." Colin beamed.

Sharidon snapped his jaw shut. Was the lass trying to make him jealous? If so, she was doing a mighty fine job of it.

Gordon returned to his seat at the table with two whiskies and pushed one in Colin's direction. "Are you sure you don't want one, lass?" he asked Cairstie.

"Positive." Her gaze darted to Sharidon, then away.

"Who's up for another round of partnership hearts?" Gordon asked.

"I'll play." Sharidon took the last remaining seat, the one opposite Cairstie. "Count me in."

"Colin and I are going to win this time, Sherwood. See if we don't." Gordon tossed back his whiskey and smacked his lips.

"Yer on," Sharidon replied, but he didn't look at Gordon; it was Cairstie he meant. And she knew it because her fair skin deepened to the hue of a ripe tomato.

Colin shuffled the deck and dealt out the cards.

Four rounds later, Cairstie and he had won every hand.

When their game broke up, Colin pulled out Cairstie's chair. "I'll pick you up tomorrow at half six."

"Verra good." She nodded and turned toward the door.

"Ta Cairstie," Nicola, a thirty-something-year-old woman with dark hair and eyes, called after her. "Lovely to meet you. Let me know when you're available to start."

"I will. Bye, now." Cairstie waved, then stepped over the threshold, the same one she and Sharidon had tumbled through a few weeks ago.

Sharidon held back until they exited the pub and started down the street for Mrs. McDougal's, walking at least five meters apart, before he let go of his pent-up breath.

"Ye played a good game. I had no idea ye were skilled at cards or the violin."

"There's a lot about me you don't know." Cairstie said, her voice cool.

"I'm beginning to realize that. A wee fairy told me that Nicola offer ye a job at The Sea Hut."

"She did, and I accepted. You did say it was best to hobnob with the islanders."

He tugged at his hair. "I didn't mean for ye to accept a job."

"Nicola knows everyone, and The Sea Hut is packed with locals and customers alike. I might hear something to help your case."

He remained silent, fighting back his frustration, and forcing himself to think logically. Cairstie's plan held merit, though it had one rather large flaw. She'd be safe enough inside the building, especially if he gave her a lift both ways. But riding in that convertible of hers or a bicycle—she was vulnerable. He hadn't forgotten that gleam reflected off metal while on their hike this afternoon.

Cairstie raised a finely arched brow. "Well?"

The last thing he intended was for that stubborn streak of hers to rear its head. "Yer right. Nicola's an amiable sort. Ye'll meet more islanders there to be sure, but I'd rest easier, especially after today's hike, if ye'd let me be yer chauffer."

"Thank you. I'd appreciate it."

An uncomfortable silence ensued, broken by the crunch of their footsteps and the occasional call of a bird.

"Yer playing was lovely." When Lady Cairstie had her nose out of joint, conversing with her was akin to prying a splinter from his wee brother's hand.

"Thank you."

"Did ye bring yer instrument to Benbecula?" he asked.

"I didn't. It was verra nice of the lad to loan me his."

"Half the single fellows in the Uists are surely besotted after that performance."

She gave him a sly smile and tossed her hair over her shoulder. "Only half?"

Not knowing how to respond, he shoved both hands into his trouser pockets while his heart drubbed like an American boxer with a speed bag. This was dodgy territory.

"Perhaps more than half," he said, entering the driveway.

"And what about you, Mr. Sharidon? What would it take for you to fall in love?"

"Who says I haven't already?"

Their walk had brought them home, and she halted to face him, the teasing light gone from her eyes. "Is she aware?"

He touched Cairstie's chin, stepping close enough to smell her exotic perfume. "My private life is my own, Lady Cairstie."

"Do you know what I think, Sharidon? I think that if you fell in love, you'd fall hard." She ignored his rebuff. "And you'd tell her you loved her a thousand times a day, so she'd never doubt you."

"Ye know what I think?" he countered.

"What?"

"That doesn't sound like me at all. I think that's what ye'd like for yerself. Yer just projecting it onto me. When I fall in love . . ." he trailed off. The vixen had almost trapped him into betraying himself.

"You were saying?" Her pretty lips curved, and she giggled at his consternation.

"Feeling proud of that, are ye?"

"Aye," she crowed, looking quite pleased. Her laughter soon died, and a considering expression had her wrinkling her forehead. "Seriously, what would you do if you ever fell in love?"

His eyes dropped to her lips, and the desire to kiss her burned within him. Before his control snapped and he gave way to temptation, he stepped back and winked. "I'd give her the use of my first name."

# CHAPTER 22

"THIRTY POUNDS, PLEASE." Cairstie smiled at the woman who had spent the last forty minutes examining every item in The Sea Hut before she settled on a small blue and green sea glass picture frame.

"Why is it so expensive?" the woman grumbled as she paid.

"Everything here is handmade by locals. It takes many hours to gather the glass to construct such a beautiful piece of art," Cairstie said.

Nicola had trained her this morning before placing her behind the counter to run the till.

Indeed, Nicola only accepted the most beautiful pieces the locals crafted to sell in her shop. Mrs. MacLeod's name appeared on a good number of them.

When she mentioned as much, Nicola touched Cairstie's shoulder. "Mrs. MacLeod might be a bit daft about those cats of hers, but she's a talented artisan. I sell more of her products than anyone else's."

Surprise ricocheted through Cairstie and forced her to rethink her opinion about her peculiar neighbor.

Despite her limited hours of operation, Nicola proved a savvy businesswoman whose clients swarmed the shop during open hours.

"How do you manage so many sales?" Cairstie asked.

"It's a mix of things. Not many souvenir shops exist in the Uists, plus I know how to advertise where tourists and locals congregate."

"But you have repeat customers. At least half are islanders."

"That's where selling quality products comes into play. I'm only open during peak hours, as I do the bookkeeping for my husband's business. I also keep up with the baking to stock our honesty box."

Sharidon had the right of it when he mentioned that most islanders held down three jobs to meet their expenses.

"We have a brief tourist season and make the most of our summers."

"What do you do in the winter to pass the time when daylight is short? Do you keep the shop open?" Cairstie leaned against the worktop of colorful stones and shells set in resin.

"Not hardly. That would be a waste of time. No tourists. We visit neighbors or hold impromptu Ceilidhs. Wintertime is when I create most of my handicrafts for the shop. If the storms aren't too fierce at sea, my husband and I often go somewhere warm for the holidays." Nicola's face lit up when she mentioned her husband.

"Do you mind my asking how long you've been married?"

"Thirteen years this autumn." A dreamy smile lifted Nicola's lips.

Thirteen years! "I thought you were newlyweds." They certainly behaved as such.

"Why?" Nicola unwound bubble wrap from a birdhouse crafted of driftwood and pottery, then set it on the worktop beside the till.

"You just seem so much in love."

A big laugh burst from Nicola. "I think that's the nicest compliment I've had in years."

"What's your secret?" Cairstie gave way to her curiosity, despite being flustered by Nicola's response.

Nicola appeared to give her question some thought. "We never stop doing thoughtful things for each other—things the other enjoys."

"That must be nice." Mother and Dad supported each other. She had taken it for granted that everyone's mother traveled with their father on business, or their fathers took an interest in their mothers charitable events.

"Marriage is hard work," Nicola said. "If anyone tells you differently, they're peddling a bucket of havers. But I'd rather be with my man than without him, even when he's tetchy."

Nicola entered the birdhouse into her computer system, then set it on a shelf beside an intricately inlaid mirror with a sea glass frame.

"Do you have a special someone in your life?" Nicola asked.

"I thought I did once, but it ended in disaster." Cairstie's cheeks burned.

"When the right one comes along, you'll know." Nicola patted her shoulder in a motherly fashion.

Sharidon's image flitted through Cairstie's mind. The fellow stirred her in ways she never imagined, more than Ahern ever had. Often, these days, she caught Sharidon's eyes on her, and the air positively thickened between them. Then he'd say something idiotic and make her long to wring his neck.

Deep down, though, Sharidon struck her just about right. The fellow had ceased heckling her to return to Torwoodlee Castle after he understood her dilemma—even though her presence on Benbecula added a kink to his mission. He taught her how to cook, clean, and operate the appliances. And it didn't hurt that he was easy on the eyes.

Too bad he was a spy. If Sharidon had a different profession, she might be tempted to act on the attraction. But after witnessing Elise's quiet worry when Harry was on assignment, Cairstie had no intention of following that route. When she married, she preferred someone who worked regular hours and didn't disappear for weeks on end, returning home with severe injuries like those Sharidon had suffered in the not-so-recent past. Nor had she forgotten that fellow in the tunnel. He had returned home in a body bag.

"Could you add these to the honesty box?" Nicola nudged a tray of soaps, cakes, stationary, and wildflower honey harvested on Benbecula.

Cairstie came out of her daze.

"Oh. Take these, too." Nicola handed her a small stack of trivets made of inlaid pottery.

Juggling the tray, Cairstie went outside and rounded the building to the yellow structure. The honesty box proved hard to miss when customers pulled into the lot. Made of brightly painted wood and fashioned into a miniature A-frame house with two latching doors to keep out inclement weather, the simple design found throughout the islands proved popular with locals and visitors alike.

Setting down the tray, she knelt and unlatched the outer doors. The chalkboards inside listed the prices. She placed the honey jars with their quaint logo on the bottom shelf beside the card reader machine, and baked cakes went on the middle shelf. She sat back when everything appeared in good order, latched the door, and reentered The Sea Hut just as the clock struck five.

"Can you lock the front door and turn off the sign while I count the till?" Nicola opened the register.

"Certainly." Cairstie unplugged the open sign and locked the door. Sharidon would be here any minute to fetch her. He felt she'd be safe enough at The Sea Hut with its cameras surrounding the exterior but too vulnerable to a potential attack when traveling to and from her job.

Nicola had ridden her bicycle, as so many islanders did.

"If you sweep out the storage room, we'll be ready to go about the same time." Nicola didn't look up from counting the till.

Cairstie located a broom in the storage closet and swept with such gusto that dust clouded the air and made her cough. Slowing her speed, she finished before Nicola completed the cash drawer.

"The Irishman's here for you," Nicola called.

Cairstie tapped the dustpan against the bin, then poked her head around the storage room doorway. "See you Wednesday."

"Ta." Nicola waved.

Cairstie let herself out the back just as an EV pulled in with Nicola's husband behind the wheel. For the life of her, Cairstie couldn't recall his name. She smiled at him as she crossed to Sharidon's van. The fellow nodded as he hopped out of the car, holding a bouquet.

"Hiya," he greeted, then turned to Nicola, who stood with her hands on her hips at the back of the shop.

"Darling, I thought you'd forgotten." Nicola beamed like he had bought her the moon.

"How could I forget my best girl's special day?"

He pulled her into his arms and kissed Nicola in a way that brought the blood rushing to Cairstie's face. Flustered, she grasped the van's door handle before Sharidon could do so and sprang into her seat. Leaning back, she fanned her face.

Sharidon cleared his throat, circled the Sprinter, and hopped behind the driver's wheel.

"Why did you use the van?" Cairstie asked to get her mind off that passionate kiss.

"I needed it for a few things."

Were the "things" he referred to weapons or his surveyor's equipment?

"How did it go today?" Sharidon might be speaking to her, but his eyes remained on Nicola and her husband before he swiveled in her direction. "Did your arm bother you any?"

"Not too much." She had changed the bandage during her break. The graze was still seepy, but it could have been much worse.

His green eyes, so unreadable at times, scanned her face before he flashed a smile that lighted his own, one that set her heart rocketing.

"Excellent." He put the van in the drive.

As they pulled out, Cairstie glanced in her rearview mirror and caught Nicola's husband staring after them, his face like granite. The hair on the back of her neck rose, and she shivered.

"Something wrong?" Sharidon asked.

"No." But the feeling persisted.

"Billow and breeze, islands and seas, mountains of rain and sun," Cairstie belted *The Skye Boat Song* lyrics as she scrubbed the last supper dish, then rinsed it under the kitchen tap. Setting the crockery on the draining board, she plunged her hands back in the warm, sudsy water.

"Cairstie?" Sharidon called from the other room.

"Aye?" Her hands stilled in the basin.

When he didn't repeat himself, she snatched a tea towel and crossed the tiled floor, halting in the dining room doorway. A higgledy-piggledy mass of paperwork lay scattered about the table. Sharidon's hair stood in disarray like he had tugged on it multiple times.

The radio blasted in the corridor between the lounge and the dining room, blanketing anything sensitive they might say.

"Could ye help me with this? I can't figure out yer writing. If you read it to me, I can add them to my document and analyze the data."

Her lungs froze partway through an inhale. "You said you didn't want me involved."

"This is social media. Anyone can access it."

"Okay." Cairstie swallowed. Was this a spy thing?

She stepped into the room and retrieved the paper in question, then squinted at the page, her heart tumbling.

Sharidon drew a chair beside him and patted the cushion. She eased onto the proffered seat.

"I thought you already did this?" She straightened the sheets, her eyes on the smudged drawings while she wracked her memory of what Sophie told her on the phone.

"The background checks took longer than I expected. I've narrowed the suspects, but adding this to the mix will likely whittle it down even further."

Her insides vaulted, then landed with a splat. He needed her list. The pictures beside the first names would hopefully jog her memory.

She glanced at the margin beside the first name. A daisy and arches. "Daisy MacDonald." One of the many MacDonalds in the Outer Hebrides.

Sharidon filled the column. "Who are her associates?"

An eating emoji alongside a male figure with light hair. "Kate Ken-Kennedy, and . . ." A picture of scrambled bits and bobs. "Bob." She squinted to make out the doodle of a cloud. "MacLeod?"

Sharidon's fingers hesitated on the keys, and his eyes remained on the monitor.

"Bob MacLeod," Cairstie repeated with more confidence.

Sharidon dropped his fingers from the keyboard and shifted in his chair, his eyes soft as new grass. "Are the letters difficult to read?"

Her hackles rose. "I can read them."

He took one of her hands and held it between his own. "Yer an intelligent woman, Cairstie. Yer cleverness and talent have brought ye fame and fortune at a young age. I'll never forget how ye discombobulated my alarms and cameras. That took serious technological skills."

He stroked her hand, rubbing circles on the back of it with his thumb. Her skin tingled at his touch.

"How long have ye struggled with reading?" he asked.

She yanked her hand from his and bolted from her chair.

"My sister has dyslexia. There are ways to help." He remained seated, his manner calm.

"Don't you think my parents have tried every means possible?" A bitter laugh escaped her.

"I'm sure they did."

"I saw specialist after specialist. Nothing worked." Her voice rose on the last words.

"Have ye tried the touch-typing method?" he asked.

"The *what* method?"

"Touch-typing. It reinforces phonics and uses muscle memory to learn word spellings that then translate into written language. It also helps make writing less frustrating."

"No." She gripped the back of her chair. Unable to remain standing, she retook her seat. "It works?" Hope stirred its gossamer wings within her.

"Tricia learned how to read and write with touch-typing. If ye'd like, I can order the necessary materials and set ye up."

"I'd—" She pressed her hands together as hope caught fire. "I'd like that verra much."

He typed in the search bar and uploaded the materials and program, then hit the order button. A smile stretched his mobile mouth.

Without thought, she leaned forward and kissed him, a simple peck of thanks. No one had ever bought her anything that mattered more than this. Shot with euphoria, she grinned at him like a loon.

Sharidon's expression switched in one blink. His green eyes sparked, then flamed to life. Her breath whooshed from her lungs when she read his intent. He hesitated for an agonizing second while her pulse thrummed. At length, he leaned in, and his breath stirred her skin.

Was he deliberately driving her mad?

His nostrils flared. Cupping her face, he kissed her cheek, then dropped his hands to her shoulders and skimmed his fingers down her arms. The effect shot tingles to every extremity.

They stared at one another, teetering on the threshold of no return.

Pain twisted Sharidon's features. "Yer the death of me." He gripped her waist, rested his hands on the small of her back, and lowered his mouth to hers.

Shivers of pleasure shot through her, and her entire body buzzed. He tasted of sweet melon, his mouth warm as a summer's day. Her heart raced at his touch. He drew back the merest millimeter. A soft moan escaped her lips, and her eyes fluttered open.

His eyes pinned her in place, needy with a desire that mirrored her own. He covered her mouth once more. She expected roughness but gasped at the tenderness of his kiss.

This was nothing like his hard manhandling at the pub to keep her from betraying his identity. This one held promises. Comfort. Respect. And need. Giving way to temptation, Cairstie wound her fingers in his hair.

Sharidon dropped his hands as if burned, and his chest heaved. "I've just broken my cardinal rule and deserve to be drawn and quartered."

"What rule?" Her brain cleared from the fog of his kisses.

"Not to get emotionally involved on a case." Sharidon lifted his computer and transferred it to the opposite side of the table—a definite retreat.

Cairstie opened her mouth to argue, but the longing in his eyes told its own story. He meant what he said and was paying for it.

She'd scolded herself once too often about not falling for a spy, but her heart had betrayed her. What she felt for Sharidon was no schoolgirl crush.

"I'll do my best not to let it happen again, but I'm warning ye when this case concludes, I'll be coming for ye."

The promise in his words settled the fears churning inside her. She returned his hard stare with one of her own. "And I'll be waiting."

She might be young and unable to read well—yet. But she knew her own mind. Those kisses they'd shared were not born of lust but of something deep and abiding. Moreover, Sharidon didn't strike her as a fellow who toyed with women's affections.

Was he a flirt? Aye. Most definitely. But sparks had shot between them since her sister's reception. Cairstie had mistaken them for something else, but the longer they spent time together, the deeper those emotions had burrowed.

Cairstie closed her eyes. Well, she'd gone and done it now. She'd fallen for a spy. Och. She was more like her sister Elise than she imagined, something that needed examining when she got over both of her sisters' betrayal.

Cairstie picked up the paper that had given up her secret to settle her racing pulse. "Are you ready to continue?" she asked.

His mouth quirked. "That's a loaded question, Lady Cairstie. Care to reword it?"

"Not in the least."

"Yer killing me," Sharidon growled, his eyes sliding to her mouth.

A table separated them, but the air crackled with enough electricity to power the appliances. To tone things down, she glanced at the paper and squinted at the next set of doodles: a branding iron and a pair of gold arches. Brand. Rand.

"Randy MacDonald."

Sharidon typed, his computer keys clicking, then looked up, his hands poised above the keys.

Cairstie glanced at her paper again. The following images were of a king wearing a crown with a Roman numeral eight and a stick figure walking. "Hank Walker."

Moving on to the last two names, she tossed her hair behind her back and focused on the cow and a fish with an arrow pointed toward its gills. "Angus Gillies."

The next doodle held a rope with sun rays. It threw her for a second. Cord. The rope was a cord, and it sounded like a gourd. "Gordon MacRae." Exhaling, she set the paper on the table. "That's the last of them."

"Only seven have social media accounts?" Sharidon asked.

"Aye. And that lot all spend time together."

"Excellent." Sharidon clicked more keys. "Hmmm. This is interesting."

"What's interesting?" Cairstie moved around the table to his side.

"Three on this list served in the navy—all in the same unit."

"Do you think one of them is our traitor?" she asked.

"Nothing's definitive, but it bears further investigation."

A honk in the drive sounded, and a car pulled up to the front stoop.

Sharidon rose and moved to the window. "Yer date has arrived." He turned, a grin curving his mouth, but the smile didn't reach his eyes.

"Gracious. Is it that time already?" All desire to attend the cinema had evaporated with Sharidon's kisses.

"Shall I answer for ye?" Sharidon's eyes danced.

"You find this amusing?"

"I do. That lad is going to try his hardest to impress ye."

"And that's funny?" She placed one hand on her hip.

"I dare ye to think of anything besides those kisses we shared." He folded his arms and winked at her.

"You conceited Irishman," she spat.

Marching from the room, Cairstie snatched her coat. The very idea of that fellow thinking his kisses were superior to anyone else's.

She'd show him.

# CHAPTER 23

SHARIDON SCOWLED AT THE SCREEN, still out of sorts because Cairstie had left him at her dining room table—only minutes after those mind-blowing kisses—to go on a date, no less, with pretty boy Colin.

Knock. Knock.

He glanced up from the computer. Had Cairstie forgotten something? She'd only been gone five minutes. Or had she changed her mind and returned?

Knock. Knock. Knock.

The lass had a key. She could let herself in.

Winkle, who lay curled at his feet, raised his shaggy head, and growled, a deep, menacing sound for such a young dog. His hackles rose along his spine, and he charged the door, barking like a thing possessed.

Sharidon got up and grabbed Winkle's collar before he opened the door.

Winkle bared his teeth at the woman on the porch dressed in black trousers and a matching coat.

"My. My. What a good doggie you are." A young woman who bore a strong resemblance to Mrs. MacLeod held out her hand for Winkle to sniff.

Winkle gave one last half-hearted bark, then wagged his tail. She patted his back. "There's a good lad."

"Is there something I can do for ye?" Sharidon asked.

"It's more what I can do for you, Mr. Sherwood." She straightened to her full height, which wasn't much above five feet.

"Come again?" What could this woman possibly do for him? Or Cairstie, for that matter?

"I saw a man dash from Mrs. McDougal's solarium when I was gathering sea glass for my auntie. He carried something in his hands and ducked behind the garage."

"When was this?" he asked sharply.

"Yesterday. I would have come sooner, but I left for work before you returned and forgot until this afternoon."

Someone broke into Muir Tigh House, and this woman only now remembered? Mrs. MacLeod's niece didn't appear overly alarmed about their visitor, save for what they might have stolen.

"I appreciate yer telling me." Anger stirred like a red-hot poker. Someone had burgled this house one too many times.

"Is anything missing?" she asked.

"Nothing I'm aware of." Sharidon combed a hand through his hair. How had their intruder avoided his cameras? This fellow knew his way around surveillance equipment.

"It was probably one of the lads out for a lark." She turned to leave. "Maybe I got it wrong. I was quite a distance from the house."

"Thank you for stopping by." Sharidon closed the door, an unsettled feeling in the pit of his stomach. Good thing he sent those encrypted files to Nigel right after discovering the secret niche. Afterward, he had locked the pen drives and documents inside the Sprinter van's safe.

Marching down the corridor, he entered the office and retrieved the plastic card from the desk. One swipe and the niche opened. He eyed the shelves, his frown deepening. He and Cairstie left two items inside the enclave.

And one of them was missing.

❖

Cairstie goggled at the blue eighteen-wheeler when Colin pulled into Balivanich's car park and set the brake. "That's a cinema?"

"Aye." Colin grabbed a shopping bag from behind his seat, and they exited his battered Ford Fiesta. "The Screen Machine stops on Benbecula every seven weeks."

"And they show movies on a real movie screen?" How odd.

"Aye. It's popular in these parts."

Chatter filled the air as people queued up, the line winding around the semi-truck with new vehicles entering the car park every few seconds.

"They play three different movies per circuit." Colin shook the bag he had retrieved from the car.

"Why have I never heard of this?"

"You're a Lowlander."

It had never occurred to her that sparsely settled communities lacked entertainment. On free evenings, she visited Glasgow or Edinburgh dance clubs with her girlfriends or the theater in Selkirk or Galashiels.

A Sprinter van pulled in as Cairstie mounted the portable aluminum steps. A flush burned across her body. What was Sharidon doing here?

"Iain." Colin acknowledged the operator, then held out his mobile to be scanned. Afterward, he took Cairstie's arm and led her inside, beelining it for the back row.

Colin's clammy hand set off red flags. Doubtless, he assumed they were here for a snogging session.

"I can't see the screen so far back." Cairstie did an about-face in the aisle.

Colin tugged on her arm just as Sharidon crossed the threshold and scanned the audience. The situation only needed that. She rolled her eyes and wished herself anywhere but here.

Cairstie pulled free of Colin and moved halfway up the aisle, plunking beside Nicola and her husband, leaving Colin no option but to join her.

"Hiya." Cairstie nodded to the married pair as Sharidon moved down the aisle and sat behind Colin. Cairstie ground her teeth. Was this Sharidon's idea of a joke?

The room darkened, and Colin slipped his arm around her.

She leaned forward, elbows to knees, and rested her chin on both fists, and sighed. Right now, she didn't know who she longed to strangle more, Colin or Sharidon. Funny. Sharidon didn't strike her as the possessive sort.

Five minutes into the film, Colin ran his hand up her thigh. She grabbed his bag of snacks, her elbow knocking his unwanted fingers away as she rummaged through the bag.

"Want anything in here?" she asked.

"I do." Colin's double entendre proved hard to miss. Then he leaned forward and kissed her cheek, leaving a trail of saliva on her skin.

"Stop it," she hissed, wiping her face. "I hardly know you."

Colin sat back in his chair, his forehead wrinkled, his bottom lip protruding. A choking noise came from the row behind her. Cairstie closed her eyes and counted to ten. Of course, Sharidon would find this amusing. He wasn't the one being slobbered on.

Undeterred, Colin stroked her arm. "Sit back, babe."

"I need to use the loo." Cairstie bolted into the aisle and rushed out the exit to use the public toilet at Spar's Grocery's, owned by the Chen family, who also ran the Chinese takeaway.

Cairstie paced the small, confined floor space until someone pounded on the loo door. "Hurry it along in there."

"Sorry." She let herself out and wandered the grocery aisles to delay her return as long as decency allowed.

With so few single men in the area, Colin dated whomever he pleased, but that did not allow him to pressure her into behavior she did not wish. She returned to the trailer, all but dragging her feet. Though aware of Sharidon's gaze, she refused to meet his eyes when she retook her seat.

The rest of the film required a series of evasive actions on her part to keep Colin's hands to himself. She gave him first-class honors for persistence, but by the time the credits rolled, she longed for nothing more than to dump Colin's bag of crisps on top of his head.

She twisted in her seat when the lights clicked on and turned to Sharidon. "Mr. Sherwood. I didn't see you there. Would you mind giving me a lift home?"

Sharidon's gaze slid to Colin, then back to her. "I've room in the van. Ye coming too, Colin?"

"I've an early start in the morning." Colin sloped off without a proper goodbye and blended with the crowd exiting the eighteen-wheeler.

The Big Screen Machine trailer emptied until only the two of them remained. Sharidon rocked back on his heels, an unholy grin stretching his mobile mouth. "That was the best entertainment I've had in years."

"So happy to accommodate you." Cairstie picked up the bags Colin left behind and exited the aisle.

Sharidon touched her arm, his fingers wrapping about her wrist, then sliding to lace with hers. "Sorry, lass. I have a tendency toward levity. My mother tells me it's one of my besetting sins."

"That's something we agree on."

"Come now. Ye must admit, tonight was spectacular. I see-sawed between wanting to punch Colin in the nose and laughing at the creative ways the two of you tried to outmaneuver each other. Ye must know, I envied him the entire two hours and seven minutes."

He slipped an arm around her and kissed her cheek. Warmth washed over her in a crashing wave. Why did Sharidon have such an effect on her? Ahern never addled her brains like this.

"And here I go, breaking my own rules again." Sharidon slid his hands to her waist, then pecked her lips with a kiss that burned to her toes.

"Hurry it along, you two. We want to close," Iain, the Screen Machine Operator, called.

"Can't blame a man, now can ye?" Sharidon grinned like a wee bairn who had snitched a pudding.

Iain winked. "Can't say that I do."

Once they reached the van, Sharidon's smile slipped as he opened her door. "I need to lock ye in the van tonight at the campground."

"Why? Has something happened?"

"Our intruders paid us another visit. I'd rest easier if ye were away from the house while I poke about."

A tremor raced through her. "You'll be careful?"

"I can handle myself." Sharidon's features hardened.

So could his friend from the tunnel, but that hadn't saved him. "Can we stop at the house for Winkle? she asked instead.

"I already moved him and his kennel inside the van."

She climbed into the passenger seat and glanced over her shoulder. Sure enough, Winkle lay inside his crate on the floor near Sharidon's bed.

So much for being flattered that Sharidon's jealousy had motivated him to follow her to the movie. More fool her. She swallowed her disappointment. "How did you intend to separate me from my date?"

"I didn't have a fully formed plan."

Lucky for him, she and Colin had played into his hands.

"How long do Winkle and I need to stay at the campground?"

"Give me until dawn. If I'm not back by then, call this number." Sharidon passed her a card with a London dialing code.

Goosebumps raised the hair on her scalp. She met his eyes and nodded. He was going into harm's way—and she couldn't do a thing about it.

In the lamplight, Sharidon kneeled in Mrs. McDougal's study and pressed the drill into the cupboard wall of the last plank. A whine erupted, and the screw dropped on the floor. He pocketed it, then stacked the wood on top of the others.

Cairstie would stay in the van, wouldn't she? Her cooperation worried him a bit, and tonight, he couldn't afford to split his focus.

He spent the next hour undoing his handiwork to access the tunnel. With summer's lengthy twilight in the Outer Hebrides, reaching The Deep Sea Range Headquarters via the open fields was not an option. If the guards caught him skulking around, he couldn't explain away his presence. Too bad Nigel hadn't made him a guard; it would have made accessing the SCIF a lot easier. Ach. He retracted that thought. The locals would have cold-shouldered him as an incomer guard. Points to Nigel. He'd provided him with the best possible cover to integrate island society.

Nigel texted the new passcode and safe combo—something Sharidon would have welcomed on his first nocturnal visit. Tossing his rucksack over one shoulder, he clicked on his torch and started down the tunnel to the base. Water dripped, and stale sea air assaulted his senses. Ninety minutes was all he had to get in and out under the cover of darkness.

How had the intruder escaped detection on his surveillance feeds in the front garden? Sharidon had hidden several cameras in the hedgerow, but the man had avoided them. The fellow must be a pro.

Sharidon suspected the man's success had more to do with surprise than ability. Now, he wasn't so sure. For a while, he'd suspected that Mansfield's murderer and Cairstie's intruder were connected. How else had the man known about the tunnel from Muir Tigh House to the base? And if he used the tunnel, doubtless, he'd dumped Mansfield's body there when he'd escaped.

Tonight's mission required checking the hard drives to see if the one he'd altered had gone missing from the safe. Reaching the metal rungs that accessed the bunker, he clicked off his light and climbed to the trap door, then strained for sounds of movement. Hearing none, he pushed up the wooden panel, leading with his gun, then scanned the building.

All remained quiet, but a partial shoe print near the exterior door, where sand gathered over time, made him pause. That shoe print hadn't been there the last time he accessed the tunnel. Someone had nosed around the place. Was this the same intruder?

He glanced out the grungy window. Jings! A few meters at best separated the SCIF from this disused building. How had security overlooked this potential danger? No wonder the traitor had disappeared with Wang and Mansfield so quickly.

Cracking the exterior door, Sharidon paused, his eyes on the rotating camera. Three. Two. One. The camera swiveled in the opposite direction. Sharidon sprinted to the main building and punched in the passcode. The door opened like the Cave of Wonders.

And he was inside the building.

Dodging security cameras until he reached the SCIF, he entered the password, and let himself inside. A temporary safe replaced the one he had cracked. Doubtless, a beefier alternative would arrive soon from the mainland. Had the traitor breached this one? If so, Sharidon needed to add a few more skill sets to the traitor's profile. That one alone ought to narrow his list of suspects.

Getting down to business, he kneeled by the safe and spun the lock. He shook his head. "A novice could hack this." He pressed the lever and swung the door wide.

After removing the hard drives inside, he exhaled. Everyone appeared accounted for—not what he expected. He pushed off the floor to relieve the strain on his leg, then examined the exterior of each plastic housing for the one he had scored. Was it still there?

When he reached the last unit, a grin stretched his mouth, and satisfaction warmed his belly.

The traitor had taken the bait.

# CHAPTER 24

"WOOF."

"Go back to sleep, Winkle." Cairstie burrowed under the covers in the back of Sharidon's van. It couldn't be morning.

The flow and ebb of the surf beating against the beach kept her up half the night. Even then, she slept fitfully. Worry had a way of doing that. She drifted into a woozy doze, sleep enveloping her in its warm embrace.

Knocking roused her.

Cairstie moaned and covered her head with a pillow to make it disappear. More tapping, this time on the window above her bed. A stream of barks erupted from Winkle.

"Cairstie. Open up. I have breakfast."

Sharidon? Her eyes flew open. She sat upright, and relief surged through her. He had survived whatever skulking, spyish thing he did last night. A naughty smirk lifted the corner of her mouth, and she lay down and smiled up at the ceiling. "I'm not hungry."

"Brilliant. More chocolate croissants and hot cocoa for me."

She tossed her pillow and sat up, pushing her tumbled hair out of her eyes, then rubbed her arms. The van was freezing. Last night, she turned off the heater when it grew too warm. Now, she regretted her decision.

Pulling on a hoodie and tracksuit bottoms, she snatched a brush and ran it through her hair.

"Hurry it up in there, lass. I'm freezing." Sharidon knocked on the side door again.

Cairstie popped a breath mint in her mouth, internally snickering as she opened the sliding door, then backed up to sit at the table.

Sharidon jumped inside and slammed the door behind him. Consternation flooded his features. "It's Baltic in here."

He placed a box of pastries and two paper cups on the worktop and started the heater. Turning, he handed her one of the hot chocolates.

"Thank you." She wrapped her fingers around the paper cup and sipped, letting the warmth seep into her bones.

He plopped down on the opposite side of the table and placed the box of chocolate croissants between them. "Yer breakfast, my lady." He reached across the narrow aisle and retrieved the napkins.

Cairstie blessed her food, then took a bite. "Mmmm. This is delicious."

"Fresh from the oven." Sharidon ate in silence, but excitement poured off him.

"Successful evening, I take it?" she asked.

"I can't be telling ye that." But his dancing green eyes provided the answer.

"Well, I'm happy you didn't end up with bullet holes in your chest." She placed her half-eaten pastry on the napkin in front of her.

He raised one brow, then eyed her uneaten roll. "Are ye finished?"

"Aye. Be my guest." She waved at her food.

Sharidon popped her half-eaten roll into his mouth in one bite.

Winkle rose inside his crate and whined to be let out just as Sharidon's watch buzzed. He glanced at it, and his eyes sharpened.

"Yer car alarm is going off at Mrs. McDougal's." He grabbed his computer from a cabinet and pulled up the video feed.

Cairstie leaned forward to view Sharidon's screen as a dark hooded figure placed a piece of paper under her Mercedes wipers, then saluted the camera, his face in shadow.

"Time to go." Sharidon turned off his computer and stored it away.

"Sorry, Winkle, wait until we get home." Cairstie climbed into the cab and buckled her safety belt.

Sharidon fired up the van and took off. They drove in silence for a few minutes. She crossed one leg, then switched them, then swapped them again. The boldness of their intruder bothered her greatly.

"Spit it out, Cairstie."

Sharidon entered a layby and let a car pass that had been following close behind. The driver raised his index finger as he overtook them.

"Do you think he's still there?"

"I'm fairly certain he's long gone." Sharidon turned off the heater once the cab warmed. "Don't follow me inside the house until I give ye the all-clear."

"Okay." Her heart thumped ever faster. What if the intruder hid in the garden?

Rather than taking the single-track B-road, Sharidon caught the A865 north with more frequent passing lanes. Zipping by one of the few filling stations, he accelerated without conversing further. They arrived at Mrs. McDougal's five minutes later.

He parked on the road and approached the Mercedes. Cairstie followed, picking her way through the wet grass.

Sharidon held up his hand for her to wait while he inspected the property.

"Nothing's moved."

Indeed, the car and garden appeared just as she'd left it, save for the paper on her windscreen. She joined Sharidon beside the fender as he withdrew a ripped-out page from a Bible, the verse circled in red. Sharidon read aloud,

"But if ye will not hear these words, I swear by myself, saith the LORD, that this house shall become a desolation." (Jeremiah 22:5, KJV).

Cairstie shivered. "I'd say he's aware one or both of us are not what we appear."

Sharidon kept his thoughts to himself.

"Let me check the house before ye enter. I'll be quick."

Grabbing Winkle from the van, Cairstie stood on the kitchen stoop, her eyes scanning the garden. A curlew cried and made her jump. What she wouldn't give for her godmother's nine iron right now.

The door opened, and Sharidon poked his head around the frame. "Come along inside, lass."

She followed him through the kitchen and stopped in the center of the lounge. Sharidon switched on the transistor radio, cranked it on high, then closed the draperies at the front of the house. Keeping one hand on his waist holster, he moved to the solarium. With no desire to be left behind, she trailed after him.

"Mrs. MacLeod's niece told me she saw a fellow bolt out of the solarium. This lock and the windows, for that matter, wouldn't hinder anyone determined to gain access."

"Do you think he'll return tonight?" Cairstie rubbed the back of her arms to dissipate the goosebumps brought on by their visitor.

"That's a question I can't answer."

"Why would he place a threatening message on my car?"

"Likely to scare us away. It's a fair bet he found the cut wires to his bomb and realized he wasn't dealing with a novice."

"He checked it?" Internal tremors shook her body and had nothing to do with the cold.

"I think so. He could have placed that Bible verse anywhere, but he chose yer Mercedes—the same location as his explosive device."

"Does he know what you were about last night?" Cairstie asked.

"I doubt it. He wants something inside the house. For yer safety, I must put my charts aside and figure out what's on Mrs. McDougal's files."

"I can help if it's not top secret."

"Two heads will be better than one. How are ye with running a portable scanner?"

"More than fair. I've used Mother's in the Command Center dozens of times."

He looked her a question.

"Mother's office," she explained. "She runs events with the precision of a general. When she goes into military mode, we're drafted into her army, so, my siblings and I dubbed it that."

"Sounds a bit like my mum. I doubt Dad could handle the farm if she didn't monitor the books and keep everyone on task."

Sharidon returned to the van for his computer, then took over the dining room—again. "I suppose this is a bit like our own Command Center." He gave her a lopsided grin.

"Let's hope we find out why this fellow shot at me and wired a bomb to my car."

Taking the file from Mrs. McDougal's secret niche, Cairstie got to work scanning article clippings and military accidents in the UK and overseas. After she worked out the dates, she noted they stretched back fifteen years or more.

"Anything interesting?" Cairstie returned the last article to the folder and placed it on the table beside Sharidon.

"This pen drive holds nothing but accidents on The Deep Sea Range," Sharidon said.

"What about the other one you took from Mrs. McDougal's study? Did that contain tests from The Deep Sea Range, too?"

Sharidon looked at her—stared, actually. Cairstie bit back a snicker.

"Ye saw me take them?"

"Aye."

"Well. Well. Well. Aren't ye a tricky one?" Admiration and a bit of something else sparked, then up went his shields. "The pen drives cover the testing on the South Uist ranges from a remote station on St. Kilda." He referred to the northernmost islands, forty miles away.

"But the headquarters are here on Benbecula. Why is everything so spread out?"

"At a guess, the Ministry of Defense keeps very few in control of the full details."

"In case someone leaks information?"

"This is a top-secret base. On the mainland, only a handful of individuals are aware of this place, let alone the testing conducted here."

Growing up near a Ministry of Defense base with military personnel and their families swelling the population of the local villages, Cairstie found the skeletal crew on Benbecula vastly different.

Sharidon turned back to the computer screen. Curiosity drove her to reopen Mrs. McDougal's clipping folder and study the pictures in greater detail. Words jumped out here and there. At first, she assumed these articles involved Mrs. McDougal's husband, but he had died long before many of the listed dates. Why had her godmother collected articles about overseas military bombings if she and her husband had never lived there?

"This is interesting." Sharidon interrupted her musings. "A missile exploded on one of the naval ships off South Uist a few months ago. The MoD suspects sabotage but can't prove it because it sank in 3500 meters of water. The debris field is almost a square mile.

"I remember hearing about that. It made national news. Over three hundred sailors died when the *HMS Lilibet* went down." Cairstie rubbed her temples. Rumors had circulated amongst locals for the past few weeks about a deep-sea salvage taking place offshore.

"Mrs. McDougal believed these *accidents* were connected, didn't she?" Why else would she compile this information and hide it in the wall niche?" Cairstie asked.

Sharidon rose and stood behind her with his hands on her shoulders. Leaning over her, he read the article as he kneaded the knots bunched under her skin. "Feel better?"

"Aye. Thanks."

He kissed the top of her head and returned to his computer.

"How do you handle crunching data for so long?" she asked.

"I've a screen to help with that. And believe it or not, I spend more of my job at a desk."

"I thought you worked overseas?"

"Sometimes." He moved his shoulders in that expressive way, so definitive of him.

She couldn't coax him to share his theories no matter how much she prodded over the next few minutes.

"Is it all right if I take Winkle for a run on the beach?" She needed to stretch her legs.

"I'd love to say yes, but I'd prefer ye stayed in the garden until I'm free."

The unspoken message rang between them, and she couldn't fault his intent to keep her safe.

"Fair enough." Still mulling over the clippings, she went upstairs and changed into exercise clothes. Unrolling her mat, she started into her Pilates routine. After three sets of stomach curls, she switched to leg exercises.

Every accident in those files occurred on a military base. Explosions. Missile malfunctions. Engine trouble. Perhaps if they compiled the information chronologically, a pattern would appear. Ditching her Pilates, she ran downstairs and burst into the dining room.

Sharidon remained hunched at his computer; his eyes narrowed at the screen.

She placed a hand on her hip. "You'll develop a squint if you keep that up."

He dragged his eyes from the computer.

"Any luck?" she asked.

"This information is common domain."

Meaning he could share it if he chose.

Sharidon indicated the clippings. "Most of the issues occurred under the command of Admiral Hastings over a period of twelve years. What have you got?"

She toyed with the ends of her hair. "It's more of an idea than anything. What if we take all the information, the explosions, missile malfunctions, and other disasters, and place them in chronological order instead of similar accidents?"

"Why? None of these appear related."

"It's likely something new will pop if we go at it from a different angle," she insisted.

"Let's do it. I'm not getting anywhere with my version."

For the next hour, they called out the dates and locations of the incidents. Sharidon placed them in a sorting grid and stuck bright sticky dots on a map where each incident occurred.

"This is interesting." Sharidon cracked his knuckles, and a grin spread from ear to ear. "Yer brilliant!"

Cairstie's heart swelled at his words. No one had ever complimented her intellectual prowess. Looks, aye, along with her athletic skills. But intelligence? Never. She could not have been more deeply moved if Sharidon handed her a gold crown.

"The incidents changed from explosives to missiles two years ago when the Ministry of Defense began developmental testing on The Deep Sea Range. The following year, the MoD handed over its operations to the

Defense and Evaluation and Research Bureau. They ran maneuvers until the MoD deemed them defunct and replaced them with Quantas, a private entity. The government then transferred the testing sites, personnel, and assets to that organization."

"It's rather like following a money trail," Cairstie said.

"Where did ye hear that?"

"Audiobooks. I enjoy thrillers."

"No wonder ye have a devious mind. For a second, I thought ye were going to tell me ye'd been eavesdropping on yer sister again."

Cairstie flushed. She *had* eavesdropped on her sister a time or two. Her stomach rumbled, growled more like, and her flush deepened to embarrassment.

"I suppose we need to refuel after missing lunch. How does MacAllister's sound?" Sharidon referred to the local chippy shop.

"Do they serve veg?"

"I doubt it." He gave her the once over. "Ye could use some fattening up."

"I'm a model; I need to watch my calories."

"One serving of fish and chips will not make ye fat." He pushed out of his chair and wrapped both arms around her. "Ye can go back to carrots and dry toast tomorrow."

"What about our intruder?" She snuggled into his embrace.

"What about him?"

"Don't you need to stay here in case he returns?" Getting out was all good and well, but the fellow had proven not only brazen but dangerous.

"If he returns, I'll be catching him on video. I reworked my cameras. He won't surprise us again," Sharidon said.

"You seem so certain."

"Yer lack of confidence in my skills is irksome, lass. Trust me. We'll be dandy. If ye fetch Winkle, then we can fill that grumbling belly of yers."

She rushed upstairs, changed into tweeds and boots, and dashed back down. Sharidon's admiring gaze spiked a flush from the top of her head to the tip of her toes.

He handed her Winkle's lead, and they started out the door, not bothering to lock it behind them. If the intruder entered through the solarium, why bother? Sharidon was right. His cameras should warn them if the intruder reappeared—unless he disabled their cameras.

Again.

# CHAPTER 25

HE KICKED the dumpster behind the pub. How had a civilian figured that out? Building a dual detonator bomb demanded skill, and even more so to deactivate one. He hadn't given Sherwood enough credit. The Irishman's easy-going charm had misled him into thinking the lad was less intelligent. How did he find the bomb, then disable it?

He couldn't ask his handler to investigate Sherwood, or there'd be accusations that he'd fouled up covering his tracks. Tearing a page from Mrs. McDougal's Bible was not the smartest thing he had ever done. Nor was saluting that camera. He'd gotten cocky. He needed to keep it together. If his handler caught wind of this, he would disappear—no doubt about it. And Nicola wouldn't be safe.

He needed to settle this quickly.

Quantas had posted signs to warn residents about an upcoming test on The Deep Sea Range. An "accident" might coincide with that. The authorities might even buy into it.

❖

Dark clouds scudded no higher than ten meters above the van, the rain a drizzle. Sharidon assessed the scarf Cairstie had draped about her head and shoulders and the tweeds she had doubtless modeled for some photo-shoot. His gaze skidded away, and he cleared his throat. Her presence proved a distraction more than he cared to admit.

Mingle. They needed to mingle.

"I'm not liking this weather much for a walkabout. Care to stop off at the community center for the Ceilidh until this storm blows over?"

"I adore Ceilidh's." A smile brightened her eyes.

"Do ye suppose Winkle will behave?" He glanced at the dog doubtfully.

"Aye. I've his rawhide bone inside my pocket. I save it for emergencies. He won't leave it until he's finished and will growl if you take it from him."

"Why would this be an emergency?" Sharidon scratched around Winkle's ears. The pup leaned into the caress, and half closed his eyes.

"He can be snarly if he dislikes someone," Cairstie warned.

"Does he bite?"

"He's never gone after anyone, save for the intruder."

"He was protecting ye then. I think we can risk it," Sharidon said.

"Is your leg up to it? I noticed you haven't been using the cane."

"It's much improved." And it was—up to a point. Before the bakery opened, he'd even gone for a brief run. Exercising the muscles contributed to his rehabilitation, despite the sleepless nights when it ached from overuse.

They headed up the road to the community center, the weather shifting between mist and light rain. When they arrived, he opened the door for Cairstie. Most women took umbrage if he held the door for them. Not Cairstie. He enjoyed dusting off his rusty manners. Mum would be proud.

"Thank you."

She peered at him, her wee smile doing crazy things to a few of his internal organs. Paddy, his brother closest in age, punched him in the gut once, and that's precisely how he felt every time Cairstie looked his way.

Breathless.

How she slipped past his guard, he did not know, but she had gone from a lovely, albeit spoiled, daughter of a Scottish marquess to someone he trusted implicitly. During her time on the island, Cairstie had matured, much like a bud opening to the sun. The metamorphosis enchanted him.

Pasting on a smile, he followed her into the overcrowded community center. Doubtless, the Scottish Fire and Rescue Service would disregard the size of this gathering.

People of all ages conversed in tiny knots, from mothers with babies cradled in their arms to a granny in a pushchair. Children darted through the assembly, playing tag. And the noise level . . . It had the potential to lift the roof. He grinned in earnest. The scene reminded him of the small assemblies in his Irish village.

Cairstie located a pair of vacant chairs and tied Winkle to one before she withdrew the bone from her pocket. Winkle sat at attention while his gaze latched onto the treat.

"Here you go, laddie." She stopped and held the rawhide before him. Winkle took it politely and slipped under the chair to gnaw to his heart's content.

She slid out of her coat as four fiddlers, an accordionist, a flutist, and a tin whistle player, started into a country tune.

"Shall we?" Sharidon held out his hand.

Cairstie removed her scarf and smoothed her hair before she placed her fingers in his. Her touch burned and fairly branded him, wiping the smile from his face as he guided her to a set of dancers forming a circle. What the blazes was that?

The musicians played the intro to the *Gay Gordons*. If the crowded dance floor was anything to judge by, the lively tune appeared to be an island favorite. With her hands in his, Sharidon barely restrained himself from stealing a kiss.

Focus, he admonished himself. Ye've a job to do. Yer looking for a traitor, one who's killed and will kill again. The self-talk sobered him.

When they reached the part of the dance where they polkaed around the room, his leg let him know he needed a break. The song ended, and everyone clapped. He limped to their chairs and waited until Cairstie sat before he joined her. The chatter resumed, much like a loud static buzz.

A flame-haired lass approached. "Miss Henderson, would ye play for Fergus so he can dance with his mum? She doesn't get out much."

Over the girl's head, Cairstie raised her brows at him, her expression a silent question. Sharidon nodded, then scanned the assembly room's perimeter and occupants.

After he'd sent Mrs. McDougal's pen drive to Nigel, he'd cross-checked all the residents' backgrounds. Three men bore further investigation: Harry, Gordon, and Randy. All three had served in the same naval unit overseas. Two of them worked at the missile range on South Uist before taking over a family-run business or venturing out on their own.

All three men were affable pillars of the community—their reputation on Benbecula spotless. If one of them proved to be the traitor, they had turned long ago. And they were careful. Very careful.

What triggered someone to betray their country to such magnitude? He understood what soured patriotism. Not all his operations progressed without a hitch. He'd be less than human if he didn't have regrets, but to destroy your compatriots? That spoke of a deep bitterness of soul or an intense need for money or power.

In his line of work, Sharidon saw it all. Whoever this traitor proved to be, he hid his reasons so tightly that no whiff had reached the community. Often, money tempted people from the strait-and-narrow, but in this instance, Sharidon believed something else motivated this traitor. He needed to figure out what drove them.

Sharidon zeroed in on the refreshment table where two suspects, Gordon, and Randy, stood conversing. Sharidon closed the distance and stopped to view the offerings.

"Would you care for a whiskey?" A woman who looked like Mrs. MacLeod's niece held out a paper cup.

"No thanks." He didn't care for alcohol. It tasted of rotted things, fuzzed his mind, and burned like the devil. But the Scots? Distilleries dotted the country, even in the smallest villages, offering tours and tastings, much like the vineyards of France.

He shoved his hands inside his pockets and joined Randy and Gordon.

"That's a bonnie lass, Sherwood." Randy nodded toward Cairstie, who tuned up a fiddle among the musicians.

"Aye," Gordon agreed and raised his whiskey cup to toast her.

"Did the two of you patch things up?" Randy asked. "The lads are hoping not, as they'd like a chance with her."

Sharidon shifted. He fancied Cairstie, and the idea of her dating other men brought on a bout of possessiveness foreign to his nature. He intended to pursue her after this mission wrapped—but would she wait? A lass like Cairstie Henderson didn't grow on trees. What if she tired of waiting on him between missions? Distance was a factor as well. He lived in London, and she in Scotland. That might cause issues.

Cairstie glanced his way and smiled, her eyes twinkling as she raced her bow across the fiddle's strings when the band started into a dance. The connection between them tautened as surely as if she had tossed a life preserver to his drowning self.

"The lads' hopes are dashed again." Gordon thumped his shoulder, his gaze straying across the room to the grocer, Mr. Chen, and his young wife, Grace.

Randy tossed back his drink, then dumped his cup into the bin beside the refreshment table. "I'd best go ask my wife for a dance, or I'll never hear the end of it when we get home. Cheers." He ambled off.

"Family man." Gordon saluted Randy, then downed the last of his drink.

"I take it yer single?" Sharidon asked.

"Aye. One marriage was enough for me. I don't care to tie myself down again." Gordon's attention wandered once more to Mrs. Chen.

The grocer's young wife spoke to her husband, who stood in deep conversation with several gentlemen. He waved her away without a second glance. She picked up her coat and slipped out the side exit.

"Nice chatting with you, Sherwood." Gordon tossed his cup in the bin, snagged his jacket, and left by the front entrance.

Interesting. Sharidon returned to Winkle as the song ended. Cairstie handed back Fergus's fiddle and whispered in his ear. The lad nodded, then picked up his bow and spoke to the other band members. A few seconds later, *The Pride of Erin Waltz*, an Irish tune, filled the assembly room.

Cairstie rounded the dance floor, a smile curving that oh-so-pretty mouth of hers. Sharidon placed his elbows on his knees and stared at the floor. A lass like Lady Cairstie deserved more than a farmer's son. She had grown up with every privilege. She'd not toss that aside for the likes of him, a lad who had plowed fields and fed livestock. Cairstie's residual income as an influencer and model doubtless exceeded his own.

Residing here, at the world's edge, where class and money held no sway, had muddied the waters. For a time, he had dreamed of a different outcome, one that included her. But he'd woken from his fancies. He and Cairstie inhabited different worlds—hers, one of luxury. And his?

His could end as swiftly as Mansfield's.

He didn't want that for Cairstie. She mattered too much. He respected her too much. Shocked at the direction his thoughts had taken, he sat back. That's when it hit him.

He wanted her—for forever.

"They're playing your song, Sherwood." Cairstie reached him, her blonde hair shining under the lights and a naughty glint in her eyes.

His resolve melted in a heartbeat, and he allowed her to drag him onto the dance floor. He took his position on Cairstie's left and started into the dance. Heel-toe. Heel-toe with the outside foot, then forward three steps. Turn. Then, they repeated the same moves in the opposite direction.

Unable to resist Cairstie's smile, he snatched her close, improvising the next turn with a three-step spin before they started up the line again. Heel-toe. Heel-toe. Cairstie followed his lead, light as thistledown on her feet.

Since he had signed on with MI6, he had locked his heart and kept a clear head, earning a few less-than-desirable nicknames from fellow agents —Flirt being the kindest. But now? He'd do anything to fill those blue eyes of Cairstie's with joy. Why? Because he loved her.

"Why so solemn?" she asked.

"Ye keep distracting me, lass."

"And that's bad." It wasn't a question. Cairstie might be young, but the lass didn't have a dim bone in her body.

"I've a job to do." Over her shoulder, he skimmed the room, tracking Harry and Randy on the floor dancing with their wives. While he spun Cairstie, he searched for Gordon, but the fellow had not returned. That bore investigation.

He pressed his mouth to Cairstie's ear. "Can ye sit with Winkle and not leave the building until I return?"

"Of course."

At the end of the song, Angus waylaid them.

"Will you give me a dance, Miss Henderson?" Angus bowed in a courtly fashion.

"I'd be honored." Cairstie hooked her arm through Angus's.

"I'll leave ye to Angus, then." Sharidon stood aside for Angus to lead Cairstie onto the dance floor.

Pivoting, he moved toward the loo, the only room in the center where Gordon might hide. The painted green door squealed when Sharidon pulled it open. Empty. Doubling back, he grabbed his coat off his chair and exited the building.

Late evening sunlight filtered through the clouds and bathed the island gold. He scanned the empty lot and surrounding *machair* for his quarry, but Gordon had vanished.

With the Ceilidh the only activity in town, Sharidon had a good idea where Gordon had gone. On foot, Sharidon headed for the center of Balivanich. The wind shifted and stirred the long strands, much like ocean waves.

The village appeared deserted as he moved down the main street close to the buildings. When he rounded the bakery, a door at the Chinese takeaway closed across the street. Grace Chen drew the draperies a few seconds later, but not before Sharidon caught sight of Gordon standing inside.

Sharidon turned away—none of his business. At least Gordon's nefarious activity had nothing to do with national security. His Mandarin had obviously been used in other ways. Shoving his hands inside his jacket pockets, Sharidon rejoined the Ceilidh.

Gordon might not be the traitor, but Grace Chen certainly was—to her marriage vows. Mr. Chen had returned from China two-and-a-half years ago with Grace, doubtless, having paid a handsome bride price for someone so young and lovely. Last year, Chen placed her in charge of the Chinese takeaway's daily operations after her English improved.

Most of Benbecula's inhabitants struggled financially. With winter storms and rough seas often canceling ferry service, supplies to the islands were often sparse. Not for the first time, he questioned how Chen earned such a good living with semi-empty shelves.

A thorough analysis of Chen's background might prove illuminating after all.

# CHAPTER 26

CAIRSTIE DIDN'T HAVE the plague, but she might as well have.

Afternoon light streamed through Mrs. McDougal's kitchen windows. Seated at the table, Cairstie hit the replay button on her video for the fourth time that afternoon. How could she focus on her dyslexia lessons when Sharidon was acting strange? For the last few days, he had inhabited the snug until noon, then closed himself off in her dining room until she retired.

He paused only for meals—meals for one.

Her temper stirred. How could he behave that way after the mind-blowing kisses they had shared? Sharidon didn't have time. He needed to focus. Even though she understood his reasoning, resentment bubbled close to the surface as each day passed.

She pushed away from the table and grabbed the kettle. Flipping on the tap, she filled it, then set it to boil. She needed Mother's herbal tea, a panacea for all ills. With her back to the cooker's edge, she folded her arms and tapped her shoe.

Her life comprised dyslexia lessons, watching a kettle boil, and drinking pots of tea that kept her up at night running to the ladies. She was bored. Bored. Bored. And a wee bit heartsick.

When sleep eluded her at night, she wrapped herself in a blanket and curled by the window to watch the moon arc across the sky, its silvery light casting a highway upon the Atlantic. A slight noise outside captured her attention. She twitched the curtain aside in time to see Sharidon, dressed in black, slip inside the house. The fellow had doubtless returned from another one of his spying forays.

The kettle whistled. She filled her teapot and set the herbs to steep. Then, she made finger sandwiches with a store-bought spread and sliced cucumbers for the tray because she needed something to do. She might not be the world's best cook, but she was able to make things pretty.

She retrieved one of her godmother's teacups and luncheon plates and returned to the table.

Sharidon entered the kitchen a few minutes later. He noticed the table and paused. "I didn't see ye there." He moved toward the fridge and pulled open the door to stare inside.

"Would you have avoided the room if you knew I was here?"

"Why would I do that?" He didn't look at her.

"I don't know, Sharidon. Why don't you tell me? You're the one who's kept away the last few days."

He closed the fridge door and opened his mouth, denial written on his face.

She held up a hand. "Spare me your platitudes. If you regret kissing me, be honest. I can take it. I'm not some China doll. I don't break." "Liar," her heart cried.

Sharidon entered the corridor and clicked the radio on high before he returned to the table, taking the chair across from her. "It doesn't work."

"What doesn't work?"

"Me. Ye." He moved his index finger back and forth between them.

"And how did you come to that brilliant assumption?" She kept her tone icy, mimicking Mother on a scold, but inside, cracks raced across her heart.

"Benbecula isn't the real world, Cairstie. We're isolated here. Cut off from society. When this mission ends, I return to London. That's eight hours from Torwoodlee and a world apart from what yer accustomed to."

He would not use the differences of their upbringings as an excuse. "I have no issue moving to London." She did not have plans to chase him.

Not really. She needed a broader pool to gain sponsors after she left Benbecula.

"That's just it, lass. I'm not asking ye to."

She winced, his comment more like a slap. She kept her poise and refused to show the devastation his words stirred within her. "So, you've decided for both of us? Don't I get a say in this?"

"I disappear for months at a time. I can't tell ye where I am or when I'll return. That's no life for ye." He touched her hand, the connection burning fire all the way to her shoulder.

"I determine what's best for me." Though wildly attracted to him, she dared not call this thing between them love. Not yet. Sharidon had never declared himself.

"That's true, but not when I'm part of the equation."

"So, you're deciding for the both of us?" If so, she had a serious problem with that, one that needed immediate rectification.

"No. Far be it from me to tell ye to do anything ye don't wish to. I'm saying, I can't be with ye. I'm sorry." No light shone from his eyes.

She read the finality in his expression. Her throat tightened, making it hard to breathe. "I am, too." She rose and gripped the table's edge to keep herself upright. "I hope you don't mind, but I need you to stay in the van from now on."

"Yer not safe," he protested.

"I didn't ask you to leave the premises, only to vacate the house. It will be too awkward having you inside. You're welcome to use the laundry, water, and electrical hookups for the remainder of your stay." Spinning, she left the room with her head high and her heart a shambles of broken fragments.

When she reached the stairs, she dropped all pretenses and fled to her room, locking the door behind her, unable to avoid the mortal blow he had delivered. Her eyes watered, and she dashed a lone tear away with the back of her hand.

Sharidon held her birth against her and refused to see who she had become. No longer the spoiled darling of social media, she gloried in caring for her own needs. She had learned how to wash her clothes, handle basic meals, and even clean the house under Sharidon's tutelage. And her online course had already made inroads with her dyslexia.

Her self-worth had blossomed, something her life of parties and travel had never accomplished. If someone had shone a spotlight on her former self and illuminated what a hollow world she existed in, she never would have believed them. Her discovery left her nauseated at the falseness of it all.

Why couldn't Sharidon see how much she had changed from the frivolous socialite he met in that restaurant? Is that why he denied them the opportunity to explore a future together? Or did her money bother him? He mentioned their lives being worlds apart. So, what? Look at Elise and Harry. His parents were servants, but no two people could be more in sync. Sharidon came from a family of Irish farmers. Landowners. Not so different from her parents, surely? Educated at a prestigious university with a job that required physical stamina and intellectual prowess, Sharidon outdistanced her in every way that mattered.

She flopped onto her bed and stared up at the ceiling. His reference to her family dealt more with something she could not control: her aristocratic birth. Sharidon needed to get over himself.

Muffled noises rose from the snug below where Sharidon slept. She swallowed. He must be packing his things.

She raced down the stairs without planning her words. All she knew was that she deserved to be heard. Sharidon couldn't have it all his way.

Balling her fist, she rapped on the snug door loud enough for him to hear over the blasting radio. Did he intend to ignore her? She raised her hand to rap again when the door swung open.

Sharidon's hair stood up as though he had tugged it several times. The truth hit her in the face. He didn't care for this separation any more than she did. The revelation knocked her sideways.

Without thought, she stepped forward and wrapped her arms around him, like a mother comforting a hurt child. His arms remained at his sides, unresponsive.

"Why did you do it?" she asked.

"Because we don't work," he parroted his earlier words.

"Not good enough. Look at Elise and Harry."

"They're different." Sharidon stepped back, out of touching range.

"That's a hard sell, Sharidon. I'm not buying it."

"Elise understands Harry's world. She's lived it as a former agent."

"And you've blocked me from yours. What is the real problem?"

The corner of his mouth quirked. "Ye don't give up easy, do ye?"

"No. Elise and I butt heads for that very reason. We both want our way."

The slightest spark flashed inside the green depths of his eyes. Cairstie narrowed the distance between them until she caught a whiff of his aftershave, something woody and aromatic. "What's the problem, Sharidon?"

"Give me strength." He glared up at the ceiling as though petitioning God. "I can't think when yer this close."

She slipped her arms around his neck. "Tell me first why we don't work."

His Adam's apple bobbed. "I never said we didn't work physically."

"Then how don't we work? Help me understand."

"Yer, a lady. And I'm me." He shrugged in that Gaelic way she found endearing.

"How is that a bad thing?"

"Yer an aristocrat. Ye live in a castle."

"My father inherited a castle and a title, which he did nothing to earn. His money came from Border reivers, men who stole cattle and married rich women. I'm twenty years old, and I can barely read. When I leave Benbecula, it's unlikely anyone will offer me modeling contracts." She touched the hair at the nape of his neck, which flipped at the ends.

"But I know one thing . . . Two."

"What?"

"No intruder is driving me off this island."

"And?"

"I care about you, Sharidon. Quite a lot." There, she'd said it. "I won't curl up and die if you end us, but I thought you should know how I feel before we part ways."

He backed up further and scrubbed both hands up and down his face before he lifted his eyes. "I'm not fancy in the least. I work out, read, go hill walking, or shoot in my downtime. I'd rather do anything than dress up for a party. They're the worst sort of torture I can imagine."

"Dressing up is all about showing off, don't you know? It's rather like one of your spy games." Ah. She had his focus now. "You track something while appearing to be doing something else. Parties are much the same."

"I can think of better ways to show off." He folded his arms, making his biceps bunch.

"Such as?"

"Beating Harry Benson on the shooting range." Sharidon flashed his white teeth.

"Or?" She inched closer and kissed his scratchy jaw.

"Taking ye out to eat with my friends. Ye have a way of turning heads, lass."

"I'll assume there's a compliment in there," she said, her tone rough as sandpaper.

"I crossed boundaries I shouldn't have on this assignment." He grimaced, his lips turning down.

"I thought James Bond kissed all the girls."

"James Bond doesn't get emotionally involved with them." Sharidon wrapped her in his arms.

At last.

He shook his head. "We'd be a mesalliance. Whoever heard of a farmer and a socialite?"

"I think it's more a case of the spy and the unemployed influencer," she murmured, reveling at being held again. She touched his jaw, the dark scruff tickling her fingers.

"How about the lady and the cow herder?" He leaned back and tilted up her chin. "No one will ever take us seriously."

"I disagree. And it's more a case of the linguist and the illiterate. People will wonder why such an academic ended up with me."

"Now that's enough. Yer not illiterate." His arms tightened. "Yer learning how to work around an issue that keeps ye from reading. That takes determination. Yer doing a fine job of it, too. I'll say one thing about ye, lass. When ye commit to something, ye stick to it like a burr. That's downright admirable."

Sharidon cupped her face and kissed her. "I can't fight ye any longer." He kissed her again with an intensity that made her cling to him like a drowning woman with the only solid anchor in an unstable sea. He bent her across his arm, her head spinning from his kisses. His mouth shot tremors straight to her nerve endings, and his lips told her things he had not put into words. She responded in kind, answering his demands with assurances of her own.

Then, as quickly as it started, Sharidon drew back, his pupils almost black as he broke the connection.

Her chest heaved.

"As much as I'd like to, I shouldn't do that again." Sharidon paced away, then glanced at her, a smirk lifting the corners of his mouth. "But I give ye fair warning. Be prepared when I do."

# CHAPTER 27

SHARIDON STOOD ON THE BEACH, the rollers hitting the shore, then flattening and racing toward his feet. He jumped back to keep his boots from getting soaked and grabbed his sat phone from his pocket.

With one eye on Cairstie up the beach with Winkle, he hit speed dial.

"Thatcher."

"Hiya, Nigel. Can Cyber run names through the system and see if any of them pop?"

"Any progress?" Nigel asked.

"Aye. Narrowing the field considerably."

"Cyber's backlogged with a situation in Russia just now. Elise Benson is handling the overflow. She has the necessary clearances. I understand you've used her."

Sharidon barked a laugh before hanging up and pressing Elise's number. She picked up partway through the second ring.

"Fancy hearing from you, Sharidon," Elise greeted, sarcasm edging her words.

"I love ye too, Elise. Nigel verified that yer handling overflow with Cyber." Nigel should have kept her in Cyber instead of allowing her to leave for the private sector. No one hacked the way she did.

"Aye. It's nice not having secrets with Harry."

"Can ye run a few names through the system? I'm hunting a mole." Sharidon eyed the sea foam on the wave's edge, which frothed like heavy cream.

"Sounds fun. Let me have them." Computer keys clicked.

"Gordon MacRae, Randall MacDonald, and Hank Walker. All three served together in The Royal Navy's Bravo Squadron. They're highly skilled divers and explosive ordinance disposal experts," he said. "All three speak Mandarin."

"This is interesting," Elise murmured after a few seconds of mobile silence. "MacDonald, MacRae, and Walker were all moved to a unit later declared defunct by the Ministry of Defense. Quantas took over those contracts. They're running top-secret tests on The Deep Sea Range for the Ministry of Defense." She had obviously read the information from a secure source.

Down the beach, Cairstie spoke to their neighbor, Mrs. MacLeod, whose manner of dress could pass for a homeless lady when she foraged for bits and bobs. Winkle zipped around the newcomer's feet, tail wagging. His yipping barks reached Sharidon between the sound of crashing waves.

"Were any of them employed by Quantas?" Sharidon asked as the swells turned dark gray under the growing cloud bank.

"Checking." Keys clicked. "MacDonald and MacRae both worked for Quantas. MacRae still does—in the purchasing department, but MacDonald left and opened a pub. When the pub floundered, MacRae came on as part owner a few years back."

"What about Walker?"

"He expanded his father's fishing company after he left the navy. He also skippers deep sea fishing excursions."

Sharidon turned back toward the women on the beach. Cairstie's long blonde hair whipped around her as she unclipped Winkle's lead, then tossed a piece of driftwood for him to fetch. Winkle darted after it, his tail streaking behind him. The pup grabbed the stick and trotted back to her, refusing to let go. A game of tug-o-war ensued until Winkle dropped the driftwood so she could repeat the entire process.

"It's a shot in the dark, but I need credit card signatures on all three men on the night of July twenty-fourth. That's the night our two agents disappeared. Despite limited CCTV in the Hebrides, he could pinpoint their whereabouts if the suspects spent money that night.

"Hmmm."

"That doesn't sound good." Sharidon zipped up his coat against the biting wind that flapped his clothes.

"I hope you have another hypothesis." Elise cleared her throat. "Walker, MacRae, and MacDonald were in Oban the night of July twenty-fourth."

Sharidon stopped pacing. "That can't be right."

"It is, I'm afraid. The charges indicate their presence at a pub called the Markie Dans on Victoria Crescent. Each one of them paid for a meal about nineteen hundred."

If that was true, then the person who killed Mansfield was someone else. Sharidon tugged his hair. He had run stats multiple times. One of those three was involved. His gut never lied. If that trio were in Oban the night of the break-in, then who blew off the SCIF door and killed Mansfield? A hired assassin?

"Elise, if I send you an encrypted file, can you run a few scans through your sorter? I'm hoping it will pick up something I missed."

"Sharidon, it can't be one of your suspects," Elise said.

"I disagree. The night of the break-in, we had a storm. High seas closed the causeways, and CalMac canceled the ferry service. No one could get on or off Benbecula."

"What about a private boat?" Elise asked.

"It's possible, but a small craft would have floundered with those seas. I checked mainland marinas, along with those on Skye and Mull. No one paid to dock nor called for help."

"This is interesting." Elise's typing picked up speed. "How's my sister getting on?"

"Famously. She's made friends with the neighbor and has even cooked a few meals."

"You've mixed up my sisters. This is Cairstie we're speaking about."

"Yer sister's grown up since her arrival. She clobbered an intruder and scared him off." Sharidon couldn't hold back the pride. For all her glamor, Lady Cairstie was no pushover.

"Do I detect admiration?" Curiosity colored Elise's words.

"Ye might." The lass had bewitched him.

"Be careful. She's headstrong."

"Rather like someone else I know."

Elise laughed, a husky sound full of warmth. "I suppose we Henderson's have a tendency toward that trait."

"She's quite a lass."

"Don't be messing with her emotions, Sharidon. She's had a bad time of it."

"Is big sister warning me off?" Surprise rattled his core. Why was Elise poking her nose in? She and Cairstie didn't get on.

"You're a terrible flirt. Don't hurt her."

"Where yer sister is concerned, my intentions are honorable."

Silence stretched, then, "So that's the way of things?"

"The attraction's mutual." He intended to see where it led after he caught the mole.

"If Cairstie suffers at your hands, Harry and I will come after you," Elise promised, her tone deadly earnest.

"I'm quaking in my boots." Sharidon laughed, but Elise didn't deliver idle threats. She meant every word, and they both knew it.

He placed two fingers between his teeth and whistled, the sound carrying to the figures on the beach. Winkle swung in Sharidon's direction, and Cairstie followed suit. He raised his arm and motioned for her to join him. Cairstie said something to Mrs. MacLeod, then caught Winkle by the collar, snapped on his lead, and started up the beach.

"Be on the lookout. I'll be sending ye that file in less than five minutes." His gaze swept over Cairstie's approaching form. "And stop worrying. If anyone is liable to be hurt, it's me."

He disconnected just as Cairstie reached him, a welcome smile on her lips. The wind had whipped her cheeks to a rosy hue, making her blue eyes sparkle. Elise and her concerns faded to nothing.

With reverent fingers, he touched a strand of her hair. "Let's go home, lass."

❖

A breeze whistled down the corridor when Cairstie unclipped Winkle's lead just inside the kitchen door. The cold air from the nearby sitting room led her down the hallway, where she found the Solarium door open. A spurt of unease made the hair on her arms rise. She stepped into the hall.

"Sharidon, did you leave the Solarium door open?" she called over her shoulder as he hung his jacket beside the kitchen door.

He came up behind her. "What's that?"

"Did you leave the Solarium door open?"

"No."

"That's odd. I'm positive I locked it earlier." A frisson slithered up her neck. Had the intruder returned?

Sharidon held a finger to his lips and removed his weapon from his waist holster. Soft-footed, he entered the lounge, scanned the room, and then moved into the corridor beside her. Not about to be left behind, Cairstie rushed back to the kitchen and grabbed a knife from the drainboard and caught up to him as Sharidon exited the study.

"Anything?" she whispered.

He shook his head and started upstairs. She trembled, disquiet stirring. First, her nocturnal visitor took several potshots at her within her home and attached a bomb to her car. Then, Sharidon's tackle at the Sunday School outing when he thought he saw something suspicious. Now this. The longer it took to find the intruder, the more nervous she became.

Was he after something specific, or were they dealing with a local bampot?

She trotted halfway up the stairs before Sharidon started back down. His eyes dropped to her hand, where the blade glinted.

Amusement shimmered. "Were ye going to protect me with that?"

"If necessary."

He placed his hand over hers and removed the knife. "I'll just put this away."

With a simple touch, the air shifted between them and deepened to something more. He kissed her cheek and continued downstairs. Turning, she went up the remaining steps to her room to put away her scarf. The door hinge squeaked when she entered. Toeing off her shoes, she padded to the window to savor the moment on the stairs. As she pushed aside the curtains, she stepped on something pliant.

Cairstie glanced down just as a snake with a dark zig-zag pattern down its back sprang and struck her calf, its fangs sinking deep into her flesh. Needle-sharp pain hit her. She shrieked and jumped backward.

The snake slithered across the floor and disappeared under her bureau, where her reflection stared back at her, wide-eyed with horror.

Feet pounded up the stairs, and Sharidon burst into her room.

"Be careful. There's an adder under the bureau. It bit me." She pointed underneath the piece of furniture across the room.

Sharidon snatched her up and carried her into the next bedroom.

"Where did it bite ye?" He laid her on the bed.

She pointed to her calf, where two red marks appeared. The flesh was already swelling.

"Yer sure it was an adder?"

"Aye. Zig-zag on the back. Diamond marks on the sides. One bit our dog a few years ago."

"Yer right. That's an adder. We need to immobilize yer leg to slow the venom from spreading around yer body. I'm going to carry ye downstairs and take ye to the hospital. Okay?"

She nodded. "Can you contain the snake in my room? I don't want Winkle to find it."

"Lass. We need to get ye to the doctor."

Her leg throbbed, and her body ached. "I know. Please. Winkle first. Please protect him."

Sharidon's brows clashed in the center of his forehead, and a stream of Irish Gaelic poured from his lips. Grabbing pillows off the bed where she lay, he stomped from the room. If her leg hadn't hurt abominably, she would have laughed. A second later, her bedroom door slammed.

She glanced at her leg where the skin around her anklet had tightened. She unclasped the fastener and dropped the anklet on the bedside table to keep it from cutting off her circulation.

Sharidon returned, only marginally in a better frame of mind.

Without a word, he scooped her up and carried her out to the van, laying her tenderly on the mattress in the back. "Don't move." He fired up the engine and backed out the drive.

Cairstie gripped the cubby beside the bed to keep from being flung onto the floor as Sharidon took the corners triple the posted limit. Four blocks later, he squealed to a halt in front of the Accident & Emergency entrance.

He jumped from the driver's seat, flung the van's back doors wide, and lifted her gently. She bit her lip as he rushed her inside the building. The small lobby was deserted, save for a medical receptionist seated behind a desk.

"May I help you?" The receptionist looked familiar.

"A poisonous snake has bitten this woman," Sharidon spoke in Gaelic.

The receptionist's eyes widened, and Cairstie identified her as the accordionist at the Ceilidh.

"Poisonous snakes do not exist in the Outer Hebrides." The receptionist informed him with amusement tingeing her tone.

"An adder struck my dog a few years ago. I know what they look like." Cairstie gritted her teeth as pain radiated and nausea roiled. She needed the loo if her stomach didn't settle soon.

The receptionist hit a buzzer and spoke into the com, "Dr. Smith. You're needed."

Sharidon placed Cairstie in a chair and pushed another in front of her so she could prop her leg on it. Cairstie fought back the tears as the throb in her leg increased, and the receptionist entered her information.

Sharidon didn't pace the lobby, instead, he stomped as the minutes lengthened. He approached the receptionist. "When do you expect the doctor?"

"He's a busy man." The receptionist pursed her lips.

"I can see that." Sharidon motioned toward the empty lobby.

Despite the pain racking her, Cairstie snorted, amused by Sharidon's sarcasm, until he stopped beside her and cleared his throat. She longed to ask him to go outside and cool down, but the sudden reversal of his cheery disposition made her pause. When she arrived on the island, Sharidon wanted nothing more than for her to leave. He insisted he needed to focus on his mission even after a few shared kisses. So, his behavior kind of threw her. Was he upset about her welfare?

A nurse opened a side door. "Cairstie Henderson?"

As she was the only female in the minuscule waiting room, the woman's gaze landed on her. Sharidon lifted her into his arms. Cairstie clenched her teeth to keep from crying out from the movement as they followed the nurse to one of the two examination rooms.

Sharidon set her on the bed and touched her arm. "I'll be back soon. I need to capture that wee visitor of yers," he said.

"Where do you believe the snake bit you?" the nurse, a woman in blue scrubs and overlapping front teeth asked, looking up from her electronic pad.

Cairstie rolled up her trouser leg and exposed her swollen, discolored calf.

"Oh." The nurse examined the puncture wounds. "That looks painful."

"It is," Cairstie assured her.

Dr. Smith, a small man with gold-rimmed specs, drew back the curtain. "I hear we have a snake bite. Is there a possibility you were mistaken? We've only had one adder bite in the Uists."

"Now we have two," Cairstie ground out. Why didn't they give her something for the pain?

"It appears to be a bite of some sort." Dr. Smith noted the puncture marks on her calf. "Any nausea?"

"Aye." Cairstie winced as he touched the flesh beside the bite marks.

"Let's sanitize the bite and start with an intravenous bag. She's having a reaction of some sort." Dr. Smith left the room.

"Aye, a right good reaction to the venom in my leg." Cairstie was fast losing patience with the medical staff. Why didn't anyone believe an adder had bitten her?

A nurse swabbed her arm in preparation for an IV and sterilized the punctures.

Cairstie averted her gaze. She hated needles. A sting, not unlike the adder's, then the worst was over. The nurse started an intravenous fluid and connected two bags to the drip line.

Dr. Smith returned with a packet in his hands and gave it to the nurse.

"Luckily, we have confab left over from the previous bite, so we're going to administer antivenom and pain medication through your IV," Dr. Smith said. "You'll experience relief shortly."

Brilliant.

The doctor held Cairstie's wrist and compared it with the blood pressure monitor. "That's a wee higher than we like."

# Chapter 28

Kitted out with a broom and pillowcase, Sharidon swiped the long wooden handle under Cairstie's bed. "Here, snakey, snakey. Come out and play."

Not finding his target, he flipped the straw end of the broom under the bed and made several passes to ensure the snake hadn't evaded him. However, he refused to put his face on the same level as the adder's. The reptile was here somewhere; he just needed to find it, if for no other reason than proving to the hospital that adders had infiltrated the Outer Hebrides.

And he intended to give them proof.

Next, he swished the broom under the bureau, stepping back to see that nothing lay underneath. He scratched his head. Where had it gone? The window remained closed, and he had stuffed pillows underneath the door.

Pivoting, he eyed the tall, painted wardrobe. Could the snake have slithered inside? Cautiously, he swung the door wide and ran the broom over the floor, knocking Cairstie's shoes and boots onto the rug. Jabbing the handle inside each boot, he came up empty. No evil serpent.

That left the chair. Would an adder climb so high?

He gazed at the clothes draped with care across both chair arms. It appeared that Cairstie removed them to select an outfit. Gearing himself for battle, he approached the overstuffed piece of furniture. He extended the broom handle, lifted a tweed suit by the hanger, and then shook it.

No snake fell from the folds. He returned the blazer and trousers to the wardrobe, then addressed the second ensemble: a tweed skirt and a silky blouse. Stretching forward, he raised the hooked end of the coat hanger the same way he had the suit. Sharidon shook the hanger, and a writhing, hissing snake fairly leaped at him.

Sharidon jumped out of striking distance and pinned its head with the coat hanger. "Gotcha ye, ye wee beggar."

The adder, now thoroughly upset, coiled around the plastic. "Ye think biting a lady is good and proper? I'll show ye what that'll get ye."

He exchanged the coat hanger for the broom. Pressing the snake's head into the floor with the handle, he scooped the reptile into the pillowcase. "And there ye'll stay, me laddie."

Sharidon tied the bag with twine while the snake writhed like a thing possessed. Holding the pillowcase away from his body, he hightailed it to the hospital and marched into the Accident & Emergency entrance.

"This is the wee laddie who bit Cairstie Henderson." Sharidon extended the pillowcase to the medical receptionist.

"I'm not taking that thing." The receptionist scooted away on her rolling chair.

Seeing he would get nowhere with the woman, Sharidon bypassed her and entered the observation corridor, holding the sack away from his body.

"You can't go back there."

"Watch me." Sharidon reached the corridor beyond. The doctor stood partway down the hall and glanced up from his electronic pad. "Dr. Smith?"

"Aye?" Dr. Smith asked.

"I brought ye the adder that bit Cairstie Henderson."

The doctor's specs flickered under the lights. Sharidon tromped toward him, his footsteps slapping against the laminate floor. With all the dignity of a medieval knight, he handed Dr. Smith the bag containing the adder.

The doctor untied the bag and peeked inside, then hastily secured the top. "That is most definitely an adder. What's it doing out here?" Dr. Smith asked.

Sharidon shrugged. "I haven't the foggiest, but the wee monster is now yer problem." Though adders were rarely deadly in the UK, their bites caused severe pain.

He left the doctor to sort the issue while he checked on Cairstie. Pumped with meds, she lay fast asleep. Grateful she'd found relief, he went in search of sustenance.

Outside, the sun poked out from between the clouds. He joined the queue at the local chippy shop, a white building with red trim, and inched forward behind three missile site contractors.

"What's the latest on the wreckage?" a round man with hair that reached his shoulders asked his burly companion.

"The dive team retrieved the *HMS Lilibet's* circuit board this morning," Burly Man said. "They were lucky to find it. The debris field extends for miles inside the Rockall Trench."

The *HMS Lilibet*? Sharidon perked up. He'd been at the hospital with Cairstie and hadn't caught up on the retrieval mission.

"I don't know what good recovering a circuit board will do. Saltwater has likely destroyed it." The third man, a fellow with big shoulders and thick, light brown hair, wiped perspiration from his temples and flicked it from his fingers.

"Aye." Burly Man nodded in agreement.

"Are you doing okay, Gordon?" Round Man asked.

Sharidon shifted to the left and got a side shot of the fellow's mug—Gordon MacRae—one of his suspects.

"I'll go save us a table." Gordon started toward one of the picnic tables, his face blotchy.

"Do you want me to order for you?" Round Man called after him.

"I've lost my appetite." Gordon waved Round Man off without turning around.

"He seemed fine a moment ago," Round Man commented to his companion.

Sharidon tossed a casual look in Gordon's direction. He sat slumped at the picnic table, his head in his hands.

If he were a betting man, it appeared that MacRae's "sudden illness" had everything to do with the *HMS Lilibet*.

His breath rasped as he edged around a containment pod. He didn't have a plausible excuse to enter The Deep Sea Range. If anyone spotted him, they'd arrest him for sure. Then what would Nicola do?

Footsteps sounded, moving his way.

He ducked behind another containment unit as two men rounded the corner of a hangar. Had they seen him? He held his breath, his heart banging like a drummer on meth as he reached for his weapon. The men drew close, their feet crunching on the gravel.

His breathing stopped altogether when they halted not ten meters from where he crouched and lit up. Cigarette smoke tickled his nose. Nasty stuff. What an unhealthy habit.

"When do you get off?" the first man asked in the local Gaelic.

"My shift ends in two hours. You?"

"Nineteen hundred."

The second fellow laughed. "Just came on, eh?"

"Something like that." They smoked without speaking, then pitched their cigarette butts and moved off.

A sigh escaped him—smoke break. Hunching low, he peered through the gaps between containers to ensure it was clear. Beyond them, on a slight rise, he spotted the white evidence tent off by itself. Doubtless, the dive teams had stored the *HMS Lilibet's* wreckage there until they shipped it to London.

An accident did not occur on the *HMS Lilibet*—not one of such magnitude. When the naval ship first sank, he assumed, like everyone else, it was due to a malfunction. But one of the divers let it slip at the pub about altered circuit boards last night.

Though he had parted ways with the navy, his former responsibilities with protective procedures told him that the premature missile detonation aboard the *HMS Lilibet* was deliberate. The navy held too many readiness activities to prevent or reduce impacts of such magnitude.

He narrowed his eyes. Only one explanation stood to reason. The Chinese had another plant in the Western Isles—one he knew nothing about. Did they intend to replace him?

The only way to counteract this was to identify and remove their operative first. Then, he'd take Nicola and move to the Cook Islands. No one would find them there.

# CHAPTER 29

SNAKES SLITHERED ACROSS HER BODY. Pain. Beeps. Men's voices. Someone holding her hand and smoothing her hair. Nausea.

Cairstie shifted on the pillow and opened her eyes.

Harry Benson, her brother-in-law, a tall man with gray eyes, sat beside her, reading. He glanced up and marked his place. She squinted at the book's cover and applied the new technique from her type-touch course.

The words took shape. *Behind the Bamboo Curtain: China and her Weapons.*

"A wee bit of light reading?" She touched the tube, blowing air into her nose.

"How are you?" Harry turned the book away from her.

"I'm better than I was. Why are you here?"

"I was in the area and stopped by."

She rolled her eyes. "No one stops by the Outer Hebrides."

"I was on Raasay when I heard about your accident and promised Elise I'd hop over and check on you."

"Raasay, huh?" Cairstie fiddled with her blanket. Not for one instant did she buy it. What was Harry doing out there? And why was he reading a book about Chinese weapons?

"I've never seen anyone get under Sharidon's skin." Harry grinned, exposing a crooked incisor.

"Where is Sharidon?" she asked.

"I sent him home to feed your dog and get some rest. Your neighbor, Mrs. MacLeod, has been feeding Winkle till now. Sharidon's been here for thirty-eight hours or thereabouts."

"I don't remember much."

"That's probably a good thing," Harry said.

She flipped back the blanket and uncovered her lower legs. Her affected calf looked swollen and bruised around the bite mark. "Why am I on oxygen?"

"You kept passing out." Harry lifted his mobile off the tray table. "I told Sharidon I'd give him a ring when you woke."

"Let him sleep."

"He won't thank me for disobeying instructions, but it won't hurt him to get some shuteye."

"Did he make any headway in finding our intruder?" Cairstie leaned against the pillows.

"Perhaps."

"Harry," she threatened with a stern note. "You're getting on my verra last nerve. I've been shot at, almost blown to bits, and bitten by a poisonous serpent. There must be something you can tell me."

"You aren't much easier to deal with than your sister." They both knew it wasn't Sophie Harry referred to, but his new wife.

"You might as well tell me. I've figured out most of Sharidon's mission already. I was with him when he discovered his mentor's body. And I connected islanders of interest on social media for him."

Harry drummed his fingers on the book in his lap. "Not a word of this to anyone, and don't ask for more than I give you."

"I promise." Once given, Cairstie kept her word.

"Sharidon thinks two separate issues are taking place on Benbecula."

"Why?"

"Sharidon's positive we're dealing with a rogue operator or a deep plant with their own agenda and another that destroyed the *HMS Lilibet*."

A rogue operator from where? She held her tongue, though. The last thing she needed was for Harry to stop sharing, so she kept her questions to a minimum. "So, Sharidon's assignment has nothing to do with what's happened to me?"

"Not really. Divers retrieved a circuit board off the *HMS Lilibet*, a naval class destroyer that sank in the Rockall Trough. It's all over the news, so I'm not giving away government secrets. The cold water didn't erode one of the circuit boards. The UK purchased them from the United States."

"Is the U.S. guilty?"

"Doubtful. Sharidon is almost certain the two incidents are linked."

"It sounds like you've both been verra busy while I was sleeping."

Harry tipped his head, his keen eyes assessing. "You seem different. More settled."

"It's the drugs in my intravenous bag." Cairstie indicated the IV beside her.

Harry bottled up after that. She might not be the world's best reader, but she had a good idea of where electronics originated. China. And China was not an ally.

"I thought you'd return to Torwoodlee after that first attack." Harry crossed his ankle over the opposite knee.

"I'm not a quitter." Cairstie folded her arms across her chest.

"You're right. Quitting isn't part of a Henderson's genetic code."

"What did Sharidon find on those pen drives he swiped from Mrs. McDougal's?"

"What makes you think Sharidon took anything?" Harry moved his foot, his manner relaxed. He had a brilliant poker face, but it didn't fool her for one second. Elise teased him once about his foot twitch being a giveaway during a game of cards.

And Cairstie had never forgotten.

"I saw the niche shelves before Sharidon blocked my view. The pen drives were missing when he stepped back."

"Did you ask Sharidon?" Harry's foot shifted again.

"Don't play Switzerland with me. You're my brother now. You're supposed to be on my side. Those pen drives are my property. In the eyes of the law, Sharidon stole them."

"Not if those drives pertain to national security." Harry opened his sat phone, pressed a number, and handed the device to her. "Let Sharidon know you're awake."

"Nice way to deflect, Agent Benson." Cairstie placed the mobile against her ear.

"Hullo." Sharidon's voice sounded husky from sleep.

"Hiya," she said, her tone apologetic. "Sorry to wake you."

"Sleeping beauty has risen." The slurring cleared as Sharidon woke. "I'm on my way."

The line clicked, leaving Cairstie with a darkened screen. She returned the sat phone to Harry.

"May I suggest you don't address this topic until only the two of you are present?" Harry asked.

Though his words were mild, they irked Cairstie beyond belief. Yet again, a family member censured her like someone without common sense.

"You don't know me verra well if you think for one instant that I would expose people I care about or endanger our national security." Cairstie dug her nails into her palms. "Do you mind waiting outside, Harry? I need to use the ladies."

"Not at all." Harry looked as though he intended to say something more, hesitated for a second, then left.

Picking up the controls looped around her bedrail, she pressed the call button for the nurse. Nothing had changed with her family. They still didn't trust her and treated her like a bairn. She sighed and stared out the window, a painful lump squeezing her throat.

Grim determination filled her. She intended to prove her trustworthiness.

Then they'd take her seriously.

⁂

Sharidon kicked at a pile of seaweed near the edge of Mrs. McDougal's back garden, a souvenir from last night's high tide. "The mole has explosives experience. They blew the door off the SCIF and wired a rather sophisticated bomb to Cairstie's Mercedes."

He glanced at Harry. "They're also an exceptional shot. Mansfield took two in the chest, the bullets close together. And if I hadn't seen that flash of sun on metal when we were out hill walking, Cairstie wouldn't be here."

"Sounds like someone called in a hit." Harry Benson stood beside him as the wind plastered the sleeves of his jacket to his arms.

Having warned Harry about the bugs inside the house, they moved their conversation outside, where the Atlantic rollers disguised their words.

"I agree, but I'm not tossing out the option that our shooter is military or has prior military experience. I've run checks on all the residents. MacDonald, MacRae, and Walker keep rising to the top. All three served on the Bravo Squadron and were skilled divers and bomb detonators. And each of them has firearms training."

"What's their motive? Money?" Harry asked.

Sharidon tightened his jaw. "No money trails. Whoever our deep plant is, they haven't received large deposits. My guess is they used an alias to set up an account, or they've an offshore one."

He rubbed his face as though the movement would clear his mind. "All three suspects are business owners. Start-ups take funds. That alone raised my suspicions, but when I checked their whereabouts, the night Mansfield was killed, all three were in Oban."

"How do you know that?" Harry's eyes sharpened.

"I traced their credit cards on the night in question." Sharidon tapped his temple. He refused to throw Elise under the bus. Harry could recon that on his own time. "Something keeps nagging at me about that night, though."

"Did Elise locate a CCTV feed on them that night?" Harry's question clued Sharidon in that he was aware of his wife's involvement.

"What are ye getting at, Harry?"

"If your gut is telling you one thing, I'd check the CCTV relay station and get eyes on the ground. Verify your facts."

"Elise won't like this."

"Doesn't matter if she does." Harry's jaw bunched inside his cheek. "We're dealing with national security. How many lives were lost when the *HMS Lilibet* sank?"

"Three hundred," Sharidon growled. "Yer right. I owe those families another look." Sharidon withdrew his sat phone and rang Elise.

"Hiya, Sharidon. How's my sister?" Elise asked.

"Much better. They sent her home today. She'll be back to her old self in a few more weeks." Indeed, save for the swelling and discoloration on her leg, Cairstie refused to be kept down. "Yer husband's doing good, too."

"Harry's there?" Elise's voice went up a notch.

"He was in the area and popped by," Sharidon said.

"Popped by my backside. What are the two of you up to?" Suspicion, sharp as a blade's edge, shot through the line.

"I need a favor. Could ye tap into the CCTV relay station and check the video feed outside the Markie Dans pub in Oban on July twenty-fourth? It's on Victoria Crescent."

"What am I looking for?" The sound of computer keys clicked through the line.

"Remember those fellows I had ye run credit card checks on?"

"Aye."

"Things aren't adding up. I'd be much more comfortable if I had eyes on them for the night in question."

"On it. I'll call you back when I locate the CCTV feed."

"Thanks. Ta."

Sharidon pocketed his mobile and glanced up at Cairstie's bedroom window. Hopefully, the meds the doctor gave her helped her sleep. That bite caused her a great deal of pain.

"Adders don't live in the Outer Hebrides," Sharidon stated.

"I wasn't aware of that. There's plenty of them in the rest of Great Britain." Harry shoved his hands inside his jacket pockets.

"I wasn't aware either, not until the hospital gave Cairstie a bad time, so I searched her room for the snake. The thing tried to bite me when I caught it."

"What did you do with it?"

"Presented it to the doctor." Sharidon grinned at the memory of Dr. Smith's appalled expression when he handed him the writhing pillowcase. "Someone planted that snake. It didn't wander in from the garden." Anger boiled at the deliberateness of the action. He checked his watch.

"Time for Cairstie's meds. Hungry?" Sharidon pivoted and started for the house.

Harry fell in step beside him. "So, you like her, eh?"

"If I did, I sure wouldn't tell ye."

"She's young, Sharidon."

He didn't miss the warning in Harry's tone. "Don't ye think I know that?" The five years between him and Cairstie might as well be one hundred when it came to life experience.

"Relax." Harry clamped a hand on his shoulder. "I fell for Elise when she was eighteen. The Henderson girls pack a wallop—no matter their age."

"Yer telling me." Sharidon sighed, the air whooshing out. "Her presence is about to drive me mad. Another thing. She refused to go home when I explained how dangerous it was to stay here."

Harry laughed. "Sounds like you're the one who needs anti-serum."

"It's no laughing matter."

Sharidon's sat phone vibrated. He held up his index finger. "Hold on. It's Elise." He pressed the mobile to his ear. "What do ye have for me?"

"Nothing."

"What?" Sharidon snapped his brows together. He couldn't be hearing her right.

"All the CCTV cameras in Oban are in perfect working order, save for the one outside Markie Dans. It stopped operating twice on the night in question—for less than three minutes apiece and fifty-seven minutes apart. The second time was right after your three suspects paid their bills. Someone must have used an infrared light and overwhelmed the sensor." Admiration lit Elise's words.

Sharidon disconnected, then pressed both hands to his temples and corroded the air with Irish Gaelic. One of those three men was a mole, but he couldn't prove it.

Yet.

# CHAPTER 30

SAVE for the occasional trip upstairs to check on Cairstie, Sharidon spent the next eighteen hours tracking the three men in question until his eyes blurred and watered so much, he couldn't see the monitor, forcing him to apply wetting drops every few minutes to continue skimming Balivanich's CCTV footage.

Elise could have whipped through these in a quarter of the time. Unfortunately, she had other obligations. As for Harry, he left after their conversation on the beach and returned to Raasay in pursuit of his own investigation.

Of Sharidon's three suspects, Gordon MacRae's connection to the grocer's wife grated against his sense of morality. And Grace, a Chinese national half her husband's age, did as well.

And unlike MacDonald and Walker, who were Uist natives, MacRae hailed from Shetland. He also worked on The Deep Sea Testing Range.

Since leaving the navy, MacDonald returned to Benbecula and owned and operated the local pub from a converted crofter's cottage. Walker, the last of the three men, had expanded his father's tourist and fishing business and was married to the local schoolteacher.

Now that he had narrowed the suspects, he needed a thorough

analysis of their pasts. Too bad he couldn't haul them in on some trumped-up charge until he proved their connection to the Chinese.

Sharidon slipped out to the van and rang Nigel.

"Thatcher."

"Hey, Nigel. Can Cyber access the Naval records on Gordon MacRae, Randy MacDonald, and Hank Walker ASAP? All three men served on the *HMS Clairmont*. I'd also like some digging on the local grocer's wife, Grace Chen. She's a Chinese national who is spending time with MacRae."

"Sounds like you're making progress," Nigel said.

"Could be."

"Think you'll find answers?"

"I'm following a hunch." Something must have happened to one of those men to twist their loyalties. He wasn't buying money as the only reason for a betrayal of such magnitude.

"Anything else?" Nigel asked.

"No, sir."

"How's Lady Cairstie?"

"Sleeping." When he caught the man, Sharidon did not intend to go easy on him for hurting Cairstie.

"That's probably a good thing. Cyber will get right on it."

"Thank you, sir." Sharidon rang off and returned to the house.

If something spiked in one of these men's backgrounds, he couldn't leave Cairstie behind while he ran a recon. She needed to come with him —only this time, he'd see to it that she didn't disable his alarm system.

That leg of hers wouldn't stand up to rigorous activity. Nor would his, for that matter. Cairstie needed another form of protection.

Kneeling on the van's floor, he pried off a wall panel beneath the table and exposed his arsenal. Cairstie had missed it when she searched his van for tools. Bypassing two handguns, a knife, and several explosive devices, he retrieved his shotgun. After dumping ammo into his trousers' cargo pockets, he locked the van and glanced up at Cairstie's bedroom window.

Time to wake the sleeping beauty and see what she could do with a gun.

⚜

"Why are we doing this again?" Cairstie eyed Sharidon from the passenger seat as they headed south on the B888.

"We both need a break."

Winkle whined from his crate in the back.

"You too, Winkle." Sharidon glanced over his shoulder at the dog. "A wee leprechaun whispered that ye helped yer father thin his pheasant population."

"Everyone helps. Otherwise, Torwoodlee would be overrun with wildlife." Same with the deer. Grandfather let things go when he got up in years, and the deer multiplied so much that they ate too much of the vegetation, and erosion resulted. It wreaked havoc on the estate.

"What do ye do with the meat afterward?" Sharidon hit the blinker and exited the B-road onto a narrow track with a sign posted, "South Uist Clay Pigeon Club."

"We host a medieval event at the castle, and Dad contributes the pheasant and venison."

"No waste?" He glanced at her briefly, then focused on the road.

"Never. Dad's the biggest softie when it comes to wildlife. He only kills what's necessary."

"How much land does yer father own?" He pulled into the club's car park, and Sharidon set the brake outside a single-story white building.

"Twenty-seven thousand acres, plus he leases a few smaller estates."

Sharidon whistled. "I had no idea."

She shrugged. It wasn't something she liked to spread about. "My father considers himself more of a caretaker than an owner and manages the estates like a business. They're all tied to the title."

"Primogeniture laws are outmoded."

"Agreed, but no one desires to be known as the marquess who mismanaged the estate."

"I did not know yer father worked so hard." Sharidon jumped out of the cab and rounded the bonnet to open her door.

"Dad's companies employ hundreds of locals who would otherwise be forced to relocate if he shut down. He's been after Roddy for ages to come home and learn how to manage them."

Sharidon retrieved a shotgun from behind her seat. "Well, my deer-stalker, let's see how ye are at shooting clay pigeons."

They left Winkle in the van and trudged to the white building.

Fifteen minutes later, their attendant, a stocky fellow with weather-beaten skin and eyes the color of peat, set them up, facing a hill covered in bracken and gorse.

Sharidon loaded the shotgun while Cairstie placed protective coverings over her ears.

"Ladies first." Sharidon handed her the shotgun, the hint of a dare in his laughing green eyes.

So, he didn't think she could shoot? Bring it on. Cairstie stepped away before she betrayed herself with an eye roll. All the members of her family were excellent shots. They'd certainly had enough practice.

With the safety off, Cairstie stared down the gun barrel and noted the wind. "Pull," she yelled.

The attendant launched the clay pigeon from the trap with a clang.

She followed the disc as it arced across the gray sky, then positioned the shotgun to pick-up point. When the clay pigeon reached the apex over the northwest quadrant, she followed it to the break point. Holding her breath, she squeezed the trigger.

Boom.

The disc shattered, and a smile of satisfaction touched her lips as she placed her gun on the portable rack beside the trap.

"Not bad." Sharidon appeared unaffected by her shot.

Right. If that's how he chose to play this—fine. She set her jaw as he took his turn, a little late on pick-up point, but his shot rang dead center, shattering the pigeon to smithereens.

She retrieved her gun from the portable rack beside the attendant and snapped it together.

The wind gusted over the hilltop and whipped across the bracken. Cairstie placed weight on her lead leg, and called, "Pull."

Aware of the breeze's force, she adjusted her stance as the disc spewed from the trap. It whisked through the sky. She followed it to the break point and squeezed the trigger. The pigeon exploded.

Sharidon's eyes widened.

Warmth filled her. Never had she competed against anyone outside her family. Elise might be a better shot with a handgun and untouchable with knives, but Cairstie beat her sisters on the rifle and shotgun.

"Marvelous shot." Sharidon's tone sounded his approval.

"Thank you." As an influencer and model, she never shared this part of her life on social media, nor did she consider it a talent, simply a necessity for the estate. People who didn't grow up on farms rarely comprehended the precarious balance between wildlife, crops, and erosion. Keep everything in balance, and property thrived. Otherwise, the entire ecosystem would fail.

The wind picked up, and in seconds, the heavens opened, dousing them with the force of a firehose.

Cairstie squealed and tossed on her hood. She removed the ammo from her gun and pocketed it. Leaving the attendant to sort the equipment, she dashed to the clubhouse. Sharidon joined her a second later, carrying his shotgun with rivulets of water running down his face.

"I don't understand this. I checked the weather before we left; this storm was not expected until tonight," Sharidon said.

A tickle formed inside Cairstie's throat, and she bit the inside of her cheek to hold back a laugh.

Sharidon caught her expression. "What's so funny?"

"You, for believing a meteorologist's forecast. The Western Isles have some of the most volatile weather in the world." She chortled.

The attendant battled to open the door. "It's Baltic out there." He wiped his face with the back of his hand.

"There might be towelettes inside the ladies to dry yerself with," Sharidon said.

"Brilliant idea." Cairstie crossed to the ladies and eyed the hand dryer on the wall. Though not what she expected, she turned on the old-fashioned unit, and a blast of warm air burst forth. Bending, she stuck her head beneath the nozzle, and in no time, her thick, fine hair had dried.

With the help of a mirror, she finger-combed her tangled tressed and tossed it up into a messy bun with an elastic she found inside her jacket pocket. The sound of a dryer in the men's made her grin. Doubtless, Sharidon had done the same thing.

He rejoined her, his dark hair looking a bit wild but dry. She longed to run her fingers through it, but Sharidon had built a wall between them since the adder incident, keeping their relationship solely professional.

Some wee imp made her long to break that barrier, even when she knew he was right.

He needed to focus on his mission. Though he threatened more kissing in the future, she doubted things could remain status quo between them forever.

When the rain lessened, Sharidon, who had planted himself in front of the trophy case, looked up. "Shall we make a dash for it?"

"Aye," she agreed.

Tossing on their hoods, they sprinted through puddles to the van. Instead of opening the passenger door, Sharidon used the sliding one and bundled her inside, then slammed it shut behind him.

"Let me get the heater going. I have something ye can wear until the weather clears."

"Aren't we going home?" That seemed the logical option.

"I promised a break from our troubles and intend to keep my word."

He removed a tracksuit from a cupboard over the bed, with trousers of soft jersey material that tied at the waist. "Ye'll need to roll up the sleeves, but this will at least be warm."

Hesitantly, she took the tracksuit and bit her bottom lip—internally squirming at her present dilemma.

"I'll change in the cab." Sharidon grabbed a jumper and jeans, then squeezed himself between the two front seats and pulled the dividing curtain between the cab and the camper section closed between them.

In privacy, Cairstie peeled off her soggy clothes, then tugged on the overlarge tracksuit. Sharidon had narrow hips, but even though she stood five feet nine in her bare feet, he beat her by more than eight centimeters. She rolled up the sleeves and draped her wet clothes over the back of one of the chairs.

The van had warmed by the time Sharidon reappeared. His hair looked as though he did something to his dark, shiny locks. Her fingers prickled to touch it, and she glanced away before he read her expression. The fellow was much too perceptive for his own good.

He dumped his clothes inside a bag hanging in the shower. She crinkled her nose that he kept his laundry in the same space as his composting toilet.

"What?" Sharidon clicked on the overhead lights supplied by the solar panels outside the van. "I keep smelly things in there until they're clean."

"I hadn't considered how you handled life in such a compact space." Cairstie eyed the van in a new light. "This layout is well thought out."

"I agree." Sharidon washed his hands in the basin and turned off the tap. Beside him stood a two-burner cooker built into the base cabinet. "All the mod cons of home."

She raised a brow.

"It's not wild camping, which I thought I'd be doing on this assignment." He brewed a pot of tea, filled her cup, and added her favorite herbal packet without asking. Sharidon accessed an overhead cupboard, withdrew a deck of cards, and tossed them onto the table before her.

"Poker, Hearts, or Kings in the Corner?" he asked.

"I haven't played Kings in the Corner since childhood."

He rubbed his palms together. "Prepare to lose."

"Not hardly." She laughed.

And they were off, battling one against the other throughout the next two games. He won the first. She took the honors for the return match.

"Last and final?" She tipped her head and dared him to give up.

"Yer on."

She shuffled the deck and distributed the cards, setting them on the table between them.

"How'd ye get so good at this?" he asked.

"Lucky, I guess. Why?"

He glanced at his hand while pink tinged his ears.

Then it hit her.

"Did you think that because I struggle to read, it spills over onto everything else?" She refused to let him off easy.

While he had holed up inside the dining room, she practiced her lessons, and her reading steadily improved.

"Lass, I'm sorry. Forget I said anything."

"I don't think so, Sharidon. You wouldn't have asked if you weren't curious. Numbers and pictures aren't an issue; I have an excellent memory."

"Do ye count cards?"

"No. But I can, if necessary." She had a knack for it.

"To win?" he asked.

"Only when I play against my brother." She lowered her voice conspiratorially.

"Why only him?"

"Because he told me and my sisters that when he inherited Dad's title, he intended to send us to the gatehouse and lock us out of the castle."

"And ye believed him?" Sharidon chuckled, the deep sound turning her insides to jelly.

She shrugged. "Perhaps."

"That was a young lad trying to exert power over one too many sisters. The three of ye outnumbered him."

"Roddy holds his own. He once bound Elise and threatened to burn her at the stake."

Sharidon's hands stilled on his cards. "How old was he?"

"I don't know. I don't remember the incident, but when Dad found out, he shipped Roderick off to public school."

"Not too old then."

"Old enough," she argued.

"My brother and I were forever boasting about who was stronger, smarter, or braver than the other. Once, we jumped off the barn loft after Dad removed the hay bales below to prove our manliness."

"What happened?" She leaned forward and accidentally brushed his hand, erupting a plethora of electric sparks.

"I broke my leg, and Paddy fractured his collarbone."

She rolled her eyes. "You were lucky to survive. Are boys always so idiotic?"

"Almost always." He winked, setting the twinkles dancing in the green depths of his eyes. "We believe we're invincible."

"Did that spill over into your present-day profession?" Had he felt the same jolt she had?

"Ach." He screwed up his face and huffed a laugh. "I should have seen that one coming." He glanced out the window at the rain. "It doesn't appear to be letting up. I'm sorry our shooting match ended in such a shamble. From what I saw, though, yer a dab hand with a shotgun."

"We're all decent shots, even Mother. She's surprisingly good with firearms."

Sharidon gathered their mugs, washed them in the basin, and put them away.

"I suppose it's back to the house." A sinking sensation filled her at the idea of returning.

Sharidon eyed her for a second, then squeezed her shoulder. "We're both tired of being cooped up. Why don't we try out that restaurant on North Uist, the one that opened last month?"

Any slight change was big news in the Uists.

"That would be grand." She brightened at the mere mention of not returning to the house.

"Brilliant." He checked his sat phone. "The worst of the storm isn't due until later this evening. We've plenty of time."

Scottish weather didn't always cooperate, but Cairstie refused to share that tidbit, so she climbed into the passenger seat.

Outside, the drenched landscape and low-lying clouds appeared ominous. Puddles saturated the earth, and the rain showed no sign of slowing. If the wind kicked in, the electricity would go right along with the internet masts.

# CHAPTER 31

HORIZONTAL RAIN BEAT against the restaurant's windows, and fierce gusts rattled the panes. The power flickered. Sharidon polished off his trifle and glanced at Cairstie—who looked exceptionally chic in his over-large tracksuit. He didn't want to rush her, but the causeway between the two islands would be undrivable if they didn't leave soon.

Cairstie set down her fork, and her gaze flitted to the ocean booming against the rocky beach, not twenty meters from where he'd parked the van. The center of the storm had roared in hours earlier than predicted, and most of the patrons had cleared the restaurant within the last few minutes.

"Are ye finished?" Sharidon indicated her half-eaten sticky toffee pudding.

"Aye."

Sharidon motioned for the bill just as his sat phone vibrated. He checked the number and groaned. Nigel. He couldn't avoid answering.

He placed his card on the table. "I'm dreadfully sorry, but I need to answer this."

Cairstie nodded. "I understand." But a pucker of worry furrowed the skin between her brows, and her gaze darted to the storm outside the windows.

It had strengthened during their meal.

He pushed back from the table. "Sorry for the rush."

The interaction between him and the home office remained minimal on most assignments, but this case had too many moving parts and required constant information sharing. Too many lives were at risk if they didn't find this mole.

He entered the men's and checked every stall to ensure he was alone before he rang Nigel back. "Hiya, Nigel."

"This case has more layers than an onion," Nigel greeted him. "We did a deep dive on your sailors. All three served together with Agent Wang."

Sharidon whistled through his teeth.

"Wang, MacRae, and MacDonald were members of the same detonation team—all skilled marksmen too."

"That explains the explosives and the cluster shots on Mansfield's chest," Sharidon said.

"It gets better. Bo Chen, your Chinese grocer? His wife's father is head of China's Ministry of State Security."

Brilliant. Sharidon tugged at his hair and paced to the far wall. Gordon MacRae was involved with a woman who had links to China's intelligence community.

Anger bunched inside his jaw. MacRae worked for Quantas, the contracting firm that ran The Deep Sea Range for the home office. Was he linked to the sinking?

"Did they find anything on the recovered electronic boards from the *HMS Lilibet*?"

"The MoD purchased circuit boards from a supplier in the States, but that was just a pass-through. The boards were manufactured in China."

Sharidon's right eye twitched. "Can we prove the Chinese blew up the *Lilibet*?"

"Affirmative."

"How?" If China disabled or destroyed the UK's firing power, they could easily take over the country.

"Not twenty minutes ago, long-distance transmitters with the capability to adjust missile controls were discovered on the *Lilibet's* warheads. We dispatched a brief to the admiralty and our other military personnel to cease all live-fire drills until every electronic circuit board is inspected."

"That will take forever. Have you sent someone to pick up MacRae?" Sharidon's eye twitch picked up an irritating rhythm.

Thatcher's voice heated. "MacRae's gone missing."

"On it." Sharidon started for the exit just as the power flickered, browned out, popped back on, then went out, leaving him in utter darkness. "Any details I should know?" He edged forward with his left arm in front of him to guide his way to the exit.

"MacRae slipped his lead while on The Deep Sea Range. He's not at home or the Chinese takeaway in Balivanich."

"What about Grace Chen?" Sharidon reached the wall and followed it until he found the door, then pushed it wide.

"She's missing too," Thatcher said.

And he'd been sitting here like a gombeen with the traitor in plain sight. Ach. For a while, he'd even suspected MacDonald—an error on his part. Had his feelings for Cairstie distracted him so profoundly that it put him off his game?

He rubbed his temple where a headache throbbed, then left the loo for the restaurant's main dining room. Weak light filtered through the windows. He scanned the tables for Cairstie. She stood near the exit, her focus on the fierce sheet of rain.

"Any more surprises?" he asked Nigel.

"Negative. With what you had to work with, you've done a brilliant job narrowing it down. That was a stroke of genius to dive into old military records."

Sharidon grunted his acknowledgement. "I've got to run." He pocketed his sat phone, crossed to Cairstie, and touched her back.

"Thank you for the meal. Here's your credit card. The server ran it through before the power went." Cairstie's gaze sharpened on him as she passed him the plastic. "Are you quite all right?"

"Yeah, but we won't be if the causeway is underwater."

She indicated the causeway through the window. "We'll be drenched by the time we reach the van. I'm hoping you have another tracksuit for me to wear." Wry humor tinged her words.

"Then it's a good thing I do. Ready?" Taking her hand, they darted outside to the van.

Rain pelted them, stinging any exposed skin with icy water. A wave hit the shore and spewed salt spray into his eyes. He opened the side door and climbed aboard on Cairstie's heels.

With his mind still on Nigel's conversation, he retrieved another tracksuit for Cairstie and a T-shirt and pair of trousers for himself.

"Thank you." Cairstie accepted the suit.

Dripping water, he climbed into the cab, shut the curtain, between the cab from the camper, and then tugged off his clothes. Where would MacRae have gone to ground? The ferries were canceled, and no one with an iota of sense would attempt to cross The Minch in a small watercraft.

But then, desperate people often did foolish things.

At first light, he slipped down to the marina and jumped aboard Walker's boat, storing his rifle and scope under the seat. Rumors had circulated that *Miss* Henderson and Will Sherwood had not returned from North Uist last night.

With everyone out searching for the MacTavish family, he intended to handle some hunting himself.

He pressed the key fob and let the engine tick over. Did *Miss* Henderson think no one would check on her? He snorted.

The Marquess of Roxbury's youngest had taken up residence here in the Uists, doubtless to hide from the British press due to her association with Lord Ahern, a man sentenced to fifteen years for attempted murder and horse doping.

And the silly chit worked for his wife!

No one made Nicola a laughingstock. No one. As for the blasted Bible that he removed from Mrs. McDougal's, it had proven entirely worthless. He chucked it in the fire after scouring every page for a micro-dot.

Whatever Mrs. McDougal's list had once contained, nothing remained of it. And just in case *Lady* Cairstie Henderson had seen something that night in the old woman's study, she was a loose end and might give him away.

And he always tied up loose ends.

# CHAPTER 32

CAIRSTIE PRESSED a hand to her chest and fought to get her breathing under control. She and Sharidon needed to reach the causeway. She clung to the hand grip as the van jounced along the lollipop, a circular carriageway on North Uist's outer rim road that connected the causeway to the long single track down the Uists' spine.

"Stop. Stop," Cairstie yelled over the storm, beating against the van's metal interior door.

From the passenger seat, she could see what Sharidon could not: the water had destroyed the road on her side of the van.

Sharidon backed up and turned around, then started along an alternate route. Rain cascaded in waterfalls down the hillsides and covered the road.

"There's too much water. We'll never reach the causeway. We need to find high ground." Sharidon turned around yet again, leaving the low-lying plain and starting up a deeply rutted track, the tarmac little more than a stream.

"What if the hillside collapses?" Cairstie clenched both hands, her gaze riveted on the farmhouse at the crest.

"Too much granite. I doubt there's enough earth up here for a mudslide," Sharidon spoke with confidence.

Cairstie prayed he was right. One of her childhood friends had drowned when a riverbank crumbled beneath her while out hillwalking with her family. Though the current situation had nothing in common with her friend's passing, torrential downpours and flooding made Cairstie anxious.

Sharidon took the hill at a slow crawl. A few hundred meters below the farmhouse, he pulled into a level area beside a dilapidated outbuilding and set the brake.

"We should be fine here until the storm abates." Sharidon gave her a reassuring smile. "Why don't ye try and get some sleep."

"What about you?"

"The passenger seat reclines."

Winkle whined from his crate.

"I need to let him out, or neither of us will get any rest." Cairstie slipped into the back of the van and clipped Winkle's lead to his collar before she opened the side door.

The dog might still be a puppy, but he was no fool. He looked at the rain, did his business, and jumped inside. Before he could shake off the excess water, Sharidon draped a towel over the dog and gave him a thorough rub down.

Cairstie cocked her head to the side, her brows rising in surprise.

"What?" Sharidon asked.

"How did you know he was going to shake?"

"When I was a lad, we had a Labrador who loved to swim in our pond. She had a habit of waiting to shake until after she came inside. Mum was forever hollering for one of us to grab a towel before Lucy splattered the floor and tracked mud through the house."

"Your mother trained you well."

"I'll be sure to pass that on to her when she scolds me for dirtying her floor."

His ludicrous comment eased some of the tension the storm brought on.

"Do you think Mrs. McDougal's house will flood?" The question had burned in her mind as they struggled to find higher ground. Water damage took forever to repair in the Uists and would likely force her off Benbecula with the white flag of failure tucked between her legs.

"Ye should be in good form. The electronic pump is wired to the automatic generator."

"How do you know all this?"

"The day I replaced the cord on yer cooker, I checked the house for other issues. I came across it then. A lot of the lads up at the pub install them in their homes, doubtless due to the frequency of power cuts."

She exhaled. The Hebrides had their fair share of storms. Their backup power gave her a tremendous sense of peace. If Mrs. MacLeod had one of her own, Cairstie would worry less about her eccentric neighbor.

"Let me grab one of the blankets off the bed, and we'll be set for lights out. I don't want to use up the battery power. We might be stuck here for a few days."

Sharidon reclined in his chair, and Cairstie clicked off the lights beside the bed.

Never one to brood and emboldened by the dark, she rolled onto her side, facing Sharidon, and voiced the question uppermost in her mind. "Have I done something to set you against me?"

"How do ye mean?" he asked.

"Have I offended you?"

"Not in the least."

"I must have done because you've shut yourself off from me."

He groaned. "Lass, if ye knew how much I long to kiss ye, ye wouldn't be saying this. I've a job to do and can't muck it up just now with courting ye."

His unloverlike declaration made Cairstie smile. She shifted onto her back and stared at the ceiling above her. "I was just making sure."

He must compartmentalize, much like Dad. For some reason, that assured her more than any romantic affirmation ever could.

Winkle whined, then let out a disgruntled woof.

"Sharidon?" she pleaded.

"Let him out. He'll keep us awake if ye don't."

Leaning over the side of the bed, she fumbled for the latch on Winkle's kennel and freed him. The dog scampered to Sharidon, who scratched his ear. "There's a lad. Tired of your cage?"

A rustle and a creak from Sharidon's chair, and he stepped across the van and placed Winkle on the mattress beside her. "Never thought I'd be jealous of a dog," Sharidon grumbled as he returned to his makeshift bed.

Winkle snuggled beside her and placed his head on her stomach.

"Thank you, Irish." The body heat emitting from Winkle was nothing compared to the warmth around her heart. Smiling, she drifted off to sleep.

Winkle's nasty breath woke her. The storm had passed, and intermittent sunshine dappled the window. She glanced to the passenger seat where Sharidon slept. Quietly, she slipped on her boots and jacket, then eased open the door and climbed out to relieve her dog.

A chill breeze tangled her hair, so she gathered it and tucked it inside her hood. The hills at the island's southern end led to flat bogs and multiple lochs. An impressionistic sea sparkled in the distance like blue topaz.

What a difference a day made from yesterday's storm. Movement up the drive drew her gaze as she turned away. A woman ambled down the lane toward her.

Cairstie made a wild grab for Winkle's collar, but he darted to the newcomer. On reaching her, instead of jumping or barking, he wiggled his tail and emitted high-pitched sounds of eagerness from his throat.

"Do you mind if I give him a treat?" the woman called, keeping her eyes on Winkle.

"Not at all. I've never seen him behave this way."

"Most animals like me." The woman held a treat in the palm of her hand. Winkle took it between his teeth and swallowed it whole.

"Oh, you're a greedy one, are you?" the woman asked.

The van door opened behind Cairstie. She glanced over her shoulder as Sharidon stuck his head out, dark stubble on the lower half of his face. He removed his hand from his hip and hopped to the ground when he saw they had company. His mussed hair and whiskers stole her breath, and she longed to caress the rough texture on his chin. She slammed the lid on those thoughts and looked away, swallowing hard.

"I came down to see if you folks survived the storm." Static broadcast erupted from her pocket, and she withdrew a handheld, battery-operated device. "I'm operating the radio this morning while the community's out searching. We've a bit of an emergency."

"Can we help?" Sharidon asked.

"The MacTavish family went missing last night. Their house flooded before the power went out. They called their gran to see if they could stay with her—but they never arrived."

"Do ye know if they left the house?" Sharidon asked.

"They were seen driving toward the causeway. Two of our volunteers found their abandoned car. We've divided the rescue teams into land and sea quadrants."

A huge knot formed in Cairstie's stomach. The woman hadn't said she feared the MacTavish family had been swept out to sea, but it was implied.

"Some of the coves and caves need searching. We've men out on boats, but they can't get close enough to the caves. Most of our rescue teams are getting on in years and can't do what they once did. Do you think you can handle the out-of-way areas?"

"I've a map and am happy to volunteer if ye can ye show me where the coves and caves are located," Sharidon said.

"Aye." The woman bobbed her head.

Sharidon nipped back to the van, popped open the passenger door, and dug through the glove box, returning with a detailed map of North Uist.

Cairstie drew out her mobile. If she could access Google Maps, she could help.

"I'm afraid the masts are down." The woman indicated Cairstie's mobile. "It'll take days before the internet is working again. It's always like this after a gale blows through."

Winkle sniffed the woman's shoe. "You smell my hens." She scratched his ear. "I'm Hannah Iverson, by the way."

"Will Sherwood, this is Cairstie Henderson."

"Nice to meet both of you."

"How did ye hear about the search, Mrs. Iverson?" Sharidon's voice quieted, the way it did when he focused.

"I've a handheld radio device. We use them when we're cut off."

"How can you reach everyone? The signal only goes so far." Cairstie had used short-distance radios with her siblings when out on the estate.

"We work it like a relay system."

Sharidon flattened his map and held the corners to keep it from tearing in the breeze. "Whereabout are those caves ye mentioned?"

"Right here." Mrs. Iverson pointed to several dots along the north coast.

"How will I contact ye if we find the family?" Sharidon folded the map.

"I've a spare radio and can contact the restaurant. They'll relay to Fire and Rescue Service, and—"

"Brilliant." Sharidon took Cairstie by the elbow. "Let's go. Every minute counts if we hope to find them alive."

Mrs. Iverson spoke into her radio. "I've a few more recruits to help search. They're heading for the north coast to cover the caves and coves."

A babble of Gaelic burst through the radio.

"Aye, Fergus. I've got a spare." Mrs. Iverson dug into her capacious pocket and handed Sharidon a second radio. "It's set to the same channel." She switched back to her native tongue and spoke to the unknown Fergus.

"Come, Winkle," Cairstie called to the puppy.

He ignored her, sniffing and wagging his tail at Mrs. Iverson. Sighing heavily, Cairstie hoisted the dog in her arms. The puppy wriggled, doing his best to get down.

Sharidon took hold of him. "There now, Winkle. Be a love."

The dog licked Sharidon's chin as he carried him to the van.

Winkle whined when they backed out and started down the hill.

"Should I be insulted?" Cairstie shifted and glanced over her shoulder at her dog. He had jumped onto the bed and plastered his nose to the back window, small whimpers emitting from his throat.

"I think Mrs. Iverson's a dog whisperer." Cairstie bit her lip. She always kept her more fanciful thoughts to herself. Models were too sophisticated to be superstitious, but thanks to Nanny's bedtime stories, she privately accepted a bit of Scottish folklore.

A few years ago, when Elise was seriously injured, Cairstie visited a Clootie Well, an ancient spring where she made a wish for Elise's healing. Afterward, she tied her best hair ribbon to a tree branch beside the spring for an offering and slunk away before anyone saw her.

"Perhaps Mrs. Iverson's been touched by the fairies." A smile lilted through Sharidon's voice. "The seventh child of a seventh child and all that comes with it."

Was he mocking her? Cairstie shifted, unable to meet his eyes.

Sharidon swung the van onto a narrow, unpaved track, rattling the crockery and pans inside the cupboards.

"Who taught you folklore?" she asked.

"My mum. And ye?"

"Nanny."

"Ah. I once made the mistake of sharing my thoughts on fairies with a co-worker. It didn't go over well. Granted, he was worried about yer sister at the time."

Cairstie's eyes rounded. "You mentioned fairies to Harry?" She could only imagine how her practical brother-in-law responded to that.

"Not my best moment, I'll admit." His gaze shifted from hers. "I was trying to ease his mind."

"Has Harry mentioned it since?"

"He thought I was teasing and told me I had a double-hinged tongue."

Cairstie leaned back in her seat. "I'll bet you played right along with it."

"Of course." He winked. No mocking. No tormenting. Just acceptance.

"Hungry?" he asked while taking a circuitous route to dodge the massive lakes made by the storm.

"Aye."

"I've sausage rolls in the fridge. Not the breakfast of champions, but they're filling."

"Sounds lovely." Cairstie unbuckled her safety belt and tottered toward the kitchen. She clung to the worktop to keep from toppling over as the van bounced down the narrow track.

She opened the fridge door and spied the sausage rolls and several cans of Irn Bru. Snatching their unusual breakfast, she returned to the passenger seat.

"How much further is it to those coves, do you think?" She handed Sharidon one of the sausage rolls and set the drinks in the cup holders.

"Thanks." He bit into his roll, chewed for a time, then swallowed. "I reckon it's another kilometer, but it could take a while."

The boggy plain stretched to the sea, unlike the hills of the southern part of the island.

"If we run into too much bog, we'll need to leg it the rest of the way."

After several more jaw-jarring bounces, Sharidon rolled to a stop and set the parking brake. "End of the line." He nodded toward the rocky coves. "I can't get us any closer, or the van will sink to her axles."

Using Sharidon's map, they squelched through the muck, their shoes making slurping noises beneath their feet as they started for the first cove. Winkle raced before them, his tail waving like a standard in the breeze.

Cairstie halted at the cliff's edge. Waves crashed against the shore several meters below the high-water mark, the din unnaturally loud inside the cove. Piles of yellow-green seaweed interspersed with tangled bits of fishing twine had washed ashore from yesterday's storm, and whitecaps danced further out, the sea still unsettled after the gale. The skerries appeared reachable by foot due to the low tide.

Inside the cove, two wooden dories bobbed in the water, doubtless tied there by local lobstermen whose buoyed pots rode the swells a meter off the headland. Winkle raced after a seagull, barking like mad.

"Winkle. Come here." Cairstie whistled, but the dog ignored her. If things weren't so dire for the MacTavish family, she'd run to catch him, but after a night in the elements, every minute counted in finding the MacTavish family.

"He'll come back." Sharidon read her distress and offered his assurance. "According to the map—" Sharidon glanced at the diagram in his hands—"one of the sea caves is down there. I'll check it out and be right back."

Cairstie nodded and sent a prayer that the MacTavish family would be found. Pivoting, Sharidon started down a well-worn trail leading into the cove. She edged closer to the drop to follow his progress.

On reaching the beach, he waved, rounded a pile of debris, and disappeared into the cave. The waves rolled in as she waited, their rhythmic crashes soothing after her fears of the night.

She turned about. Where had Winkle run off to? She spun in a slow circle this time and scanned the shore.

Movement on one of the closer skerries caught her gaze, where a small dark object trotted across the rocky surface.

A holler from below.

She leaned forward as Sharidon exited the sea cave. The lower part of his jeans was wet like he'd waded through the water.

She cupped her hands around her mouth. "Anything?"

"No." He motioned for her to join him.

Picking her way to the trailhead, she descended, careful of her leg, stepping over clumps of sea pinks and loose stones to attain the beach. It had already taken thirty minutes for her and Sharidon to gain the cove and search the cave.

The wind whistled in off the sea. Sharidon sat on a boulder and removed his wellies. Tearing off his socks, he wrung them out, the water streaming onto the sand beside him before he tugged them back on and shoved his feet inside his rubber boots.

"The tide's rising. We'll be blocked if we don't investigate the next cove quickly."

She swallowed. What a fine time for Winkle to have run off.

"There's a small trail against the sea stack on the far side of the cove that leads to the next cave." He pointed to an arched stack they needed to traverse to reach the adjoining cove.

She bit her lip.

"What's wrong?"

"Winkle's out on one of the skerries."

"He can swim, can't he?"

"Aye, but the ocean currents..." The tide was coming in, not out, and Winkle was still a pup, albeit a large one.

"He'll be fine. If you're up to helping, this shouldn't take much over thirty minutes."

Sharidon had the right of it when it came to a choice between people or animals, but that didn't ease the worry knotting inside her. Winkle might not be the brightest dog, but she loved him.

They picked their way across the boulder-strewn cove to the trail under the narrow archway into the adjoining inlet. Here, rocks rose steeply above them, with no exit save for how they entered. Sharidon stopped to pull up his sock. She passed him, anxious to check the cave and return to Winkle.

Halfway across the rock-strewn beach, a man appeared on the rim above her with a rifle slung over his shoulder. His back was to the light and obscured his features.

"Take cover," Sharidon yelled.

Her heart pounded like mad as she darted for the cave. Something pinged beside her. An explosion followed. It echoed off the cliff walls a beat later. Leaping over a mound of seaweed, she landed on loose rocks and jarred her ankle.

Gasping, she limp-ran, her eyes on the cave's opening. *Please. Please. Please,* she prayed.

More shots.

A sting as she entered the dark crevice in the rock wall. Water covered the cave floor. The tide was rising. Her leg buckled, and she fell onto her knees, her chest heaving from the run.

Only then did she notice the blood.

# CHAPTER 33

SHARIDON CROUCHED beside the stone arch and reloaded his firearm. The cartridge snapped into place as he scanned the rim. He had drawn the fellow's fire so Cairstie could gain the cave. That last shot had been close. Much too close.

The shooter possessed serious skills but hadn't allowed for the wind. With Cairstie tucked safely out of the line of fire, Sharidon skidded to a halt behind a boulder.

His pulse throbbed like his motorbike at top speed. He scooted forward and peeked around the massive stone. The man stood on the cliff with his rifle barrel aimed at the inlet. He appeared a mite too tall for Gordon, but Sharidon was uncertain at this distance.

He gauged the gap to the next boulder. Too far. He'd never make it. He retreated to the arch and sloshed through the rising water, colored stones under his feet. The rocks gave him an idea, not a spectacular one, but the only one he could come up with.

Fishing about the chill sea water, he grasped a stone the size of a tennis ball, drew back, and lobbed it. The rock clattered as it struck the beach.

The man jerked and aimed his rifle where the stone landed. Sharidon got a look at his face and shook his head. Well. Well. Well. MacDonald—

the bartender. He and Agent Wang had not only served on the same detonation team, they'd also been partners.

Randy edged along the rim in Sharidon's direction, his rifle still aimed at the cove. Sharidon gripped another rock and chucked it closer than the first. It landed in a clump of heather a few meters away.

Hunching, Randy zipped along the rim toward the heather and sprayed bullets into the bushes where the pebble landed.

Satisfaction welled within Sharidon. The fellow had come undone.

Randy approached the edge above the clump of heather, bringing himself within Sharidon's handgun range. He drew himself up, his heart pulsing in his ears. He cocked his gun and stepped out from behind the stone arch.

Ethics kept him from shooting. "Drop your gun, Randy," Sharidon called. "I don't want to kill you."

He swung in Sharidon's direction, raised his rifle, and aimed.

Sharidon squeezed the trigger. Pop.

Randy's eyes widened, and he toppled backward.

Sharidon inhaled sharply, his hand shaking. He detested taking a life, self-defense or not.

Crossing under the arch, he entered the first cove, ran across the beach to the trail, and climbed the path to the rim, his leg straining at the steep incline. Winded, Sharidon reached the top and jogged to the next cove, his gun arm extended.

Randy lay crumpled in the mud with his rifle beside him.

Sharidon kicked the weapon out of reach, knelt, and unzipped the fellow's jacket to see if he could save him. The hole in his left breast had him zipping it right back up.

"Why?" A lot of people died at this traitor's hands. "Why betray yer country?"

Randy struggled for breath. "Naval coverup outside Shanghai. Poisoned water. So many died . . ." he rasped.

Unfortunately, that happened. Sharidon himself witnessed one or two egregious things that had tried his patriotism, but overall, the UK had the better good in its sights. Randy lost his perspective over one horrendous incident and lost the big picture—and his betrayal led to disastrous results.

Randy opened his mouth, wrestling to speak.

Sharidon crouched beside him, the rocks digging into his bad knee.

"Tell Nicola I love her." Randy's breath rattled, and his breathing slowed. "Sorry about . . . Wang," he whispered.

Randy's chest rose twice, then stilled. Sharidon checked for a pulse but found none.

He sat back on his heels as his stomach roiled. He had killed a traitor, yet no elation stirred, only relief that Cairstie and the test facilities were safe from China's insidious plans.

With effort, he struggled to his feet, pulled out his sat phone, and pressed Nigel's number. His gaze slid out to sea where birds circled, their discordant cries mirroring his emotions.

"Thatcher."

"Nigel. I found our traitor. He's dead. Self-defense."

"I'll send a chopper. I've got your coordinates."

"Thanks." Sharidon pocketed his sat phone with shaky fingers and exhaled.

It was over. Cairstie was safe. He descended into the first cove and sloshed through thigh-high water through the arch to reach the inlet beyond.

The Atlantic had not paused its tidal race during his shootout with Randy. His heart stopped. The ocean had swallowed the cave's entrance—the one where Cairstie sheltered. He rushed across the rocky beach and skidded to a halt. His nostrils flared, and his breath rasped. Only a dive team could enter the cavern under these conditions.

Had Cairstie noticed the rising water? Or was she too afraid to leave the cave?

Though futile, he cupped his mouth and yelled, "Cairstie. Cairstie."

His heart tumbled, mimicking the waves breaking on the shore, and he stared unseeing out to sea. Cairstie. Tears blurred his vision. He had given her his word that he would protect her.

He might have killed a traitor, but he was responsible for the death of the woman he loved.

Sharidon spun away and floundered through the water to the arch. A head bobbed in the sea, then disappeared behind a swell. He reached the beach beyond, his eyes scanning the water. A seal?

Or was it... Sharidon squinted, his heart galloping. Someone was in the water.

He shot across the beach, tripping in his haste. Had the tide carried Cairstie out past the end of the cove? A few minutes in that water caused hypothermia.

Gaining the cove beyond, he untied one of the two wooden boats and shoved off, grasping the oars. His stomach churned as seasickness took immediate hold. He couldn't be sick. The person in the water needed help.

His stomach kinked. Unable to keep the nausea at bay, he hurled, upchucking his breakfast without taking his eyes off the spot where he had last seen that head.

Another swell, and he was sure. Cairstie lay on her back, barely above the water, the rip tide taking her.

His mouth watered, and he leaned over the side and hurled again. Blast this queasy stomach of his. He wiped his mouth with the back of his hand, then took up the oars and cleared the cove.

Dip. Pull. Dip. Pull. Dip. Pull.

Once more, his stomach rebelled. He gagged and retched until nothing was left but bile. He didn't have time to be sick. Cairstie could die.

Barking drew him from his misery. Cut off by the tide, Winkle raced to the end of a skerry not three meters off his port bow. Sharidon reapplied the oars and drew alongside Cairstie.

"Cairstie. Can ye hear me, lass?"

She opened her eyes, her face white as death, her lips blue.

He leaned over the side and extended an oar. "Grab this, and I'll pull you in."

"I can't," she mouthed.

He dumped the oars into the bottom of the boat, tore off his jacket, shoes, shirt, and sat phone, then horizontally balanced himself across the narrow, wooden boat, bracing his toes on one side. He leaned over and grasped her under the arms.

Cairstie didn't weigh much, but she was tall, and dragging her into the boat took some doing. While he hauled her aboard, they drifted further out. On seeing them, Winkle yipped, his high-pitched cries carrying across the water. He zipped back to the opposite end of the skerry and tugged at something blue.

"Winkle," Cairstie murmured as Sharidon wrapped her inside his jacket. Her feet were bare. She must have lost her wellies. Then he saw the blood.

He opened the coat he had wrapped around her. Blood dripped sluggishly from her side. "Father in Heaven, save this lass," he prayed.

Closing the coat once more around her, he snatched both oars. Cairstie needed immediate attention. Angling the boat, he ran it aground on the skerry. Winkle rushed over and hopped inside. Wriggling and yipping like a tiny pup, he first licked Cairstie in the face, then him.

"Sorry, old man." Sharidon pushed him aside, ripped both sleeves from his shirt, and created a pad from the main torso section of his top to quench the flow. Then, he eased the hem of Cairstie's tracksuit and applied the compress to her flesh.

Randy had shot her.

All that time, he thought she was safe inside the cave. Fool. He chastised himself as he knotted the sleeves together and tied them around Cairstie's waist to hold the pad. He needed to get her to the van. She was too cold. "Oh, Lord. Please help us."

Winkle barked, drawing his attention.

"Winkle." He glanced up from Cairstie long enough to spot a ratty blue tarp similar to the one that had covered Mansfield's body. Long dark hair waved in the water where the body had snagged on the skerry's jagged rocks. He did not doubt that he had just discovered Agent Wang.

Fury surged, driving away his nausea.

Sharidon climbed from the boat and dragged the corpse by the heels onto higher ground, where the incoming tide couldn't wash it away. Winkle followed him. With the dog's collar clutched in his hand, he climbed back.

Cairstie lay where he'd left her, barely conscious. He adhered to first aid guidelines, supporting her against his body and positioning Winkle to lie against her back. Any warmth the two of them produced might save her.

He picked up the oars and rowed to shore, the tide, for once, in his favor, and the waves helping run them aground near the van. The wind whipped mercilessly. He tugged on his wellies, pocketed his sat phone, then lifted Cairstie in his arms.

Winkle trotted beside them, whining profusely and nudging Cairstie's legs with his nose until they arrived at the Sprinter. Once inside, he laid Cairstie on the bed, wrapped her in a blanket, and cranked up the heat.

Only his sat phone worked, and he rang the hospital on Benbecula.

"Uist and Barra Hospital," a harried woman answered.

"I need medical assistance immediately. Can you prepare a bed? I'm coming from North Uist. The victim has a gunshot wound and is suffering from hypothermia."

"Sir. The storm weakened the causeway. They closed it thirty minutes ago."

"Can ye send an air ambulance?" Sharidon tugged his hair.

"We can, but we've so many emergencies. The wait time is nearly two hours. I'm sorry. That's the best I can do until they arrive. I'll have a nurse coach you through triage."

"I understand." He gave her the coordinates for the air ambulance.

"I'll have a nurse call you when one is available. Ring if anything changes."

Triage. He inhaled several times. With anyone else, the situation wouldn't rattle him. This was different. Very different. Sharidon's brain kicked into gear after his initial panic subsided. Like all agents, he had triage training, and Cairstie needed every bit of it to survive.

By now, the van had warmed to a comfortable temperature, so he locked Winkle inside his kennel. The last thing he needed was a growling dog if Cairstie cried out in pain. Her eyes remained half open, but she didn't speak.

Inside his first-aid kit, he located the antiseptic, suture packet, a pair of surgical forceps, and gloves. He had no idea if the bullet had grazed her or lodged in something vital. With trembling hands, he unfastened the pad over her wound—then prayed he wouldn't kill her.

The next ten minutes were some of the worst of his life until he dropped the bullet into the mug. It was done.

Shaken more than he cared to admit, Sharidon dabbed Cairstie's wound with antiseptic. She had passed out partway through his barbaric surgery—a good thing. Her soft cries turned Winkle into a wild, snarling beastie. For a time, he feared the dog would break out of the kennel and attack. With her silence, the pup settled into low-throated growls.

Tossing the bloodied gauze in the bin, Sharidon turned on the tap and scrubbed his hands with hot soapy water. He leaned against the kitchen worktop, his leg weak as reaction set in.

He eyed the needle in his packet with distaste. Cairstie needed suturing. Sewing her back together did not appeal in the least. As a model, he doubted she'd be pleased with his handiwork. Stalling, he created a compress and applied it to her wound. Even while unconscious, Cairstie's brow twitched.

"Sorry, love," he murmured.

He avoided the sutures. They needed doing, but his stitches would forever mark and doubtless pucker that smooth skin of hers, but as the minutes passed, he set his jaw—no hope for it. He retrieved the packet and threaded the needle.

A whirl of blades followed by the deep throb of an engine made him pause. The air ambulance had arrived. Hallelujah. Relief oozed from his very pores as he reapplied the compress to Cairstie's side.

A tap sounded outside the van, and he had everything ready to hand over.

"Come," he called.

Agent Burke opened the side door. "I'm here to collect a body."

Sharidon blinked. MI6 had arrived for Randy MacDonald. In all the kerfuffle, he'd almost forgotten about ringing Nigel.

"Do you have medical training?" Sharidon asked. "We've an injured civilian in here."

"Dillardson was a military medic before he joined us."

"Excellent."

A few seconds later, Agent Dillardson entered the van and squeezed past Sharidon to reach the bed where Cairstie lay.

"What have we got?" Dillardson asked.

"Gunshot wound and possible hypothermia. I don't know how much blood she's lost. I fished her out of the ocean."

"Exit wound?" Dillardson pushed past him and washed his hands, his manner all business.

"No. The bullet was spent when it hit her. I removed it." Sharidon jerked his chin toward the cup on the worktop beside the basin.

"I'll have a look." Dillardson leaned over Cairstie and carefully removed the gauze pad. "You cleaned it?" Dillardson used the torch on his sat phone to inspect the injury.

"Yes."

"It doesn't appear that anything vital was hit. I'll suture her up. I'm more worried about her loss of blood."

On that, Sharidon heartily agreed. Another worry was how long she'd been in the water.

"Can ye . . ." Sharidon hesitated.

"Can I what?" Dillardson shot him a disgruntled look.

"She's a model. Can ye make the stitches even so they don't pucker her flesh?"

"Got it bad, eh?" A smile lifted the corner of Dillardson's mouth.

Sharidon quit the van. Dillardson could razz him all he wanted later, but he couldn't bear watching someone poke more holes into Cairstie's flesh.

# CHAPTER 34

Seated at her dressing table, Cairstie fumbled with the buttons on her cuffs, then picked up her matching black hat and gloves.

"Cairstie, darling. Are you sure you are up to this? You just left the hospital." Mother worried the clasp of her purse handle.

"I'm sure. I need to show my support. This community is in mourning."

"Army," Mother opened Cairstie's bedroom door. "I can't talk any sense into her. She insists on attending that funeral for the family who were swept out to sea."

Dad ducked to avoid the lintel as he entered Mrs. McDougal's small bedroom. "Janet, my dear, I think Cairstie's old enough to make her own decisions."

"She's only just left the hospital, and we're not prepared to attend a funeral dressed as we are." Mother indicated their clothing.

Dad winked at Cairstie, then scooped her up and carried her downstairs to her temporary pushchair. She was too weak to walk more than a dozen steps after her recent shooting and dip in the sea. The doctor insisted she needed to rest until her strength returned.

Mother clattered down the stairs behind them, protesting all the way.

"She must come home where she can be tended properly. This is a horrid place to convalesce."

Once, Cairstie might have rolled her eyes, but she had learned a thing or two since leaving home—one being that her parents had her best interests at heart.

"Mummy, I'm sorry I gave you a scare, but I'm not a wee bairn. I'll be careful."

Mother, the Marchioness of Roxbury, drew herself up to her full height, which wasn't much, but her commanding presence made up for her lack of inches. Her soft blue eyes misted, betraying very real concern. She kissed Cairstie's cheek and clung to her for a second before she let go.

"You'll always be my bairn, lass, even when you have children of your own." Mother's smile wobbled. "Well, what are you waiting for, Army? We have a funeral to attend."

"The general has spoken." Dad saluted, then pushed her outside to his Range Rover. Mother assisted her into the passenger seat while Dad stored her chair in the back.

"I assume you know where the chapel is?" Dad climbed behind the wheel and started the engine.

Cairstie bit the inside of her cheek at her father's method of gaining information. Mother used the direct method of attack, but Dad had a more subtle approach. His was no idle question but a fishing expedition to see if she attended church.

"Aye. Don't bother with the satnav. I can guide you there."

"Do you suppose that handsome friend of Harry's will be in attendance?" Mother leaned forward to buckle her seat belt on the bench behind them. "I quite liked him. He's a pleasant fellow. Very amiable. It was he who called us."

Sharidon? He had only popped by once to check on her last week.

"What was his name, again?" Mother's innocent tone didn't fool anyone. She met Sharidon at Elise's wedding.

Cairstie caught her father's smirk before she twisted in her seat to answer. "I call him Irish." She should warn Sharidon about using his alias around her parents. Is that why he had made himself scarce?

St. Mary's Chapel stood on a rise, surrounded by tall grass. It had a commanding presence for such a wee chapel—much like Mother.

Cars lined both sides of the unpaved road, and islanders dressed in subdued colors queued outside to enter the vestibule.

"Goodness. I've never seen so many turn out for a funeral." Mother gazed at the large group of mourners.

"The islanders are a tight-knit group. The MacTavish's loss has hit them hard. When they went missing, everyone helped."

The clouded expressions and downcast eyes expressed deep mourning. Cairstie spotted Nicola MacDonald, dressed in black and veiled, entering the building. Her heart ached for the woman. She and Randy shared a close relationship. His death must have devastated her, yet here she was, lending her support despite her own loss.

Nicola's presence exemplified the Uists' spirit. The islanders might share their unsolicited opinions freely and, at times, rather heatedly, but when disaster struck, they united, much like her family.

Dad parked on the verge of the road and then set up her chair.

"Thanks, Dad." Cairstie situated herself.

She grasped the arm rests on her chair as Dad pushed her up the incline toward the chapel. Mother walked beside them.

The ushers took one look at her parents, then glanced at each other.

Cairstie's heart plummeted. Brilliant. They'd pegged Dad.

"Right this way, milord." One of the ushers escorted them inside the brick-and-mortar church to the pews directly behind the section reserved for the bereaved family.

"Marquess of Roxbury." Whispers carried through the conclave due to the magnificent acoustics.

Cairstie lowered her head, cheeks flaming. Her secret was out. Mother and Dad never introduced themselves by their titles. Perhaps one of the ushers' family members worked in the hospital. Dad had drawn on his account. Doubtless, the family crest had raised comment.

Och. This ruined everything, and on a day when the focus should remain on the bereaved. There'd be no end to the bowing and scraping now. Or the cold disdain—no happy mediums for the titled. After overcoming the initial shock of living on her own, Cairstie grew to enjoy her anonymity and the independence of caring for herself. For the first time, she understood why Elise changed her name when she moved to London.

The pipe organ's notes swelled to the rafters inside the chapel's interior. All rose as the three caskets were wheeled in, followed by the remaining members of the MacTavish family: Alicia, the grandmother, her two sons, Dan and Michael, and their wives and children.

The priest, dressed in a scarlet robe, gained the rostrum, the only bright spot of color in the chapel, save for the stained-glass windows behind them.

He motioned for them to sit. "We gather today to mourn the loss of Ewen MacTavish, his lovely wife, Matilda, and their son, wee Carl. No one could have foreseen this tragedy . . ."

Cairstie's heart ached, and many openly wept. A huge lump formed in her throat. Why did God spare them when this sweet family had been lost? Wee Carl's life had barely begun, while she continued to enjoy everything the world had to offer. A weight pressed upon her, and she bowed beneath the guilt. She and Sharidon could have died that night if he had not sought higher ground.

During her hospital stay, she'd heard the sad tale. At some point that night, the MacTavish family fled their home when the wind and tide drove the Atlantic up over the beach to the threshold of their house. Rocks were later found in their front garden, thrown by the sea. Taking the narrow, single-track road, they headed for extended family a mile away. A storm surge swept them off the road between their house and safety.

From under her hat brim, Cairstie sought the tall, dark-haired Irishman. She spotted him in the back, seated beside Angus Ghilcrest. His presence soothed her troubled spirit. What cover had MI6 crafted for Randy MacDonald's death? She needed to know before she approached Nicola. As it turned out, she needn't have worried. By the end of the service, Nicola had disappeared.

And so had Sharidon.

⚜

Sharidon stood beside the canopy over the freshly dug graves, his eyes on Nicola MacDonald as she made her way to her car. Despite her husband's confession to killing Wang, things weren't adding up, and unfinished business always set Sharidon on edge.

He wandered the cemetery, reading tombstones and keeping an eye on

Benbecula's most recent widow. Nicola reached her car and climbed inside, but instead of driving off, she tossed her veil aside and bent over her steering wheel, her shoulders heaving.

Training taught Sharidon to distance himself from his emotions while on assignments, but sometimes things got under his skin, like that funeral. That small coffin had gutted him.

He tipped his head and narrowed his eyes at Nicola's form. As the wife of a traitor, he took a more objective stance. Her grief appeared genuine. Either that, or she deserved a BAFTA for such a convincing performance.

Eventually, Nicola mopped her face, then drove off as the first mourners exited the chapel. Curious, he followed, slowing the Nova to a crawl when Nicola pulled into her drive, then speeding past when she entered the house.

Once the mainland coroner dealt with Randy's body, Nicola's funeral arrangements consisted of close friends and family only. Gossip about Randy's sudden demise had not yet reached the Uists.

Parking at the community center, Sharidon slouched in his seat and waited until people arrived, carrying food for the bereaved family. Sharidon picked up the store-bought container of millionaire's shortbread and followed them inside.

Buffet tables loaded with roasted chickens, hams, haggis, scones, jams and clotted cream, pots of soup and chowders, tatties and neeps, venison, and homemade bread groaned under their weight, their scents making his mouth water. He shifted a few puddings aside and added his dessert to the mix. It was a wonder the table didn't collapse.

Sharidon paused when Nicola entered the building just before the family arrived, carrying paper goods and utensils. Her puffy eyes were devoid of make-up, but she pasted on a smile and carried on.

Cairstie, whom he had yet to greet, hesitated when she saw Nicola. Then, lifting her chin, she wheeled through the human obstacle course to reach her. The two embraced for a very long time. Sharidon tugged his hair. How could Cairstie comfort her when that woman's husband had almost killed her? His admiration ticked up another notch. What a woman.

Gordon came up alongside him.

"Gordon, I thought ye had deserted us."

"I visited the mainland and only just returned. Terrible. Terrible thing, that storm. And Randy . . ." Gordon shook his head. "I just can't take it all in."

"Were ye visiting that pub in Oban I've heard about?" Sharidon probed. "The one ye visited a few months back? What's the name? Markie, something on Victoria Crescent?"

"Must be new." Gordon's brow furrowed in confusion. "I've never tried that pub. Save for this trip, I haven't been to Oban since the spring."

"My mistake." Sharidon's hinky feeling that something wasn't right returned with a vengeance.

Gordon clicked his tongue and motioned toward Nicola. "I dinna ken how she'll get on. Randy was her whole life, and she was his. They never had any children."

Whatever else Randy MacDonald had done, he loved his wife. His last words were for her, words Sharidon couldn't pass on.

Gordon moved off, but Sharidon kept an eye on him, his thoughts unsettled. If Gordon spoke the truth and had only visited Oban in the spring, who ran his credit card at the Markie Dans pub the night of Mansfield's death? Had someone stolen it?

Not leaving anything to assumption, he put on his jacket and left. Randy admitted to killing Wang. The coroner's report mentioned a hematoma on Randy's shoulder that coincided with Cairstie's golf club attack, which seemed conclusive.

He still couldn't work out the sinking of the *HMS Lilibet*. How had Randy handled that? Not for one second did he accept a ship with such strict precautionary measures would blow itself to bits, with not one, but four defective missiles.

Doubtless, Harry or Nigel could update him on the circuit boards.

Turning about, he searched the room for Hank Walker, the third member of the trio, to visit the Markie Dans pub that fateful night. The man stood alongside his wife, their hands clasped, as they spoke to Mrs. MacTavish.

He went outside and rang Nigel instead.

"Can Cyber check Gordon MacRae's bank to see if he ordered a new credit card in the last seven weeks?"

"What's this regarding?" Nigel asked.

"I just spoke to Gordon MacRae. According to him, he hasn't visited Oban since the spring."

"He was certain about that?"

"Affirmative. All I can figure is that Gordon either lost that bank card or someone else used it on the night in question."

If Gordon spoke the truth, who was the third person at the Markie Dans pub the night Mansfield and Wang disappeared?

# CHAPTER 35

"I NEED to order flowers for Nicola MacDonald." Cairstie picked up the magazine lying on the kitchen table the day after the services at St. Mary's.

No one had seen her since Randy's funeral. To complicate matters, Nicola closed her business, one which the locals depended on to supplement their income.

Cairstie opened the fashion magazine Mother had brought from the mainland. An article about Stella Walker's fashion show lauded Cairstie's replacement, making Cairstie's temples throb. She closed the magazine and pushed it away.

"Didn't that woman's husband almost kill you?" Mother added cream to the pot on the cooker.

Cairstie's mouth watered for Mother's famous Cullen Skink, a smoked fish chowder the entire family enjoyed.

Dad slipped behind Mother, rested his hands on her waist, and bent over her shoulder. "Smells delicious, Janet."

"Army, if you're looking for a sample, you had best think again," Mother scolded, but her lips curved at his compliment.

"Come now, my love, just one eensy weensy bite," Dad wheedled, flashing the saddest puppy-dog eyes Cairstie had ever witnessed.

She snorted. The two of them flirted like teenagers at times.

"Oh. Verra, well." Mother scooped up a ladle full and tipped it into a mug.

Dad grinned like a wee lad with a double helping of pudding. He snatched a spoon from a drawer and sat opposite Cairstie at the kitchen table.

"You're good, Dad. How'd you manage to get that out of her?" Cairstie asked.

"Years of practice." He wiggled his brows, then took a bite. "Delicious."

"I think you should stay far away from that MacDonald woman," Mother said.

Cairstie sighed. Dad's interruption had only paused her mother's rant.

"Here we go again," Cairstie said to her father. "Nicola has no idea what her husband did, and we'd like to keep it that way."

"We, being?" Mother paused her stirring.

Her parents knew Sharidon's name and why people called him Sherwood. They hadn't questioned him, which only added to Cairstie's suspicions. Mother and Dad grasped their family's secrets more than they let on.

Best to bypass that question. "Nicola's in that house all alone."

Mother held up her ladle and sampled the Cullen Skink. "Just a few more minutes, and we can eat." She set the ladle on the worktop and busied herself with setting the table. "I think that's verra kind of you to be so thoughtful, considering her husband almost killed you."

How many times was she going to mention that? Cairstie closed her eyes, not bothering to hide her irritation.

"I saw that young lady." Mother waved a spoon at her disapprovingly, then laid it on the table. "Now that Sharidon's caught the fellow who did this to you, you can return home."

"You've forgotten the reason I'm here. I have almost four months left on Benbecula before I can collect my inheritance."

"I'm sure Mr. Anderson will revoke those horrid stipulations after the dangers you've encountered." Mother met Dad's eyes.

"I'd like to stay." Cairstie looked at her lap.

Dad thunked his mug on the tabletop.

"I intend to stay," Cairstie added in a firmer tone.

"Why? This island is the back of beyond. There's nothing to do here. No decent shops of any sort." Mother shook her head, and that Command Center look glinted in her eyes.

"I like Benbecula." Here, she could play her violin, work part-time at The Sea Hut, and talk to Mrs. MacLeod—who might be a bit daft about her cats, but her crafts were of the best quality. The woman's oddity touched a protective chord within Cairstie.

Besides all that, the community had welcomed her. A fluke for an incomer, one she treasured. In Clovenfords, she would always be Lady Cairstie, but she could be herself on the island. And that was enough.

She no longer yearned for the glamorous parties and jet-setting friends whose goals lacked depth and purpose. In the Uists, she associated with people of real substance.

And Sharidon?

What would happen to them when his mission wrapped? Since her release from the hospital, she had not seen him except at a distance. Did he still intend to pursue her?

For that, she had no answers.

The wind gusted in off the sea, but for once, the sun shone from a brilliant blue sky. Sharidon gazed through the theodolite, his mind juggling facts. A car slowed on the B892 behind him, its wheels leaving the tarmac and coming to a halt near his position.

He turned from his "day job" and glanced at the driver.

Harry Benson? Again? That could only mean one thing, Benson's mission linked to his somehow.

"Slumming it, Benson?" Sharidon greeted, a broad smile stretching his mouth.

"Maybe." Harry came alongside him and slapped his shoulder in man-hug fashion.

"What brings ye to our humble island?" Sharidon asked.

"How's your case?" Harry by-passed the question.

"About to get interesting; if yer visit is the omen, I think it is."

Harry pressed his eye to the surveyor's lens. "This thing isn't focused."

"So?" Sharidon shrugged. "I have my numbers. The government owes the islander's land. I don't need a clear image for that."

"That wasn't your mission." Harry rested his hand on top of the theodolite.

"Consider it a bonus. Anytime the underdog wins, I'm all for it." Sharidon scanned the windswept fields. "I'm positive I located our traitor, but I can't work out how he sabotaged the *HMS Lilibet*."

"What makes you think the *Lilibet* wasn't an accident?"

Sharidon didn't answer. Harry was toying with him, and he knew it.

Harry jingled the keys in his pocket. "We've done some digging on those circuit boards Quantas purchased from the Americans."

"And?" Sharidon folded his arms and waited.

"The Americans didn't manufacture them. They were a passthrough."

Electronics. Sharidon's gut tightened. "They're Chinese."

"We found an interesting mechanism embedded inside." Harry's jaw bulged as though he clenched his jaw. "The circuit boards were monitored and manipulated remotely."

"The Americans are our allies. I'm not buying that they tampered with those parts."

"China sold the Yanks electronics at vastly reduced prices, and Americans passed the deal on to us."

"The Chinese are behind the *HMS Lilibet's* sinking."

"I'm afraid so."

"Ye'll forgive me if I say I am not entirely surprised." Sharidon stomped several paces into the *machair* before he circled back. "By any chance, do ye know who ordered those parts from the Americans?"

"What are you getting at?" Harry's eyes darkened.

"Just following a hunch." Perhaps the Chinese had not one, but two deep plants on Benbecula. "Can Elise do some digging and keep it on the down low? I'd hate to accuse an individual or company of working for the Chinese until I'm certain."

"She would if I asked her." Harry removed his sat phone and rang his wife. "Hey, babe."

"Harry," Elise's husky voice sounded through the line. "Do you know when you'll be home?"

"I've got you on speaker," Harry warned. "Sharidon's here, and we need your help."

"What have you got?" The change in Elise's tone flipped like a switch.

Harry motioned for Sharidon to take the "floor."

"Hey, Elise. Can ye hack into Quantas's purchasing department and find out who ordered the circuit boards for the *HMS Lilibet*? Quantas is a government contracting corporation here on Benbecula," Sharidon said by way of explanation.

"I know who they are." Elise didn't snarl—not precisely.

"How long will it take ye to dig?" Sharidon asked.

"Rushing me, Sharidon?" Computer keys clicked. A long pause. "Well, this is interesting."

"Ye know yer wife's skills are wasted in the business sector," Sharidon murmured for Harry's ears alone.

Harry cleared his throat, his eyes shifting away.

"Elise isn't exactly working in the business sector. She's on indefinite loan to C." Harry named the head of British Intelligence.

"Huh." No wonder Elise hadn't put up a fight when he reached out for assistance. Not only did she have the necessary clearances to hack, but her uncle's blessing as well. Elise's cyber skills had drawn the attention of one of the toughest men in the UK. Sharidon couldn't fault C for taking her on. Uncle or no uncle, her skill sets were downright scary.

"It's hush hush. So, I'd—"

"Of course. Of course."

"How fascinating," Elise's voice interrupted their little tête-à-tête.

"What do ye mean?" Sharidon asked.

"Every circuit board, plus their related components on the *Lilibet*, was of Chinese origin."

"And?" There must be an "and" involved.

"All were ordered by Gordon MacRae from Quantas's purchasing department."

"No one else?" Sharidon leaned forward, adrenalin bubbling like a fizzy drink.

"No."

"MacRae's not the only person who works in purchasing, is he?" Sharidon needed to cover all his bases.

"Negative."

More keys clicked, then Elise chuckled. "Gotcha, MacRae. It appears he altered several orders to obtain those specific electronic boards."

Sharidon punched the air. His hunch was right. Benbecula had two deep plants. The question was, did Randy and Gordon work in tandem or separately? He mulled that over for a time. "You should know that Gordon MacRae's been seeing Grace Chen, the local grocer's wife. She's a foreign national whose father is over China's State Security Ministry."

Harry whistled.

"You've landed in a hornet's nest, Sharidon." Elise was more explicit.

He agreed with her. "Chen visited Beijing two-and-a-half-years ago and returned with a young wife in tow. I wonder what bride price he paid to marry her."

"Bride price?" Elise snorted. "China handed her to Chen on a golden platter so they could place an intelligence officer near our top-secret testing range to sabotage our programs."

"My thoughts exactly." Sharidon tugged his hair. Doubtless, Mrs. Chen had encouraged MacRae to order those circuit boards for personal favors.

"Out of curiosity, how long ago were those parts ordered?" Sharidon needed to cross every T before demanding their arrests. The last thing they needed was to incarcerate an innocent person, especially if that individual's father ran the Chinese intelligence community.

"Two years," Elise said.

Sharidon narrowed his eyes. Mrs. Grace Chen arrived on Benbecula six months before that. It appeared he had located a second mole and an intelligence officer, as well.

# Chapter 36

"AND WHAT AM I to call you now?" Mrs. MacLeod tucked a blanket around Cairstie's shoulders.

"Thank you." Cairstie leaned back into the lounge's overstuffed chair. "Miss Henderson or Cairstie, whichever you prefer."

"That's not who you are." Mrs. MacLeod seated herself on the floral sofa inside the lounge, ready for a chat.

First, the home care nurses, now Mrs. MacLeod. How many times was she to have this conversation? The entire island knew her identity after Mother and Dad's recent visit.

"That's who I am."

"You're a proper lady. What are you doing here anyway? Aren't you a model or some such thing?"

Cairstie stroked the soft, cream-colored Minky blanket. Mrs. MacLeod had looked her up and, typical to form, had no issue poking her nose into Cairstie's business.

"I inherited this house and need to live here to prove my intention to keep it."

"And that young man of yours? He's down in that campground. Did the two of you row?"

"None of your business."

Instead of growing angry, like most nosy people who overstepped their boundaries, Mrs. MacLeod cackled and slapped her knee.

"I like you, lass. You've got backbone." She glanced around the lounge. "I miss your godmother. She was much like yourself. Spunky."

"I didn't know her well. Did she work on the RAF base?"

"Aye. We were friends, she and I. Both of us are widows. I had a standing tea invitation here once a week for many years until the last few months."

"Why did that stop?" This was news to Cairstie.

"Something was troubling her."

"Did she mention what it was?"

"No, I thought at first it might be her health, but found out later it had something to do with work. That ship's sinking was a horrible business. Those poor sailors." Mrs. MacLeod clicked her tongue and shook her head. "A terrible tragedy."

Cairstie struggled to keep her eyes open as exhaustion claimed her. Each day, she stayed up a bit more, but regaining her strength after heavy blood loss took time.

"I've tired you out, haven't I? I'll be by this afternoon to let Winkle out for a run and fill his water dish." Mrs. MacLeod rose and started for the front door.

"Mrs. MacLeod?"

"Aye." She turned around.

"Thank you for your help. I'm sorry you lost Mrs. McDougal." A shadow passed over Mrs. McLeod's face and made Cairstie add, "You're welcome here any time you'd like to stop by. Perhaps we could resume your weekly afternoon teas?"

The woman's eyes misted. She opened her mouth, then nodded. "That's right, nice of you . . . Cairstie." Then, in typical fashion, she bustled to the door. "Good day."

Cairstie stared at the closed door. Mrs. MacLeod had called her by her Christian name. Not Lady Cairstie. Or Miss Cairstie. Simply, Cairstie.

Odd duck or not, Cairstie had a friend—a real one.

❖

Sharidon unzipped his hoodie and edged forward in the queue to pick up his takeaway. Mrs. MacLeod and her niece, a lass whose name he could not recall, stood directly in front of him, and Angus Ghillies, directly behind.

Tourists and villagers milled about, taking advantage of the first sunny day in over a week. Children squealed and tossed balls to dogs while their parents waited for their orders.

"Don't let me forget. I've a bag of sea glass in the boot for you, Auntie," Mrs. MacLeod's niece said.

"I can't use it. Nicola's gone to her sister's on Harris and closed The Sea Hut for the season."

"When did that happen? I saw her yesterday, and she said nothing about leaving the island." The niece's eyes widened, and she turned and fully faced her aunt.

Sharidon pricked up and edged toward the ladies, anxious not to miss their conversation.

"She took the ferry this morning. Losing your spouse is hard, lass. She misses Randy something fierce," Mrs. MacLeod murmured.

With Nicola MacDonald off the island, a prime opportunity loomed to investigate the MacDonald home.

"MacLeod," a lad called from the pickup window.

Mrs. MacLeod shuffled forward and clasped the takeaway bag, turning from the pickup counter. "Good to see you, Will."

"And ye, Mrs. MacLeod," Sharidon said.

"Sherwood," the lad called from the window.

"That's me." Sharidon stepped forward and glanced over the worktop into the takeaway's kitchen. Grace Chen stood beside the cooker, mincing veg.

She had returned.

He didn't have enough evidence on Grace Chen to incarcerate her. Though a suspect, evidence remained circumstantial, even if his gut said otherwise.

Grace's husband bustled through the connecting door to their house, his face like a thundercloud. Sharidon dithered over selecting duck sauce to slow his exit.

Mr. Chen glanced at him and their young Scottish employee, then switched to Mandarin. "Are you seeing Randy?"

Sharidon dropped his duck sauce packets on the ground and bent to retrieve them, taking his time.

"No," Grace said.

Sharidon rose and added the packets to his takeaway bag. Then, he thumbed through the other packets on the worktop, ears straining.

Mr. Chen tugged his wife toward the doorway adjoining their house, his fingers pressing into her upper arm. "I don't believe you. You are seeing someone, Grace. And Randy is missing. Did you meet him somewhere?"

Sharidon selected several napkins and added them to his bag.

"He's your friend. Not mine. I have customers." Grace yanked her arm loose and picked up her knife.

"You are my wife, and you answer to me. Stay away from Randy. He works for me." Mr. Chen stormed through the adjoining door and banged it shut behind him.

Sharidon helped himself to chopsticks and stepped away from the window. Instead of joining the villagers at the picnic tables, he crossed the road to the car park and climbed inside the Nova.

Mr. Chen suspected his wife, but of what, Sharidon wasn't exactly sure.

Stars dotted the dark, velvety sky, and the moon had yet to rise. Sharidon dumped his motorbike behind a dune and crossed the *machair* toward the MacDonald house. With Nicola visiting her sister on Harris, he couldn't pass on the opportunity to glean more information on this case.

Lying prone on the grass, he adjusted his night vision goggles and pulled on his gloves. He checked his weapons, then edged around the house and unlocked the door. The house was cold. Nicola must have shut off the heat. Good move. Electricity prices had risen exponentially in the last few years.

The snug and kitchen echoed hollowly, the house soulless without its owners. On the kitchen worktop stood an assortment of advertisements, bills, and letters. He riffled through them, but nothing of consequence raised suspicions. He checked the cupboards and drawers, then headed for the lounge, where he spotted a small paper calendar pinned to the wall.

Most people used electronic calendars these days. To each their own. Precise writing noted dental and doctor appointments, birthdays of people who meant something to the MacDonalds, and a blocked-out holiday in Majorca next month. He turned back a month. The Sunday School outing up Reuval jumped out at him. Flipping back to the previous month, he stopped.

On the date of Wang and Mansfield's murders, Nicola had scheduled a shopping trip to Oban, followed by a hen's night with Freya Walker and several other islanders at the Markie Dans pub. Pulling out his mobile, Sharidon took a screenshot and sent the images to Elise.

Sharidon: What do you make of this?

A few minutes later, his mobile dinged.

Elise: I assume that date is important enough for you to wake me?

Sharidon: Yes. Very.

He pressed her number and rang her.

"Ahhh," Elise yawned.

"Sorry to wake you."

She yawned again. "It's all right. Harry's still on assignment. I'm not sleeping all that well with him gone. What do you need?"

"Two MI6 agents were killed at The Deep Sea Range headquarters on the night of that shopping trip to Oban. I had you search credit card statements on Randy MacDonald, Hank Walker, and Gordon MacRae for the night in question."

"I remember. We ruled them out because they were off island even though we had no CCTV feed to verify their presence on the mainland," Elise's voice sharpened.

"According to this calendar, they weren't off the island—their wives were."

"What about MacRae? He's not married, is he?"

"He didn't report a lost credit card or order a new one. Could you check ferry records around that date to see if Grace Chen boarded the ferry?"

Another yawn. Footsteps. Then the computer keys clicked.

"Grace Chen took the ferry. The ferry scanned her ID when she boarded. Are you thinking she used MacRae's card?"

"Yeah."

"What are you going to do?"

"I'll have the local police question the ladies who attended the hen do that night. I need you to do one last thing for me if you can."

"Aye."

"Dig deeper into Bo Chen and Hank Walker. He's MacDonald and MacRae's buddy. I'm missing something."

"On it."

"Thanks, Elise."

"No problem. Night."

Nothing else in the MacDonald house shed light on the mystery. Doubtless, Randy had been so used to the calendar hanging on the wall that he forgot about its existence.

Checking the time, Sharidon let himself out and jogged to the beach to retrieve his motorbike. The wind had calmed, and the crisp air did not penetrate his clothes as he started the engine and headed up the road. Night vision goggles allowed him to run without lights and not call attention to himself.

Bo Chen roused Sharidon's suspicions when he had purchased his takeaway and overheard the grocer's conversation with his wife. Sharidon received the impression that Chen suspected his wife, but of what, that remained to be seen.

Keeping in second gear, he reached the pub, driving past to ensure no one was about, then parked his motorbike two streets away and doubled back. Staying in the shadows, he tried the doors. *Ach.* Both had deadbolts.

With hands on his hips, he circled the one-story building that contained an alarm system. That seemed rather curious in an area that boasted little to no crime. A small attic window under the eaves drew his attention. He eyed the metal drainpipe and judged its distance to access it. Clasping the cold pipe between both hands, he shimmied up the side of the building, pushed away from the pipe, and grasped the window sash. For a moment, he teetered on the narrow ledge, his weak leg nothing but a hindrance before he regained his balance. He searched for an alarm and got lucky. None on the attic level. He tugged on the frame. Jammed.

Holding his breath, he let go with one hand and reached inside his pocket for a small file. A fall could undo the surgery on his leg, so he slid the metal piece between the two sashes where years of grime had sealed the frame. Thankfully, MacDonald had not painted it shut. Scraping the file, he worked it around the casing.

Inside, the unlocked latch taunted. He rattled the sash and shoved at the lower frame. No good. Putting more muscle into it made his foot slip on the sill, and he flung out his arms and dropped the file.

Grabbing the drainpipe, he stopped his fall, his heart scrambling. Sweat beaded his forehead, and his leg shook from the exertion as he glanced at the file on the tarmac below. His leg would never handle another climb.

He shoved the frame, then rattled it some more. His muscles screamed. He couldn't hold on much longer. Using the last of his strength, he muscled it one last time, and casing gave way.

Sharidon climbed inside onto a bookcase topped with glass aquariums. The closest one housed a familiar patterned snake. The adder lifted its head, and its tongue darted out. Sharidon jumped off the bookcase and landed beside a brass floor lamp and a folding table. Any doubt about who placed the snake in Cairstie's room fled.

Dust coated every surface and tickled his nose. The attic needed a good cleaning. Inside the aquarium next to the adders, a dozen frogs stared at him from beady black eyes. An empty tank in the corner gave Sharidon a good idea of its former occupant.

Stepping back, he scanned the rest of the room, his gaze landing on an electronic device on the folding table. He pressed play. Soft breaths from the speaker filled the attic. Someone sleeping? Sharidon rewound the recorder halfway, and Cairstie's voice jumped out at him. "Winkle, let's go for a walk."

Sharidon snapped off the unit and erased the recording, then pried open the compartment and smashed its inner mechanism. He needed to remove the bugs from Muir Tigh House.

Righting the unit to appear unharmed, he perused the rest of the room. Nothing else gave credence to Randy's links to the Chinese. MI6 had already passed Randy's mobile to Cyber. Doubtless, they'd find something.

A car slowed on the road and pulled into the lot below. The engine cut. With only a side window, Sharidon couldn't make out the occupants, but at this time of night, it could only mean a robbery or Randy's Chinese officer had arrived to retrieve incriminating evidence that would betray his or her identity.

Adrenalin pulsed as Sharidon scanned the folding ladder used to access the attic from the ground floor. Grasping the floor lamp, he removed the glass shield and bulb, then shoved the pole between the hinged ladder, extending it from one side of the opening to the other. That would hold the searcher off for a bit.

He climbed onto the bookcase, gun in his hand as glass shattered on the ground floor. An alarm blared, cut off half a second into its bleat, then two sets of footsteps entered the supply room beneath him.

"Check the shelves. I'll look here," a man spoke in Mandarin, his accent difficult to follow.

Long minutes ticked while Sharidon stood, unmoving.

"It's not here." A woman spoke, her Mandarin excellent. Grace Chen.

"You're sure he had it?"

"Yes. All of it. The bugs, burner, everything," Grace said.

"They must be here. They aren't at the house."

"Do you think his wife found them?" Grace asked.

Sharidon cocked his gun, the metallic click the only sound in the room. He could not identify the man. Gordon had served overseas for several years and spoke Mandarin, so did Hank Walker. Bo Chen did as well.

"If Nicola found them, the police would have retained her for questioning," the man grunted.

Shuffling. A groan of wood. "What's this?" Grace tugged the cord to pull down the attic's folding ladder.

"Attic access," the man said.

Heavy footsteps. Another tug, this one much harder.

"It's jammed," the man said.

Sharidon breathed through his mouth, his pulse hammering. He could shoot the first person up the ladder, but the second would escape, undoubtedly the officer who ran this operation—the one he intended to interrogate.

"Do you think MacDonald hid it up there?" Grace asked.

"Perhaps. Help me carry a table. I'll get it open."

Two sets of footsteps moved away.

Easing open the attic window to a blast of cold air, Sharidon gripped the drainpipe and slid to the ground, landing soft-footed on the gravel. He snatched up his file and sprinted for his motorbike, frustrated he couldn't stick around to identify Grace's companion.

But one pressing need drove him. Cairstie.

If Grace Chen intended to retrieve anything that could prompt an investigation, she was running scared and covering her trail. He needed to destroy the bugs inside Muir Tigh House in case Grace determined that he or Cairstie were persons of interest after she discovered her recording device hooked to Muir Tigh House was destroyed.

He mounted the bike, and within seconds, it roared to life. Not many owned motorbikes in the area. If they heard the engine, it wouldn't take much to determine who it belonged to. His nocturnal visit confirmed Grace's guilt. Even though he longed to arrest Grace and identify the second Mandarin speaker, tonight was not the night for that. If he remained, a shootout would have ensued. Shootouts didn't provide answers. Interrogations did.

Keeping the lights off, he pulled onto the road and sped toward Muir Tigh. Grace Chen worked with a Mandarin speaker.

The question was, who?

# CHAPTER 37

---

AFTER TWO DAYS OF SUNSHINE, dozens of families descended on Benbecula's empty beaches. Children shrieked and chased each other up and down the white sand. Cairstie slathered sun cream on her face and laid on the mat, her shoulders wrapped in a blanket. The island's few vacation rentals limited visitors, but every rental in Balivanich was booked.

A dozen steps away, Mrs. MacLeod, dressed in her usual black, wandered the beach, poking around for her bits and bobs while Winkle raced after any bird that dared to land.

The soothing lull of waves did nothing to calm the storm that raged inside Cairstie. She picked up her mobile and checked her texts for the thousandth time. Five days. Sharidon hadn't contacted her in five days. Surely, he had a few spare minutes for her. Didn't he?

Had she offended him? Mother and Dad insisted on clearing the air after a disagreement. She and Sharidon had not quarreled. He had vanished.

That was it. Cairstie curled on her side and used her mobile's voice to text.

> Cairstie: Are you okay? Or are you avoiding me?

She might as well hit this thing head-on.
Dots on the screen.

> Sharidon: Miss me, lass?

> Cairstie: Have you closed the case?

> Sharidon: New developments have arisen. Are your parents still here?

Relief crested, then tumbled through her.

> Cairstie: They left yesterday.

> Sharidon: Are you following the doctor's orders?

> Cairstie: Aye. I'm lying on the beach resting.

> Sharidon: Which beach?

She laughed outright at his question.

> Cairstie: Why?

> Sharidon: I might wander that direction.

> Cairstie: You just want to see me in my bathing suit.

She glanced at the jogger suit that covered her body and the blanket wrapped around her shoulders, then laughed again.

> Sharidon: Am I so obvious?

More dots typing.

> Sharidon: So, where are you?

Still smiling, Cairstie answered:

Balivanich Beach.

Seven minutes later, a shadow blocked the sun above her. Cairstie scrunched her nose and looked up. Sharidon grinned down at her. Just his presence set happiness bubbling inside.

"That's a mighty fine bathing costume." Sharidon's green eyes danced. "My great granny would approve."

"I thought you might appreciate it."

He wore a hoodie and a pair of short trousers, exposing the scar on his leg, which had faded to a dark pink. He plunked on the sand beside her and faced the sea, both wrists on his knees. He leaned sideways and bumped his shoulder into hers. The touch, though slight, sent her heartbeat into jackhammer heaven.

"Feels like an age since I saw ye last," Sharidon murmured.

"Aye." Her throat dried, and she swallowed while her heart fluttered so fast that black dots danced across her vision.

He wrapped his hand around hers, entwining their fingers and squeezing hers tight. "Ach, lass. This is no good. I can't think when I'm around ye."

"Is that why you kept away?"

"That, and I didn't want yer parents to betray my moniker by accident."

"Sensible." She had assumed as much.

"I'm not the least sensible around ye." Sharidon faced her, his eyes solemn.

"Have you made progress on the case?"

"Some, but it hasn't stopped me from wanting this." He tugged her into his arms and rested his chin on her head.

"This is what you wanted?" She ran her fingers lightly down the side of his face.

"Yer killing me." He groaned.

"Maybe you'd prefer this instead." She traced his mouth with a featherlight touch.

He closed his eyes and shuddered. Then his mouth crashed onto hers, his lips demanding. Hungry. The brush of his whiskers against her skin. The tenderness of his touch. Nothing but Sharidon existed. His kisses melted her insides, making her heart bang like a kettledrum on parade. This time, her lightheadedness had nothing to do with blood loss.

His woodsy fragrance enveloped her, and she clutched his shoulders and hung on for dear life. His fingers twined through her hair. Sharidon. His name echoed through her soul. Sharidon—the fellow she loved.

Her heart stuttered at the revelation. She loved him. He wasn't anything like her usual. She couldn't bend or manipulate this hard-headed man. Didn't want to. His laughing eyes and helpful nature had stolen her heart unaware.

Sharidon nuzzled her neck, and tingles buzzed her body. She pushed against his chest to cool things a bit.

He leaned back, his pupils so big they almost swallowed the green. "Ach. I'm sorry, lass." Sharidon tugged on his hair. "I've no excuse except for the way I feel for ye. I'm afraid my good behavior flies right out the window with ye."

"I was a verra willing participant."

He rubbed his eyes as though trying to clear his vision. And her heart melted even more at the endearing action. She took his hand, and they faced the Atlantic swells.

"I'll be leaving soon," he said.

Her heart squeezed. "Wrapping up the case, aye?"

Unless Mother and Dad convinced Mr. Anderson to change the stipulations in Mrs. McDougal's will, she'd be here several more months.

"I don't know how to make this work between us, Cairstie. Ye must know, long-distance relationships don't work well."

"Some do." Her heart stumbled as a new fear arose within her.

Sharidon nodded slowly. "Yer right. It won't be easy, though. I'm often gone for months at a time. Even if ye lived in London, it's not ideal."

"Are you breaking up with me?"

"No, lass. I'm just telling ye what yer in for when ye date a bloke like me." Sharidon gazed at her. The long, black lashes surrounding his green eyes made her heart flutter.

"I'm willing to risk it."

He squeezed her hand, then gazed at her as though putting her face to memory. "If I can, I'll call ye before I go."

"Sharidon?"

"Eh?"

"I forgot to tell you something. Mrs. MacLeod said that my godmother was worried about something at work just before she died."

His eyes sharpened. "Did Mrs. MacLeod mention what it entailed?"

"No."

"That's no good. I was hoping to prove Mrs. McDougal's death was a homicide."

"Even if we can't, I'm convinced it was."

"With Randy MacDonald dead, we'll probably never know. If it's any consolation, my vote's with ye." He rubbed his jaw. "Mrs. McDougal's newspaper clippings and pen drives have raised suspicions that go back many years."

"Is the home office looking into those?" She stood beside him, the blanket slipping off her shoulders and falling to the sand at her feet.

He chucked her under her chin. "Ye know I can't tell ye that." Bending, he kissed her, chaste and quick. "I'll be in touch."

Then he was gone, leaving her with a knot inside her throat the size of Bass Rock.

⁂

With Cairstie at the beach, Sharidon drove straight to Muir Tigh House to remove those bugs before Grace Chen linked them to another listening device. Capturing Grace Chen and her unknown accomplice remained his top priority in wrapping this case.

Sharidon pulled into Muir Tigh's drive and set the brake, his eyes sweeping the orderly garden. The place had improved one hundred percent since Cairstie's arrival. He'd mowed the weeds, but someone had set the flower beds to rights during his absence. Cairstie wasn't up to that yet, was she? Perhaps she'd hired a gardener.

He unlocked the kitchen door and let himself inside with his tool kit. The place smelled of beeswax and furniture polish, and the floors appeared scrubbed.

"Hello?" he called.

Had Cairstie's parents hired a housekeeper and gardener? If so, were they still about?

He inspected the ground floor before he took the stairs. On entering Cairstie's bedroom, he retrieved the listening device. Rather than disposing of it, he checked the other bedrooms and family baths for any surprises installed during his absence. Not finding any, he crushed the bug under his heel, then flushed it down the loo. Before he clattered back to the ground floor, Elise rang him.

In his eagerness to access the much-needed news, Sharidon bypassed the usual greetings. "What do ye have?"

"Hello, Sharidon." Elise sounded tired, her voice strained.

"What's wrong?"

"Harry's in hospital."

A chill swept over him. "How bad?"

"Critical." Her voice shook. "He took some shrapnel in a shootout on Raasay."

"When?" Job injuries occurred among operatives, but this news struck too close to home. Harry was a mate. He and Elise had just married.

"Two days ago."

It now made sense why she had delayed her response.

"Does Cairstie know?" he asked. She hadn't appeared burdened when they met at the beach.

"No. Mother and Dad don't want anything upsetting her while she convalesces. Besides, she can't visit Harry, anyway."

"Cairstie won't thank ye for keeping her out of the loop." The lass was tired of being treated like a baby.

Elise hiccupped, a sure sign of tears.

"I'm sorry, love. What can I do?" he asked. He could stand anyone's tears but hers. And maybe her sister's.

"Catch the people sabotaging our defense programs." Anger licked through her words.

"I intend to." He set his jaw. Now, this was personal. "What do ye have for me?"

"Walker's not an issue. He's a local who joined the navy. It's MacRae you want."

"Excellent. I wanted to arrest him earlier, but that would have blown my cover."

"Drives me bonkers when that gets in the way," Elise muttered.

"And Chen?" he asked.

"That's where this gets interesting. He's Mongolian, not Chinese. The Chen family adopted him, and he attended school with his wife's father."

Sharidon whistled as another puzzle piece clicked into place.

"Chen entered the UK as a university student, then surfaced on Benbecula a few years later when he purchased a grocery store."

"The Chinese love a long game." The patience involved in such an arrangement often blew his mind. "Chen must have monitored MacDonald. What about the wife? Are they married, or is that a cover?"

"Married. Her father gave her to Chen."

Sharidon shook his head. Favors. "So, when Grace arrived on Benbecula two-and-a-half years ago—"

"She upped China's game," Elise said.

Bingo. That time frame aligned with MacRae's ordering of those circuit boards and the attempted thefts on base. Chen might suspect his wife of infidelity, but he'd bet his life that both Chens were up to their ears in this mess.

Still mulling that over, he pressed Nigel's number and relayed the information. If anything happened to him, it was best to keep his officer updated.

"Sending a team to scoop up MacRae," Nigel said. "Good work. Let me know when you get concrete evidence to bring in the Chens."

Glass shattered, and the Solarium door opened on the ground floor. Mandarin reached Sharidon, spoken in whispers.

Sharidon's heart took off like a jet. "Gotta go."

He withdrew the gun from his holster and inserted a fresh clip. Seven rounds. That's all he had. His extra ammo was in the van. A floorboard groaned when he shifted weight.

The speaker quieted. Instead of leaving, two sets of footsteps moved through the Solarium. A man's voice raised, followed by a slap. A woman cried out.

Sharidon edged toward the stairwell and took cover at the top of the narrow-walled stairs. He tracked both sets of footfalls as they moved out of the Solarium, then checked the snug and study, and converged at the base of the stairs. Why were they here? Had someone tipped them off as to his identity? Or had they seen him leave the pub? Neither of the Chen's were daft. Doubtless, the broken recording device helped them connect the dots.

A rung groaned halfway up the stairs. Sharidon cocked his weapon, the metallic sound a giveaway to his presence.

Gunfire burst up the stairwell.

Classic startle tactics.

Sharidon crouched as one of the Chen's reached the top step, weapon raised. Sharidon squeezed his trigger. Pop.

Chen fell face-first onto the hall's tartan carpet, his legs dangling over the narrow stairwell.

Only six bullets remained in Sharidon's clip. He had to make them count.

The second person discharged a volley, the ammo chipping plaster beside Sharidon's ear. Sulfur and plaster fogged the air. He used the cover to roll across the corridor and lay prone, his gun extended.

A slender figure rushed him, spraying bullets as she charged. One ricocheted off his weapon and grazed his shooting hand, knocking the firearm loose. He grabbed it, but she kicked it out of reach.

Grace Chen stood over him, her dark eyes shining with triumph. Instead of finishing him, she checked her companion's pulse.

"Thank you," she said. "Bo's a beast."

If he kept her talking, perhaps he might outwit her.

"Yer very clever," he said.

"You British. You so stupid." Grace's accent dripped with derision. "I am smarter than Bo. I am smarter than all of you."

What an egomaniac.

"My father will be pleased." Grace's eyes gleamed with a twisted amusement.

"Will he? Ye've lost yer team. Gordon's in custody, and Randy and Bo are dead."

She narrowed her eyes. "Lies. Gordon is home." She stomped Sharidon's wounded hand with her boot.

One of his fingers snapped. He grunted. "Did you kill Mrs. McDougal?"

"Mrs. McDougal was nosey woman. She followed Gordon everywhere. Bo sent Randy to Muir Tigh House to retrieve her pen drives and stope her meddling." Grace paused. "You killed him?"

"Someone did. He's in the morgue." Sharidon had no intention of aggravating a woman with a gun pointed at his head.

"I will get that file. It's here somewhere."

"If Gordon's in custody, and MacDonald is dead, why do ye want that file? Shouldn't ye leave the area?" he asked.

"I must erase proof of my connection so my father can use me. If people know I involved. . ." She shook her head. "I need that file."

"Gordon might talk." Sharidon was grasping at straws. Any second, Grace would pull that trigger.

"He is loyal."

A scuffling outside on the stoop reached them, then the kitchen door opened. "Winkle," Cairstie called. "Put that nasty thing down. No. No. Bad dog."

Cairstie. Fear pole-axed his mind. He needed to warn her.

"Your girlfriend returns." An icy smile curved Grace's mouth. She pressed the gun once more to his temple. "Not a word."

Winkle, who usually charged for his food dish upon arrival, was immediately locked in his kennel. Had Cairstie heard the gunfire? She must have smelled it the second she opened the door, yet she did not call out.

With Grace's attention divided between him and Cairstie, Sharidon swung his good leg and knocked Grace's feet out from under her. Her gun went off, the roar deafening as a bullet embedded in the plaster above his head.

Sharidon whipped his arm to block Grace's aim as he sprang to his feet. She stepped back and raised her weapon.

Everything slowed. Words. Movement. Time.

The cock of a large gun at the base of the stairs. "Put down your weapon," Cairstie demanded.

Grace swung in Cairstie's direction, her semi-automatic peppering the wall as she turned. Cairstie held her ground and squeezed the trigger. Fire belched from both shotgun barrels. Grace collapsed, her bullets making an arc on the floor as she fell.

Sharidon pounced, then grasped the weapon from Grace's unmoving hand. He checked her pulse. She was still breathing. He punched emergency services on his sat phone, then glanced downstairs at Cairstie.

Her face was set, and her blue eyes glittered.

"I told you I could shoot."

# CHAPTER 38

SHARIDON KEPT a keen eye on the hospital screen, tracking Grace Chen's surgery—seven hours to pick out the buckshot and repair the damage of Cairstie's shot.

Still weak after her own blood loss and dip in the sea, Cairstie rose from her seat beside him, her face pinched. "I'm going home for a bit now that you're patched up." She indicated his splinted hand.

He gazed up at her, an overwhelming desire to kiss her welling within him. She had saved his bacon back there at the house. "I owe you big time."

"I'd say we're even. See you soon?"

"Hope so."

She waved, then exited the hospital lounge.

The police declared the crime scene a B&E with a determination to harm when they arrived. If only. MI6 had loads of paperwork for him to muddle through after they took Grace into custody—if she survived.

His sat phone vibrated.

Nigel: Meet me by the van.

Using his unbandaged hand, Sharidon pushed out his chair and took the Accident and Emergency's exit, zipping his jacket against the wind. He crossed the tarmac and found Nigel beside his vehicle.

"You completed this mission with an exclamation point." Nigel greeted him.

"Hardly. Lady Cairstie took care of Grace Chen. Her husband's in the morgue."

"So, I understand. How's the hand?" Nigel nodded toward his bandaged and splinted appendage.

"It'll heal." Sharidon lifted his hand and glared at the splint.

"But will it shoot?"

"I'll be fine in a few weeks. The police have posted a guard on Grace; if she survives, she won't get away."

When Cairstie heard shots inside the house, she broke into the van and helped herself to his arsenal. If not for her quick thinking, he wouldn't be here.

"When do you interrogate Mrs. Chen?" Sharidon longed to listen to what should prove an interesting conversation, given the woman's propensity to chatter about her superior mental prowess.

"She has diplomatic immunity." Nigel's nostrils flared.

"I should have known. Dear old Dad's pulled strings." Sharidon fisted his left hand and itched to punch something.

"Major ones. The home office is exchanging Grace for Yen Zhan." Nigel named one of the most notorious spies in China. "She leaves as soon as she can travel."

"I hate politics," Sharidon growled. "We had her. We could have interrogated her to ferret out China's plans."

"I doubt Grace knows more than her assignment." Nigel slapped his shoulder.

Sharidon was not so sure about that. "My cover's blown."

Nigel's poker face told him nothing.

If they had the option of keeping Grace Chen in custody, his cover would have remained intact. No more days in the field for him. At least he had language skills to fall back on. Doubtless, Nigel would post him to a foreign embassy. The idea did not sit well with him.

"I'm recalling you to headquarters and promoting you to officer trainee," Nigel deadpanned.

Sharidon's brain scrambled. "What?"

"You heard me. You'll report to me but have a small team of your own. I've a job that requires your skill sets. I need you in London ASAP for a briefing. The fashion industry is passing information to enemies of the state. We need to infiltrate their circle to find the leak. Unfortunately, the agent we use is on another assignment, so you'll need to build and monitor your own team."

Too bad Cairstie no longer worked in that industry. She'd be fabulous. He didn't know the least thing about the fashion world.

"Is this an overseas job?" Was Paris part of the deal? His mouth watered suddenly for a chocolate croissant.

"The shows start in London. If things go as planned, no further traveling will be required."

"Where do I find a model with training to infiltrate that industry if ours is unavailable?"

"Use that Irish charm of yours and recruit one." Nigel grinned, showing all his teeth.

The first rumblings of anticipation coursed through Sharidon. "It just so happens that I have someone in mind." Perhaps he could rehab Cairstie's reputation and restore her to the profession she loved at the same time.

"I was hoping you might. Resourceful is your middle name."

"She'll need training," Sharidon warned. "And she isn't available for a few months."

"That won't work then. We need her sooner."

"Let me see if I can pull a few strings." Excitement rippled through Sharidon, and his mouth curved.

"You're up to something." Nigel's eyes narrowed.

"Trust me. If this works, it'll be more than interesting." Sharidon's smile widened into a grin.

"We have a flight in forty minutes. Think you can pack in twenty?" Nigel returned to the business at hand.

"Yes, sir." Did the man have a life outside SIS?

"Agent Snodgrass will return the van to London. No more ferry crossings for you." Nigel slapped his shoulder.

"Excellent, sir." Oh, sweet relief. After fishing Cairstie out of the sea, he had no intention of voluntarily entering a boat anytime soon.

Then it hit him, and his heart bottomed out. Would there be time for a proper goodbye before he left?

⚜

Cairstie rested her head on the back of a hard plastic chair in the local constabulary's "interrogation room," an alcove off the minuscule lobby.

At this point, Mrs. MacLeod, who heard the gunfire from the beach while out foraging for sea glass, arrived at the station to lend her unique form of moral support—by playing cat videos—until Cairstie closed her eyes in self-defense.

"I'd best get back and feed my fur babies." Mrs. MacLeod patted Cairstie's arm and left, the cold air whooshing inside from the open sliding doors.

"Miss Henderson?" the receptionist called.

"Aye?" Cairstie rose and approached the woman's desk.

"You'll need to stay here while the forensics team 'clears the site' before you return to Muir Tigh House."

The images of Sharidon with a gun to his head, of Mr. Chen's dead body, and Grace falling by Cairstie's shot replayed over and over inside her mind. How could she spend several more months in a home where so much carnage had occurred?

Maybe Sharidon would lend her his van, or she could buy a tent, anything rather than stay inside that house. She took a seat.

Earlier, when she returned from the beach with Winkle, she reached the driveway as shots rang inside her house. Without thought, she broke into Sharidon's van, disengaged his alarms, and tore the place apart to access the weapons cache. Having previously searched the van, she knew where they weren't located. That had likely saved his life.

The outside door burst open, and Sharidon darted inside, a duffle bag slung over one shoulder. One look at him, and Cairstie knew. He was leaving.

She straightened in her chair. Sharidon noted the movement and turned in her direction, his green eyes lighting. He plopped on the seat beside her.

"You're leaving?" She touched the duffel bag.

"Yeah." He gripped her hand. "This wasn't how I pictured our goodbye."

"Me neither." Her throat tightened and threatened to strangle her.

"Ach, lass. Don't look so sad." Sharidon dumped his canvas bag on the ground and tugged her into his arms. "I'll be back. I'm like a bad penny. I'll turn up when ye least expect me."

He kissed her hard and quick, then grabbed his duffel and bolted out the door as fast as he'd entered.

She closed her eyes to keep the tears at bay, but the second she did, everything that had occurred inside Muir Tigh House rushed at her. After a time, she dozed, but nightmares woke her.

Hours later, heels tapped on the floor in a familiar pattern. Cairstie cracked open an eye as her mother bustled up to the receptionist's desk.

"May I help you?" the receptionist asked.

"I was told my daughter, Cairstie Henderson, is here," Mother said.

"Mummy?" Cairstie straightened in her chair. Before she stood, her mother embraced her.

"Darling, your neighbor rang us. She said there had been a shooting inside Muir Tigh House. I came immediately."

The concern in Mother's soft blue eyes crumbled Cairstie's defenses, and the tears she had held inside dripped down her cheeks. Mother kissed her and pushed the hair out of her face.

"There now. Everything is going to be lovely. I've brought Mr. Anderson along to see how unsafe this island is. After viewing the crime scene, he's revoked that horrid six-month mandate in Mrs. McDougal's will. Haven't you, Mr. Anderson?" Mother raised both well-arched brows at the gentleman in question.

Mr. Anderson had halted several meters away to give them privacy.

"I'm going home?" Cairstie gazed at Mr. Anderson, hoping he'd validate Mother's words.

"Mr. Anderson accompanied me to ascertain that we were not attempting to trick him," Mother said, her voice fake as artificial sweetener.

"I'm doing my job, Lady Roxbury." The solicitor shifted, his expression wary.

"Of course, you are, just as I am here to handle my responsibilities as a mother. My daughter will not live in a house where so much violence has occurred."

Cairstie's heart tripped. Wasn't that information top secret?

"Aye, milady. Malicious robberies such as this are rare." Mr. Anderson bobbed his head.

Robberies? Was that what Sharidon had let about? Thankfully, she had kept her words to the bare facts and didn't contradict Mother's information.

"Considering the mental anguish of such an incident, I intend to release Lady Cairstie's inheritance with no further demands," Mr. Anderson declared.

"Thank you, Mr. Anderson." Mother inclined her neck as though granting a royal favor.

Cairstie's lips twitched, and she averted her face to save Mr. Anderson embarrassment.

"I'll be off now. Lady Roxbury. Lady Cairstie." Mr. Anderson dipped his head, then left by the entrance door. They whooshed shut behind him.

Silence reined for two beats.

"Where's Dad?" Cairstie asked. Her parents always visited in tandem.

"He's with Elise. Harry's in hospital." Mother said.

"Why?"

"He's doing better. The doctor expects a full recovery. It was touch and go for a while."

"Harry almost died?" Cairstie's heart squeezed. "When did this happen?"

"A few days ago."

"When did you intend to tell me? At his funeral?" Hurt and anger warred within Cairstie. She had shot a Chinese spy, almost died from blood loss and hypothermia, fallen in love, and learned to take care of herself. She could even cook scrambled eggs and a few other basic dishes. And to top everything, she had just said goodbye to Sharidon.

But when it came to her family, nothing changed. They still treated her like a bairn.

"Cairstie, love, you were recovering. We thought it best to keep it from you until you were stronger."

"Mother, please don't spare my feelings. I'm no longer a child, and I'd appreciate not being treated like one." Cairstie ran her hand over the vinyl chair.

Her mother blinked several times. Cairstie was not deceived. Behind that facade, Mother's mind clicked at hyper-speed.

"You're right, darling. We have shielded you from unpleasantness. It's hard to accept that you're a grown woman. Will you forgive me?"

Cairstie's anger dissolved like water on spun sugar. "It's forgotten." And it was. Mother would see that no one in the family treated her thus again.

"What really happened to Harry?" Cairstie asked.

"Shrapnel," Mother said.

"Another word for guns." Cairstie leveled her mother with a stare. "It seems to be a family pastime."

Mother returned the favor with a hard stare of her own.

"How's Elise?" For a newlywed, this could not have gone over well.

"Your sister is an emotional disaster. If I ever questioned her love for Harry, her behavior has put any lingering doubts to rest."

Elise a mess? That didn't sound like her tough-minded sister.

"Harry's wounding has sobered us all." Mother slipped her arm around Cairstie's shoulder. "We have much to be grateful for. The Lord has been so good in sparing you and Harry."

Tears of reaction seeped down Cairstie's cheeks. Mother fished inside her purse and drew out a tissue.

"Thank you." Cairstie took it and mopped her face.

"Where's Sharidon? I thought he'd be with you?"

"I haven't the faintest notion. He's gone."

# CHAPTER 39

## LONDON, THREE DAYS LATER

"AFTER YOU, MR. SHARIDON." The buying agent, a middle-aged woman with bright pink hair, unlocked the flat on the top floor of his building. He already owned the remaining two across the hall.

Sharidon stepped into the open lounge onto the thick mauve carpet and crossed to the window overlooking the Thames River. He acquired land in East Cambridgeshire last year and planned to build a house when he retired from MI6.

Until that time, the value of this apartment would increase significantly after he converted it, along with the two other flats he owned on this floor, into a large penthouse. Right now, though, he intended to sublet the spares which paid all three mortgages.

"Nice view," he commented for something to say after the long pause.

"I know it's outdated, but the view *is* splendid. I understand there are two neighbors. One works nights, and the other, as far as I could gather, keeps to himself," the buying agent added.

"Brilliant." Sharidon bit the inside of his cheek to keep from laughing. He'd planted that information. "How many bedrooms?" He paused in the minuscule corridor off the entrance.

"Two bedrooms, both with ensuite bathrooms, and there is an additional toilet next to the laundry," the agent said.

Lovely. His own flat contained one family bath. With plumbing already installed, he'd save a bundle on the eventual remodel. Moving to the kitchen, he stared at the almond-colored appliances and dark cabinets. The last remodel occurred in the eighties, long before his birth.

"I didn't see a washer in the kitchen." He returned to the lounge.

"The owners didn't care for the noise while they entertained, so they moved the washer into the pantry."

Not a bad idea.

Sharidon stepped to the master, a spacious room similar to his own, then crossed to the ensuite. Women's pantyhose draped over the shower door conjured images of Cairstie's laundry adventures in the bathtub.

A call came through an unlisted number. "Sharidon," he answered.

"Agent Sharidon?" a woman asked.

"Speaking."

"This is Maxine Aldershot, the Ministry of Defense's undersecretary. The home office has reviewed your packet and is pleased to inform you that Benbecula's community-owned co-op has been awarded the oversight in acreage."

Sharidon punched the air. "When will they receive it?"

"The packet arrived by certified mail yesterday. We received an acceptance call first thing this morning. C thought you should know. We're also reviewing that rather unique set of clippings compiled by Mrs. Caroline McDougal." Click.

His mobile went black.

Governments made mistakes. Sharidon's heart swelled with thankfulness that this time, MoD had rectified a wrong, and also intended to investigate Mrs. McDougal's files.

Sharidon stared, unseeing, at the flat's artwork. If he had let a few of his questionable missions' fester, as Randy had done, he'd be a SIS target instead of an operative. Too bad Randy had given way to his baser actions, thus endangering the lives of his own countrymen and women. And Gordon was no better. Hundreds of sailors had died on the *HMS Lilibet*.

He shook his head. Randy and Gordon–traitors both.

According to Nigel, the home office had shut down all military testing until the electronic warhead components were changed out. They'd notified their allies of the issue, and similar precautions were underway in the United States and Australia.

"What do you think of the bedrooms?" The estate agent called to him from the corridor.

"Just a sec." Sharidon pulled himself from his thoughts and entered the flat's second bedroom, a nursery with floating shelves loaded with colorful books and a plethora of lion stuffies. He stepped to the bureau, where a photo of a blonde tot with bright blue eyes smiled at the wee rabbit in his hands.

The lad's coloring, so like Cairstie's, sucked the remaining air from his lungs. Jings. He missed her, but his surprise should be happening just about now, one he had left in Nigel's capable hands.

"If this doesn't tick all your boxes, Mr. Sharidon, I have other flats we can view." The agent fidgeted with her purse.

"This one is perfect."

# Chapter 40

Sunshine streamed through the tall casement windows as Cairstie entered Torwoodlee Castle's breakfast room. Goldfinches flitted in and out of the holly outside the glass, their bright colors vibrant against the dark green foliage.

Still a bit peely-wally from his injury, Harry sat beside Elise, chatting with Uncle Roger and a fellow Cairstie did not recognize. All four turned in her direction, and the men rose as one.

"Morning, Cairstie. We've waited ages for you to come down," Elise said.

"Sorry. I was unaware that we had visitors. I was up late and had a lie-in." Cairstie moved to Uncle Roger's side and kissed his cheek in greeting.

"No worries." Harry rescued her. "We were just catching up. Meet Nigel. He's an old friend."

Nigel, a man of average height and no remarkable features, held out his hand while his gray eyes assessed her. "I've heard positive things about you, Lady Cairstie."

Though Cairstie couldn't define it, everything inside her sprang on high alert when she shook Nigel's proffered hand. Uncle Roger rarely visited, and this Nigel fellow gave her the impression that his assessment of her somehow mattered.

The anniversary clock on the mantle chimed. Turning to the sideboard, Cairstie helped herself to a fruit bowl and bypassed the full Scottish breakfast of poached eggs, beans on toast, bacon, Lorne sausage, mushrooms, and tomatoes. The odd feeling persisted as she rounded the table to Harry's side and took her seat.

"Sophie left a sample of the bridesmaid fabric." Elise pushed a piece of yellow material in her direction.

Cairstie glanced at the fabric, and her stomach cramped at the canary yellow lace backed with white satin. The intense color would make her, and Elise look positively bilious. She glanced at Elise and met her knowing gaze.

Instead of commenting, Cairstie stabbed a strawberry and popped it into her mouth, stalling for time.

"She's dead set on this?" Cairstie asked after almost choking on the berry.

"Aye." Elise tossed her long red hair over her shoulder, amusement glinting.

"I'm sure Sophie will be quite happy with it," Cairstie said. *Sophie's wedding. Sophie's choice.*

Neither of Cairstie's sisters were what she'd term fashionable. Though, lately, Elise had upped her game. Sophie, their middle sister, who hung about in barns and smelled of horses, could do with a professional stylist and a full-time dresser.

"She said it reminds her of sunshine." Elise made air quotes, careful not to jostle Harry's arm that hung in a sling against his body.

"I can see why she would think that." Cairstie placed the gown sample on the tablecloth beside her fruit.

Elise blinked, her surprise apparent. Cairstie hardly blamed her. The old Cairstie would have pitched a fit and refuse to wear Sophie's selection, but Cairstie had learned a thing or two during her stay on Benbecula.

A naughty smile curved Elise's mouth. "I'm glad you approve, because Sophie's already ordered the material."

*The rat.* Elise knew their gowns would be dreadful and had deliberately baited her. Cairstie pressed her lips together and refused to say more. Subject closed.

Elise blew her a kiss, one of genuine affection and respect. "Sorry, I twitted you."

Miracle of miracles. Elise had apologized? Their sisterly dynamics had done an about face, indeed.

Elise bent her head to Harry's and whispered, the pair making googly eyes at each other. Since Harry's release from the hospital, Elise never left his side. Perhaps his close shave with death had softened her hard-edged sister but their cuddles and kisses set Cairstie's teeth on edge. Good thing Sophie and Zander were in England buying a horse, or she'd go stark raving mad, surrounded by all the loved-up couples.

"Cairstie, it's been some time since we chatted. It's come to my attention that you believe Elise and Harry work for the government." Uncle Roger raised his teacup and sipped.

She shot Elise a dirty look for giving her away. Mother and Uncle Roger were similar in one regard; both gave their opponents little time before they attacked.

"Along with other family members." Cairstie placed a tea bag in her cup and poured hot water over it from the porcelain pot in front of her. She lifted her chin at Uncle Roger, the head of British Intelligence.

"You stand by your convictions on this?" Nigel asked her, his tone mild.

"Aye." Cairstie set her cup in its saucer and folded her arms. Why had Uncle Roger broached this subject in front of a visitor?

"Who else have you voiced your concerns to?" Uncle Roger asked.

"Only Elise, Sophie, Harry, and Agent Sharidon." Cairstie's stomach muscles tightened. "If you're afraid I'll give away state secrets, think again. I won't betray them. It would be like betraying my country."

"I thought not." Uncle Roger glanced at Nigel.

The fellow nodded slowly, then focused on her once more. "Your instincts do you credit, Lady Cairstie. SIS has been alerted to a recent development in the fashion industry."

A little zip of excitement coursed through her. She was right! Elise, Harry, and Uncle Roger worked in the intelligence community.

"I understand that you have modeling experience," Nigel said.

"That's in the past, I'm afraid." Cairstie's cheeks burned.

"We can work that out if you're interested in what I have to say. I need someone on the inside to be our ears. The agent I normally use for this type of assignment is overseas. Would you be interested in filling her shoes? It would require a move to London and working under a junior officer on this project."

"London?" Cairstie's heart leaped, then sank like a boulder. "I'd love to help, but my prior association with Lord Ahern ostracized me from the fashion industry."

Uncle Roger winked at her. "We'll get you on the catwalk. Never fear. The officer you'll report to has already paved the way for your return. All you need do if a cheeky reporter digs into your past is state that your relationship with Lord Ahern ended before his arrest."

Cairstie's gaze darted from Uncle Roger to Nigel and then to Elise and Harry.

"Is this something you feel confident you can handle? If you're hesitant, now is the time to voice your concerns." Uncle Roger dabbed his mouth with a linen napkin.

Once, she thought that life had ended and she'd been content, but with this new offer, a frisson of excitement coursed through her. And working in intelligence meant more time with Sharidon, wouldn't it?

But before she could accept, she needed to come clean. "You must understand I'm dyslexic. I've started a program that has helped me tremendously, but if literacy factors into this assignment, you would be better off using someone else."

Elise draped her arm across the back of Harry's chair and squeezed her shoulder. Warmth suffused Cairstie at the unexpected support.

"I appreciate your honesty; however, literacy is not a major proponent of this mission. You will report your findings and suspicions to your officer; even the smallest things will be scrutinized." Nigel removed a piece of paper from the interior of his sports jacket and placed it on the table. "Please look this over. If you are still keen after reviewing the particulars, sign the contract and give it to Harry. He'll see that I receive it." Nigel rose from his chair. So did Uncle Roger.

Cairstie followed suit. Their interview appeared at an end.

"I hope you'll join us, Lady Cairstie." Nigel shook her hand with a firmer clasp than during their initial greeting. And this time, genuine warmth emanated from his smile.

Uncle Roger was less formal and tugged her in for a hug. "You'll do us all proud, Cairstie. Your family breeds patriots. For your information, Elise is temporarily working for me."

Cairstie glanced at her sister, who winked at her instead of gloating.

"Then you're not a spy?" Cairstie had difficulty accepting that she'd got it wrong.

"A hacker, more like," Elise said.

Elise treated her like an adult. This was an absolute first in their relationship and a new beginning for them both—not to mention a return to her career.

"Proud of you." Harry winked.

Warmed by her family's unexpected support, Cairstie accompanied Nigel and Uncle Roger to the entrance hall. Nigel stopped near a starburst pattern of medieval weaponry and turned to her.

"If you should choose to sign, your officer will be in touch." Nigel shook her hand, then jogged down the steps to a waiting sedan.

"And if you join us, you may be sure I'll monitor your progress from the sidelines." Uncle Roger kissed her cheek and followed Nigel, taking the seat behind the driver.

Cairstie stood on the top steps as the vehicle started up the lane, passed the loch, and headed for the gate.

The acidic scent of early fall carried on the breeze, the leaves vibrant from the rain. Smiling to herself, Cairstie took in the dappled light filtering through the trees as multiple emotions tumbled inside her chest.

*London!*

She had her old job back—with a difference—and what a difference. Ripples of anticipation pinged through her. The home office trusted her skills.

But as her reading continued to improve, so did her long-term plans. Her lack of education, a sore spot in the past, now beckoned. She intended to obtain a degree, even if it took her a decade.

And when she acquired one? What then?

Her chin quivered. She'd teach others to read. Oh, she intended to help the home office, but modeling careers lasted only so long. Men and women aged out of that field reasonably young. After her time on Benbecula, she no longer based her self-worth on a glamorous lifestyle.

She, Cairstie Henderson, was enough.

No longer would she hang her head in shame for her lack of literacy or being dismissed from her profession. She longed to tell Sharidon about this development but, after a moment's consideration, determined to wait until she received a green light from Uncle Roger.

Here, away from the glitz and glamor of high fashion, she had learned what mattered most, and though she enjoyed the finer things the world had to offer, they were simply things without the power of lasting happiness.

Her family mattered. Relationships built on trust mattered. Sharidon mattered.

Sharidon saw her, shortcomings and all, and accepted her anyway. He found her intelligent and, best of all, treated her like an adult.

With her hand on the rail, she descended the stone stairs to the drive below, then cut to the graveled path that encircled the wind-whipped loch. She zipped her jacket and followed the trail through the rustling trees to a rustic bench overlooking the water. She settled in, prepared to besiege the Irishman.

Grinning, she estimated how many calls she'd place before he picked up. Five? Six? She pressed his number. It went straight to messages. Hmmm. She rang him again and experienced the same result. By the eleventh time, her ire had risen.

"Sharidon. You ornery Irishman. Give me a bell," she all but yelled into the mouthpiece.

By the twenty-seventh call, Cairstie's determination deserted her. She slumped on the bench and stared at her feet, the ache inside too great to ignore. Had she misread their time together?

Pain, more potent than any ostracism or abandonment, seared her breast. Tears stung her eyes and clung to her lashes. She wiped them hastily as footsteps alerted her that she was not alone. One of Dad's gamekeepers was doubtless out touring the estate.

The fellow stopped a few meters from the bench and dropped a rucksack at his feet. She glanced up, and her breath froze.

"Yer a lovely sight, lass." Sharidon's eyes twinkled.

Cairstie gripped the seat to keep herself from bounding off the bench and wrapping her arms around him. Instead, she remained seated, cloaked in the hurt of her unanswered calls.

Sharidon held up his mobile. "What was so important?" He glanced at the screen. "Ye called me twenty-seven times?" His dark brows shot up.

"Why are you here?" She took the offensive rather than answer his question.

"I couldn't go another day without seeing ye, lass. It's the truth." Sharidon stepped closer. "I'm miserable without ye."

"Why didn't you answer when I rang?"

"I had just landed in Edinburgh and was on my way here. I wanted to surprise ye. Why did ye ring me twenty-seven times?"

"I've taken a modeling job in London and need to find a flat." She could share that much with him, at least.

"London, eh?" A wide smile split Sharidon's features and made her heart race.

"Aye. How do you feel about that?"

"I think God has answered my most fervent prayer." He shortened the distance between them. "So, yer coming to London?"

"I am." She nodded. "How did you find me?"

"That stuffy butler of yers told me where ye were."

She bit the inside of her cheek at Sharidon's description of Dad's butler. McFarlane's stuffy behavior hid a fiercely loyal heart.

He joined her on the bench. "Have ye signed Nigel's contract yet?" He leaned forward and rested his elbows on his knees.

"How do you know about that?" She jerked in his direction and narrowed her eyes at his nonchalant pose. He didn't fool her for a second.

"I asked ye first." He cocked his head and gave her a side-eye.

Were all MI6 agents such a pain?

"To answer your question. No, I haven't signed it."

Sharidon's shoulders slumped, along with some of his bravado.

"But I'm planning on it." She grinned.

"Would this help speed it along? He bent and pressed a firm kiss to her mouth, one that snatched her breath.

When she recovered, she gripped the bench's wood slats beneath her.

Sharidon retrieved a file from his rucksack, his mouth quirking with suppressed humor as he passed it along with a pen to her.

"What's this?"

"A contract with SIS. Want me to read it to ye?"

She tapped the paper. "Sharidon, why do you have a copy of my contract?"

"Because I'd like to work with ye, lass."

Suspicions triggered. "Are you my . . ."

His green eyes sparkled.

"You're the officer I'd report to?" Excitement zipped through her body.

"Sign it first, then we'll chat." He nudged her.

"Not until you read it out loud and explain all the rhetoric first."

"Ye drive a hard bargain." He sighed.

After he went over every clause in great detail, he met her eyes, his own wiped of mirth. "Have I scared ye off?"

"No. It's more than fair."

"Ye know. That's one of the first things I liked about ye. Yer no pushover."

Picking up the pen, Cairstie signed and dated the contract.

"Yes, I'm yer officer, and ye'll be reporting to me."

"I knew it!" She squealed and launched herself at him. "You're behind this, aren't you?"

"Nigel didn't take overlong to come 'round to my way of thinking." Sharidon grinned.

"When do we start?" she asked.

"As soon as ye can pack yer bags."

She drew back. "So soon? Will I have time to find a flat?"

"I know just the place as it happens. The rent is reasonable, and it's near the Underground with a view of the Thames."

"That sounds nice. What about the landlord? I understand some inspections can be quite difficult. I don't know how to scrub floors yet, but I can do the washing up and laundry, thanks to you. Will they mind?" She could always hire a housekeeper, but after her time on Benbecula, she preferred to do the cleaning herself.

"If ye like the space, I think he can be persuaded to take ye on." Sharidon dragged out the words as though considering the situation.

"It sounds perfect. Is it close to headquarters?"

"I doubt ye'll be going there much. Aren't ye interested in hearing more about the flat? What about the mod cons?"

"I'm not overly particular about those. Can I bring Winkle?" she asked.

"I don't see why not. Would he be happy in the city?"

Her face fell. Winkle had always lived in the country with loads of room to run. "Probably not." She needed to think more on that.

"What about the neighbors. What if I don't get on with them? Or their dog barks all day when I'm trying to sleep after a show? Is it possible to meet them before I sign?" She bit her lip.

"There are two neighbors." Sharidon scooted so close that she caught a whiff of his woodsy cologne.

"Do you know anything about them?" The idea of nosy neighbors who peeked inside her windows made her a bit leery. But perhaps it would turn into a beautiful friendship like the one she shared with Mrs. MacLeod.

"One is a radio presenter who works nights. The other's a loyal government sort who sometimes travels. Most people like him well enough," Sharidon said.

The teasing note in his voice alerted her that something was afoot. "How much will I like him?" Her heart pounded unnaturally fast.

"I have it on good authority, that ye'll love him almost as much as he loves ye." Sharidon trailed his unbandaged fingers across her cheekbone.

Goosebumps rippled across her flesh. "What's his name?" she whispered, holding her breath until she grew lightheaded. Would he tell her?

"Nollaig Sharidon."

"Nollaig." Her heart tumbled, and tenderness filled her as she absorbed the full implication of his words.

"It means merry in Gaelic." He pronounced it the Irish way. "I was born on Christmas day."

"It suits you."

Sharidon took her hand in his and stared into her eyes. "A mhuirnín," he murmured.

"What does that mean?"

"My darling." He touched her hair. "I'm yers, Cairstie. My heart—it's yers, lass." His voice choked with emotion as he enfolded her in his arms.

And she was home.

# Also by Paige Edwards

**PRESSLEY-COOMBES SERIES**

Catherine's Intrigue #1

Deadly by Design #2

Danger on the Loch #3

Skye Fall #4

**ROXBURY HEIRS SERIES**

Facing the Enemy #1

Flat Deception #2

**ROXBURGH SCIONS SERIES**

Traitor in the Scottish Isles

**STAND-ALONES**

Heirs of Falcon Point (creator)

**ANTHOLOGY**

Sinister Secrets

**SOLDIERS LEAP SERIES**

A Royal Request (Coming 2025)

# A ROYAL REQUEST

SOLDIER'S LEAP SERIES

**COMING 2025**

## PAIGE EDWARDS

# CHAPTER 1

## BUCKINGHAM PALACE GARDENS,
## LONDON, ENGLAND – PRESENT DAY

A SUDDEN GUST ballooned Annabelle's dress, and she smoothed the chiffon into place as rain peppered the sea of umbrellas around her. The shower switched to a drizzle, and the feather in Mother's once jaunty hat fluttered in Annabelle's direction and tickled her nose. She stifled a sneeze, then leaned toward Dad and peeked at his watch. He winked and adjusted his wrist for her convenience. Seven more hours until her flight left for Wales. All she had to do was survive the Queen's Garden Party first.

How her siblings managed to finagle out of it, she'd never understand.

Shifting her weight onto the ball of her right foot, she lifted her heel from the grass it seemed intent on aerating. In general, Annabelle avoided society events, but when HM The Queen invited their family to honor Mother's years of service on behalf of the crown, one did not decline, nor bypass an event of such magnitude for a beloved parent. So, despite her heavy work schedule, Annabelle flew home to lend her support.

All about her, men clad in morning suits and women, in dresses and fancy hats, had stood for hours on Buckingham Palace's private lawn awaiting Her Majesty's arrival. The Queen's equerries, her appointed military attendants, had arranged all six thousand guests into "human lanes."

Another gust lifted Annabelle's hemline and blew mist under her umbrella. The palace door opened, and the band struck up as the royal family appeared, then descended into the garden. How the royals managed to greet so many people on a regular basis astounded Annabelle. Never good with idle chit-chat, and existing on the fringe of palace fetes, she was grateful not to have been born a royal. Life in a fishbowl, with every move and word speculated on by the press seemed a horrid way to live. The Windsor's held her deepest sympathies.

Her mobile dinged with a text inside her father's suit pocket.

"Dad, can I check my mobile? It might be work."

Keeping an eye on Mother, Dad passed it to her when Mother was otherwise occupied. Shielding herself from Mother's prying eyes, Annabelle opened her device and squealed—as much as one could without calling the attention of the poshly dressed people around her.

"Laurence is engaged! Look." Annabelle shifted the screen toward her father. Missy, Laurence's intended, held up her hand, displaying a gorgeous diamond." Annabelle squelched the urge to give Laurence a bell this very instant and offer her congratulations.

"Have they set the date?" Dad looked every bit as delighted for Laurence as she felt.

"Not yet. I couldn't be happier for them." Annabelle enlarged the image on her screen, her eyes misting at the stunning picture. Doubtless, Laurence had taken it himself, being an amateur photographer and designer for a prominent London jewelry company.

Her cousin Laurence, along with Annabelle's three siblings, Wills, Jecca, and Cressida were not only family, but her closest friends. She couldn't be happier for Laurence, but sadness tinged her heart. Would his nuptials prevent the fabulous five, as they called themselves, from spending as much time together?

"Annabelle, please put that away," Mother said under her breath.

"Sorry." Annabelle scrunched her nose and handed the mobile back to her father.

The rain started up in earnest this time and beat upon their umbrellas, the ground growing soggier by the minute. Annabelle shivered and shifted to her left foot and extracted her heel from the lawn, teetering for balance.

"Stop fidgeting," Mother hissed. "The Queen is coming our way."

"Bother," Annabelle muttered. Of course, Her Majesty, and not one of the lesser royals, chose their "lane." And Annabelle knew why. She narrowed her eyes at the woman behind the king's wife. Grandmama, the Lady Barbara Poole, the seventy-two-year-old Dowager Countess of Seybourne, was one of The Queen's six companions. She habitually steamrolled everyone in her path, including Annabelle, who, despite working in Wales for the last year, had agreed to stand three hours in torrential rain in the hope that Mother might receive a royal handshake.

"It will be over before you know it, and then you'll be on your way back to Beckham." Dad patted Annabelle's arm.

Beckham might be her boyfriend, but he was also her current boss. Genesis, her employer had placed him in charge of converting her father's Welsh estate into a resort.

"I'd be lying if I said I could wait. Doubtless, you're pining for home every bit as much as I am for Beckham." She slipped her arm through Dad's. He disliked royal events as much as she did and rarely left Castleton Hall, his estate in the Lake District.

"You'd be right." Dad flashed her one of his rare smiles.

The Queen progressed up their "lane," with Grandmama on her heels. Dad might be a prosperous landowner and businessperson with a title of his own, but Mother's family had long served the crown in one capacity or another.

Her Majesty, wearing a pale-yellow dress and a chic matching hat with a wide black brim, stopped to chat with a fellow next to her but one. Mother pasted on a bright smile as she waited her turn. Dad patted Annabelle's back, and she, too, amidst the sudden churning in the pit of her stomach, put on her party manners. Her mother might be comfortable with this, but she was not.

The Queen stepped forward and shook hands with the lady next to Mother, a retiring crusader for a mental health charity that Annabelle supported.

Then Her Majesty shifted toward Mother, who immediately dipped into a curtsy.

"Lady Eliza. How lovely to see you again. Thank you for your service," The Queen said.

"How kind of you, Your Majesty." Mother gripped her hat from to keep it from flying off in a sudden gust.

"And how are you, Lord Harding?" The Queen asked, while Grandmama fought with her umbrella, one that appeared intent on flipping inside out.

"Can't complain, ma'am." Dad bowed.

"I haven't seen Peter lately. Where's he been keeping himself?" The Queen referred to Mother's second cousin, the Duke of Devon.

"I believe his arthritis objected to the rain." Dad's quiet charm sparkled through his words.

"Peter always did enjoy his creature comforts." The Queen lowered her voice. "Good for him. It's a foul sort of day for a Garden Party, don't you think?"

"Indeed." Dad bowed, his lips curving at Her Majesty's comment.

Grandmama swung in Annabelle's direction. "And you remember my granddaughter, the Honorable Annabelle Cavender?"

Annabelle dipped into a curtsy, her knees fairly knocking together. She caught Her Majesty's eyes as they glinted with humor. Charmed, despite herself, a genuine smile stretched Annabelle's lips.

"I do indeed. Lovely girl. Such dazzling blue eyes," The Queen spoke to Grandmama as though Annabelle weren't standing before her.

She squirmed, feeling rather like a specimen under a microscope. The Queen tilted her head, and Annabelle's stomach cramped. *Bother.* Her Majesty hadn't finished with her yet.

"You must visit London more often, Miss Cavender. Barbara tells me you are to be married. May I offer my congratulations? I should very much like to attend."

Annabelle's tongue swelled and all but choked her. She opened her mouth to respond, but no sound came out, so she curtseyed. All those years of ballet lessons had finally paid off.

The Queen, along with her entourage of attendants and bodyguards, moved off.

Mother squeezed her arm. "Annabelle, did you hear? The Queen is doing us a great honor by attending your wedding."

Annabelle swallowed. She had a problem—one of epic proportions.

She was not engaged.

# Stalk me

Paige Edwards is an award-winning and best-selling author of inspirational romantic suspense novels. Due to her deep British roots, Paige's books are often set in the UK, and she hops the pond whenever she gets the chance. When she isn't writing, she consumes too much Dr. Pepper Zero and is currently converting a Sprinter van into a camper so she and the hubs can visit every U.S. National Park. Paige loves to connect with readers. Reach her at authorpaigeedwards.com.

Amazon: Paige Edwards
Goodreads: Paige_Edwards
BookBub: Author Paige Edwards
Instagram: Instagram.com/authorpaigeedwards
Facebook Group: Paige's Page Pals
Facebook Page: Author Paige Edwards
LinkedIn: Paige-edwards-a3a38841

www.ingramcontent.com/pod-product-compliance
Lightning Source LLC
Chambersburg PA
CBHW052022240626
47153CB00006B/1922